Praise for *New York Times* bestselling author
Katee Robert

'Her writing is unspeakably hot...but its true
turn-on is the emotional beats.'
Entertainment Weekly

'A tension-filled plot...and sizzling love scenes will make
it impossible for readers to set the book down.'
Publishers Weekly

'Robert's world-building, the clear set of rules within,
the action and the strong heroines made
me really love this book.'
Smart Bitches, Trashy Books

Also by Katee Robert

Illicit Temptations

KATEE ROBERT

FORBIDDEN GAMES

MILLS & BOON

Mills & Boon
An imprint of HarperCollins*Publishers* Ltd
1 London Bridge Street
London SE1 9GF

www.harpercollins.co.uk

HarperCollins*Publishers*
Macken House, 39/40 Mayor Street Upper,
Dublin 1, D01 C9W8, Ireland

This edition 2025

1
First published in Great Britain by
Mills & Boon, an imprint of HarperCollins*Publishers* Ltd 2025

Forbidden Games © 2025 Harlequin Enterprises ULC

Make Me Want © 2018 Katee Hird
First published in 2018. This edition published in 2025.

Make Me Crave © 2018 Katee Hird
First published in 2018. This edition published in 2025.

Katee Hird asserts the moral right to be identified as the author of this work.
A catalogue record for this book is available from the British Library.

ISBN: 9781848459489

MAKE ME WANT

To Tim.

Second chances make for the best stories.

1

GIDEON NOVAK HAD ALMOST CANCELED THE
meeting. He would have if he'd possessed even a shred of honor.
Some things in this world were just too damn good for him to
be associated with and Lucy Baudin topped that list. To hear
from her now, two years after…

Focus on the facts.

She'd called. He'd answered. It was as simple as that.

The law office of Parker and Jones was the same as it had
been the last time he'd walked through the doors. The small
army of defense attorneys took on mostly white-collar crimes—
specifically the ones that paid well—and that showed in every
element of the interior. Soothing colors and bold lines projected
confidence and created a calming effect.

Pale blue walls and good lines didn't do a single damn thing
to dial back the pressure building in his chest with each step.

He usually didn't contract out with law offices. As a headhunter, Gideon preferred to stick to tech companies, various
start-up corporations or, literally, anyone except lawyers. They
were too controlling and wanted their hands on every detail,
every step of the way. It was a pain in the ass.

This is for Lucy.

He kept his expression schooled on the elevator ride up.

When he'd known her, she was somewhere around floor six, proving herself by working cases not big enough for the lawyers with seniority to want but that were too big to turn down. Now she was on floor nineteen, only a couple below Parker and Jones themselves. She'd done well for herself in the two years since he'd seen her last. Really well.

The elevator opened into a large waiting room that didn't look anything like an actual waiting room. The more money people had, the more care was required in handling them, and the coffee bar and scattering of couches and trade magazines reflected that. The hallway was guarded by a large desk and an older woman with tasteful gray shot through her dark hair. Surprising. He'd expected a bottle-blond receptionist—or perhaps a brunette if they were feeling adventurous.

But then the woman looked up and he got the impression of a general surveying her domain. *Ah.* They'd chosen someone who couldn't be bulldozed, if he didn't miss his guess. Useful to keep unruly clients in line.

Gideon stopped in front of the desk and did his best to appear nonthreatening. "I'm here to see Lucy Baudin."

"She's expecting you." She turned back to her computer, effectively dismissing him.

He spent half a second wondering at her qualifications—and if she was amiable to being poached for a different company—before he set it aside. Stepping on Lucy's toes by stealing her receptionist wasn't a good way to start off this meeting.

He'd spent the last week trying to figure out why the hell Lucy would seek *him* out. New York was rife with headhunters. Gideon was good—better than good—but considering their history, there had to be someone better suited for the job.

You could have said no.

Yeah, he could have.

But he owed Lucy Baudin. A single meeting wasn't much

in the face of the fact that he'd more or less single-handedly brought her engagement down in flames.

He knocked on the dark wooden door as he opened it. The office was bright and airy, big windows overlooking New York, the only furniture a large L-shaped desk and two comfortable-looking chairs arranged in front of it. Gideon took in the room in a single sweep and then focused on the woman behind the desk.

Lucy sat straight, her narrow shoulders tense, as if she was about to step onto a battlefield. Her long dark hair was pinned back into some style that looked effortless but probably took a significant amount of time to accomplish. She raised her pointed chin, which drew his attention to her mouth. Lucy's features were a little too sharp to pass for traditional beauty—she would have made a killing on a runway—but her mouth was full and generous and had always been inclined to smile.

There were no smiles today.

"Lucy." He shut the door behind him, holding his place to let her guide the interaction. She was the one who'd called him here. It didn't feel natural to take his lead from someone else, but for her he'd make an effort.

At least until he heard her out.

"Gideon. Sit, please." She motioned at the chairs in front of the desk.

Maybe she could pretend this was like any other job interview, but he couldn't stop staring at her. She wore a dark gray dress that set off her pale skin and dark hair, leaving the only color present in her blue eyes and red lips. It created a striking picture. The woman was a goddamn gift. She always had been.

Jeff, you fucked things up beyond all recognition when you threw her away.

Focus.

She hadn't arranged this meeting because of their past. If

she could be professional, then he'd manage, as well. It was the least he could do.

Gideon sank into the chair and leaned forward, bracing his elbows on his knees. "You said this was about a job."

"Yes." A faint blush colored her pale cheeks, highlighting the smattering of freckles there. "This is confidential, of course."

It wasn't quite a question, but he answered it anyway. "I didn't put together a nondisclosure, but I can do that if you need to make it official."

"That won't be necessary. Your word that it stays between us will be enough."

Curiosity curled through him. He'd had clients insist on confidentiality in the past—it was more the rule than the exception—but this felt different. He set the thought aside and focused on the job. "It would help if you'd describe the position you want filled. It gives me a general idea of what you're looking for, and we can narrow it down from there."

She met his gaze directly, her blue eyes startling. "The position I need filled is a husband."

Gideon shook his head, sure he'd heard her wrong. "Excuse me?"

"A husband." She held up her left hand and wiggled her ring finger. "Before you get that look on your face, let me explain."

He didn't have any *look* on his face. *A husband. Where the fuck does she think I'm going to find a husband?* He opened his mouth to ask exactly that, but Lucy beat him there. "The timing isn't ideal, but gossip has come down the grapevine that I'm being considered for partner at the end of the year. While that would normally be a cause for celebration, some of the old guard have very strong beliefs about single women." She rolled her eyes, the first *Lucy* thing he'd seen her do since he'd arrived. "It would be laughable if it wasn't standing in the way of what I want, but I watched Georgia get passed over for a promotion last year for this exact reason. She wouldn't bend and they chose her male competition instead."

She was dead serious.

Gideon took a breath, trying to approach this logically. Obviously she'd put a lot of thought into the idea, and if she was misguided, that didn't mean he had to verbally slap her down. *This* Lucy, put-together and in control, was a far cry from when he'd seen her last, sobbing and broken. But that didn't change the fact that they were one and the same. He could handle this calmly and get her to see reason.

But calm and reasonable wasn't what came out of his mouth. "Are you out of your goddamn mind, Lucy? I'm a headhunter—not a matchmaker. Even if I was, getting married to secure a promotion is bullshit."

"Is it?" She shrugged. "People get married for much less valid reasons. *I* almost married for love before, and we both know how that ended. There's nothing wrong with handling marriage like a business arrangement—plenty of cultures do exactly that."

"We aren't talking about other cultures. We're talking about *you*."

Another shrug. As if it didn't matter to her one way or another. He *loathed* that feigned indifference, but he didn't have a goddamn right to challenge her on it.

She met his gaze directly. "This is important to me, Gideon. I don't know about kids—I love my job, and having babies would potentially interfere with that—but I'm lonely. It wouldn't be so bad to have someone to come home to, even if it wasn't a love for the ages. *Especially* if it's not a love for the ages."

"Lucy, that's crazy." Every word out of her mouth cut into the barrier of professionalism he fought so hard to maintain. "Where the hell would I find you a husband?"

"The same place you find people to fill the positions normally. Interview. We're in New York—if *you* can't find a single man who's willing to at least consider this, then no one can."

Gideon started to tell her exactly how impossible it was, but guilt rose and choked the words off. He thought this plan was bat-shit crazy, and the thought of Lucy in some loveless marriage irritated him like sandpaper beneath his skin, scratching until he might go mad from it.

But it wasn't his call to make.

And he was partially to blame for her single status right now. *Fuck.*

Gideon straightened. No matter what he thought of this plan, when it came right down to the wire, he owed Lucy. He knew that piece of shit Jeff had cheated on her, and Gideon had kept his mouth shut for a full month before he'd told her the truth. That kind of debt didn't just go away. If she was coming to him now, it was because she'd exhausted all other options, and his saying no wasn't going to deter her in the least—she'd find a different way.

Really, he had no option. It might have been two years since he'd seen Lucy Baudin, but that didn't change the fact that he considered her a friend, and he'd never leave a friend hanging out to dry when they needed him. Gideon might have questionable morals about most things, but loyalty wasn't one of them.

She needed him. He'd have found a way to help her even if he didn't owe her.

At least if he was in the midst of this madness, he'd have some ability to keep her as safe as possible. He could protect her now like he hadn't been able to protect her from the hurt Jeff had caused.

If she was crazy for coming up with the plan in the first place, he was even crazier for agreeing to it. "I'll do it."

Lucy couldn't believe the words that had just come out of his mouth. It was too good to be true. Attempting to rope Gideon

Novak into this scheme had been her Hail Mary. She was desperate and he was the only one she trusted enough to even attempt something like a search for a husband. But she hadn't thought he'd actually agree to it.

He said he'd help. Shock stole her ability to speak for a full five seconds. *Say something. You know the drill—fake it until you make it. This is just another trial. Focus.* She cleared her throat. "I'm sorry—did you just say yes?"

"Yes." He studied her face with dark eyes lined with thick lashes, which she secretly envied. Gideon had always been too attractive for Lucy's state of mind. His dark hair was always styled in what she could only call "rakish," and his strong jaw and firm mouth would have kept her up at night if he wasn't firmly in the friend zone.

At least, he used to be.

She set the thought aside because going down the rabbit hole of despair that was her relationship with Jeff Larsson was out of the question. It had ended, and her friendship with Gideon had been a casualty of war.

Until now.

Gideon shifted, bringing her back to the present. "How exactly were you planning on going about this?"

This, at least, she had an answer for. Lucy had spent entirely too much time reviewing the steps required to get to her goal with minimum fuss—a husband and her promotion. "I thought you could come up with a list of suitable candidates, I could have a date or two with each, and then we could narrow the list down from there."

"Mmm-hmm." He tapped his fingers on his knee, dragging her attention south of his face. He wore a three-piece suit, which should have been too formal for this meeting, but Gideon managed to pull it off all the same. The pin-striped gray-on-gray gave him an old-world kind of feel, like something out of *Mad Men*.

Thankfully for Lucy, he had better morals than Don Draper.

She fought not to squirm in her seat under the weight of his attention. It was easy enough to be distanced and professional when she'd laid out her proposal—she'd practiced it the same way she practiced opening and closing statements before a trial. Getting into the nitty-gritty of the actual planning and actions was something else altogether.

"I'm open to suggestions, of course." *There—look at me, being reasonable.*

"Of course." He nodded as if deciding something. "We do this, we do it on my terms. I pick the men. I supervise the dates. And if I don't like the look of any of them, I have veto rights."

Veto rights? That wasn't part of the plan. She shook her head. "No. Absolutely not."

"You came to me, Lucy. That means you trust my judgment." He gave her an intense look that made her skin feel too tight. "Those are the terms."

Terms. Damn, she'd forgotten the most important thing.

It doesn't have to be the most important thing. He doesn't know it was part of the plan, so it's not too late to back out.

But if she backed out, the deep-rooted fear from her time with her ex would never be exorcised. She'd spend the rest of her life—and her prospective marriage—second-guessing herself and her husband. It would drive her crazy and ultimately poison everything.

She couldn't let it happen, no matter how humiliating she found asking for Gideon's help with this.

Lucy managed to drag her gaze away from his. She pulled at the hem of her dress. "There's one more thing."

"I'm listening."

She smoothed her suddenly sweating palms over her desk. "Are you seeing anyone?"

"What the hell does that have to do with anything?"

It had everything to do with things. She'd never known

Gideon to hold down a relationship longer than a few weeks, but that didn't mean he hadn't somehow changed in the last two years. The entire second part of her plan leaned heavily on the assumption that he *hadn't* changed.

The Gideon she'd known before had been her friend, yes, but he'd also been a playboy to the very definition of the word. He hadn't dated seriously. He'd never mistreated women, but he hadn't kept them around for long, either. Lucy had heard the whispers in college about his expertise in the bedroom—it was legendary enough that most women ignored the fact they had an expiration date from the moment he showed an interest in them.

To put it simply, he was *perfect* for her current situation.

She just had to find the strength to speak the damn words. She forced her hands still. "I'm going to need…lessons."

"Lucy, look at me."

Helpless, she obeyed. He frowned at her like he was trying to read her mind. "You're going to have to explain what the hell you're talking about."

It was so much harder to get it out while looking at him. She pressed her lips together. She'd faced down some of the most vicious prosecutors New York had to offer. She could damn well face Gideon Novak down, too.

You know these words. You've practiced them often enough.

"I need lessons of the sexual nature." He went so still, he might as well have turned to stone, so she charged on. "This might be an arranged marriage, so to speak, but it would be a true marriage. And, as I don't cherish the idea of being cheated on by yet another fiancé, that means sex needs to be part of the bargain. It's been a long time for me, and I have to brush up on my skill set."

Not to mention the only man I ever slept with was Jeff, and he never missed an opportunity to tell me how uninspiring he found our sex life.

Or that he blamed his cheating on my being unable to meet his needs.

She didn't let what Jeff thought dictate her life anymore, but Lucy would be lying if she pretended his words didn't haunt her—that they hadn't been instrumental in her two-year celibate streak. She'd enjoyed sex. She'd thought Jeff had enjoyed it, as well. If she could be so terribly wrong on such a fundamental level before, what was to stop her from failing at it again?

No, she couldn't allow it. If she trusted Gideon enough to secure his help finding a husband, then she trusted him enough to create a safe space to teach her something she obviously needed to know to be an effective wife. His rumored sex prowess just sweetened the bargain, because he was more than experienced enough to walk her through a crash course in seduction.

He still hadn't said anything.

She sighed. "I know it's a lot to ask—"

"I'm going to stop you right there." He stood and adjusted his jacket as he buttoned it. "I will charge you for the husband hunting—the same rates of a normal client. I'm not a sex worker, Lucy. You can't wave a magic wand and acquire lessons in fucking."

She did her best not to wilt.

You knew it was a long shot.

"I understand."

"That said…" He shook his head like he couldn't believe the words coming out of his mouth any more than she could. "Come by my place tonight. We'll talk. After that, we'll see."

That…wasn't a no. It wasn't a yes. But it most definitely wasn't a no.

"Okay." She didn't dare say anything more in fear that he'd change his mind. *I can't believe this is happening.* He didn't look happy to have offered the invitation. In fact, Gideon looked downright furious.

He pinned her with a look. "Seven. You remember the address."

It wasn't a question but she still nodded all the same. "I'll be there."

"Don't be late." He turned and stalked out of her office, leaving her staring after him.

What just happened?

A thrill coursed through her. What just happened was that Gideon Novak had agreed to help her. Professionally he had a reputation for always getting his man and, personally, he had everything required to get her pending marriage off to the right start.

He said yes.

With him in her corner, there was no way she'd fail.

The promotion was hers. She could feel it.

2

GIDEON SWAM LAPS UNTIL EVERY MUSCLE IN HIS body shook with exhaustion. It didn't help. All he could see was Lucy's earnest expression as those sinful lips spoke words he would have killed to hear before. *Teach me.* His attraction for that woman had never brought him anything but trouble, and apparently he was doubling down because he hadn't told her no like he damn well should have. Instead he'd told her to come to his place.

So they could talk.

About him giving her lessons in fucking.

He pulled himself out of the pool and climbed to his feet. He'd been prepared to tell her no—to both the husband hunt and the lessons. Instead he'd invited her over tonight. What the hell was that about?

You know what that's about.

Gideon wanted Lucy.

He'd wanted her from the moment he'd seen her across that crowded bar in Queens six years ago. She'd been so fresh-faced and, even too many shots in, he'd known there was something special about her.

Unfortunately so had Jeff Larsson, and that bastard had

beaten him to the punch—meeting Lucy, dating Lucy, proposing to Lucy.

Gideon had tried his damnedest to be happy for his best
friend—and to table his desire for his best friend's woman—but
it had never quite gone away. It didn't matter how many girls
he'd dated, because his heart had never been in it. When Jeff
had made a passing remark on Gideon's tendency to find wil-
lowy brunettes with freckles, he'd shelved dating completely
and restricted his interactions to one night.

He showered and dressed quickly. It would be tricky getting back to his place before she arrived, but he'd had to do
something to take the edge off or he was in danger of throwing caution to the wind. The temptation of Lucy in his bed,
even for such a shitty reason…

He'd be a bastard and a half to do it.

No, Gideon would grab takeout, sit her down to her favorite Chinese and explain all the reasons why sex between them
wasn't an option. He'd be calm and reasonable and use whatever arguments he had to get his point across. She didn't need
lessons. No man with a pulse and a working cock was going to
have a problem with anything Lucy had to offer.

His step hitched at the thought of someone else waking up
next to her every morning. Of the long nights buried between
her thighs and the friction of sweat-slicked skin and—

Fuck.

He glanced back at the gym, seriously considering calling
the whole thing off and spending the next three hours back in
the pool. Maybe if he was too exhausted to move, his fury at
the thought of her with another man would subside.

He knew better.

If he hadn't been happy that his best friend was with her—
even before the idiot had started fucking around—he wasn't
going to be pleased with a stranger. There was no help for it.
Lucy would charge ahead with this plan of hers whether he

agreed to it or not. He might be able to talk her out of the sex bit, but he wouldn't be able to convince her that she didn't need a husband.

He'd failed her when it came to Jeff. Even as his best friend, Gideon had missed the warning signs until it was almost too late—and then he'd hesitated a full month before breaking the news to her. He'd well and truly fucked up across the board and it had cost him her friendship—something he'd valued more than he could have dreamed.

He wouldn't fuck up again.

She wanted a husband? Well, then, Gideon was going to find her the most honorable man he could to make her happy. He owed it to her to do so.

He barely had time to drop the takeout on the kitchen counter when a knock sounded. He skirted the couch and opened the door. "You're early."

"I hope you don't mind. Your doorman remembered me, so he didn't bother to buzz you." She gave a tentative smile that pulled at him despite his determination to do the right thing.

Lucy must have made it home because she'd changed into a pair of black leggings and a lightweight slouchy shirt that seemed determined to slide off one shoulder. She saw him looking and bit her bottom lip. "I know we talked about lessons, and this isn't exactly seduction personified, but I went through my closet and, aside from work clothes, I don't think I *own* anything that's 'seduction personified.'"

For fuck's sake, she was killing him. Gideon stepped back and held the door open. "You look fine."

"Fine." She frowned. "I know you're cranky about being cornered with this whole thing, but you don't have to damn me with faint praise. I asked you to do this because I trust you to tell me the truth. I've always trusted you to tell me the truth."

If she'd taken out a knife and stabbed him in the heart, it would have stung less. Gideon closed the door carefully behind her, trying to maintain his control. It didn't matter how honest she thought he was, he wouldn't agree to take her to bed. He couldn't. "This won't work if you're going to jump down my throat every time I say something. I said you look fine. You do. I didn't tell you to dress for seduction, Lucy. I said to get your ass over here so we can talk. That—" he motioned at her clothes "—is perfectly adequate for a conversation between two friends."

"Right. Okay. I'm sorry. I'm nervous." She pulled at her shirt, which caused it to drop another inch down her arm.

Gideon had never found shoulders particularly provocative before but he wanted to drag his mouth over the line of her collarbone. *Keep it together, asshole.* He cleared his throat and looked away. "You don't need lessons, Lucy. Not from me. Not from anyone. You're beautiful and any man would be lucky to have you in his bed."

"If you don't want to teach me, that's fine. I did say that this morning." She wandered farther into his apartment and circled the couch he'd bought six months ago. It was slate gray with dark blue accents, and the saleswoman had insisted it would pull the room together in a way he'd love. He was still waiting to love it. Lucy picked up one of the ridiculous blue throw pillows and hugged it to her chest. "I'm not fishing for a compliment, by the way, but thank you. Though, beauty only goes so far. Since you haven't… We haven't…" She huffed out a breath. "Can I be perfectly frank?"

"You weren't before now?" If she was franker, she might actually kill him.

"Jeff might be a cheating bastard, but that doesn't change the fact that even before he started sleeping around, he was never…satisfied. Since he obviously found that satisfaction with those other women, it's impossible to blame the entire problem on him."

Gideon watched her pick at the tassels on the pillow while he dissected what she'd just said.

"You've been with other men since him."

"No." She still wouldn't look up. "I almost did once. But I kept hearing *his* voice in my head with those nasty little comments that he always wrote off as a joke and I just couldn't. I know that's pathetic, but after a while, the risk of finding out that Jeff was really right all along wasn't worth the potential pleasure. So I focused on work instead of dating—and now here we are."

Gideon wished he could go back in time and deliver a few more punches to Jeff's perfect face. He'd known things weren't perfect with Jeff and Lucy, but he hadn't realized just how much of a dick his friend had been. "He's a piece of shit."

"I'm not arguing that, believe me." She gave a faint smile. "Thank you again for saving me from marrying him. I don't know if I ever said it before, but it couldn't have been easy to say something. You two had been friends for so long."

Gideon scrubbed a hand over his face. He read people for a living—both his clients and the people he found to fill the open positions. He was damn good at it, too. That skill made him the best in the business and ensured that he almost always got the secondary bonus for the position still being filled for a year after the initial contract.

Every instinct he had was insisting that Lucy's sheepish smile covered up a soul wound. If he was a good man, he'd let someone else help her heal from that—someone who'd be there for the long term. Likely that theoretical husband he was supposed to find her. But Gideon wasn't a good man.

He didn't want it to be anyone else.

He wanted it to be *him*.

"Sit down."

She dropped onto the couch, still clinging to the pillow. "Okay."

There wasn't a convenient playbook for how to go about this, but they *did* need to have a conversation before it went any further. "I will give you…lessons. On two conditions."

"Agreed."

He shot her a look. "Hear the conditions first and then decide if you're good with them. First—you communicate with me. You like something? Tell me. You aren't into it? You need to speak up. You fake anything and we call the whole thing off. I can't help you if you aren't honest with both yourself and me."

She wrinkled her nose. "Fine. I'm an adult. I can talk about sex."

He didn't comment on the fact she seemed to be trying to convince herself. The confidence and ice queen bit she'd played in the office was nowhere to be seen now, which made him wonder who was the real Lucy—the cold and professional lawyer or the unsure woman sitting in front of him now.

Gideon leaned forward. "Second condition is that you're not with anyone else for the duration."

"Why?" She held up a hand. "I have no intention of being with anyone else, but I'm curious."

"It's respect." *Liar. It's jealousy.* He smothered the snide little voice and kept his tone even. "We're exclusive—both of us—until the expiration date."

"Exclusive." She said the word as if tasting it. "When's the expiration date?"

Never. Fuck, he was already in over his head and sinking fast and he hadn't even touched her. "When you decide on a candidate for a husband, we end it."

Lucy nodded. "That seems reasonable. Should we start now?" She reached for her shirt.

"Holy fuck, slow down." He made an effort to lower his voice and held out a hand. "You want lessons? We start with the basics. Come here."

She reluctantly let go of the pillow and rose to cross over to his chair. Lucy eyed his hand, but ultimately placed hers in it.

Gideon drew her down slowly, giving her plenty of time to see where things were going. She obliged him by climbing into his lap, though she held herself so stiffly she felt downright brittle.

He kept hold of her hand and set his other on her hip. It would have been innocent if not for the fact that she was straddling him and his cock had not gotten the memo about moving slow.

She shifted, her eyes going wide. "Ah…"

"Are you uncomfortable?" He spoke before she could think too hard.

"No…" She bit her lip. "Right. Honesty. Okay, yes, this feels weird. Awkward. I don't know where to put my hands and I can feel you, and it's making me nervous."

She was right. It was awkward as fuck. But Gideon wasn't going to throw her off the deep end on the first night, no matter how surreal this whole thing was. She trusted him to take care of her and he'd do whatever it took to be worthy of that trust. *Do whatever it took to keep her from changing her mind.* He kept his voice low so as not to startle her. "I'm going to kiss you now."

"Okay." She licked her lips and carefully tilted forward.

Gideon moved his hand from her hip to cup her jaw, guiding her down as he leaned up to brush his mouth against hers. She smelled of citrus and he had to fight to keep a growl internal. *Nice and easy.* He nipped her bottom lip and then soothed it with his tongue. She placed her hands on his biceps and relaxed against him, bit by bit. Gideon took it slow. He kissed her, keeping it light, until she shifted restlessly against him.

Then, and only then, did he slip his tongue into her mouth.

His first taste of Lucy went straight to his head. He used his hand on her jaw to angle her to allow him deeper and stroked his tongue against hers. Slow and steady was the name of the game.

Lucy whimpered and went soft against him. Her body melded to his, her breasts dragging against his chest with each inhalation. She shifted her grip and tentatively sifted her fingers through his hair. As if she wasn't sure of her welcome.

He wanted her sure.

Gideon shifted back to lean against the chair. The move settled her tighter against him as her knees sank into the cushion on either side of his hips. She gasped into his mouth and he ate the sound. He kissed her like he'd wanted to since that first night, when he'd heard her infectious laugh across a crowded bar. She tasted just as sunny as she smelled, as addicting as a summer's day in the midst of winter.

He couldn't get enough.

3

LUCY'S AWKWARDNESS WENT UP IN SMOKE THE
second Gideon kissed her. She'd expected… Well, she wasn't
sure what she'd expected. For him to take her into the bedroom and strip them down and just go for it. Preferably with
the lights turned off to hide her mortification.

He stroked his hands up the sides of her face and tangled his
fingers in her hair. The move pulled her out of their kiss, but
Gideon didn't let the distance stand. He dragged his mouth
down the line of her neck, raising goose bumps in his wake.

A deep, hidden ember inside her burst into flame.

She was doing this. She was straddling Gideon Novak with
his mouth on her skin and his hands on her body. Something
she'd never even allowed herself to *think* about until she'd come
up with this plan.

"You're thinking too hard."

"I can't believe this is happening."

He set his teeth against her collarbone. "If you change your
mind—"

"I won't." She'd never dared fantasize about him—she hadn't
let herself cross that line, even in her mind—but she wasn't missing this opportunity for the world. Warmth flared with each

breath, the heat centered at her core, where she could feel his cock lining up right where she wanted it.

I want it.

The realization startled her, though it shouldn't have. Gideon was sex personified and having all his considerable attention focused solely on her was a heady feeling. She wanted... More. All of it. Everything he could give her. She moaned. "More."

Gideon took her mouth. There was no other way to put it. He claimed her, establishing dominance with a stroke of his tongue, engulfing her entire world in that single contact. He tasted like peppermint—a shocking sensation against her tongue. Unexpected.

Just like the man himself.

It wasn't enough. There were too many clothes between them. She could feel his broad shoulders flexing, could test the definition of his muscles as she slid her hands down his chest, but his button-up shirt barred her from the skin-to-skin contact she craved.

Her breasts felt too tight, her nipples pebbling until they almost hurt. At least her yoga pants didn't offer much in the way of a barrier as she rocked her hips against him. His slacks did little to hide the size of his cock, and that little movement felt deliciously good. Intoxicating. So she did it again.

Gideon dropped one hand to her hip. For one horrifying moment she thought he'd stop her—maybe tell her that grown adults did not dry hump in the middle of one's living room—but he just urged her on. He never stopped kissing her, never stopped exploring her mouth. As if kissing was his be-all and end-all rather than just the first step to get to sex.

God, I am so messed up.

He squeezed her ass and nipped her bottom lip. "How we doing?"

"Good." Was that her voice? She sounded like she was doing something requiring a whole lot more exertion than kissing

Gideon Novak. *If this is what* kissing *is like, am I going to survive actual sex?*

Who cares? It'd be a glorious way to go.

He used his grip on her hip to pull her closer yet, lining up his cock with her clit. "And now?"

She hissed out a breath. *Please don't stop.* She could come like this if they kept it up. "Really good. But—" She didn't want to talk about it, didn't want to do anything to make this stop, so she went in for another kiss.

Gideon tightened his hold on her hair just enough to prevent her from moving. "But?"

His insistence on honesty had seemed like a good idea at the time—how could she improve if she didn't know what she was doing wrong?—but in practice it felt like he was stripping her bare in a way that had nothing to do with sex. She closed her eyes, because it was easier to answer when she wasn't meeting his gaze. "Isn't dry humping kind of juvenile?" *Are you going to mock me if I orgasm from this? Maybe make a joke about cobwebs or how long it's been for me?*

His chuckle pulled at things low in her stomach. "Does this feel juvenile to you?"

"No." It felt hotter than it should have and even a little dirty. She wanted it too much, and that was the problem. She forced herself to open her eyes and found him watching her with a contemplative expression. "What?"

"Pleasure isn't something you can put limits on, Lucy. There isn't a right way to go about it. Would you tell someone who was eating one of those double-chocolate-death desserts you love so much that they were eating it wrong if they did it differently than you?"

"Of course not." She blinked. How had he possibly remembered her favorite dessert?

"Then why is *this* wrong?" He urged her to rock against

him again. "Feels good to me. Feels good to you. No reason to overthink it."

When Gideon put it like that, it sounded so simple. Deceptively simple. She started to ask another question but forced herself to silence it. This insecurity wasn't her. This was the ghost of her relationship with Jeff coloring the current interaction.

Exactly what she'd been afraid would happen.

"Thank you for agreeing to this, Gideon. You didn't have to and—"

"Lucy." He framed her face with his big hands, preventing her from looking away. Those dark eyes were so incredibly serious. "Stop thanking me for this. The matchmaking shit? Sure. Not this. You're crazy if you think I'm not getting something out of it—same as you. Enjoy it. Enjoy *me*. It's as simple as that."

Easier said than done. The malicious voice that had spent far too many years lurking in the back of her mind wouldn't be silenced. Not completely. *Pity fuck.* She pressed her lips together. "I want to have sex now."

"No."

She frowned. "What?"

"No." He sat up, forcing her to grab his shoulders to stabilize herself, and then stood, taking her with him. "You want me to teach you? Then we're doing this on my terms. You were enjoying the hell out of this and something tripped you up." He laid them down on his ridiculously comfortable couch. She sank into the cushions as his weight settled over her. It felt good. Right.

It scared the shit out of her.

"Gideon."

"My terms, Lucy." He kissed her again. Before it had been sweet, and then intense, but she hadn't realized he was holding back until that moment. Gideon kissed her like he owned her. He took her mouth, urging her to meet him halfway.

She held back for all of one second; it was impossible to

maintain distance with his very presence overwhelming her. So she let go, tangling her tongue with his. The second she did, he started to move.

It had felt good when she was on top, but it was nothing compared to him pressing her into the couch as he stroked his cock against her clit. One long slide up and then another back down. The desire that had been put on hold while she'd let her insecurities get the best of her seared her—with interest. As if it'd been waiting for her to just let go and enjoy this moment for what it was. *Pleasure. No questions asked.*

She arched up to meet him. "That feels good."

Gideon hitched a hand beneath her knee and drew her leg up and out, opening her farther. He kissed her again and kept up that slow drag that had sparks dancing at her nerve endings. Her body wound tighter and tighter with each stroke until she teetered on the brink. Lucy writhed against him, trying to get closer, to get him where she needed him, to do whatever it took to reach that edge. "Gideon, *please.*"

He shifted back and she sobbed out a breath at the loss of him. But he didn't make her wait long. He slid a hand beneath the waistband of her yoga pants and into her panties. His rough curse would have made her smile under other circumstances, but she was too busy holding her breath. *So close. Please just touch me.*

He did.

He made a V with his fingers and slid it over her clit in the exact same motion he'd been doing with his cock before. She lasted three strokes before she came apart in his arms, her pleasure drawing a cry from her lips and blanking out her mind into delicious static. He softened their kiss to the barest brushing of lips and then shifted to the side so his weight wasn't completely on her.

Lucy blinked at the pale gray ceiling and tried to reconcile what had just happened with reality. *I just came. Without pres-*

sure. Without having to force it or fake it. A world-ending orgasm and *Gideon* was the one who'd coaxed it from her. "Wow." As soon as the word popped out of her mouth, she cringed. *What a stupid thing to say.* She was hardly a virgin and she wasn't an idiot teenager, no matter what they'd just done.

Gideon gave another of those low laughs. "All flavors, Lucy."

Against her better judgment, she couldn't help comparing what they'd just done to her experiences with Jeff when they'd first started dating. Night and day. Even though it'd taken her and Jeff a bit to work up to sex, he'd always had an air of impatience about him when they were intimate—like he couldn't wait to get to the next step. Add that to his competitive need to make her come multiple times every time they were together and the pressure had twisted with the desire until it made her jumpy every time they'd been alone together. Things had changed a little once they'd finally had sex, but then other elements had come into play.

Boring.

Uninspired.

Like fucking a doll.

"Lucy, look at me." Gideon's voice drew her out of the horror show that was her past.

She shook her head. *God, I can't even do this right.* What they'd just done was so incredibly perfect and she'd had to go and ruin it by letting her issues with her ex creep in. "I'm sorry."

"No, I'm sorry." He stroked a hand through her hair, the move so tender, her stomach tried to tie itself in knots. His dark eyes took on a distance as he looked at something she couldn't see. "I knew Jeff was an asshole, but if I'd known what a piece of shit he was, I would have warned you off before he got his hooks into you."

"It wouldn't have mattered." Six years ago, in the midst of her headlong rush into adulthood, she was so sure that she knew better, she hadn't listened to anyone. Not her sister, not her friends, not her fledgling instincts. As nice as it was to think otherwise, she wouldn't have listened to Gideon, either.

Being this close to him, talking like this while her body still sang from the pleasure he'd given her… It was too intimate. Too revealing. Just plain too much.

She slid off the couch and stood. A quick look at the front of his slacks confirmed that he was still, in fact, painfully hard. *Nice job, Lucy. Bask in your post-orgasmic bliss and ignore the fact he's still in need.* "Do you want me to…?"

"These lessons aren't about me." He sat up. "They're about you. And you need space."

Yeah, she did. His airy living room was suddenly too small, the walls closing in even as her heart beat too fast. "I asked for this."

"You don't have to explain." He gave her a half smile that didn't reach his eyes. "We poked at some old wounds tonight. If that means you need some distance from the whole thing, then so be it. You're being honest, and fuck if I'm going to punish you for that." He grabbed his phone off the coffee table. "But if you're headed home, I'm calling you a cab."

She should push back. She was more than capable of calling her own damn cab and the subway would be running for hours yet. But if Gideon could respect her need to flee without his pride being injured and throwing a fit, she could respect his need to get her home safe. "Okay."

He made the call quickly and set the phone down. "What's your schedule look like tomorrow?"

The change in subject left her discombobulated. "I have court in the afternoon, so I'll be doing last-minute preparations beforehand." It was as close to an open-and-shut case as such things got. The cops had mishandled the evidence and the lead detective had an established vendetta against her client. She had every intention of getting the whole damn thing thrown out.

"I know that look on your face. You have this one in the bag."

Her stomach gave another of those flutters that wasn't altogether uncomfortable. He'd said that with such confidence, as if there wasn't a single doubt in his mind that she would win. Lucy tucked a strand of hair behind her ear. "I should be free in the evening." *For another lesson?* She didn't know if she'd look forward to it or dread it. *Liar. You haven't even left yet and you're already craving another hit.*

"Good." He stood, suddenly taking up too much space. She tensed, half expecting him to touch her. But Gideon headed for the door. "I'll have a list of preliminary candidates ready for you, and we'll go over them at dinner."

"That I'll pay for." She cast a pointed look at the way his jaw tensed at her words. "Don't be like that. If I was a normal client, I'd pay and you wouldn't blink because that's how things are done."

"You aren't a normal client, Lucy. There's nothing *normal* about this." He motioned between them.

She couldn't really argue that, but that didn't mean he'd win this battle. "I'll handle the reservations and text you the details."

"Stubborn."

The twisting in her stomach took on a sour edge. Jeff had thrown that word at her like a curse more often than she could count. *Stop it. Oh, my God,* stop. *He's in the past and he's staying there.* "It's my best trait."

"I wouldn't dream of arguing that." He held the door open for her. "Until tomorrow."

"See you then."

She headed for the elevator, stopping several steps down the hallway and leaning against the wall as she tried to calm her racing heart. She hadn't known it could be like this. He'd just... taken care of her. Both physically and emotionally. Bringing her to orgasm and recognizing and respecting the panic driving her to leave. Lucy hadn't expected that. She didn't know what to do with a version of Gideon who was different than she'd expected.

What did I get myself into?

4

"YOU'RE FUCKING CRAZY."

Gideon didn't look up from his computer. "You don't have to tell me that."

"And yet I'm telling you all the same. What the hell are you doing? *Matchmaker?* For *Lucy Baudin?*" Roman Bassani paced from one side of the room to the other, his restless energy irritating as fuck.

"I know we're supposed to have lunch, but this came up and can't wait. I'm going to have to take a rain check." Gideon wrote down another name and moved to the next candidate on his preliminary list. When Roman paced another lap around the office, he cursed. "Sit down or get out. You're distracting me."

"You need the distraction. Hell, you need a goddamn intervention." Roman threw himself into the chair across from the desk and slouched. He would have been at home in some artsy perfume ad with his brooding good looks and the way he seemed to pose without noticing he was doing it. On any other man, the affected attitude would have pissed Gideon off, but with Roman it was just... Roman. He was too honest, too brash, too comfortable in any space. It was part of what made him so good at his job—he had never met a challenge he wasn't fully confident he could tackle.

Whether his confidence was misplaced or not was an argument for another day.

"Gideon, why are you doing this? Wait—don't tell me. You're not still feeling guilty because you didn't tell her what a douche Jeff was immediately? Look, we all fucked up. You're the only one who stepped in, and that's something I have to live with." He made a face. "I convinced myself that it wasn't my place or my business."

"Jeff's good at spinning any situation to benefit him." He'd sure as hell laid on the guilt and idiotic bro code heavy enough to give even Gideon pause at the time.

"Changes nothing." Roman shrugged. "Including the fact that you are not qualified to be a matchmaker, let alone for Lucy. She's a good girl and, damn it, she deserves a professional. I know a few in the city. I can call in a favor and get her shoved to the top of the list and wrap this whole thing up without anyone crossing any lines."

He tried to be rational and actually consider it. He fucking failed. The line had been crossed last night and there was no going back now. "No. She asked me, so I'm the one who'll do it. And don't get any funny ideas, Roman. You meddle in enough people's lives. I have no interest in being added to the list."

"As if you'd let me." Roman affected a sigh. "You're as mean as a junkyard dog."

"And you're wasting my time. Unless you have something worthwhile to add to the search, get out."

He realized his mistake the second his friend perked up. "Who's on the list?"

Fuck me. "No."

"Come on." Roman shot to his feet, towering over the desk, and snatched the paper from beneath Gideon's hand. His hazel eyes went wide. "Shit, Gideon. You put Aaron Livingston on here. Shooting for the stars, aren't you?"

"She's worth it." He grabbed the paper.

Roman studied him for a long moment. "Interesting."

"For fuck's sake, Roman, don't you have some business to buy up or small children to terrify?" He still had several hours' worth of work to do before he met up with Lucy tonight. The address she'd texted him wasn't far, but rush hour would be a bitch to navigate, so he'd scheduled in extra time. That didn't mean he was going to dick around with this damn list.

His friend pointed to two names on the list. "Take Travis and David off the list. They're fuckheads with women, though they both hide it well."

Gideon crossed out their names. "I hadn't heard."

"Why would you? You don't date, and that handsome mug of yours might have people intrigued, but it's from a distance. People aren't rushing to confide in you because there's a solid chance you'll rip them a new one for wasting your time."

Gideon glared. "Are you finished?"

"Not yet." Roman gave a lazy grin. "My point is that people talk to me, so using that as a resource is a smart thing to do. Aaron Livingston is as straight as they come. If that guy has any skeletons in his closet, they're buried deep. The other two left on the list are up in the air. I'll find out what I can and let you know."

He fought down the need to snap back. The truth was that Roman was right. People didn't open up to Gideon. His clients only cared that he got the job done and had one of the highest ratings in the industry. The people he placed for his clients only cared about their endgame in a company that would pay them well to do what they loved. Friends? He had them. He just preferred them at a distance.

Roman had never been able to take that hint.

"Fine. Look into them."

"It's charming that you think I need your permission." Roman grinned. "I'll come by in the next few days and let you know what I dig up."

A call would have been preferable, but Gideon knew Roman well enough to know that arguing was pointless. His friend did what he wanted, when he wanted. He sighed. "Fine."

"Chin up, Novak." Roman paused. "All joking aside, if you're going to do this, do it right. I know your history with Lucy is complicated, but playing this straight is the only way. Otherwise, there are a lot of potential complications that could arise."

Last night had been nothing if not one long, agonizingly good complication. Even almost twenty-four hours later, he could still taste her in his mouth. It made him crave more, which was a dangerous path to walk.

Lucy wasn't for him.

He had to remember that.

If she'd wanted *him*, she would have said so. Even this al-most-timid version of her wouldn't have balked at putting it out there. She was direct, as evidenced by her plan existing in the first place. But she hadn't brought him into her office to ask *him* to step into the role of husband.

Husband.

What would that even look like?

Gideon shook his head and focused on his friend. "I have it under control."

"Keep telling yourself that." Roman headed for the door. "I'll check in tomorrow, but in case I don't see you before then, we still on for Friday?"

"Yeah." They had a standing reservation in Vortex's VIP lounge on Friday nights. It was one of the only social appoint-ments he held consistently, despite occasionally running into Jeff there. But that asshole had started coming less and less in the years since he and Lucy had broken off their engagement. Peo-ple had started to see through his charming act and called him out when he was acting like a douchebag—which was often.

"See you then." Roman opened the door and paused. "You should bring her."

Gideon tore his gaze away from the list of names yet again. "What?"

"You should bring Lucy on Friday. I know Aaron Livingston since we worked together last year. We can orchestrate a non-pressure meeting. You're on your own with the other two, but I don't think Aaron would agree to a blind date for shits and giggles."

Since Gideon had only met him in passing, he couldn't argue that. "Do it." He spoke before he had a chance to think up half a dozen reasons why it was a bad idea. It *wasn't* a bad idea. It was his issue if he didn't want to see her with someone else—not hers.

He waited for Roman to shut the door behind him before he grabbed his phone. Both Mark and Liam were acquaintances he'd come across in the last few years who had seemed like upstanding guys. He'd feel them out for interest and then take the list to Lucy to see where she stood with all of it.

The knowledge that she'd likely end up with one of these men sat in his stomach like a rock. He hesitated, his contact list staring back at him. It would be the easiest thing in the world to sabotage this. All he had to do was feed some false information about Lucy and they'd say no. Or feed her false information about *them* to prove New York had a shitty dating scene.

"No." He'd promised her to do his best and he'd damn well do his best. Gideon had lied to her once before and it had almost destroyed them both. He wasn't going to do that to her again.

Fuck, he was in this situation *because* of what happened before.

Gideon would do right by Lucy. He'd have to be a heartless bastard to do anything else. The only option was to find her a damn husband.

No matter what it cost him to do it.

★ ★ ★

Lucy was on her second glass of wine by the time she caught sight of Gideon's familiar form moving toward her table through the darkened room. He towered over the tiny host and the poor man kept shooting looks over his shoulder as if he expected Gideon to club him over the head. The thought made her smile and was almost enough to distract her from her nervousness.

She'd woken up this morning from the single hottest dream of her life, starring none other than Gideon Novak. It started identical to their encounter last night, but they hadn't stopped until they were naked and in his bed, both shaking from their respective orgasms. Her body flushed at the memory and she took a shaky sip of wine.

What was the protocol for greeting a man who'd used his fingers to make her come on his couch the night before? They weren't dating, so a kiss seemed inappropriate. They weren't even really friends anymore, so a hug was likely presumptuous. A handshake was just absurd.

Gideon saved her from having to decide by sitting before she had a chance to stand. He shot a look at the host. He probably meant it as a polite dismissal, but it actually looked scathing. Lucy watched the man nearly run from the table. "You really have to work on your attitude."

"My attitude is fine."

"Without a doubt, but you have a very intimidating persona. You know most women judge a man by how he treats the wait-staff on their first date—and you would have just nixed the possibility of a second date and we haven't even had appetizers yet."

Gideon raised his eyebrows. "Good day in court, I take it."

"We're not talking about me." She leaned forward and lowered her voice. Enjoying poking at him a little. "Though that was a very smooth change of subject."

The corners of his lips twitched upward. "Yes, it was. We're not here to talk about my dating prospects. We're here to talk about yours." He looked up as a waiter approached and she actually saw the effort he put into forcing a smile. It looked downright pained, but it was better than nothing. "I'll have a seven and seven." He glanced at her half-full wineglass. "Another?"

"Sure." She didn't drink more than two glasses often, but she'd busted her ass on today's case and the judge had been persuaded to dismiss the entire thing. It was a coup that should have been the tipping point for her promotion, but when Rick Parker had come by her office to congratulate her, he'd made a comment about the big, broody man who'd been in to see her yesterday. Because, of course, who she was or wasn't dating was just as important as her professional skill set.

Well, damn it, Parker's crappy attitude wasn't going to ruin her night.

"Tell me about the case."

She almost refocused the conversation, but the truth was that she didn't have anyone to talk to about it. Her sister was supportive and wonderful, but Becka had her own thing going on and couldn't be less interested in law. Get together for drinks and chat about life and what their parents were up to? Sure. Hash out the details of whatever case Lucy was working on? Not a chance. And Gideon actually looked interested.

She picked up her wineglass. "I got the entire case thrown out today. All they had was circumstantial evidence and a bad attitude about my guy's priors. They were so certain he did the crime, they didn't look at anyone else. Anyone on the outside would have come to the same conclusion, but it's always a crapshoot with Judge Jones."

"That's great, Lucy. Congrats."

"Thanks." She smiled and then took a drink. "How was your day?"

"Productive." He leaned over and pulled a tablet out of his briefcase. "I have some things to show you."

Disappointment coated her tongue when he slid the tablet across the table to her. They'd barely gotten their conversation started and now they were back to business. *You hired him as a business decision. You don't get to have it both ways.* It wasn't fair to ask him to go back to being her friend along with her being his client.

She picked up the tablet and found pictures of three men. She clicked on the first one—a blond guy with a close-cropped beard and a seriously expensive suit—and found a file. "'Aaron Livingston, born May thirteenth...'" He'd compiled a list of information ranging from where Aaron was born to where he graduated high school and college—and his GPA at both. There was also a notification about possible likes and dislikes. "Wow, Gideon. You really don't do anything halfway, do you?"

He had compiled the same information for each of the other two men. Interestingly enough, all three of them were local and had gone to prestigious business colleges, graduating close to the top of their class. All three had moved on to respected companies and seemed to be doing well for themselves.

Using their information and ignoring their pictures, she wouldn't have been able to pick any of them out of a lineup. "This... Wow."

"You said that already." He frowned. "Is something wrong? I assumed that you were looking for someone in the same financial class as you, and leaning toward white-collar businessmen. That *is* why you came to me, correct?"

Yes, at least in theory. In reality, this whole thing was playing out much differently than she'd expected. It didn't make a bit of sense, especially because it was proceeding *exactly* how she'd hoped. "No, it's fine. They're excellent candidates."

Seeing them laid out like this, the situation just became so much more real. In a very short period of time she'd be sitting across the table from one of these men, rather than Gideon.

She'd be torturing herself with wondering if they'd kiss her after dinner—if maybe they'd expect more to happen.

I'm not ready.

She took a gulp of her wine. "Can we get dinner to go?"

5

NERVES STOLE LUCY'S VOICE AS SHE AND GIDEON walked to her apartment. She'd intentionally picked a restaurant close to her place so that they wouldn't have to worry about a cab ride to get from point A to point B. She nodded at the doorman as he held open the door for them and then she strode to the elevator and pushed the button.

Gideon followed her inside and leaned against the elevator wall. The food in the paper bag smelled divine, but her craving was solely for the man holding it. She clasped her hands together to keep from touching him. "I want to progress tonight."

He raised his eyebrows. "I'm listening."

Why was it so challenging to say these things aloud? She was an adult. She should be able to express her needs honestly without fear of being laughed out of the building—or rejected. Lucy fisted her hands and raised her chin. The mirrors in the elevator walls and door reflected a version of her that looked ready to go several rounds on the courthouse floor. "I don't want to wait anymore. I want everything."

That predatory stillness rolled over him and his eyes seemed to flare with barely banked heat. "Bite-size steps are the smart option."

"Nothing about *this* is smart, and I think we both know that." Last night had made her skittish in a way she hadn't expected, and if she was shrewder and less stubborn, she would have called the whole thing off as a result. Instead she was pushing them toward something neither could take back.

The elevator door opened and she wasted no time walking into the hall and down to her door. There were only four apartments on this floor, each occupying their respective corner of the building. Hers faced southeast, so she often woke to the early morning sunlight streaming through her windows. At least on the days she wasn't up before dawn.

She unlocked the door and held it open for Gideon. He stopped just inside the entranceway, barely leaving room for her to slide inside behind him. She tried to see the place through his eyes. The open floor plan showcased the big floor-to-ceiling windows. The kitchen lay just to the right of the front hall, the white cabinets set off with little turquoise handles she'd found online. The living room contained a decent-size TV that she rarely used and two short couches arranged in a loose V. Her cat, Garfunkel, lifted his head and gave Gideon a death stare.

Gideon moved to the kitchen counter—white marble shot through with pale gray—and set the bag of food on it. He turned and crossed his arms over his chest. "Why the change of pace?"

"Maybe I just want you." It was the truth, but not the full truth.

He shook his head. "Honesty, Lucy."

Why had she agreed to that particular term? She pulled at the hem of her fitted blue dress. "I'm nervous. Last night was good, but I didn't expect that level of reaction, and I'm afraid if we don't get it over with, I'm going to change my mind."

"Get it over with," Gideon murmured. "Sex isn't something

you 'get over with.' If you think of it that way, there's a problem somewhere."

A problem he was determined to fix if the expression on his
face was anything to go by. She sliced her hand through the air.
"No problem. That's not what I meant at all. My issue is that
the anticipation, the will-we-or-won't-we, is driving me nuts.
I want to rip it off right now—like a Band-Aid."

He stared at her for a long moment and then burst out laughing. "A Band-Aid. Fuck, woman, you really are going to kill
me." He ran a hand over his face. "The anticipation is meant
to be enjoyed."

She could think of a lot of words to describe how she felt
standing in her apartment with Gideon and knowing they were
alone and could do what they wanted for hours. *Enjoyment*
didn't top the list. Her body was too hot, her lungs too tight,
her core aching from need. But she knew that look on his face.
If she didn't do something rash, he was going to put the brakes
on and sit her down and coax her to talk through it. For someone with such a ruthless reputation, Gideon was overwhelm-
ingly careful with her. She knew why—he had residual guilt
over not telling her immediately about Jeff's cheating ways. But
she didn't care about any of that right now.

All she cared about was getting through this interaction so
she could go back to breathing normally again.

Before she could talk herself out of it, Lucy unzipped the side
of her dress and slid it off. She didn't look at him as she kicked
the silky fabric to the side. If she thought too hard about the
fact that she stood in front of him in only a pair of nude-lace
panties, she might die on the spot.

A second passed. Another.

Still, he didn't say anything.

What is he doing?

Probably looking for a way to gracefully exit that wouldn't

have her throwing herself from the nearest window. *Stop that right now.* She was stronger than this. Lucy looked good. She ate relatively well and hit the gym at least three times a week. Last night Gideon's physical reaction had proved that he'd wanted her. He might not have taken his release, but he wasn't remotely unaffected.

So why was he standing there without saying a word?

Stop waiting for him to make the first move.

Do it yourself.

Gathering her courage, she lifted her head and looked at him. Her first step took more effort than she could have dreamed, and the intense look on his face didn't help her any. He held himself perfectly still, every muscle coiled. Though, for the life of her, she couldn't tell if it was to keep from jumping her or to stop himself from fleeing.

Only one way to find out.

She took the last few steps that brought her close enough to touch. Tentatively she reached out and laid her hands on his chest. *Why isn't he saying anything?* She waited another few seconds but the only sound in her kitchen was the soft rush of their quickened breathing.

Maybe she'd misjudged the situation. *Oh, God, what did I do?* "If you've changed your mind, just tell me. We can pretend this whole thing never happened."

Gideon couldn't look away from Lucy. She was fucking perfect. He'd known that, of course, but seeing it without clothes barring his vision was something else altogether. Her breasts were small and high, capped with dark rose nipples. He forced himself not to reach for her as she stroked her hands down his chest and back up again.

"Gideon?"

She'd asked a question, hadn't she?

"What?" His gaze snagged on her narrow waist and the nude-lace panties that were so sheer, he could see a shadow of her slit beneath them. He cleared his throat and jerked his attention back to her face.

She frowned a little. "Did you change your mind?"

"No." He finally allowed himself to move, reaching up and covering her hands with his. "Fuck me, but you can't expect a man to be faced with the sight of you naked and still be able to hold down a conversation."

"That's sweet."

But she thought he was lying. He could read it all over her face.

It struck Gideon that he'd been playing this wrong. He'd known Jeff had hurt Lucy with his actions, and then she'd told him that she hadn't been with anyone since, and he'd gone straight to treating her like an innocent virgin. She was innocent in some ways, but by being so careful with her, he'd created room for her to doubt herself—and him.

Fuck that.

He guided her hands to his shoulders and then started unbuttoning his shirt. "You don't believe the words, and I don't blame you for that. But if you won't listen to me when I tell you that you're a fucking goddess personified, then I'll show you."

She kneaded his shoulders slightly, her eyes glued to his hands as he finished with his shirt and started on the front of his slacks. "I believe you."

"You don't." He kicked off his shoes and shoved down his pants. Lucy shook her head as if fighting off a daze and pushed his shirt off his shoulders. He let it fall to the floor and then the only barriers were their respective underwear. He snagged the lace with a single finger. "These have to go."

"Yours, too."

He took a step back and hooked his thumbs in his boxer

briefs. A single, smooth movement and he stood before her naked. Watching Lucy's jaw drop was ridiculously gratifying. She took in each part of his body, starting with his head and moving over his neck, his shoulders, his chest, his stomach and, finally, settling on his cock. He grew harder in response to her hungry expression.

Gideon had never had a woman look at him the way Lucy did. As if he was a present she'd found under the Christmas tree—just for her. It threatened to turn this interaction into something it could never be, so he smothered the thought. She wanted him physically. End of story.

"Gideon, you're beautiful." She shucked off her panties, never taking her gaze from him. "I mean, I'd seen you in a swimsuit, but this is different." She closed the distance between them once more, a small line appearing between her brows. "Is it weird, though? I never considered you a brother or anything like that, but you were family."

Family.

He'd forced himself to forget that feeling of belonging that Lucy seemed to extend wherever she went. When he'd hung out with her and Jeff, he'd never felt like a third wheel—he'd just been part of the unit. Of all the things he'd missed when she'd cut off communication between them, that might be the highest on the list. "I never saw you as a sister."

"I know." She laughed softly. "I'd catch you watching me sometimes—not often—and you never made it weird. But… I know."

He thought he'd hid it better than that. Gideon shoved the past away just like he shoved aside so many inconvenient feelings that seemed to arise the more time he spent with Lucy. "It's not weird."

"I guess it's not." She carefully slid her hands up his chest and around his neck, taking that last step to bring them chest to chest. He rested his hands on her waist, but she felt too good to limit the contact. Gideon stroked up her back and down again to cup her ass.

There was nothing left to say. They'd reached the point of no return the second Lucy's dress had hit the floor. Gideon lifted his head. "Bedroom."

"This way— *Oh!*"

He swept her into his arms and strode across the living room to the door she'd indicated. Her bedroom was purely Lucy: a pretty wood headboard, more pillows than one woman should require, and a bright yellow floral bedspread that brightened the room even in the low light of the single lamp she must have left on.

He laid her on the bed and settled between her thighs. Gideon had every intention of slowing things down and having a very specific conversation about how this would proceed.

Every. Intention.

But Lucy wrapped her legs around his waist and arched up to meet him, and that honorable plan disappeared as if it'd never existed. Maybe it hadn't and he'd just been lying to himself all along. It didn't matter. There was only her soft skin beneath his palms, her body sliding against his and her mouth on his neck.

He kissed her. Gideon might never get enough of her sunny taste, and he wasn't about to miss a chance to immerse himself in the feel of her. This was happening. They would cross the line he'd never once considered anything other than insurmountable.

He stroked a hand down her waist to squeeze her ass and hitch her up to fit tighter against him. The temptation to sink into her was almost too much, but this wasn't about him, his wants, his needs.

This was about Lucy.

Gideon hadn't leashed himself and his desire for her this long to skip over for anything less than the full experience. He didn't want to miss a single thing. He kissed down and across her collarbone and palmed her breasts. "Perfect. Every single thing about you is fucking perfect."

She laughed a little nervously. "You said that before."

"I'll say it again." He tongued one nipple. "Pretty and pink and...fuck. Just fucking perfect."

"Don't stop." She laced her fingers through his hair and drew him back down. "Harder."

He set his teeth gently against her nipple and then increased the pressure slightly when she went wild beneath him. Through it all, he kept his eyes open. Gideon wanted it all, every nuance of expression, every reaction. All of it.

A flush stole across her freckled cheeks and over her chest, and her small breasts heaved with each sobbed breath. He moved to give her other nipple the same treatment but kept stroking the first, pinching it with the same amount of pressure he'd applied with his mouth.

She shuddered against him, her hips grinding. "Gideon. Oh, God. I think I could come from this alone."

"I'm not done yet." He pressed one last kiss to each nipple and then slid back until he knelt on the floor next to the bed. He grabbed her hips and jerked her to the edge. This close, he could see every part of her. Gideon drew his thumb over her slit. "You need more."

"Yes."

He used his thumbs to part her. "Next time, you'll tell me exactly what you want."

"Next time?" She lifted her head to give him a dazed look. "Why next time?"

"Because I'm a selfish bastard." His mouth actually watered being this close to the most private part of Lucy. Her pussy was as flushed as the rest of her skin, wet and wanting and practically begging for his tongue. There wasn't a single damn reason *not* to give her exactly what he wanted. "I hope you're ready."

6

LUCY HAD NEVER ENJOYED ORAL. NOT REALLY. It was yet another area where Jeff's competitiveness soured any inkling of pleasure she might get from the act. He had a series of moves he'd go through, the goal being to get her wet enough for sex. Truth be told, she'd always suspected he didn't like the act any more than she did, but the one time she'd brought it up, it had been one of the worst fights they'd ever had.

The first rasp of whiskers against Lucy's inner thigh drove thoughts of her ex right out of her head. Gideon didn't immediately go for her clit. Instead he dragged his cheek against her other thigh, using the motion to spread her legs farther.

She lifted her head just as he dipped down and drew his tongue over her in one long lick. Then he did it again—as if she was his favorite flavor of ice cream. Considering their frenzied making out, she'd expected this to be just as quick…

Should have known better than to make assumptions about Gideon. Especially after last time.

He spread her folds and thrust his tongue into her, his low growl making the act unbearably erotic. Lucy's thoughts slammed to a halt and her mind went gloriously blank. "Holy shit."

He didn't appear to hear her. Gideon fucked her pussy with

his tongue as if he couldn't get enough of her taste. He gripped her thighs with his big hands, holding her open to his ministrations even when her muscles shook with the effort to react, to move, to do *something*.

She thrashed her head from one side to the other, the sensations too much and not enough—and she didn't know how to put it into words. *Honesty.* Words crowded in her throat, too raw and vulnerable to give voice, but then she felt his teeth and they burst forth in a rush. "My clit. Gideon, suck on my clit. Use your teeth." Like he had with her nipples. Like he was doing right now with her labia.

Her entire body coiled at the thought, and the feeling intensified when he did exactly as she asked. There was no macho posturing or telling her that he was more than capable of pleasing her without an instruction manual. Gideon just…listened.

He sucked her clit into his mouth and set his teeth against the sensitive bundle of nerve endings. She arched almost completely off the bed, and he used the move to slide his hands under her ass and lift her so he could feast more effectively.

Because that was exactly what he was doing—feasting.

There was nothing gentle or teasing about his touch now. He went after her clit in a way that was just shy of pain, sending little zings of pure bliss through her. Her body coiled tighter yet, so close to the edge, she didn't know how much longer she could hold out.

Gideon lifted his head just enough to speak, his lips brushing her heated flesh with every word. "Do you want to come like this?"

Asking that question was the single sexiest thing anyone had ever done to her. Choice. Control. Who knew it could be such a turn-on?

She almost said yes. Lucy was so close to orgasm, she shook with need and had to focus entirely too hard to create verbal words beyond *yesyesyesyesyes*. Did she want him to keep doing what he'd been doing? Hell, yes.

But she wanted him inside her more.

She licked her lips. "I want…" How did she want him?

Every way.

Right now, though? "I want to ride you."

A muscle in his jaw ticked and his grip on her thighs twitched. "You have condoms."

"Yes." She pointed a shaking finger at her nightstand.

The ones she'd bought after her breakup had expired ages ago, victims of her self-esteem issues, so she'd picked up a new box this morning. She'd also unwrapped the box so they could save time. It had felt presumptuous in the extreme when she'd been sitting alone on her bed, Garfunkel staring at her in feline judgment. Now she wished she'd already had one of them on Gideon.

He slowly released her, as if it pained him to move away. She sat up and scooted back so she could watch him pull open the top drawer. It wasn't until his dark eyes flashed that she remembered what *else* was in the drawer. "Ah…"

He held up her pink vibrator. "We'll talk about this later." He dropped it back in the drawer and pulled out a condom. "Scratch that. We're not going to talk. I'm going to stroke myself while I watch you use it."

Her eyes went wide at the image his words painted. Him, sitting against the headboard with his cock in his hand. Her on her back with her legs spread, using her toy. Her core clenched. "I want that. Later."

"Later," he agreed. He ripped the wrapper open and proceeded to roll the condom down his length.

She stood and pushed him to sit on the edge of the bed. "Like this." Lucy climbed into his lap and reached between them to notch his cock at her entrance. With her desire driving her, it was easy to speak things that would have stoppered her words with embarrassment in any other situation. "Kiss me while I ride you."

"You have no idea how fucking sexy it is that you know exactly what you want." He scooted back enough that she could brace her knees on the mattress. Then he hooked one arm around her waist while he dug his other hand into her hair. He tugged a little. "Yes?"

She moaned. "Yes." She loved when Gideon didn't treat her like she was breakable. He didn't so much as hesitate when she urged him to bite her harder, to grab her tighter. Things she hadn't even known she craved until he gave them to her.

Lucy slid down until he was completely sheathed inside her. She had to pause to adjust to the almost uncomfortable fullness. The sensation passed quickly, dissipating to sheer pleasure as her body accommodated his size. She wrapped her arms around his shoulders and kissed him as she started to move. Their position had him rubbing against her clit with every stroke and, despite trying to hold out, her orgasm loomed all too soon.

Her strokes went choppy. *"Gideon."*

He shifted his hands to her hips, helping her maintain the rhythm that would get her where she needed to go. "You feel so fucking good."

"You...too." She opened her eyes, not sure when she'd closed them, and the expression on his face stilled her breath in her lungs. *Possession. Desire. Need.* It was too much.

Lucy cried out his name as she came. He kept her moving, kept the orgasm going, until her muscles gave out and she slumped against him.

He carefully pulled out of her and shifted them back onto the bed. Gideon spooned her, lightly stroking her arm, her hip, her stomach. She stared at the art print on the wall next to her bed for several long moments while she relearned how to breathe. Gradually she became aware of a very specific part of him pressed against her ass. "You didn't come."

"Not yet."

Not yet.

Who knew those two little words would be the sexiest thing she'd ever heard?

Gideon kept up his light touching until Lucy arched back against him. Judging her to be recovered enough, he hooked one knee and lifted her leg up and over his legs, leaving her open to him. He slid a hand carefully between her thighs, testing her tenderness. "Tell me what you want."

"You."

He kissed the back of her neck. "You have me." *For now.* "Tell me what other fantasies you've been harboring." The image of her using that toy on herself would be enough to keep him up at night for the foreseeable future. He was a goddamn idiot for feeding his imagination more images, but he craved them the same way he craved her.

"You want my sexual bucket list?" Her amused tone turned into a gasp as he idly stroked her clit. "You can't expect me to think when you're doing *that*."

"Consider it inspiration." He liked the idea of being the one who helped her cross items off that type of list. Fuck, he liked the thought that he was in her bed right now and would be for as long as she felt he had something to teach her.

Lucy reached back to sift her fingers through his hair. "I haven't really thought about it."

"Liar." He took the move for an invitation and slid his other arm beneath her so he could palm her breasts. "There's at least a few things you have lurking in the back of your mind about this—something you've always wanted to try." Something he could be the only one to ever give to her.

At least for now.

She hesitated and he could practically hear her thinking it over and considering laying herself bare in this way. Gideon could have pointed out that they were already bared to each other, but this was different.

He stilled his hands, waiting for her answer.

"Don't stop." She covered the hand between her legs with one of her own, guiding him back to her clit and then lower, to push a finger inside her. Lucy moaned. "High-end dressing room. I've always wanted to have sex in a high-end dressing room—lingerie, maybe, if that's not super cliché." She tensed. "Crap. I'm doing it again. God, it's so hard to turn *off*."

"I think we could make that happen." He kissed along her neck to growl in her ear. "I want to see you in green—that bright jewel tone."

She tilted her head forward, giving him better access. "I think we could make that happen." She echoed his words back to him.

"Charitable of you." He paused his stroking long enough to guide his cock into her. She clamped tight around him and he barely bit back a curse.

As many times as he'd slipped and imagined what it would be like to have Lucy in his bed, his fantasies hadn't come close to the bliss of reality. She was fucking perfection. Every move, every word, every gasp—Gideon stored them all away in his memory. He only had a limited time to accumulate enough to last him a lifetime.

A worry for another day.

Tonight he was inside Lucy.

Tomorrow could wait until tomorrow.

Gideon sat in Lucy's living room and ate reheated leftovers. She had a bright throw wrapped around her shoulders and her cat in her lap as she tried to arrange her food in an order that she could actually eat. He reached over and plucked the cat out of her lap.

Or he tried.

In reality, Garfunkel had no intention of going anywhere against his will. He let loose a yowl that raised the small hairs on the back of Gideon's neck. Before he could react, the cat hissed and swiped claws across his forearm. He cursed but managed not to chuck the horrid little beast. Instead he dropped the animal the short distance to the floor.

"Oh, my God!" Lucy shoved her food containers to the side and grabbed his wrist. "What were you thinking?"

He gritted his teeth as she dabbed at the blood welling in the scratches with a napkin. "I was thinking you'd have an easier time eating if he wasn't taking up so much space on your lap."

"You weren't wrong." She dabbed a little harder. "But if you haven't noticed, Garfunkel is territorial. And he doesn't like men much."

"You think?" He took the napkin from her and pressed it hard against his arm. "It's fine. I should have known better." His lifestyle wasn't one that allowed for a pet, but if it had, Gideon would definitely be a dog person. Cats seemed to be little assholes as a general rule, and he had a feeling if he tried to adopt one, he'd pick the biggest asshole of them all through sheer karma.

Though Garfunkel has a solid running for that title.

"I'm really sorry."

"Lucy, it's fine." He grabbed his food and joined her on the couch. "How are you feeling?"

"Unwound." She leaned her head against the back of the couch and gave him a sleepy smile. "I'd forgotten how relaxing good sex could be."

Good doesn't begin to cover it.

He bit the comment back. It was sheer pride that made him want to say it and he didn't have a right. Not in the current situation. He was here for a specific purpose and he couldn't afford to forget that even for a moment. Lucy wasn't for him in any permanent way. This was a window into the world of what could have been in another life, if things had fallen out in a different sequence of events.

But they hadn't. So here he and Lucy were.

"What made you pick those particular men?"

It took him a few seconds too long to make the subject change with her. He didn't want to talk about other men while he still had the memory of her body against his and the smell of her on his skin. It felt wrong on a whole hell of a lot of different levels. An intrusion.

Except it wasn't.

Lucy had asked him for a specific set of things, and sex had been an afterthought. Just because it wasn't an afterthought for Gideon didn't mean he could snap at her for keeping her head in the game. So he did his best to do the same.

"They're all ambitious men who have reputations for being honest and are old enough that they're likely thinking about settling down with one person. I've personally placed both Mark and Liam in jobs, so I did all the research and then some. They have solid histories. Neither has any record of being a cheater or abusive in any way. They're good guys—as good as anyone is." And he'd checked. Even with only twenty-four hours at his disposal, he'd done extensive research and even gone so far as to call a few of their exes, though Gideon wasn't about to admit that to Lucy. None of the women had said anything to raise red flags.

She speared a green bean with her fork. "And Aaron?"

"He's the best of the best. I actually tried to poach him for a client last year and he wouldn't give me the time of day." When she raised her eyebrows, he shifted, something like embarrassment sifting through him. "There's more to it than that, of course. He's got an excellent reputation, and Roman is actually friends with him."

"Your pitch is overwhelming." She laughed softly. "But then, this is what I asked for, isn't it?"

He didn't like seeing that look on her face, as if she was resigning herself to a life half lived. "Lucy, if you want to change directions on this thing, we can do that. Even if you go on dates with these guys, nothing is set in stone."

"I know you mean well, but I would very much appreciate it if you'd stop trying to talk me out of this."

He tried to rein in his temper, but he'd held himself too tightly under control the last two days. Too careful. It wasn't Gideon's natural default, and it had started to wear on him. He glared. "I'm not trying to talk you out of shit. I'm giving you options. You want this to have a chance in hell of working, you need to stop being so goddamn defensive. I'm helping you with this bat-shit-crazy plan, so I need you to throw me a bone once in a while."

She set down her fork. "I think you should leave."

Fuck. He started to apologize but stopped. Lucy might be fragile in some ways, but she wasn't broken. He had to remember that and stop treating her with kid gloves. And yet letting her make what might be the biggest mistake of her life because he felt guilty over her last relationship was a shitty thing to do.

He wasn't sure what his other options were, but he'd have to figure it out. Fast.

In the meantime he needed to get the hell out of there before he said something they'd both regret. Gideon stood and buttoned the last few buttons on his shirt. "I'll email you the details tomorrow."

"Okay." She still wouldn't look at him.

He hesitated, but there was nothing left to say. Sex had changed things. Having concrete proof of how deep the connection ran between them was enough to set him back on his heels. She felt it, too. There was no way she didn't.

Now he just needed her to actually admit it.

7

"I'M SORRY—DID YOU JUST SAY THAT YOU HAVE a *date*?"

Lucy swirled her white wine, not looking at her little sister. "You don't have to sound so shocked by it." She hadn't wanted to confess her plan, but it twisted her up inside not to be able to talk about it with at least one person. Gideon hardly counted, especially since his reactions were hardly consistent with what she'd expected—and *her* reactions weren't cooperating, either.

"I *am* shocked. You've been all work, work, work. When did you have time to set up a date?" Becka leaned over and snagged a chip from the plate in the middle of the table. "That's not a dig, by the way. That's just facts. I'm on three freaking dating websites and *I* have trouble finding dates who aren't candidates for 'but he seemed so nice.'"

Lucy sighed. "They can't all be serial killers, Becka."

"It only takes one." Becka frowned. "Besides, we aren't talking about me. We're talking about you."

Now that push came to shove, she didn't know where to start. Or if she even should confess any of it. In truth, if she hadn't had these drinks set up with Becka already, she'd be at home, moping. It had been two days since she'd seen Gideon and, aside from a few emails confirming her first date, they hadn't talked, either. She knew she'd been an ass, but it wasn't like Gideon to avoid a conflict.

Not that there had to be a conflict. There didn't. She just didn't want him to think that their having sex meant he could push her into not going through with her plan. She'd made the decision. He had to respect that. If that meant he didn't want to continue with their lessons… Well, that was something she'd just have to deal with.

Unless he doesn't want to continue for a different reason…

"You okay?"

She blinked and tried to focus on her sister's face. Becka changed her hair color with the seasons and today it was a bright blue that was the exact shade of her eyes. Her lip piercing glinted in the light of the little hipster bar where they always met up. She had the cute-alternative look down to a science. *She* never had problems with men, despite her lamenting about dating.

Lucy tried to smile. "Just a crisis of faith. You know, the usual."

"Don't do that. If you don't want to tell me, that's cool, but don't pat me on the head. You don't have to protect me anymore, Lucy. You know that, right?"

"It's not about protecting you." And it wasn't. They'd had a fine upbringing. Decent—if distant—parents. A solid middle-class lifestyle. Nothing traumatic happening to make waves in their lives.

But Becka was still her little sister. When they were growing up, Becka had been the shy one, the bookworm who was a little too odd to fit in with the rest of the kids in her grade. It led to bullying and, when their parents had failed to notice, Lucy had taken care of it.

She'd been taking care of her little sister ever since.

Though these days, Becka fought her own battles.

But her sister had a point. Holding on to the turmoil inside her wasn't doing Lucy any favors. She'd talked about it to Gideon, but he wasn't exactly a neutral party. Neither was Becka, for that matter. "I just… I know it's been two years, but I still have Jeff's comments rattling around in my brain. It's pathetic and I should be over it by now, and I *am* over *him*. I don't know what's wrong with me."

"Nothing's wrong with you." Becka grabbed the wine bottle on the table and refilled her glass. "It's not like you had a monthlong relationship and turned around and let it mess you up for the rest of your life. You and Jeff were together for… what, like four years? You were going to marry him." She narrowed her blue eyes. "Though he better hope we never cross paths, because I'm going to kick his ass one of these days."

"Becka."

"Lucy." She mimicked her voice perfectly. "But that day is not today. Either way, I'd say you were having a normal reaction and that's that. Why's this coming up now? The whole matchmaking thing is kind of out there, but it's not like you're jumping into bed with these guys to give them a trial run." Becka grinned. "Though *there's* an idea."

She tried to imagine it—taking a single night with each of the guys on Gideon's list—and instantly rejected the idea. "No way." It felt wrong and she didn't want to spend too much time thinking about why. *I promised Gideon to be exclusive.* Sure, that was it. Definitely.

"Worth a shot." Becka ate a few more chips. "You'll be fine, Lucy. I promise. Dating is weird and it's hard to get to know people, but you have a matchmaker in your corner. It'll all work out."

She couldn't tell her sister that Gideon Novak was the so-called matchmaker in question. Becka had met him on several occasions and she'd lose her shit if she knew. Since they'd managed to get through this conversation without her thinking Lucy was out of her mind, she'd like to keep it that way. "I'm sure you're right."

"I am."

Lucy's phone rang and her heart leaped in her throat at the sight of Gideon's name on the screen. "Hello?"

"I'll meet you there ten minutes early, so be ready."

She blinked. "I'm sorry—what?"

"The date, Lucy. Please tell me you haven't forgotten about it."

She bristled at the irritation in his voice. "Of course I haven't forgotten. But I was not expecting you to be attending." She was nervous enough about going out with Mark Williams without having to do it under the watchful eye of Gideon. "That's unacceptable."

"My rules. Be there ten minutes early." He hung up.

Lucy set her phone carefully on the table and looked up to find her sister watching her. "What?"

"I know that move. The 'gently set your phone down so you don't chuck it across the room' one. Who pissed you off?"

"It's a long story and, unfortunately, I have to leave in order not to be late." *Not to be late to being early. I'm going to kill him.* She dug out her wallet and flagged down the waitress. "Same time next week?"

"Sure. You're the one with the crazy schedule." Becka finished her drink and set it on the table. She grinned. "And whoever that was that just called you, give 'em hell, sis."

"I plan on it." She set the appropriate amount of cash on the table under the ticket and rose. She accepted Gideon's direction in the bedroom because that was exactly what she'd asked for. She accepted his list of men for the same reason.

She refused to accept him taking control of every aspect of this matchmaking situation.

He vetted and picked the candidates, yes, but ultimately it was up to her and the individual men to see if it was something that could actually work. Gideon's role in this ended the second she and one of the men came to an agreement. She tried very hard not to focus on the way her stomach dropped at that thought.

It didn't matter.

What mattered was his trying to steamroll her on this. She had to have some freedom to figure out if she could stomach the thought of spending her life with the man across the table from her, and she couldn't do that with Gideon standing at her shoulder.

If he did, she couldn't shake the feeling that she'd compare every man to him and it would skew her perception.

Against Gideon Novak, who could compare?

Gideon checked his watch for the third time in as many minutes. Where the hell was she? He turned to look down the street again just as Lucy walked around the corner. She didn't seem particularly concerned to be running late—or happy to see him. He motioned to his watch. "We had an understanding."

"Wrong. You told me something. I disagreed." She crossed her arms over her chest, which drew his attention to her dress.

"What are you wearing?" It was a pale blue lacy thing that gave the illusion of showing more than it actually did. It clung to her body, the gaps in the lace showing a nude lining the exact same shade as her skin. At a glance, she might as well have been naked beneath it.

He loved it.

He fucking hated it.

"A dress." She touched it, a frown drawing a line between her brows. "Don't take that overprotective tone with me, Gideon. It's a good dress."

"It's inappropriate for a first date. He's going to sit across that table and spend the whole time thinking about fucking you."

Lucy gave him a brilliant grin, her plum-colored lips mirroring the darkness of her hair, which she'd left in waves down around her shoulders. "Then it's doing its job. Now, if you'd please get out of my way, I can take it from here." She strode past him and through the door to the restaurant.

Jealousy flared, hot and poisonous, down the back of his throat. He didn't have a right to it any more now than he had before, but it was a thousand times more powerful now that they'd put sex on the table. Gideon followed her inside and hooked a hand around her elbow, towing her sideways into a small hallway that led to the coat check.

It was dimmer there than in the main entrance—more intimate. He pressed his hands to the wall on either side of her shoulders. "You make me fucking crazy."

"That makes two of us." She poked him in the chest. "You might be calling the shots in some things, but you have to give me enough space to breathe. The compressed timeline is already going to play havoc on my instincts—I don't need your constant presence doing the same."

He'd think about how his presence affected her later. Right now all he could focus on was the first part of the sentence. "If the timeline is too tight, then extend it. The only person who put this deadline in place was *you*."

"And it stands." She lifted her chin. "I'm already late for this date. I don't want to have this conversation for the seventh time. Just give me some space to breathe."

He pushed off the wall even though it was the last thing he wanted to do. The truth was that he wanted Lucy, and it was fucking up his head space and messing with *his* instincts. He knew better than to push her, but he couldn't help doing it all the same. He wanted her and she wanted him—at least physically.

What if it could be more than just physical?

What if I actually played for keeps?

The thought stopped him in his tracks.

He watched Lucy greet the hostess and follow her deeper into the restaurant, but he couldn't move. This whole time, he had been letting Lucy take the wheel and guide things—at least to some extent. Gideon had handled her so goddamn carefully because he was well aware of the damage Jeff had caused her and he blamed himself, at least a little, because of it. That guilt was the same reason he hadn't pushed her to face the fact that there was more than just friendship between them.

But what if he did?

He couldn't hit this head-on—Lucy would tell him to get lost, and with good reason. She had her eye on the prize and she wouldn't be deterred by an outside force, even if it was Gideon.

If he could get her to change her mind, that would be a different story.

Gideon smiled.

Let her have her date with Mark. The guy was nice enough, but Gideon fully intended to take her to bed until she was so wrapped up in him that she forgot Mark's fucking name.

A man looked up as Lucy approached the table the hostess had indicated. He was cute in a hipster sort of way, his close-cropped beard and glasses a combination that would have been strange five years before. Now it seemed like everyone had them. The only thing missing was suspenders or a bow tie. Instead, he wore a nice button-up shirt and a pair of slacks. When he rose to pull her chair out for her, she got an eyeful of his broad shoulders and clearly outlined muscles.

Too many muscles. Too much facial hair.

Oh, my God, stop. *What is wrong with me?*

He resumed his place and grinned at her, his teeth white and straight. "Lucy, I presume. Otherwise, this is about to get incredibly awkward."

That startled a laugh out of her. "Yes, I'm Lucy." She extended her hand. "That would make you Mark."

"The very one." He gave her a firm handshake, which she appreciated. Too many men—especially men who worked in corporate jobs—tended to give handshakes like they thought they'd break her. It drove her crazy.

Mark leaned back, his gaze roaming over her face.

Another mark in his favor—not ogling my chest. Lucy gave herself a shake. She had to stop overanalyzing every second of this date. Mark was most definitely not Gideon, and that didn't have to be a tally in the negative column.

It was just hard to focus when she could still smell Gideon's cologne from where he'd pressed her against the wall a few short minutes ago. It wasn't musky and strong like so many men she knew—it was light and clean and reminded her of... She couldn't place it.

Focus.

She gave a polite smile. "Thank you for agreeing to the date."

"When Gideon called me and explained the situation, I'll admit I didn't believe him." The corner of his mouth hitched up. "And then I asked him what was wrong with you."

She tensed and then admonished herself for doing so. He was joking. He didn't really think there was something wrong with her. "As you can see, I'm in possession of all my teeth."

"Not to mention beautiful and successful." Mark's easy smile made the words fact rather than a throwaway compliment. "I've heard of marriages of convenience, but I assumed they were the stuff of fiction. This whole situation is kind of strange."

"I can't argue that." She'd known it was a reach the second she'd called Gideon to put the plan into action. That didn't change the fact that she had no other option. "But I have to ask. If you think it's so strange, why are you here?"

He sighed. "I'm fucking up this small talk, aren't I? That was way too heavy to start in on."

"I don't mind. This isn't exactly the most conventional situation." She appreciated the frankness, even if there was something missing from this interaction that she couldn't quite put her finger on. Mark was attractive—there was no denying that—but… Lucy didn't know. It was off.

"In that case, I agreed to this because I've worked eighty-hour weeks for several years and that won't be stopping anytime soon. I don't know if you've been to a bar lately, but meeting people there is a joke. Everyone is on their phones or with their friends or not interested. Dating apps are even worse, in large part because women have so many nightmare encounters that they're edgy and distant. It makes it hard to really get to know a person when they're sure that you're going to turn on a dime and send a dick pic or freak out because they cancel the date." He shrugged. "It comes down to time. I don't have much of it to meet new people and jump through the hoops of first dates and second dates—and balancing the knife edge of showing that I'm interested without being too goddamn pushy." Mark sighed. "Sorry. It's a sore spot for me."

There was a story there—perhaps several.

The waitress appeared to take their order and then disappeared as quickly. Lucy leaned forward. "Tell me some of your dating stories."

He raised his eyebrows. "If there was a playbook for first dates, I'm one hundred percent sure it wouldn't include recalling dates with other women."

"This is hardly your textbook first date." She smiled. "My little sister runs the gauntlet of online dating, and some of her stories defy belief."

"I wish I could say she was making it all up." Mark relaxed a little, just the slight loosening in his shoulders. She hadn't realized he was tense until it disappeared. He grinned. "If she's half as beautiful as you, she's seen more than her fair share of crazy on those sites."

"I'm sure she has." Lucy knew all too well that Becka had kept plenty of it back, sharing only the funny stories. That was what gave her away—there only seemed to be funny stories.

Nothing dark, nothing worrisome. Nothing indicating she'd met anyone she had more than a passing interest for. "Tell me about them."

He hesitated, surveying her expression, but he must have seen only the interest she felt there because he chuckled. "I'd rather know more about you. Gideon said you're a lawyer."

"I'm a defense attorney." She had to wonder what else Gideon had told Mark and the other men he'd managed to get to agree to meet her. Lucy looked good on paper. She was confident in that, even if she wasn't in any other romantic aspect of her life.

But a lot of women looked good on paper and weren't going about marriage in such an odd way.

Mark leaned forward, expression attentive. "Do you like it? I've been fascinated with the court system since I was a kid. Too many *Law & Order* marathons, you know."

"It's not much like that in real life. There's a truly unglamorous amount of paperwork, and research can be tedious to the point where I've believed more than once that it might kill me." She forced herself to relax a little. "But actually being in court is exhilarating. It's like a game of chess but with higher stakes. I wouldn't trade it for the world."

Their food arrived and the conversation proceeded easily, her work moving into his work as a cybersecurity expert, and then sharing a bit about their childhoods. Mark was as nice as he was handsome and Lucy waited through the entire meal for her heartbeat to pick up at the sight of his smile, or for her mind to leapfrog into what it would be like to get naked with him.

There was nothing but a vague pleasant feeling of spending her time in friendly conversation.

No sizzle whatsoever.

She'd asked for that, but she couldn't help comparing him to Gideon. They were different in so many ways. Mark was built lean like a blade—a very well-muscled blade—whereas Gideon looked like a Viking who had decided he'd bring his pillaging to the corporate world. His broad shoulders created a V that tapered down to a narrow waist and there was no way he'd be able to buy a suit off the rack with those powerful thighs.

Mark was attractive but missing a vital component she couldn't put her finger on. A sizzle. A flair. Something that screamed *life*.

I've been reading too many romance novels.

Or maybe she was trying to rationalize something that couldn't be rationalized. She didn't have a connection with Mark. That didn't mean there was something wrong with her—or with him. It just wasn't there.

Mark seemed to notice it, as well. He paid for their meal and sat back with a rueful smile. "This has been fun, but I won't be hearing from you for a second date, will I?"

She liked his frankness. She just wished she felt some kind of pull to the match.

Lucy pressed her lips together. "I can't say for certain."

"I get it." He stood and moved around the table to pull out her chair. "I'd love to get to know you better—as friends."

That was exactly it. She'd enjoyed the dinner. She wouldn't mind spending more time with him. She just couldn't imagine walking down the aisle to him, even in an arranged setting. "Thank you for a wonderful evening."

Mark pressed a quick kiss to her cheek. "You're something special, Lucy Baudin. I hope you get what you're looking for."

"You, too. She's out there. Don't give up yet."

He squeezed her hand. "Good night, Lucy."

She followed him to the door and allowed him to hail her a cab. It was only when she was on her way back to her apartment that she took out her phone and texted Gideon.

Heading home.

I'll be there in thirty.

Her stomach dipped pleasantly and she clenched her thighs together. There was no mistaking what would happen the second he walked through her door, and her skin heated just thinking about it.

She couldn't wait.

8

GIDEON STORMED THROUGH LUCY'S DOOR WITH-
out knocking. He found her pacing nervously around her living room, practically wringing her hands, and stopped short.
"What did he do?"

Her blue eyes went wide. "Excuse me?"

"Mark. Obviously he did something." He sliced his hand
through the air to indicate her current state. "Tell me what
it was and I'll take care of it." He'd thought Mark was a safe
enough bet for the first date, but Gideon shouldn't have taken
it for granted. If he'd stayed, he could've stepped in.

Lucy was still blinking at him. She burst out laughing. "Mark
was a perfect gentleman."

"You don't have to smooth it over. It's my job to ensure
you have solid dates, and if something went wrong, I need to
know." He very pointedly ignored the fact that he almost hoped
something had ruined the night. Mark was fucking perfect. If
he wasn't essentially married to his job, he would have found a
girl, gotten married and had a couple of kids by now.

She crossed to him and put a hand on his chest. "Gideon,
stop. Nothing happened. We had a nice conversation and decided to leave things at that."

Leave things at that.

Call him crazy, but he hadn't spent much time dwelling on what would transpire during—and after—the dates. Jealousy reared its ugly head and, even as he fought for control, his words got away from him. "Did he hold your hand?"

She blinked. "I don't know if I'd call it hand-holding—"

"Help you into your coat?" He took a step closer to her, crowding her and unable to stop. "Kiss you?" The thought of Mark in Gideon's current position, leaning down to take Lucy's mouth, made him crazy.

And, damn it, she saw it.

Lucy frowned. "What's wrong?"

"Nothing." *Fucking everything.* He kissed her to keep from saying anything else. Lucy responded instantly, her hands sliding up his chest to loop her arms around his neck, her body melting into his. Her instant yielding should have soothed him.

There were far too many "shoulds" when it came to Lucy Baudin.

He grabbed the hem of her dress and yanked it up as he tumbled her back onto the couch. Gideon had the presence of mind to catch himself so she didn't bear the full brunt of his weight. The break in their kiss gave him the chance to say, "You want this."

"That wasn't a question. But yes." She jerked his shirt out of his pants and went to work on the buttons. "I want to feel you."

He palmed her pussy. "Then feel me." He spread her and pushed a single finger into her. Lucy made one of those sexy fucking whimpers that he couldn't get enough of and yanked his shirt apart, sending the last few buttons flying.

She shoved the shirt down his shoulders. "I need you, Gideon."

He'd give every single dollar he owned to hear her say those words every single day of his life. It wasn't his destiny, but he sure as hell planned to coax her to say it as often as he could during their time together. "Tell me. Guide me."

"I, uh…" Her eyes shut for a split second as he circled her clit with his thumb. When she opened them again, there was new purpose there. "I want you in my mouth."

He froze. "Lucy—" *Fuck me, it's like she pulled a fantasy right out of my goddamn head.* He saw the exact moment her confidence wavered and bit back a curse. He was so determined to give her everything, he was missing signs.

Gideon shifted to sit next to her on the couch. He stopped her from going to the floor with a hand on her shoulder. "Open my pants."

She didn't hesitate. Lucy undid the front of his slacks and withdrew his cock. She stroked him once and then sucked him into her mouth. Gideon had expected some sort of cautious exploration, but she went after it like she was desperate for him.

As desperate for him as he was for her. He pulled her hair back so he could see his cock disappear between her deep purple lips. A sight he never thought he'd stand witness to. She opened her eyes and pinned him with a pleased look, and he couldn't stand it a second longer. Keeping one hand holding her hair back, Gideon pulled her dress higher, baring her ass completely. He squeezed her ass and then ran his hand down until he could push two fingers into her.

Her eyes went wide then slid shut and she sucked him harder, faster.

"You like that? You like me playing with your pretty pussy while you have my cock in your mouth." It wasn't enough. He was so goddamn desperate for her that feeling her come on his fingers wouldn't do a thing to take the edge off. He kept thinking about her wearing that peekaboo dress across the table from Mark and laughing at that fucker's jokes, and inspiring a lifetime of filthy fantasies. "Give me a taste."

He grabbed her around the hips and lifted her until her knees rested on the back of the couch on either side of his head. Gideon waited for her to start sucking his cock again before he ran his cheek up her thigh to her pussy. "So beautiful." He licked her, teasing.

Or at least that was the plan.

She was so fucking drenched and tasted so fucking sweet, he lost his precarious hold on his control and gripped her thighs where they met her hips, raising her to his mouth and spreading her wider in the same move. She moaned around his cock and the sound drove him wilder. He licked and sucked her folds, growling against her hot skin. *I've got my face buried in her pussy.* Me. *Not that asshole she went to dinner with.*

Lucy reached between his thighs and cupped his balls, slamming him back into the present. She twisted up off his cock enough to say, "You like this?"

"Hell, yes, I do. I like every single thing you do to me." His world narrowed down to the taste of her on his tongue and the feel of her mouth wrapped around him. Her whimpers and moans drove him on, leaching every bit of rational thought from Gideon's head. He needed her to orgasm.

Needed to claim her.

Lucy couldn't tell which way was up—and not just because Gideon had her in the most impossible and erotic position. She'd barely made it home before him and now he had her upside down on the couch with his face buried between her legs as she sucked his cock. She took him deeper. He made her so damn crazy.

For once, she wanted to return the favor.

She shifted her hold of his balls, squeezing lightly. He made a sound she felt all the way to the back of her throat. Nothing mattered but the next slide of his tongue over her clit and the way his fingers dug into her hips, effortlessly holding her in place.

Her orgasm rolled over her from one breath to the next, and she sucked him with unmatched desperation, needing Gideon with her every step of the way. She could *feel* him holding back, trying to outlast her just like he had every other time since they'd started. If she didn't do something drastic right this second, he'd move them somewhere else and she wouldn't get a chance to finish him like this.

So she played dirty.

Lucy pressed two fingers to his perineum. She'd read in so many books that it was a hot spot for men as well as women, but she'd never had the courage to try.

Gideon's response made the risk worth it many times over.

His back arched and his balls drew up. He hissed out a breath that made her clit tingle. "Fuck. I can't hold out."

She sucked harder, not willing to lift her head to tell him to go for it. She wanted this. She *needed* this.

He hesitated but she circled her middle finger against him and that was all it took. Gideon cursed long and hard against her skin, his grip spasming as his hips bucked up to meet her mouth. She took him as deep as was comfortable and then took him deeper yet. He growled her name as he came. Lucy drank him down, sucking him until he shuddered and gently lowered her to the couch.

Only then did she raise her head.

The look on Gideon's face could only be described as shell-shocked. He opened his mouth, closed it and shook his head. "Come here." Without waiting for a response, he pulled her onto his lap and tucked her against him.

She settled her head onto his shoulder. "That was…"

"Yeah."

How to put it into words? She might not be the more experienced of the two of them, but she wasn't stupid. That hadn't been like the other times. There was no lesson here that Gideon wanted to teach her. He'd come through her door like a jealous boyfriend and then delivered one of the most devastating orgasms of her life and now he was holding her like he…cared.

Of course he cares. He wouldn't have agreed to this if he didn't.

Just because he considered her a friend didn't mean the lines had blurred for him.

She clung to the thought with a stubbornness born of desperation. Lucy had a plan and she knew better by now than to deviate from it. The last time she'd done that, she'd ended up with Jeff, and that entire experience had screwed her up, at least emotionally.

It would have screwed her up professionally, too, if she processed pain in any other way than powering through it out of spite.

Gideon stroked a hand down her back. "Did I hurt you?"

"What? No." She leaned back to look at him. Not as shell-shocked now and the thread of guilt in his dark eyes made her heart hurt.

That was the other reason she couldn't allow the lines between them to blur. Gideon might be someone she cared about, and he might make her body sing, but he would never forgive himself for his role in Jeff's shitty choices.

He'd never be able to look at her without seeing his friend's ex-fiancée. The one *he'd* had to take aside to let know she was being cheated on—and everyone knew.

Gideon frowned. "Tell me what put that look on your face."

"It's nothing." The very *last* thing she wanted to do was to bring Jeff into the room with them. It was hard enough to banish the memory of him without inviting him in. She almost settled back against Gideon, but the moment had passed. Cuddling and soft words wasn't what this was.

Lucy climbed to her feet on shaking legs. "Give me a few minutes to change."

"Sure."

She retreated to her bedroom and threw on a pair of leggings and one of her knitted sweaters. It felt too comfortable, but as he'd been quick to point out before, this wasn't about seduction. If he wanted her to dress the part, he would request it so he could help her strike the right note. She closed her bedroom door behind her and made her way back into the main room. "I need to go shopping."

"This instant?"

"Don't be silly. Of course not." Her laugh felt forced, mostly because it was. Lucy pulled a newly purchased bottle of wine out of her cabinet and took out two glasses. "Wine?"

"Yeah."

She poured them, still not looking at him. "The date with Mark was nice enough, but I think it's best I meet the rest of your list. That said, I'd like to be as prepared as possible, and I think I mentioned before that I have nothing in the way of seduction clothing."

Gideon snorted. "*You* are seduction enough, Lucy."

He didn't get it. But then, she didn't expect him to. She turned and offered his glass, then took a sip of her own. "This may sound strange, but I dress well."

"I noticed."

She ignored that. "Walking out to face a judge or jury—or both—is terrifying. It's exhilarating, too, but taking that first step is like jumping out of a plane and hoping you remembered your parachute. Or, more accurately maybe, it's like stepping onto the dueling grounds and hoping like hell you prepared your weapons and they won't malfunction. I know that sounds dramatic, but it's what it feels like for me. My clothing is both armor and weapons combined. It allows me to take that first step without fear crippling me. I'm going to need that in the bedroom, as well."

There. He might laugh in her face, but at least she was being honest.

Gideon didn't laugh. He studied her with those dark eyes, mulling over what she said and the implications behind it, no doubt. She'd revealed far more of herself in that little tidbit than she had in a long while. Becka knew, of course—she was the one Lucy always dragged along on her shopping trips—but everyone at the office assumed that Lucy was just extremely into fashion and expensive clothing.

Finally he took a drink of his wine. "Do you have free time next weekend?"

Next weekend? It was Thursday. "That's eight days from now."

"I'm more than capable of counting, Lucy." He set the glass down. "Tomorrow, you'll meet Aaron Livingston at the weekly event Roman puts together. I'll be out of town most of next week meeting with several potential fits for a client."

Disappointment soured her stomach but she did her best not to show it. Of course Gideon wasn't exclusively focused on her predicament. From what she remembered, he usually had multiple clients at any given time and there was no reason to expect to be the exception to the rule.

It also meant almost a full week that she wouldn't see him.

No lessons for seven days.

Stop it.

She managed a smile. "I'm free next weekend, aside from a lunch date with Becka."

"We'll go shopping afterward."

Which would give her a chance to imbibe enough alcohol to feel a little fearless at the thought of picking lingerie with Gideon. Lucy wasn't feeling anything resembling fearless at the moment. She swallowed hard. "Okay."

His gaze sharpened on her face. "Tomorrow, wear something appropriate."

Just like that, her nerves disappeared. She drew herself up straight. "Excuse me?"

"You know damn well that you were playing with fire with that dress tonight. I don't know how the fuck Mark kept his hands to himself, but it's a small miracle. No other man would."

Meaning *he* wouldn't, which he'd more than proved by walking through the door and ravishing her right there in her living room. *I did a bit of ravishing myself.*

That wasn't what they were discussing, though, and she didn't appreciate his attitude. The whole point of this was to market her—for lack of a better word—to these men, and he was acting like she'd been out of line. It wasn't a dress she would have worn for work, but it was a far cry from indecent. He was acting like she'd shown up in a minidress with all her goods on display. Lucy glared. "I'll wear whatever I please."

"Wrong. You'll wear something that doesn't project sex."

"You can't be serious." She threw up a hand. "I am more than capable of dressing myself. The lingerie excepting, I don't need or want your opinion."

Gideon set the wineglass down and advanced on her, a forbidding expression on his handsome face. A muscle in his jaw jumped and her stomach leaped in response. He stopped mere inches away. "You wear some shit like you wore tonight and you won't like the results."

She could barely catch her breath with him so close. "What are you going to do, Gideon? Put me over your knee? I don't think so."

"Put you over my knee." His hands came down on either side of her, bracketing her in. Still, he didn't touch her. "Yes, Lucy, that's exactly what I'll do. And after I've spanked your pert little ass red, I'll bend you over the nearest surface and fuck you, date with another man or no."

9

_____

"YOU KEEP STARING AT THE DOOR LIKE THAT, you're going to start scaring guests away."

Gideon didn't look away from the door. He couldn't relax. Truth be told, he hadn't managed to relax since he'd walked out of Lucy's apartment last night, his words ringing in his ears. They hadn't talked today, other than his text with the address and time to be here and her reply that she would show up.

The question of _how_ she would show up was driving him crazy.

He didn't know which outcome he wanted. It would be best if Lucy listened to him and dressed in something that was less of a goddamn tease.

But a part of him wanted her to challenge him—to push him to follow through on his threat. It crossed the line and he knew it, but he was past caring. If Lucy's date with Mark had made anything clear, it was that Gideon couldn't stand the thought of her with another man.

He'd stepped aside for Jeff.

He wasn't about to step aside now. Not again.

None of those other fuckers would care about her the way he would. Their chemistry about set the apartment on fire, and they had a history of genuine caring between them—all of which Lucy said she wanted with whatever husband she picked.

He was the right choice.

He just had to find a way to make Lucy see that.

"Shit," Roman muttered. He stepped to the side, blocking Gideon's view of the door. "Don't make a scene. I invited Aaron here in good faith and you look like you're about to rip someone's head off if they glance at you wrong."

"I'm not going to make a scene." As long as Lucy didn't test him.

He hoped like hell she *did* test him.

"The expression on your face is about to make a liar out of you." Roman slid his hands into his pockets, still looking on edge. "You've already crossed the line with Lucy, haven't you?"

He'd crossed so many lines, he'd lost count. But Roman wasn't bringing this up now just for shits and giggles. Gideon jerked his chin to the side. "Get out of the way."

"No. Scene."

Roman stepped out of the way and Gideon went still. Lucy made her way through the tables toward the VIP section, drawing stares in her wake. She had on a little black dress, but to call it that didn't do it justice. It was so short, it made her already long legs look even longer. It was also strapless, the heart-shaped bodice adding extra curves to her body. Her hair was down in a carefully messy wave that made him think of fucking, and her bloodred mouth only drove the image of hot sex home. She nodded at the guy manning the entrance to the VIP section and then strode straight to Gideon. Closer, he realized there were little beads sewn into the skirt of the dress, giving an extra shift of movement with each step.

Without looking away from Lucy, he handed Roman his beer. "We'll be right back."

Roman cursed. "Whatever you're going to say to her, make it quick. Aaron will be here in thirty."

Thirty minutes was more than enough time to thoroughly

make his point. He stood and prowled the last few steps to her. "Follow me. Now."

She wet her lips, her eyes already a little hazy. "And if I don't want to?"

"You do." He turned and stalked back through the VIP section to the hallway that led to bathrooms and two rooms for meetings or private parties. One held a table and chairs and Gideon had used it on more than one occasion. The other had several couches for a more informal touch.

He chose the boardroom.

He opened the door and walked in, Lucy on his heels. She shut the door behind her and glared. "This is ridiculous."

"If you really thought that, you wouldn't be here right now." He grabbed her hips and pulled her against him. She instantly went soft, even as her blue eyes sparked. Gideon dipped his hands beneath her dress and froze. "What the fuck, Lucy?"

"Hmm?"

"You know exactly what I'm talking about." He pulled her dress up, though he didn't need the confirmation. "You come in here with that cock tease of a dress and you aren't wearing panties." Jealousy and desire twisted viciously through him. "Were you going to give Aaron a little show?"

"Oh, please. Give me a little credit." She lifted her chin. "I'm proving a point. You, Gideon Novak, don't get to make my decisions for me. I appreciate your help, but that's where it ends."

She didn't want him.

He was good enough to fuck but not good enough to listen to.

He kept a white-knuckled grip on his temper because having a knock-down, drag-out fight here and now wasn't an option for either of them. Not to mention the fact that he didn't have a *right* to be pissed. She'd laid out the terms that first day, and if he chose to ignore them, that was on him—not on Lucy.

It didn't make how shitty this situation was any easier to swallow.

Gideon stepped back. "The table. Bend over it."

Her eyebrows inched up. "You can't be serious."

"As a fucking heart attack. I told you what would happen if you showed up like that, and you were all too eager to pick up that gauntlet. Choices have consequences, Lucy. This is one of them."

She backed toward the table. One step. Two. "The consequences being that you'll spank my ass red and then fuck me right here."

She wants it.

It didn't soothe his temper. If anything, it ratcheted it up a notch. She might want *it* but she didn't want *him*. "The table."

Lucy turned and, prim as a princess, bent over the table. She seemed to consider and then lowered her chest farther until the top half of her body was flush against the polished wood. The position left her ass in the air and had her skirt riding up so he could *see* how turned on she was by this.

"Which part is getting you?" He stood between her and the door and pushed her dress the last few inches to bare her completely. "The spanking, the defiance, or the fact that we're in an unlocked room where anyone could walk in—including your fucking date?"

She tilted her ass up, just a little, an offer that made his mouth water. But it was her words that sealed her fate. "All of the above."

Fuck me.

He placed a steadying hand on the now-bare small of her back. "Brace yourself." Gideon wasn't into pain play, and he didn't think Lucy craved more than some rough-and-tumble shit, so he delivered a smack to her ass designed to sting without any lasting pain once they were through. Her gasp was almost a moan.

Gideon alternated smacks, giving each of her perfect fucking cheeks three. Enough to redden them as promised, but not more than that. He slipped a hand between her legs and groaned when he found her drenched. "You're going to fucking kill me."

He pulled out his wallet and retrieved the condom he'd stashed there this morning. The crinkle of the wrapper sounded unnatural in the silence of the room, but he could barely hear it over the roaring in his ears. He nudged her legs wider and notched his cock at her entrance. "Next time, obey."

"Not likely." She used her forearm to muffle a moan when he shoved all the way into her.

Damn him to hell, but he loved that she pushed back. She'd been so timid in some ways their first couple of times together, and this defiance was more like the Lucy he used to know. He gripped her hips and pulled almost all the way out before he slammed back into her again. It was good—so fucking good— but it didn't satisfy the feral edge of rage he'd been riding for damn near twenty-four hours.

Gideon pulled out of her and flipped her around. She barely caught herself on his shoulders when he hooked the back of her thighs and lifted her onto the edge of the table. *Better.* But not enough. He yanked down her dress, baring her breasts. "Fucking *hell*, Lucy." He spread her legs wide and shoved into her, his gaze glued to the way her small breasts bounced with each thrust.

It wasn't enough to erase the image of her wearing that dress while chatting up Aaron.

Don't have a right to be jealous.

Don't give a damn if I have a right or not.

"Touch yourself. I want to feel you coming around my cock." He maintained his hold on her hips as she reached between her thighs and stroked her clit. Every thrust ground him against her fingers, the sensation as unbearably erotic as the sight of her touching herself while he fucked her.

Her body tightened around him and she cried out as she came. Gideon tried to hold out, but there was no fighting against the intoxication that was Lucy. He came with a curse. His breath tore from his lungs and he had to keep a death grip on the table to keep from hitting his knees.

It had never been like this for him before. He'd cared about women—even loved them—but the insanity Lucy drew out of him without seeming to try all that hard blew his fucking mind.

He stared into her bright blue eyes and wondered how the hell he was supposed to go back out into that club and pretend like he hadn't just been inside her.

As soon as she had control of her legs again, Lucy climbed off the table and fixed her dress. She could feel Gideon watching her, but she ignored him and pulled a pair of panties she'd stashed earlier out of her purse. She slipped them on and double-checked to make sure she wasn't in danger of indecent exposure. She straightened and froze. "What?"

"You just pulled panties out of your purse."

Heat flared over her exposed skin, but she forced herself to meet his gaze. "Yes, I did."

He didn't move, but he seemed closer. "I don't know whether to be impressed or pissed the fuck off. You baited me on purpose."

"Yes, I did," she repeated. "I was also proving a point. I won't allow you to control every aspect of these dates, but this thing between us is separate from that. For the duration, I'm yours." The words felt funny, as if she was declaring more than she intended, but she couldn't take them back without sounding ridiculous and giving them more weight than they deserved. *It's the truth. We're exclusive.*

But only sexually. There wasn't—couldn't—be anything more between them. She had her plan and Gideon hadn't held down a relationship for longer than two weeks the entire six years she'd known him. Even if Lucy was willing to bend on this—and she couldn't afford to be—Gideon would lose interest right around the time she needed him the most.

There would be no change of plans. They might fit better sexually than she could have dreamed, but that didn't mean anything in the grand scheme of things. She'd let good chemistry sideline her before—or what she'd *thought* was good chemistry. She wouldn't do it again, even if this felt as different from that as night to day.

"Mine for the duration." It sounded funny coming from him, too. Or maybe those were the butterflies erupting in her stomach.

She couldn't manage a smile, so she nodded. "Now, can we please go out there and meet this guy? Not to mention I haven't seen Roman in years and you hustled me past him so fast, I didn't even get to say hello." As ridiculous as it was, the thing she'd ended up missing most about being with Jeff was his friends.

Gideon had disappeared the second she'd broken up with Jeff and the rest of that group hadn't put up more than a token effort to keep in touch. To be fair, she hadn't tried, either. It was hard to look them in the face and know that they'd all had at least some idea of Jeff's extracurricular activities well before she had.

It doesn't matter anymore. I won't let *it matter.*

She didn't wait for Gideon to answer before she marched to the door and back the way they'd come. There was no helping her flushed cheeks, but she'd purposefully styled her hair a little wild in the event that Gideon was good on his threats. She might not be willing to admit it aloud—to him—but she was so very glad he had. The first two times with him had been wonderful beyond measure, but last night and tonight felt like the *real* Gideon. The man beneath the carefully controlled exterior.

She wanted more.

In fact, the last thing she wanted to do was exactly what she was doing—walking back into the VIP section. Much more enjoyable to slip out the back door with Gideon and go to one of their apartments to relieve the tension that only continued to rise the longer they were sleeping together.

It wasn't an option.

She ignored the way Roman glanced over her shoulder to where Gideon had no doubt just stepped into the room, speculation in his hazel eyes. Lucy gave him a big smile. "Roman, how have you been?"

"Well. Really well." He took her hand and stepped a little too close to be comfortable, his handsome face severe. She tensed and his next words did nothing to dispel the feeling. He kept his tone barely above a whisper. "I'm so sorry. If I'd have known he was going to be here, I would have passed on the information."

It took her pleasure-drugged brain several seconds to catch up. He wasn't talking about Aaron.

He was talking about Jeff.

She turned horror-movie slow toward the sound of a painfully familiar laugh. Jeff sat next to a pretty redhead and the entirety of his attention appeared to be on her. Lucy hadn't seen him in nearly two years—not since she'd thrown every single item he'd owned out their second-story apartment window—and she hated that he looked good. There was no extra weight, no puffy face that would indicate alcoholism, no slovenly appearance.

In fact, Jeff looked better than ever.

Lucy, no doubt, looked like she'd just been up to illicit activities in the back room—because she had been.

She looked up at Roman and didn't know what she was supposed to say or do. Jeff hadn't seen her yet, but it was just a matter of time before he did. She wasn't ready. She'd fought long and hard to get past the damage he'd done to her, but occupying the same space as him was enough to bring the truth flashing in front of her eyes.

She was still making her choices because of Jeff.

A hand pressed against the small of her back and Gideon's crisp scent wrapped around her. He stepped into view, blocking Jeff from her sight—or her from Jeff's. If Lucy felt off center, Gideon looked ready to shoot fire out of his eyes at Roman.

"Hey, man, like I just told Lucy—I didn't know he'd be here or I'd have let *you* know. He just showed up."

She pressed a hand to her chest. *I can't breathe.* An invisible band closed around her, tightening with each exhalation until black dots danced across her vision. Two years later and he still had so much power over her. She hated it. She hated *him*.

"Holy shit. Look what the cat dragged in." Jeff's voice came from directly behind Gideon.

Roman and Gideon looked at her, identical expressions on their faces. Asking how she wanted to handle this. If Lucy so much as blinked, she had a feeling Gideon would sweep her out of there without hesitation—and Roman would block Jeff from following if he tried.

But that was what she was so very tired of—letting Jeff's bullshit dictate how she handled any given situation.

Lucy lifted her chin, giving a slight nod. Gideon frowned, but he and Roman parted, taking up positions facing Jeff and only leaving a small sliver of a gap between them—standing sentry between her and her ex.

For all his pleased tone, Jeff's blue eyes were cold. The redhead on his arm didn't seem particularly happy, either, and Lucy spent a worthless few seconds wondering what he'd told her about this encounter. It didn't matter. *Jeff* didn't matter.

Or at least, he shouldn't.

She put all of her not inconsiderable willpower into appearing surprised. "Jeff. I had no idea you came here anymore."

"Not often." The look he shot the men in front of her was downright lethal.

Apparently his friendship with them hadn't lasted any longer than hers had. Lucy had known that about Gideon, but it comforted her to think of Jeff feeling just as abandoned as she had, even on that small scale.

He didn't jump in to say anything else, so she went with the first thing that popped into her mind. "You look well." *Meaningless chitchat.*

"I am well. Better than ever, really." His gaze jumped between her and Roman and Gideon. "You three look cozy." There was no mistaking the undertone of the statement. *Which one are you fucking?*

Looking too much into this. Get hold of yourself.

Gideon surprised her by taking a step back and pressing his hand to the small of her back. "We were just leaving."

At that, Jeff's mask slipped. His brows dropped, the first indication of what had always turned into a huge fight—one she had no chance of winning. Jeff seemed to take in her dress for the first time, his gaze leisurely raking over her body, pausing at her breasts and her bruised-feeling lips. "You and Gideon, huh? You took a pretty high-and-mighty stance with me when you broke off our engagement, and now you're fucking my best friend. Classy, Lucy, really classy."

No matter how much she told herself that his opinion didn't matter, it still felt like he'd sucker punched her. "It's not like that."

"It's exactly like that." Gideon spoke over her. He slipped his arm around her waist, pulling her against his side. "You fucked up and lost her. That's not on anyone but you, so don't start spouting that bullshit." He looked down at her, his expression hard. "You ready to go?"

"Please." She didn't want to stand there any longer than strictly necessary. The fact she hadn't sprinted for the exit was a win, as far as Lucy was concerned. Asking anything more of herself was out of the question.

Gideon nodded and glanced at Roman. "Next time."

"For sure."

He didn't give her a chance to say anything further before he steered them out of the VIP section and through to the front door. But what else was there to say? Anything she could come up with on that short walk sounded defensive, as if they'd done something wrong.

Well, I am sleeping with him.

But not dating him. Even if I was—it's been two years.

Two incredibly long and lonely years.

Lucy couldn't stop her shoulders from sagging the second they turned the corner away from the club. "That was terrible."

"I'm sorry, Lucy." His hand on her hip tensed, as if he wasn't sure whether he should pull her closer or release her. "I didn't know he'd show up. If I'd thought for a second it was a possibility, I wouldn't have taken you there."

"It's fine." It wasn't, but she should be stronger than this. Being brought to her knees emotionally just from running into her ex was inexcusably weak.

It wasn't even *Jeff* that was the problem. It was the fact that with one look, one carefully worded sentence, he could trigger every insecurity she fought so hard to banish. *He* wasn't the issue.

She was.

"It's not fine." Gideon stepped to the curb and flagged down a cab. "Your place or mine?"

If she let him, he'd talk through this with her. Gideon might be gloriously rough around the edges with a temper that would do a Viking proud, but he never failed to be careful around her.

Except when she pushed him hard enough that he forgot he was supposed to handle her with kid gloves.

There'd be no pushing him tonight. He'd pour her a glass of something alcoholic, sit her down and demand nothing but perfect honesty about how screwed up she was in her head. He'd pull out her issues and do his damnedest to fix them. Or, worse in some ways, he'd be wonderfully understanding and tell her it was okay.

She just…couldn't.

So incredibly weak.

Lucy didn't look at him as he pulled open the back door of the cab. "If it's all the same, I'd like to go home alone."

Gideon tensed and, out of the corner of her eye, she watched him fight an internal battle. Finally he shook his head. "If that's what you want."

It's not. "It is." Maybe if she got some distance, she could get her head on straight again. It was so hard to think with Gideon so close, his presence overwhelming her in every way. She couldn't handle it.

Lucy just needed time.

He stepped back, releasing her from her internal debate over whether she'd like him to force the issue or not. "Text me when you get back to your place."

"I will."

He waited until she slipped into the cab to say, "See you Saturday, Lucy."

10

GIDEON MADE IT UNTIL WEDNESDAY. THREE LONG-ass days in Seattle while he met with the first of the prospective fits he had for one of his clients. The guy was an advertising genius, though he was a little too free spirited for Gideon's straight-edged client. It might not be a deal-breaker, but it was something to take into account.

He shrugged out of his suit jacket and stared at his phone. Lucy hadn't called and she hadn't texted after the one letting him know that she was safely home. He had left New York with every intention of giving her the space she obviously wanted, but three days out of town had given him clarity.

She was running scared.

Seeing Jeff had screwed her up, and Gideon understood that. She hadn't wanted to further break herself open for *him*, and he respected that.

But she was closing him out.

He tossed his jacket on the bed and dialed her before he could think of all the reasons it was a bad idea. She hadn't brought him into this to work her shit out—she just wanted a husband and sex lessons. *Too damn bad. She signed up for* me—*and that's what she's going to get.*

"Lucy Baudin," she answered.

"Hey."

A long pause. "Hello, Gideon."

He hated the awkwardness seeping into this conversation before they'd exchanged half a dozen words. If he let it, it would become downright painful. Unacceptable. Gideon had never met a challenge he wasn't willing to go around, over or through, and a simple conversation wouldn't be the thing that stopped him in his tracks. "How's your week going?"

"Long, and it's only Wednesday. One of my clients is being difficult, and I'm having to work around her just to help her, which makes everything twice as challenging."

"You'll figure it out."

"I always do."

He dropped into the chair next to the desk. This wasn't working. Lucy held herself distant—polite—but there was none of the intimacy they'd started building. He hadn't even realized it was happening until that softness disappeared. *One way to put them back on solid ground.* "You home?"

"Yes. Hanging out with Garfunkel and wading through some old accounts for my current case—and drinking wine. This kind of investigating always requires wine."

"Naturally." He settled back into the chair and kicked off his shoes. "What are you wearing?"

Her surprised laugh was music to his ears. "Phone sex? Really, Gideon? Isn't that a bit juvenile?"

"We already had this discussion."

The amusement faded from her voice. "I suppose we did."

"On second thought, don't tell me what you're wearing. Show me. You by your computer?"

"Always."

"Give me two seconds." He grabbed his laptop and brought it online. A few button pushes later and he had a video call going through to Lucy.

She answered, looking unsure. "I guess I can hang up now."

"Yeah." He set down the phone and shifted to get comfortable. She looked good. She sat on her couch in the middle of several stacks of files, one housing her cat, and wore a fitted tank top and sleep shorts. Her shirt was thin enough that he could see the faintest outline of her nipples through the white fabric, and her sleep shorts gapped around her upper thighs in a way that made his mouth water. "Hey."

"Hey." She spoke just as softly. "Nice shirt."

"Thanks." He pulled his tie loose and tossed it onto the bed. "Have to look the part, though this guy isn't formal at all. He's a big fan of flannel, hair gel and skinny jeans."

She laughed softly. "Poor Gideon. You'd look downright fetching in flannel, but I like you without a beard. I'll hold out judgment on the skinny jeans, though they present some interesting possibilities."

His cock went rock-hard at the desire warming her expression, but he kept his tone light. "I'll be sure to pick up something while I'm here."

"You don't have to."

"I know." But he wanted to show her that he valued her opinions. Gideon had never owned a piece of flannel clothing in his life, but if Lucy thought she'd like the look, he'd give it a shot. He noted the hesitance in her body language and refocused. "You always lounge in that sort of thing?" He waved to her clothing.

"This? Yes, I guess so." She shrugged. "It's comfortable."

"It's sexy as hell." He set his computer on the desk and leaned forward. "Let those thin little straps slide off your shoulders. I want to see you."

"Right now?" She looked around as if expecting him to jump out of a closet and tell her it was a joke. Lucy tucked a strand of her dark hair behind her ear. "I don't know if I'm ready for this."

She might very well not be, but if she didn't want to talk to him, then he'd keep them in the roles she'd set out for them. "Close your eyes." He waited for her to obey. "How do you feel when you take everything you think you *should* be feeling out of the equation?"

"Warm. Turned on." She hesitated. "A little intimidated. It's different when you're here with me, touching me. There's no room for being self-conscious."

"I've been thinking about you for five long-ass days and thinking about all the things I want to do to you when we're alone again."

"Things…" She licked her lips, one of her tells. Oh, yeah, she liked this when she stopped remembering the reasons she shouldn't.

He kept going, pitching his voice low and intimate. "That lingerie shopping date we have? I've been thinking about sitting there and watching you come out of that room wearing one of those getups. Maybe you'll tease me, make me wait for it."

"Like this." She used a single finger to inch first one strap off her shoulder and then the other. The upper curve of her breasts caught the fitted fabric and he had to bite back a curse.

"Exactly like that. You know how bad I want it—want you— but I think you've got a little sadist in you because you like pushing my buttons. Making me crazy."

"I do." Her lips quirked up in a smile. "You're so controlled all the time. I like seeing what happens when the leash snaps."

He liked that she liked it. Gideon spent most of his days aware of how he presented himself and how everything from his tone to his appearance to his walk could be interpreted by clients and prospectives alike. He never let himself relax, because even in a social setting, there was no telling who was around.

There wasn't anyone around now—no one but him and Lucy.

"If I was there, I'd tug that top of yours a little lower. Yeah, like that." He watched, mouth dry, as she inched it down, stopping just below her nipples and then baring her breasts completely. "Exactly like that."

"This feels so dirty." She opened her eyes and pressed her lips together. "Would you…?"

"Tell me what you want and it's yours." He craved her words as much as he craved her touch. One was out of the question for the next few days—the other she gave him after the briefest hesitation.

"Unbutton your shirt." She leaned forward, the move making her breasts bounce a little. "I love your shoulders. Your suits have this way of masking how muscled they are, and seeing you shirtless makes me feel like it's my birthday."

He straightened so he could slip his shirt off and drop it on the floor. They stared at each other for a few seconds, Gideon drinking in the sight of her while she appeared to give him the same treatment. He spoke the second he saw doubt start creeping into her blue eyes. "Your breasts look like they ache. Palm them for me."

She instantly obeyed and then took it a step further and lightly pinched her nipples. This time he couldn't hold back his low curse. "Yeah, just like that."

"Are you…? Will you…?"

He instantly understood what she meant. "You want my cock?"

"Yes. Show me." She writhed a little, her hands moving with more purpose on her breasts.

He tilted his computer screen so the camera took in his lower half. He moved slowly, teasing her, and undid his slacks to withdraw his cock. He gave himself a long stroke and was rewarded with Lucy's moan. "You like that."

"I like that a lot."

"Take off your shorts. I want to see you stroking that pretty pussy until you come for me."

She barely hesitated this time before she released her breasts and lifted her hips to slide the shorts off.

He stroked himself again idly. "Spread your legs—yes, like that. Show me how you like it the same way you did that first time."

She slipped her hand between her thighs, parting her folds to draw a single finger over her clit. It was the single most devastating thing he'd ever seen.

Gideon watched avidly, taking in every detail and imprinting it into his memory. It was shitty not being able to be there and touch her, but it allowed him a perfect view and the distance to appreciate it in a new way.

Lucy was fucking magnificent.

After the first halting touches, she gave herself over to her pleasure—to both their pleasure—and stroked faster. Her head fell back against the couch and her body bowed as she pushed two fingers into her pussy. "I wish you were here."

"Saturday. I'll make it worth the wait."

"I don't know if anything is worth the wait." Her words were breathy and her breasts quivered with each exhalation. She managed to open her eyes. "I'm close, Gideon. Are you close?"

He'd been teetering on the edge the second she'd taken off her shorts, holding on through sheer force of will. "I'm close." He spoke through gritted teeth. Pressure built in his spine and his balls drew up, his cock swelling at the sight of her stroking herself to orgasm.

Lucy let her head hit the back of the couch again, but she kept her eyes open and on him as she fucked herself with her fingers. Her breath turned even choppier.

"Next time…" He had to stop and restart the sentence when she gasped. "Next time, you'll bring out that toy of yours. I want to see it sliding into you, vibrating and making you crazy."

"*You* make me crazy." Her back arched and every line of her body stood out as she came with his name on her lips.

Gideon couldn't hold on after that. He stroked faster, harder. She lifted her head in time to see him come in several spurts onto his stomach. He stared down at it marking his body and wondered when the hell his life had taken a hard right turn. A month ago he would have laughed someone out of the room for suggesting he'd be participating in a video call with mutual masturbation, let alone with Lucy Baudin.

And yet…here they were.

He reached down to grab his shirt and wipe himself off, and checked on her. Lucy had slid down to lie on the couch, and she watched him with a sleepy smile. "You've got that look on your face."

Her smile widened. "What look is that?"

"One that says you're thinking filthy thoughts." He liked that look. A lot.

She swept her hair off one shoulder and it pooled around her head on the cushion. "That's because I *am* thinking filthy thoughts." She bit her lip and then rushed on. "What time do you fly in Friday?"

"Our appointment is…" He stopped short. A slow tendril of pleasure that had nothing to do with sex rolled through him. "You want to see me Friday night."

"If that's okay. I know you'll be tired."

"It would take a whole hell of a lot more than a few hours' plane ride to make me too tired to see you. Though I don't fly in until after eleven."

She smiled. "I'll leave the key with the doorman."

Fuck yes. He damn well knew he was reading more into that choice than he should be, but it was hard not to. That simple sentence, more than anything else they'd done to this point, signaled her trust in him. "I'll stop by my place to drop my shit and then I'll be there."

"Perfect." She stretched. "Thank you for this, Gideon. All of it."

Strangely enough, he felt like *he* should be thanking *her*. He'd spent a long time just going through the motions and, for better or worse, Lucy had woken him up. He wanted to keep talking to her, but a quick glance at his phone showed that it was well past ten on the East Coast. "Don't let those files keep you up too late."

"I think I'm done for the night." She pulled on her shorts and resumed her comfortable-looking spot. "I had this really gorgeous guy call and talk me to orgasm just now, and I'm feeling all loose and relaxed, so I'm going to jump in the shower and head to bed to read for a bit. One of my favorite authors has a book out and I've been dying to start it."

I wish I was there. He didn't say it again. It was one thing to put those words out there when talking about sex—it was entirely another to do it now that the desire had cooled.

It was the truth, though.

He wanted to be there to pull her into a relaxing shower, to exchange small talk about nothing important while they got ready for bed, to settle in while she read her book and he finished answering the last few emails of the day. Gideon wanted it so bad, he could barely breathe past the need.

He couldn't say any of that now without scaring the shit out of Lucy.

But he managed a smile. "You'll have to tell me about it when I see you."

Lucy gave him a strange look. "You want to hear about my book?"

"Sure." If only because it was something she was interested in and obviously passionate about—and had been for as long as he'd known her, though she used to hide them under a pillow when he and Jeff would walk into the room. Jeff had always made snide comments that he covered up as joking, and Gideon should have paid more attention to Lucy's reaction to those comments. He'd known his friend was a jackass, but he hadn't realized the depth of the damage Jeff was dealing her.

"That's nice of you to say, but we really don't have to talk about my romance novel addiction."

Damn it, she was doing it again. He leaned forward until his face filled the video screen. "I wouldn't ask if I didn't want to know. Nothing but honesty between us, remember? It interests you, so I want to know more. It's as simple as that."

She opened her mouth, seemed to reconsider arguing with him and shut it. "That makes sense."

"Because it's the truth." He stomped down on his anger. Hard. It wasn't directed at Lucy, and it wasn't fair to take his fury at himself and Jeff out on *her*. Gideon kept his tone low and even. "Enjoy the rest of your night, Lucy."

"You, too." She looked away and then back at the camera. "If you change your mind about Friday, I'll understand."

God, she was fucking killing him. "I'll see you Friday night."

11

LUCY HAD EVERY INTENTION OF STAYING AWAKE
to greet Gideon. If nothing else, she was sure nerves would keep
her alert until he arrived. She hadn't counted on the long day.

It had started at 5:00 a.m. when she'd gotten a call from the
office that there was a new client on retainer and that Lucy was
needed at the woman's home immediately. Things had only
gone downhill from there. The client—accused of money laun-
dering—was as high maintenance as they came, so Lucy'd had
her work cut out for her.

Throw in the partners dragging her into a boardroom for a
progress report the second she'd set foot in the office, and she
was exhausted. Her other clients couldn't be shoved to the back
burner, no matter how important the new one was, so she'd
worked late to ensure she was ready for court on Monday.

All of it had added up to an exhaustion she couldn't fight,
no matter how entertaining the newest episode of her favorite
medical drama. Her blinks became longer and longer, and the
next thing she knew, she roused to the feeling of strong hands
sliding up her thighs.

That alone should have scared the crap out of her, but Gideon's scent wrapped around her, setting her at ease even before

she was fully awake. She blinked down at him as he hooked his arms beneath her and lifted her off the couch. "I can walk."

"Humor me." He strode down her hallway without turning on any lights and toed open the door to her bedroom. She hadn't bothered leaving lights on in her room and Lucy regretted that when Gideon set her on the bed and stripped in quick, efficient movements. She moved to do the same, but he beat her there, carefully pulling her oversize T-shirt off. Since Lucy had been expecting him, she hadn't worn anything else.

His quick intake of breath was a reward in and of itself. She ran her hand up his chest. "Hey."

"Hey." He guided her to lie on the bed, quickly put on a condom and covered her with his body. "You looked comfortable on the couch."

"I was." She wrapped her legs around his waist and arched up to kiss his throat. "This is better."

"Agreed." He laced his fingers through her hair and guided her mouth to his, kissing her lazily, as if he had no idea of the need already building in her core. Need that only Gideon seemed to be able to sate. He took his time reacquainting himself with her mouth before he moved to her neck and collarbone. "I was going to wake you up in a very specific way."

"Mmm." She reached between them to stroke him. "This is better." She notched his cock at her entrance. "I need you."

He slid into her in a single move and kissed her again with them sealed as closely as two people could be. Pressure built between them, but his big body kept Lucy pinned in place so she couldn't do anything more than shake. Even that tiny movement ratcheted up her desire until she couldn't stop a whimper of need from escaping. "Gideon, stop teasing me."

"I know I'm not supposed to say it, but I missed the fuck out of you this week."

Her breath got tangled somewhere between her lungs and throat. The words she was supposed to say lingered on the wrong side of her lips. *That's not what we are.* It might be the correct thing to say, but it wasn't the *right* thing to say—or the truth. "I missed you, too."

He finally moved, rocking against her. It wasn't enough, but that made it all the hotter. She did her best to arch, fighting against the weight of his body and loving every second of it. "More."

"Demanding," he murmured against her lips. "I waited seven fucking days to be inside you again, and I'm going to take my time and enjoy it." He dragged his mouth down her throat, his whiskers rasping against her sensitized skin. "I like having you like this."

"Furious?"

He chuckled, the low sound vibrating through her. "Needy. Wanting. As close as you'll ever come to begging."

"Would begging make a difference?"

His lips brushed the shell of her ear. "No."

Lucy shivered, her breath releasing in a sob. It felt too good and she needed more. But he was right—she loved every second of this. Their bodies slicked with sweat as he kept up those slight rocking movements, every single one inching her closer to oblivion. His pelvis created delicious friction against her clit, and she found herself talking without having any intention of doing so. "That feels so good, Gideon. Don't stop. Never stop." She dug her fingers into his ass, loving the way he growled against her neck. "I love this."

"I know." He slipped one arm beneath the small of her back and the other up her spine to cup her head. She'd thought they were as close as two people could be. He proved her wrong. Lucy slid her feet down to hook around his calves, grinding against him. Gideon kissed her as if he couldn't help himself. His tongue stroked hers, plunging deep, the way she wanted him to elsewhere. Right when she caught his rhythm, he withdrew and then stroked deep again, starting the process over. It made her crazy—crazier.

He knew. He always seemed to know exactly how close to the edge she was.

Gideon began to move. His hips mirrored the movements his tongue had made, stroking deep and then withdrawing before slamming home again.

Lucy couldn't think, couldn't move, couldn't even breathe. Her entire existence boiled down to the places Gideon touched her and his cock between her thighs. Pressure wound tighter and tighter, turning her into a wild creature with no thought but her own pending orgasm.

It hit her like a freight train and she let loose a keening cry that didn't sound human to her ears. Lucy couldn't do more than cling to Gideon as his strokes became more and more ragged and rough until he orgasmed with a curse. He dropped slightly to the side of her, but shifted to pull her leg up and over his hip, keeping them close.

She tried to get her racing heart under control. "That was some wake-up."

"It's good to see you, Lucy." Such a polite thing to say considering their current position.

I think I prefer hearing that you missed me.

With the post-orgasm bliss numbing her common sense, she couldn't quite shut that thought down. She crossed the line they'd drawn in the sand. "Stay."

"What?"

She ran her hand up his arm. "Stay. It's almost morning and there's no point in you cabbing back to your place and turning around to do it again in a few hours. Just…stay here with me."

"You sure that's what you want?" There wasn't a single thing in his voice to indicate what *he* wanted.

"Yes. If you want to, of course." *Maybe I misheard him and I'm wrong about this entire situation.*

Gideon delivered a devastating kiss and climbed off the bed. "Give me a few."

"Sure." She waited for him to walk into her bathroom and shut the door before she relaxed and sighed, staring at the ceiling. *What am I doing?*

He was back before she could muster the energy to second-guess herself. Gideon pulled down the comforter and waited for her to climb beneath it before he followed suit. She tensed, waiting for the inevitable awkwardness, but he just slipped in behind her and guided her so he could spoon her. He kissed the back of her neck. "Sleep."

Lucy thought it impossible, but the heat of him and the feel of safety being tucked against his big body lulled her circling thoughts to a standstill. Between one breath and the next, she slipped into a deep sleep.

Gideon woke to the smell of bacon. For one disorientating moment he didn't know where he was, but then the events of the night came rushing back to him. Lucy. Her apartment. Sleeping here. He sat up and scrubbed a hand over his face. *I told her I missed her and then I stayed the night.* For all his intentions of respecting *her* intentions, Gideon was doing a piss-poor job of following through.

Worse, he'd been so focused on himself, he hadn't stopped to ask her how she was doing after seeing Jeff again—a week ago. *Fuck me.* He stopped in the bathroom to brush his teeth as best he could with a finger and pulled on his pants.

He found Lucy in the kitchen, opening a series of take-out containers. She looked fresh and happy, her hair back in a low-key ponytail, and wore black leggings and a blue sweater that matched her eyes. She smiled when she saw him. "Morning."

"Morning." He took in the spread. "What's all this?"

"I think we can both agree that cooking isn't one of my strengths, so I popped out and grabbed something edible." She grabbed two mugs from one of her cabinets. "Coffee, however, I am capable of throwing together."

"Survival skill."

"Exactly." She passed him a full cup and her expression turned serious. "Can we have today?"

Gideon took a careful drink of the scalding liquid and contemplated her. For all that she appeared relaxed on the surface, there was an underlying tension there. "And after today?"

"I figure we're due a conversation, but we have plans today and I don't want to ruin them by talking this to death. I'm happy and I want to hold on to that."

Meaning that this talk wouldn't make her feel happy—or him, for that matter. Gideon already knew what was coming. He'd muddied the waters by showing up last night, and taken it a step further by staying and holding her while they'd slept. They hadn't talked about lessons after that first time they'd had sex, which was supposed to be the whole purpose of this exercise. She'd also been on exactly one date.

He had to fix that.

He would rather chew off his own arm than set her up on any more dates, but that was what he'd given his word he'd do. Lucy trusted him and he couldn't betray that trust. *Not again.*

Gideon forced an easy smile onto his face. "Sure, we can have today." He didn't want to have that talk any more than she appeared to want it, so he wasn't going to worry about a few hours spent without overthinking things. "I thought you had lunch with your sister?"

"She got called in to cover a class and had to cancel." Lucy gave him a small smile. "I know we had planned for this afternoon, but I'm free all day if you are."

"I'm free." Gideon had been looking forward to this date all damn week, so he hadn't put anything else on his schedule.

Because that was exactly what this was, even if Lucy didn't realize it. A date.

Maybe she does realize it and that's why she's asking to shelve the conversation we obviously need to have until tonight.

She gave him a sunny smile. "Good. In that case, eat up while I jump in the shower." She pushed the food toward him, grabbed her mug and strolled out of the kitchen.

He spent half a second considering following her and making the shower one to remember, but if Gideon read the signs correctly, Lucy needed time. It had been that way with them from the start of this—she'd take a step forward and need time to acclimate. He could respect that. He *would* respect that. If he pushed too hard, too fast, she'd bolt, and this time he'd never hear from her again. It wasn't a risk he was willing to take, especially now when it felt like they were close to something that could actually be real.

If she'd take that leap of faith with him.

He ate quickly and cleaned up the containers. By that time, the shower had turned off, so Gideon grabbed the bag he'd brought in the night before and hauled it into her room.

Lucy glanced over from where she'd just walked through the bathroom door. She had a fluffy towel wrapped around her, and though it hid her curves, the exposed skin of her shoulders and calves had him craving the feel of her. She narrowed her eyes. "You didn't go home last night, did you?"

There was no use in denying it. "Nope." He'd wanted to see her—had *needed* to see her—and the extra forty minutes it would have taken were forty minutes too many. He nodded at the bathroom door. "Mind if I use your shower?"

"Of course not. Go for it."

He didn't need to be told twice. Gideon showered quickly, pausing long enough to wish he had time to shave, but he wasn't likely to see anyone he knew professionally today. He paused in front of his suitcase. Lucy had been wearing casual clothes earlier, and it might make her uncomfortable if he used his last suit. The other option wasn't as comfortable for *him*, but he'd make do.

He had promised her, after all.

When he walked out of the bathroom, she froze. "You…" She gave herself a shake. "Sorry, I don't think I've ever seen you rumpled-looking before—not even in college."

He glanced down at his designer jeans and the flannel shirt he'd thrown over a white T-shirt. "I'm not rumpled."

"You are most definitely rumpled." She moved closer, taking him in as a small smile pulled at the edges of her lips. "You look like you should be standing on a porch on some mountainside, a steaming cup of coffee in hand while you contemplate whatever it is that lumberjacks contemplate." She ran her hands up his chest and over his shoulders. "I like it."

"Rumpled suits me."

"You don't have to sound so cranky when you say it." She smoothed down his shirt, actually leaning forward a few inches before she seemed to remember herself and took several steps back. "I'm ready when you are."

She wore a different variation of what she'd had on earlier: dark leggings, a long black T-shirt and a slouchy knitted cardigan thing. Her pants were tucked into a sleek pair of knee-high boots. *Rumpled* was not a word he'd use to describe her, but with her hair falling in careless waves to her shoulders, she looked relaxed. Almost peaceful.

He liked it.

Gideon pulled on his shoes and then they headed down to the street. Lucy paused on the sidewalk. "It's such a nice day."

He could pick up a clue as obvious as that one. "We could walk. It's only a handful of blocks."

"Are you sure? We didn't really talk about what your other plans are for the day and—"

"There are no other plans." He cut in before she could talk

herself out of the whole day. "I worked all week. I cleared today for you, Lucy."

"Oh. Well…oh." She managed to look everywhere but at him. "I'm sorry—is this weird? It didn't feel all that strange when I suggested it earlier, but I think common sense has taken hold."

"More like nerves." He pressed his hand to the small of her back. "Walk with me, Lucy. What's the harm that could come of it?"

12

WHAT'S THE HARM THAT COULD COME OF IT?

Lucy forced herself to look at Gideon. His expression was as open as she'd ever seen it, inviting her to take this first step with him. First step into *what*, though? It had been an off-the-cuff thing to tell him that she wanted today, but through her shower and then his, the importance of that statement—this plan—had grown to epic proportions.

It felt like a date.

Except she wasn't supposed to be dating Gideon. She was supposed to be dating the men Gideon set her up with.

He didn't look particularly concerned that they had left the boundary of their agreed-upon relationship in the rearview. He offered his arm, the old-world gesture so very Gideon.

She slipped her hand onto his arm and fell into step with him as if it was the most natural thing in the world. Maybe it was. She didn't know anymore. These days, it felt like up was down and down was up, and Lucy was bouncing somewhere in the middle.

"How was your trip? Other than having to fend off a city full of free spirits." She injected false sympathy into her tone. "You poor thing."

Gideon shook his head. "You mock me while you were here,

safe in New York. The people on that coast aren't anything like *our* people. They chat." He gave a mock shudder. "You wouldn't last two days."

"On the contrary, I'm not nearly as cranky and antisocial as you are. I'd be fine."

"There is that." He pulled her to a stop at the curb as cars whizzed past. "It was a productive trip. One of my prospective fits looks like she'll work out, and I managed to source a secondary backup in Portland. Those two cities are filled to the brim with tech geniuses, so if I can lure either woman over here, they'll have jobs waiting."

A barb of something like jealousy embedded itself in Lucy's throat. He'd spent a full week in endless meetings between Seattle and Portland, and a few of the people he'd met with had been women. It shouldn't matter. Lucy had no claim on Gideon. Not really. They might be exclusive for the time being, but there was a looming expiration date. He could have plans to hook up with one of those women—or both—and Lucy didn't have the right to be upset about it.

That didn't change the fact that her chest ached at the very thought.

"Maisey Graham has been married to her high school sweetheart since the month after graduation, and he owns his own business, so relocation isn't out of the question." Gideon spoke low enough that she had to lean in to hear his words, very carefully not looking at him. "Jericha Hurley will be eighteen in two months, though she's damn near a certified genius and she's got her pick of companies vying for her attention."

He knew.

The ache in her chest got worse. She managed to breathe past it—barely. "It's none of my business."

"Honesty, Lucy."

She didn't want to be honest. She wanted to shove her head in the sand. They crossed the road and kept going down the block. She tried to pinpoint exactly what the problem was. *Easy enough—I'm jealous of the thought of Gideon spending time with other women.* Not just spending time, though. Having long meetings, likely alone, on the other side of the country. "It's not that I think you'd do that after you told me we were exclusive."

"The fear is there all the same." He set his free hand over hers and squeezed. "That's not something you just get over."

Maybe she would have. If she'd put half the effort into dating that she'd put into her career, she'd have worked through what was apparently a hair trigger. *Or maybe it wouldn't have mattered.* There was no way to tell, and it was a moot point. "We have to fix this."

"What?"

"This is another issue. I can't very well marry someone if the thought of them being alone in a room with a woman is going to send me into a jealous spiral. They're all businessmen, and so that sort of thing will pop up. There's no avoiding it." She latched on to the idea, turning it over in her mind. "We can start at the lingerie shop."

Gideon pulled them out of the path of foot traffic and guided her to the brick wall of a nearby storefront. He let go and took her by the shoulders. "Lucy, stop."

"Don't take that tone with me. I'm not being crazy."

"Everything about this situation is crazy. No, don't get your back up. It is and you know it, and I'm here willingly, taking part in it." He looked like he wanted to shake some sense into her. "You're asking me to… What? Flirt with someone in front of you? More?"

More?

Her entire body clenched as if trying to reject the very idea of Gideon doing *more* with someone else. *I am out of control.* "If that's what it takes."

A muscle jumped in his jaw. "No."

"Excuse me?"

He shook his head. "Absolutely not. You pick one of these assholes and he flirts with another woman in front of you—or at all—and you get out, Lucy. You hear me? That is not normal, and no man who respects his partner would put them in that situation where they have to wonder if something more is going on. I would never so much as look at another woman if I was with you—in your presence or not."

"But—"

"But nothing. There are a lot of gray areas in relationships. This isn't one of them. Short of there being extenuating circumstances that are agreed upon by both parties, there is a clear line and no one should be crossing it."

She stared. This was supposed to be all in theory—a test run of sorts—but Gideon spoke like it was a personal attack on him. *Because it is.* She didn't know what to do, so she slipped her arms around his waist and pulled him in for a hug. "I'm sorry."

He cursed, but he wrapped his arms around her. "You have nothing to be sorry for."

"I'm blurring the lines." She wasn't even sure where the lines were at this point. Having sex was one thing, though they hadn't even done *that* right because she was too busy enjoying herself to pay attention to whatever he tried to teach her. On what was supposed to be her second date, she was more excited about pushing Gideon's buttons than she was about meeting her actual date.

And now she was getting jealous.

He pulled her tighter against him. "We'll talk about it tonight." He stepped back and reclaimed her hand. "Come on."

Lucy didn't know whether to look forward to the conversation or to dread it. When she'd initially brought it up, she'd deluded herself with the falsity that she had everything under control. Twenty minutes into this day and she'd proved herself wrong half a dozen times. Gideon was probably going to sit her down and explain how out of line she'd been lately.

Let it go. You can obsess about every word and touch and meaning once he's left tonight.

Strangely enough, that made her feel better. Or maybe it was his fingers laced through hers as they walked down the street. Two blocks later, he pulled her to a stop in front of a boutique lingerie shop. "Yes?"

She took in the window display, a perfect blend of tasteful and risqué. The mannequins reclined on a lounging sofa, both wearing jewel-toned bustiers, ruffled boy-short panties, with garters and thigh-highs. One had on a lace shrug that looked like something out of an old black-and-white movie. "Yes."

She couldn't wait to get into that dressing room with Gideon.

One minute Gideon was leading Lucy into the lingerie boutique, the next, a whirlwind of a saleswoman had stationed him in one of the private change areas and led Lucy away. He blinked at the opening leading into the rest of the store but didn't move from his assigned spot. *That was smoothly done.*

Content to leave Lucy at the mercy of the woman, he surveyed the changing area. It was a clever design, each of the three doorways leading to a small sitting area and an individual change room. The whole setup created the feeling of an intimate environment for shopping for the most intimate of clothing. He approved.

Gideon hadn't decided whether now was the time to play on Lucy's fantasy of change room sex. He'd intended it initially, but their conversation on the walk over had put things up in the air. He'd already pressed her hard just by staying last night. Her showing signs of jealousy was a sign that she felt more than just sexual attraction, but it obviously set her off balance and made her uncomfortable.

He sat back and scrubbed a hand over his face. The truth was, he didn't know how to play this. He'd made his career on being able to read people and find good fits, but he was fumbling around in the dark when it came to Lucy. He felt like he was back in high school, trying to express interest without hanging himself out to dry and becoming the laughingstock of the school.

Except the stakes were a whole hell of a lot higher now.

The saleswoman had hustled Lucy into the change room so fast, he hadn't seen more than a flash of bright colors attached to hangers before the door shut. The saleswoman—a little Goth woman who stood five feet tall, if that—emerged a few seconds later. She had purple streaks in her black hair and a lip ring. She winked at him and raised her voice. "You let me know if you need any different sizes or want to try something else. There's a button in there that will ding me, but otherwise, I'll leave you to it."

"Thank you." Lucy's voice was muffled.

The saleswoman stopped next to him. "Special lady you have there."

"Yes." She wasn't telling him anything he didn't know. She lingered for a second, something obviously on her mind, but he didn't have the patience to deal with it when he could hear the slide of cloth against skin in the dressing room. "Thank you."

"Let me know if you need anything. We have coffee and water." She waited half a beat and then was gone, striding out the door and into the main boutique.

Gideon drummed his fingers on his knee and waited.

Then waited some more.

Five minutes later his frayed patience gave out. He rose and stalked to the dressing room door. "Lucy."

"Yes?" She sounded small and unsure.

"Do you need assistance?"

"No."

He stared at the door, willing her to open it. She didn't. Gideon sighed. "Is there a problem?"

"No. Yes. I don't know. I just feel absolutely ridiculous."

He considered and discarded several responses to that. None of them was worth the breath it would take to give them voice. "Open the door."

"It's fine, Gideon. This was a silly idea. Just give me a minute to change back into my clothes and we can find something else to do today."

"Open the door," he repeated.

Her bare feet padded over the tiled floor and he held his breath as they approached the door. And then it was open and a vision from every one of his fantasies stood in front of him. Lucy wore nude-colored thigh-highs, held up by an emerald garter belt. Its decorative lace almost hid the fact that her panties barely hid anything at all. And the bustier was a work of art, offering her breasts with peekaboo lace that showcased her nipples apparently by accident. The whole thing was a goddamn tease and he loved it. "You look ravishing."

She put her hands on her hips, at her sides, and then finally crossed them over her chest. "*Ravishing* is a strong word."

"It fits." He stepped into the dressing room and shut the door behind him, unable to take his eyes off her. "If you don't like it, *divine*, *exquisite* and *breathtaking* are also accurate."

Her eyebrows inched up. "Do you have a thesaurus tucked into your back pocket?"

"Don't need one." He stopped in front of her and uncrossed her arms so he could see her. As with all things Lucy, both she and the lingerie were even better up close. Gideon stroked his hands down her sides and ran his thumb over the garter belt. What he found had him going to his knees in front of her. "Your panties are on top."

"Well, yes." A blush spread over her pale cheeks and down her chest. "I'd already decided to buy it based on the color, so I wanted the full effect."

There was only one reason to wear panties over the garter

belt; they could be removed while leaving the rest of the lingerie on.

Gideon hooked the side of the thong with his thumbs and
looked up her body to her face. "Yes?"

"Yes." The word was barely more than a stirring of the air
between them.

He slid her panties down her legs, taking his time. "I'm buy-
ing this for you. Don't argue. This isn't a disagreement that
you'll win."

"This getup is incredibly expensive." As he crouched, she
lifted first one foot and then the other so he could remove the
thong completely.

"Worth every penny." The garter belt framed her pussy to
perfection, an offering he couldn't have resisted if he'd tried—
and Gideon wasn't interested in trying. He guided one of her
legs over his shoulder, a position that left her completely at his
mercy. "Just a taste."

13

AT THE FIRST STROKE OF GIDEON'S TONGUE, LUCY forgot all the reasons this was a questionable idea. She didn't care. The only thing that mattered was his tongue lazily circling her clit. As if he had all the time in the world and they weren't in a public place.

A public place where every moan and sound could be heard by someone on the other side of the dressing room door.

She shivered, heat cascading through her body at the thought of someone listening. Someone knowing what they were doing. Someone thinking Gideon was so turned on by the lingerie that he couldn't wait for the time it'd take them to get home.

He'd had to have her right then and there.

His dark gaze met hers as he licked her again. "What are you thinking?"

She was thinking she wanted more. To be dirty. To break the rules.

Lucy reached down and tugged on his shoulders. Without saying another word, Gideon rose and let her guide him to sit on the bench that ran along the wall in the changing room. He watched her through hooded eyes as she undid the front of his jeans and climbed onto his lap. After a quick detour to her purse for a condom, she rolled it onto his length. He opened his mouth but Lucy pressed a single finger to his lips.

His eyes flashed in understanding and his lazy grin made her pussy clench. Lucy guided him inside her and sealed them together. She leaned forward until her lips brushed his ear. "Someone could hear."

"Yes." The word was barely more than a whisper. He reached up and pulled her bustier down to bare her breasts. "Hope you locked the door. She knocks on it and it'll swing right open. Give the woman the sight of a lifetime."

Her nipples tightened at the image his low words painted. It didn't matter that she knew for a fact the door was locked. It *could* be unlocked. Lucy held on to Gideon's shoulders and started to move. Each time she lifted almost all the way off his cock, her breasts brushed against his mouth and he kissed first one and then the other.

Thrust. Kiss. Thrust.

"Look at how beautiful you are." He gripped her chin and turned her face to the full-length mirror.

What a picture they made. Him fully clothed except for his cock disappearing and reappearing between her legs. Her mostly naked and riding him, her pale skin flushed with desire. Lucy couldn't take her gaze away from where one of his big hands held her hip while the other maintained its grip on her chin, to the look on his face as he stared at her in the mirror. She licked her lips. "*We* are beautiful."

He guided her back to face him. "Fuck me. Come on my cock. But be quiet or Agnes will hear."

The words unleashed the orgasm that had been building from the moment he'd slipped off her panties. Lucy buried her face in his neck and tried to muffle her cry as she came. Gideon looped an arm around her waist and lifted her to reverse their positions, sitting her on the bench with him kneeling between her thighs, his cock still buried inside her.

He held her thighs wide and proceeded to fuck her. She had to cling to the edge of the bench to keep from smacking against the wall with the strength of his thrusts. Through it all, his dark eyes swallowed her up, so full of things she couldn't put a name to. An expression almost like pain flickered over his face as he came with a muffled curse, hips still thrusting as if he never wanted to stop.

Lucy slumped back onto the bench and blinked at the reflection of herself. Gideon crouched in front of her, his dark eyes wild. He started to reach for her and stopped. "Your place. Now."

"We could…" She trailed off. *My place.* Despite the outstanding and filthy sex, she wanted more. She wanted skin on skin and Gideon's taste in her mouth. She wanted it all.

She nodded. "My place." She lifted her shaking hands to finish undoing her bustier, but Gideon beat her there. He undid the tiny clasps carefully, the delicate lace looking strange against his massive hands. He slid it off her arms and folded it neatly on the bench next to her before giving the garter belt and stockings the same treatment. The panties finished off the pile.

He ran his hands up her legs. Lucy held her breath and arched her back a little. His pupils dilated, which was a reward in and of itself, but Gideon stood. "Get dressed." Then he was gone, snatching the lingerie off the bench and striding out the door, careful to not let it open too much.

She stared after him for a long moment before she dredged up the ambition to move. It was just as well he'd shown a little restraint or she had a feeling they wouldn't have left this dressing room for several hours. She wasn't sure if she was disappointed that he'd walked out or excited for what was to come.

Excited. Definitely excited.

She dressed quickly and paused to check her appearance in the mirror. Flushed cheeks, slightly wild eyes, skin a little too glowy. It was a good look, but there was no mistaking that she and Gideon had been up to no good behind the closed door. It was becoming a habit of theirs, though Lucy couldn't say she was sad about it. She liked the thrill of knowing there were people within hearing distance.

She liked that she was experiencing it with Gideon even more.

Lucy stopped short.

There it was. The thing she'd been doing her best not to think too hard about since their first time—since *before* their first time, if she was being honest. There'd always been an attraction simmering between her and Gideon, even when she'd been with Jeff. She'd gone out of her way to ensure she'd never given him any sign of it, because she'd been in a relationship.

Because she cared about Gideon as a friend, and if something had happened between them, she'd lose him.

There was no Jeff standing between them now, and her feelings for Gideon were significantly more complicated. There was lust, definitely. Her body craved his like she'd never craved anything—anyone—before.

But there were...feelings.

She gave herself a shake. It didn't matter if there were feelings or not. She'd set out the terms and Gideon had agreed to them. Changing the rules without notice meant she really *would* lose him and she hadn't come all this way to falter now. She'd missed him terribly these last couple of years, and the thought of going back to her life without him in it felt like she had a gaping hole in her chest.

Gideon wasn't the keeping kind. A lot had changed, but she couldn't afford to believe *that* had. He'd settle down someday, with the right woman, but he wasn't there yet. Even if he tried to give them a shot for her sake, it would self-destruct sooner rather than later.

No matter which way she looked at the situation, the end result was the same—if she changed the rules now, she would lose him. If she saw her original plan through to the end, she retained the chance to keep Gideon in her life.

Lucy would fight for that, even if it meant hurting herself to do so.

She took a deep breath and straightened her shoulders. *I can do this.* Lucy opened the change room door and marched out. Gideon stood by the entrance to the boutique and she headed his way, very carefully not looking for Agnes. They might be the only people in the shop, but they'd been in that room far too long to be doing anything but exactly what they'd been doing. *Focus, Lucy.* She licked her lips as she stopped next to Gideon. "My place?"

"I changed my mind."

She braced herself. "Oh?"

"That meal might have been sweet, but it won't sustain us for what I have in mind for later." He gave her a wolfish grin that had her warming even as she tried not to read into his words too much.

It won't sustain us.

He didn't mean anything by it—of that, Lucy was sure—but it served as yet another reminder that this was temporary and any effort to make it permanent would backfire spectacularly. She put on her best smile. "What's the plan, then?"

Gideon's grin dropped away and he studied her for a long moment, seeming to see through her façade. Finally he nodded, almost to himself. "Lunch. Then we'll head back to your place to finish what we started."

Not a brush-off, then, but a detour. She kept her shoulders from sagging through sheer stubbornness. "I could eat."

"Good." He touched the small of her back and ushered her out of the building. He didn't say anything as they walked down the street, and she was too twisted up inside her own head to try for conversation. Nothing she said right now would change the truth, and the weight of it threatened to send her scurrying back to her place to barricade herself in with Garfunkel and the work files she still had to find time for this weekend.

Their destination was a little restaurant on the second floor of a converted apartment building. They'd left most of the interior walls up and designed low lighting so that even in the middle of the afternoon, it gave the illusion of a night tucked away. The hostess led them to a room that might have been a closet at one point, though it had two doorways now and space for a little booth for two.

Gideon waited for her to slide in and then took the spot next to her. The hostess left and Lucy became aware of a low jazz song playing in the background. She ran her finger over the rough tabletop. "I didn't even know this place existed."

"It's new. A friend of mine bought the building a couple years back and construction just wrapped up a few months ago. The bottom floor is split into a clothing boutique and shoe store, and the third floor is privately owned."

She'd definitely come down here to check out the shoe store in the future. She twisted to face him, but he spoke before she could. "What happened back there?"

"Excuse me?"

"You know exactly what I'm talking about. You were fine in the dressing room, and when you walked out, you'd put a wall up between us."

She desperately didn't want to talk about this, but his jaw was set in an all-too-familiar way. There would be no getting out of this conversation, short of crawling over the table and making a run for it. Since that was beneath Lucy's dignity—and she didn't know for certain that Gideon wouldn't just chase her down—she sighed. "We have clear boundaries."

"Mmm-hmm."

That response gave her no indication of what he thought of that, so she hedged. "Very clear boundaries."

Gideon drummed his fingers on the table. "Is the problem that you feel that I'm threatening the boundaries or that the boundaries themselves are the problem?"

Trust the man to just lay it out there with no qualms. She fought not to fidget. "I value our friendship. I know it may not seem like that after not speaking for two years, but I missed you terribly during that time and I feel like we're almost starting to reclaim that lost ground."

The guarded look on his face cleared. "You don't want to jeopardize our friendship."

"Exactly." She didn't mention the theoretical pending marriage or what their friendship might look like once she'd picked a man and followed through on that. The marriage might have sex included in the bargain, but it would still be a marriage without love. Having Gideon in her life, even on the outskirts, wasn't something she was willing to give up.

Not now that she'd just gotten him back.

The waiter brought their waters and took their drink orders. Once the man disappeared through the doorway, Gideon turned back to her. "That gap in communication was as much my fault as it was yours. I let guilt get the better of me and figured that you didn't want to see my face any more than you wanted to see Jeff's."

"You…weren't wrong—at least, not at first." She'd been so hurt and angry and embarrassed that she hadn't wanted to see *anyone* for months after she'd broken off her engagement. The only person who'd ignored that was Becka, and even she'd had to come to Lucy. If Gideon had tried during that time, she would have slammed the door in his face.

By the time she'd gathered the strength to get back out into the world again, it was to find that her former friends had moved on without her. It made sense, in a way. She'd lost most of her good friends when she and Jeff had started dating—a sign she should have paid more attention to. He hadn't missed a beat after their breakup, and most of their friends had been his first, so they'd moved along with him.

It was Gideon's steady presence that she'd missed the most, but she hadn't known how to reach out to him.

Or if she even should.

I'm here now. We are here now.

She held herself steady. "Regardless, I feel like I just found you again."

"And you don't want to lose that." He said it almost as if musing to himself. When she tensed, he leaned back and slung an arm over the back of the booth. "I don't want to lose it, either, Lucy. I missed you, too. I'm still missing you, if we're going to be perfectly honest."

Her jaw dropped. "What are you talking about? I'm right here."

"Yes, you are." He pulled her closer, tucking her against his body. "But we haven't stopped to have a real conversation since you sat me down in your office and told me you wanted me to help you find a husband."

Lucy opened her mouth to say he was wrong, but stopped and thought hard about it. Was he? "We've…talked." But not like they used to. There had been nights where Jeff had passed out, or was occupied playing whatever his video game of the week was, and she and Gideon had sat and just talked. Shared things about themselves, about their dreams. She'd always chalked it up to being good friends—family, even—but even if they'd restarted their acquaintance, they hadn't reestablished the intimacy they'd once had.

Sex, yes.

Intimacy, no.

She frowned. "I guess you're right. God, I'm sorry, Gideon. I've been treating you like a prize stud."

He chuckled. "I haven't exactly complained. But I do miss us, Lucy. Whatever version of your future you're aiming for, make room for me."

That startled a laugh out of her. "You're just as confident now as you were back then."

"Two years can change a person, but it can't *change* a person."

That was what she was afraid of. Lucy had fought hard to shed the timid woman she'd become while dating Jeff. She'd even mostly succeeded, if one didn't look too closely at her lack of dating. But she couldn't shake the fear that, deep down, she was still that mouse of a person who'd let her boyfriend say such horrible things to her—worse, who'd believed him when he did.

"I should have known." He spoke softly in the tiny space between them. "I said it before and I'll say it again—I knew Jeff was an asshole, but I didn't know the extent of it. I would have stepped in."

Her heart surged even as she shook her head. "If anyone should have seen the signs and stepped in, it was me. I let myself get taken in by him, and I almost married him because I was too stubborn and too naive to see him for what he was. If we're going to lay blame, there's plenty to go around." She covered his hand with hers. "I don't want to talk about Jeff anymore. He's taken up enough of both of our lives, and I don't want to give him even another second."

"I won't argue that." Gideon nudged her closer yet, until she was almost sitting in his lap. "I have the prettiest woman in all NYC sitting with me in a dark restaurant. I can think of a thousand things I'd rather say and do than talk about a piece of shit that we share a mutual history with."

She laid her hand on his thigh, enjoying the way the muscle clenched beneath his jeans. "I can think of a few things to add to the list." They were alone in this mini room within the restaurant. They could do anything they wanted to beneath the table and no one would be the wiser. "Gideon…" She slid her hand higher.

"Yeah?"

"What have you been up to since I saw you last?"

He blinked down at her as if he couldn't reconcile her ever-

sliding hand with her words. Finally he relaxed, muscle by individual muscle. "After you and…" He looked away and back.
"Two years ago, I looked at my life and decided I was done
dicking around. I went after the biggest accounts I could find
and went head-to-head with companies that had reputations
stretching back before we were born." He laughed. "I figured
I had nothing to lose, so I might as well aim for the stars."

"You've made quite the name for yourself." Even if her company didn't make a habit of contracting headhunters to fill positions, Lucy would've had to be living under a rock not to hear
news of Gideon. He'd beaten out several more well-known
headhunters and developed an excellent reputation in the process. He always got his man—or woman, as it were.

*God help the woman he finally sets his sights on. She won't stand
a chance.*

The thought was bittersweet in the extreme. Lucy cared
about him. She wanted him happy…but contemplating him
with another woman made her want to throw things. *Stop that.*

He's yours for the duration.

That will have to be enough.

But what if it wasn't?

14

GIDEON INSISTED ON DESSERT, IF ONLY TO KEEP things going for a little bit longer. Lucy must have felt the same way because she didn't hesitate before she picked a particularly delicious-sounding apple cobbler to his cheesecake. The waiter—who was getting a significant tip since he'd made himself scarce in between checking on them—took their order and hurried off. The restaurant had filled up, though the only evidence of it they had was a low murmur of conversation by people they couldn't see.

He curled a strand of Lucy's hair around his finger. "You said we needed to talk."

"Don't we?"

He'd always liked Lucy's directness. Even when she was highly uncomfortable with the subject—like sex—she still made an effort to cut through the bullshit and be as honest as possible. Now he almost wished that she was willing to let the slow slide of afternoon into evening go on without following through on her words this morning. Gideon should have known better. "Yeah, we do."

She met his gaze directly, never one to shy away from a potential confrontation. "Shall I go first or shall you?"

Though he was tempted to let her take the lead, that was

the coward's way out. Gideon knew what he wanted and the only way to give him a snowball's chance in hell was to go for it without reservation. So he let go of her hair and sat back. "Pick me."

She blinked and then blinked again. "I'm sorry?"

"Screw the others guys and screw the list I put together. They won't make you happy like I can, and you know it. I know you as well as anyone, and we match up in the bedroom and out of it. Pick me." *I love you. I've always loved you.* He didn't say it. He'd already pressed his luck by putting his cards on the table. If he threw that at her, she'd be gone before he finished the sentence.

She leaned forward and then shook her head. "What are you saying?"

"You know what I'm saying. I want you. You want me. We fit, Lucy. You can't deny that it's true." He held himself still in an effort to keep from reaching for her. Crowding her now was a mistake and using sex to cloud her judgment was a dick move. Not one that he was above, but if he wanted a chance— a real chance—with her, he had to do this right.

As right as he could do it when they'd started this thing with her dating another guy and then restarted it by bargaining for sex lessons in addition to her attempting to marry another man.

When you put it like that…

Lucy put her hand to her mouth and dropped it as quickly. "I don't know what to say."

Hell, he really had overplayed it. He didn't retreat farther physically, though he wanted to. Instead, Gideon gave her an easy smile. "It's fine. We're fine."

"No, I don't think we are." She rubbed her hands over her face and looked at him, her blue eyes so bleak, it broke his fucking heart. "Gideon, even with all the crap in our history and the two-year separation, you're one of the closest friends I have. I *care* about you. I don't know what I'd do if I lost our friendship again and…" Her hands fluttered between them. "We have irreconcilable differences."

"What are you talking about?" He reined in his reaction until she could tell him exactly what the hell she meant by that. *I was never on that goddamn list.*

"When's the last time you dated someone for longer than a few weeks?"

He froze. "That's the measuring stick you're going to use against me? Fine, Lucy. I haven't dated anyone for longer than a few weeks. I've been focusing on my career, and before that, it was school." He shook his head, frustration reaching a boiling point. "It's pretty rich that you expect me to roll with your limited dating history, but mine is the reason you won't consider me."

"That's not what I meant." She tucked her hair behind her ear. "Okay, it's a little what I meant, but the core concept is still the same. What happens when I throw all my other options out the window and say yes to you? Are you planning on marrying me? Because that's still the endgame, and rather quickly. Even if you *are* willing to take that step, what happens in a few weeks, months, however long, when you get bored—or, heaven forbid, you meet someone who you might actually love?" Lucy slumped in the booth. "No, it's not worth the risk. You'd realize that if you took emotion out of your reaction."

That was the problem—Gideon couldn't take emotion out of the equation when it came to Lucy. He'd never been able to. "I wouldn't do that to you."

"Maybe not intentionally. But eventually you'd resent me for pushing you into this choice."

He took a calming breath and then another. "You're not giving me much credit here, Lucy." She thought she had it all figured out, and he couldn't say a damn thing to dissuade her because it'd just be used as evidence of either how unready he was for that kind of commitment, or how much she valued their friendship. *Struck down because she cares about me.*

That brought him up short.

He was being greedy, but hell. The thought of her with someone else when they *fit* drove Gideon out of his goddamn mind. He took her hand, noting the tension there. "You've given me the worst-case scenario, and I respect that. Let me paint you a different picture."

Lucy hesitated. "Okay."

"You pick me. We get married, figure out living arrangements. Nothing bad happens. In fact, our quality of life improves exponentially. We force ourselves to take a few breaks from work a year and travel a bit. We start working through that list I know you've put together. We make our house a home. Fuck, maybe we have some kids, too. And every night, it's just us. You and me."

Her lips curved in a faint smile. "I like how you added in my sexual bucket list."

"It's important." He ran his thumb over her knuckles. Gideon wanted the life he'd just described. He wanted to be able to shoot Lucy a text and meet her after work for dinner and then walk home together and make love on every goddamn surface of the place they shared. He wanted the lazy Sunday mornings and the long weekends away. He wanted to be able to call her when he nailed an account or to get her calls when she was victorious in court.

He wanted it all.

Lucy pressed her lips together. "What if it blows apart in our face?"

"What if it doesn't?" He kept stroking her knuckles as she relaxed against him, bit by bit. "But let's talk this out your way. You pick someone else. We stop sleeping together, but that tension isn't going to disappear. Your new husband—" the term soured his stomach "—picks up on the tension and it makes him uncomfortable. Because it will, Lucy. Even if the guy is interested in marriage in name only, he'll have a problem with it."

"But—"

"Trust me. He will draw the line in the sand, and you'll have to choose which side of it you're going to be on." Gideon hated seeing the worry all over her face, but if they were being real, it had to be said. "You'll pick him. You'll have to."

The waiter walked in carrying their desserts. He set them on the table, took one look at Gideon's and Lucy's faces and stepped back. "Let me know if you need anything. Enjoy." He dashed out of the room.

"I don't… This is too much." She picked up a fork and poked at her apple cobbler. "You just dropped a serious information bomb on me and I don't even know how to wrap my head around it."

"Then don't."

She twisted to look at him. "What are you talking about?"

"I'm not saying you need to make the decision this second." He nudged his dessert away. "But you need to stop thinking that I'm not an option. I am. Fuck, I'm the best option."

"Arrogant to the very end."

"I'm sure of my worth. I'm even surer of how good we'd be. We've more than proved it over the last two weeks."

"One of which you weren't even on the same side of the country." But she relaxed against him and allowed him to tuck her head against his shoulder. "I'll think about it, Gideon. I don't… I don't know if I can promise more than that."

"Don't let fear win, Lucy. You've gone down that road before and you already know how it ends."

The walk back to Lucy's place happened in a blur. She couldn't get Gideon's words out of her head and his big presence at her side eclipsed all else. He made it sound so simple— the easiest thing in the world. *Pick me.*

It wasn't that easy.

The picture he painted was an attractive one. More than attractive. She craved that life, craved the connection already strung between her and Gideon. But Lucy had seen firsthand how bad things could get when she let someone close and they turned on her. Gideon would never cheat on her—of that, she was certain—but there were so many ways a person could hurt someone they cared about. Most of the time, it was even un-intentional.

If she married some near stranger and they did something careless or cruel, she could respond without missing a beat. They weren't close enough to hurt her. Gideon, though? He could cut her to the bone.

Aren't you tired of living in fear?

The voice in her head sounded a whole lot like his. She nod-ded absently at the doorman and led the way into her build-ing. Fear had controlled every choice she'd made since she'd found out Jeff had been sleeping around on her. Fear that she'd never get out had prompted her to end things in a rather re-markable fight. Fear of failure had thrust her into a career that she might love but which she'd chosen for its earning poten-tial. Fear of being hurt again kept her from giving dating more than a token effort.

What if she just…jumped?

Lucy unlocked her door and turned to him. "Come in?"

"Sure."

His presence filled her apartment, giving it a life that it seemed to miss when it was just her and Garfunkel there. The feline in question meandered up as if he just happened to be in the room at the same time they were. She bent to pick him up and turned to face Gideon. "What if we do a trial run?"

"Trial run." Neither his tone nor his body language gave even the slightest indication of what was going on in that beau-tiful head of his.

"Yes, a trial run." She warmed to the idea as she spoke. "I have a few months before I'll be down to the wire on this marriage business. A week or two shouldn't make much difference."

His eyebrows rose. "What do you think you'll know in two weeks that you don't know now?"

He had a point, but she wasn't about to admit it. Making any kind of decision right that second felt like too much too soon. She'd know in a week or two. She'd be *sure*—or as sure as Lucy ever was these days about things outside of the office. "What do you say?"

"Yes." He carefully extracted Garfunkel from her arms and set the cat free. Then he set his hands on her hips and pulled her slowly toward him until they stood bare inches apart. "I say yes, Lucy. If you need two weeks to figure this out one way or another, that's what you'll have."

Her throat tightened. "You're too good to me."

"You've got that backward." He sifted his fingers through her hair, tilting her head back so she lifted her face to him. "I'm taking you to bed now."

She blinked at the change in subject. But was it really a change at all? Anything left to say would just be rehashing what they'd already gone over. Left to her own devices, she'd drive them both crazy with her doubts. Better to let their obvious physical connection take over and push her worries to the back seat than to sabotage things before they had a chance to get started.

Gideon didn't wait for a response before sweeping her into his arms and striding back to her room. He carefully kicked the door shut, his gaze on the floor. "Woke up this morning to the damn cat watching me."

"He does that." She dragged her fingers through his hair and kissed his neck. "In his defense, you look absolutely marvelous while you sleep."

"You watched me while I slept?" He set her on the bed and

backed up enough to pull her boots off, quickly followed by her leggings. "That's very creepy of you."

"You're in my apartment—that means I'm not creepy." She pulled her shirt off and tossed it away. "If I was standing on the fire escape outside your window and doing it, *that* would be creepy."

"A fair point." He nudged her onto her back and stripped slowly.

Lucy propped herself on her elbows. "Have I mentioned lately how much I enjoy you in flannel?"

"It might have come up once or twice." He dropped the shirt onto the floor and started on his jeans. "Careful there, or you might look up one day and realize I've grown a beard and started wearing thick-rimmed black glasses."

She laughed. "You don't even need glasses."

"My point stands." He hooked the back of her thighs and slid her farther onto the bed. She expected him to follow her to the mattress, but Gideon stepped back. He pointed at her. "Don't move."

"Okay…" She froze when he went to her nightstand and unerringly opened the top drawer. When he straightened, he had her pink vibrator in his hand. She shivered. "Oh."

He examined it. "This isn't a design I'm familiar with."

"You—"

He chuckled. "Give me some credit. I can figure out how it works." He thumbed it on, his grin widening. "Brilliant." He joined her on the bed and took up a position next to her with his head propped on his hand. "Spread your legs."

"This feels…" When he didn't immediately jump in, she had to search for something to fill the space. "Naughty." It wasn't quite the right word, but it fit.

"More or less than bending over that table and offering your ass to me?"

Her entire body went hot at both the memory and his words.

"I'm not sure. It's not the same thing." There was no one here except them. No one to potentially walk in or witness. It didn't make the encounter less hot, but it had a different flavor as a result.

Gideon traced her puckered nipples with his gaze. "More or less than stroking yourself on a video chat with me?"

She gave a mock frown even as her breathing picked up. "You've made your point."

"Have I?" He ran his thumb over the circular silicone portion of the vibrator. "I still have a few points to make. Spread your legs wider."

She paused just long enough to have his brows slant down—the reaction she was aiming for—and then obeyed. The heat in his dark eyes was nothing compared to the inferno blasting into existence beneath her skin. *What if it was always like this?* He pressed the vibrator to her clit before the thought could take root. The silicone perfectly circled her clit, the vibrations drawing a moan from her lips. The fact that it was *Gideon* wielding it only made the entire situation that much hotter.

"How often do you use this on yourself?"

She arched half off the bed when he lifted it away. "Often. Don't tease me. I was so close."

He grinned wickedly. "I know."

"Gideon." She couldn't stand the teasing even as she loved it.

"Next time we go out—" he touched the vibrator to her clit long enough to have pleasure almost cresting and then took it away again "—wear what I bought you today under your dress. Halfway through dinner, I'm going to tell you to take off your panties and slip them into my pocket."

She couldn't catch her breath. "Tricky."

"I have a better idea." He set the toy aside and idly stroked her with his fingers. "There's a blackout restaurant I've been interested in trying."

How he could talk so calmly when she was in danger of going out of her skin was beyond her. "Gideon—"

He shoved two fingers into her, drawing a cry from her lips. "I'll spend the entire dinner fucking you with my fingers right there at the table. You'll have to be quiet or the other diners will hear you." He stroked her and slid her wetness up to circle her clit before pushing back into her again. "Though, if *they're* too quiet, they'll be able to hear exactly what I'm doing to you."

She reached for him, only to have him use his free hand to press the vibrator into hers. "Show me."

It took three tries to get her shaking fingers to operate it while he kept fucking her with his fingers the same way he'd described. She could picture exactly how it would feel to sit in perfect darkness, her dress up around the tops of her thighs, Gideon's big hand palming her pussy as he gave the waiter their order with none the wiser. She froze. "Don't the waitstaff have night-vision goggles?"

He guided her hand with the vibrator to her clit, waiting until she'd placed it perfectly to respond. "Yes. They'll be able to see every single thing I'm doing to you."

Her orgasm exploded through her. Lucy's back bowed and she fumbled the toy, but Gideon was there, his fingers still inside her as he repositioned it and sent another wave of pure bliss through her. "Oh, my God." She thrashed, though she couldn't say if she was trying to get away from him or closer. "Oh, God. Gideon. Please. Stop. Don't stop."

A thunk sounded as the vibrator hit the floor and then his mouth was there, soothing her oversensitized clit in long strokes. She laced her fingers through his hair, riding his face. "What are you doing to me? I don't… I feel completely out of control."

He lifted his head just enough to say, "I have no control with you, either, Lucy. I feel like a fucking animal. I can't get enough of you."

"Then get up here." She tugged on his hair. "You want me? Then take me."

★ ★ ★

Gideon hadn't bothered with a plan when it came to seduc-
ing Lucy into seeing things his way. All his damn plans went
right out the window the second their clothes came off. Now,
looking up her body into those blue eyes demanding he take
her, he wished for a plan. This whole day was special. The
start of their trial run. But more than that, it was the first time
they'd spent time together without someone else between them.

Just Gideon and Lucy.

He wanted her to know how important that was to him,
how close to perfect today had been. How much he cared about
her. How much he wanted her in every way, body and soul.

In the end, Gideon did the only thing he could do. He
crawled up her body and kissed her. She met him eagerly, her
body already shifting to accommodate his, her legs wrapping
around his waist and her hands coasting down his back to dig
her fingers into his ass. As if they'd done this a thousand times
before and would do it another thousand times.

"Condom," he rasped.

"I'm clean." Her lips brushed his with every word. "And...
well, I'm on birth control."

He went still. "What are you saying?" There was no room
for misunderstanding—not here, not now.

Lucy kissed one side of his mouth and then the other. "If..."

"I'm clean. I haven't been with anyone since the last time I
was tested." He hadn't done anything to disabuse her of the no-
tion since it'd be wasted breath, but Gideon hadn't had much
interest in sleeping around in the last couple of years. He hadn't
been celibate, but the demon driving him had disappeared right
around the time Lucy had vanished from his life.

"I don't want barriers between us. I want you—all of you."

He wanted that, too. So bad, he could fucking taste it. "You're
sure."

She wedged her hand between them and stroked his cock once, twice, before guiding him to her entrance. "I'm sure."

He didn't ask again. Gideon kissed her as he slid into her, inch by inch. There were no words to express his feelings at her trust in him. From the very beginning, she'd trusted him, but this was something else entirely. He kissed her with everything he had, everything he couldn't say. And then he began to move.

She rose to meet each thrust, their bodies moving in a dance as old as time, neither of them willing to break the kiss. He laced his fingers through her hair to tip her face for a better angle. She raked her nails over his ass, urging him to move faster, harder.

It was like flipping a switch.

He froze for one eternal second. Lucy nipped his bottom lip. "Stop being so careful with me. I can take it."

He knew that. Of course he knew that. Gideon tightened his grip on her hair with one hand, tilting her head to the side so he had access to her neck. He dragged his mouth down the line and then bit her shoulder. "Teeth?"

"Yes." She let loose a shaky laugh. "Just don't mark up where anyone can see."

Which was as good as saying that she *did* want him to mark her somewhere.

Gideon rolled onto his back, taking her with him, and slammed her down onto his cock. "Fuck me." He sat up enough to palm her breasts as she did what he commanded. Gideon sucked her nipple hard, urged on by her fingers in his hair and her hips slamming down onto him again and again. He took as much of her breast into his mouth as he could and bit her. Lucy cried out, her pussy squeezing him as she came.

He wasn't through.

He flopped her onto her stomach and yanked her to the edge of the bed. Gideon guided his cock back into her, paused to kick her feet a little wider and press his hand to the small of her back, and then he started to move.

He fucked her. There was no other word for it. She wanted it hard, and her hands fisting her comforter and the cries slipping from her lips only drove him on. He became a wild thing, slamming into her over and over again, driven toward a release he couldn't have stopped if he'd tried.

It wasn't enough. He was so damn close, and it wasn't enough.

Gideon covered her with his body, reaching around to bracket her throat with one hand while he slipped the other between her thighs and pinched her clit. "You're mine, Lucy. *Mine*." The move bent her backward and she twisted to give him her mouth.

"Yes, yes." She bucked against him, grinding herself against his hand. "Yours. Always. God, Gideon, don't stop."

"Never. I'll never fucking stop."

15

A LAZY SUNDAY MORNING WAS THE ONLY THING Gideon wanted, but he'd agreed to breakfast with Roman weeks ago. He left Lucy a note and brewed her a pot of coffee before heading out. An hour—two, tops—and he'd be back with her. Simple.

He still had to talk himself out of turning around seven different times during the cab ride—and again when he climbed out onto the sidewalk. The limited timeline Lucy gave him rattled around in his head, and he had the irrational fear that if he didn't spend every second with her that he could scrape out, it wouldn't be enough and she'd leave.

She's not leaving yet. I have time.

Not enough. Never enough.

Roman stood outside the little hole-in-the-wall place, staring at a pair of guys smoking just down the way. Gideon stopped next to him. "You quit."

"I know that. Doesn't mean I don't miss it sometimes."

"Miss the ability to breathe a whole lot more when you end up with lung cancer."

Roman rolled his hazel eyes. "Yeah, got it. Thanks, Mom."

"How's your mother doing?"

"Same as always. *Just swimmingly, darling.*" He gave a spot-on impression of his mother's breathy, high voice. Roman opened the door. "She and my old man are on that goddamn yacht somewhere. The Caribbean this week—either Saint Lucia or Jamaica."

"Worse ways to spend your retirement." He followed his friend into the brightly lit restaurant. If one could call Frank's a restaurant. There were exactly two tables and three chairs, and in all Gideon's time of coming here, he'd never seen them empty. Most people took their food to go, which was what he and Roman did. They turned left without bothering to talk about it—it was always the direction they took when they managed to carve time out of their schedules for this sort of thing.

They both finished their breakfast sandwiches by the end of the first block. Roman barely waited for them to cross the street before he started in. "What are you doing with Lucy?"

"None of your damn business."

"No, it's not, but you know me well enough to know that I'm not going to leave it alone. Explain. Now."

Gideon stopped walking and turned to face his friend. He didn't like the set of Roman's jaw or the tight way he held himself. "Why are you pissed?"

"Everyone with eyes in their head has seen the way you've watched her since she came into our group. You've had a thing for her for as long as we've known her."

He crossed his arms over his chest. "You have a point. Get to it."

"My point is that you agreed to find her a husband—that's it. A husband that is from the agreed-upon list that I helped you put together." When he didn't immediately jump in, Roman glared. "I may be pretty, but I'm not stupid. You dragged her into the back room at Vortex and you two had sex, which means you've crossed so many damn lines, you're too deep into it to realize exactly how much you're fucking up."

He wasn't fucking up. He might have changed the rules with

her, but she was on the same page he was. *More or less.* It was the "less" that worried Gideon. Lucy had put it all out there yesterday—her fears about the future and what it might mean for them—and he'd essentially steamrolled her.

Admitting that to himself and admitting it to Roman were two very different things.

Roman, damn him, knew it. He shook his head. "She gave you an opening and you just went for it, didn't you? Didn't bother to stop and think about the damage you were dealing because you were too busy thinking with your cock."

Enough was enough. "I would never hurt Lucy."

"You're hurting her *right now.*" Roman raked his hand through his hair. "We all stood by while that piece of shit ran around on her, and we have to live with that. There's no making it right—not really—but she came to you for help, Gideon. You do anything else than give her exactly the help she wanted and you're just as bad as he is."

No need to clarify the "he" Roman meant. Gideon gave his head a sharp shake. "It's not the same."

"Isn't it? You and me—and even him, though I hate to include Jeff in anything—are not good men. We're just not. We never have been—you don't get as far in the world as we've gotten without throwing people under the bus along the way. I've made my peace with that, and I thought you had, too, but you've always had a white knight complex when it came to Lucy. *She* is good—as good as anyone is. She deserves a hell of a lot better than she's gotten up to this point, and that means we owe her."

"Fuck, will you listen to yourself?" Gideon knew all that. How could he not, when he'd thought it himself over and over again for years? But hearing Roman say it felt different. Real. As if Gideon really had been deluding himself all this time by thinking things could work out between him and Lucy. "She and I just work."

Roman's eyes didn't hold a shred of sympathy. "For how long? How long until she wakes up one morning and realizes you pulled one over on her? She asked you for help, and instead of doing what you promised, you used her needing you to leverage a place in her life. That's shitty, Gideon. If our positions were reversed, you'd tell me the same thing."

He started to react, but stopped short. If Roman had come to him with news that Lucy had approached him for help, and he'd ended up sleeping with her and sabotaging her matchmaking plans… "I would have punched you in those perfect teeth."

Roman rubbed his jaw. "You have a wicked right hook."

He didn't smile, though it couldn't be more obvious that his friend was trying to lighten the mood.

Gideon tossed his garbage into a trash can and stared at the street. "I didn't set out to do this." *I love her.* But what did his feelings matter when he hadn't taken hers into account? Lucy'd had years of playing second fiddle to some asshole—she didn't need Gideon coming in and starting a replay, regardless of his intentions. He'd never cheat on her, would do everything in his power to make her happy.

She didn't choose me.

That was what it came down to. If she'd given him any indication that she had started this process with some sort of feelings for him beyond friendship, he would have a right to ask for more. Yesterday she'd even gone so far as to try to explain that she didn't want to lose him as a friend, and he'd leveraged that fear into getting her to agree to give them a trial run.

His shoulders slumped. "Fuck me, you're right."

"I'm not saying it to be a dick." For once, Roman sounded downright apologetic. "You're my friend, and if she was any other woman, I'd say to hell with her plans—play dirty. But this isn't any other woman. This is Lucy we're talking about."

And, because it was Lucy, that changed everything.

Gideon took out his phone and stared at it for a few moments. He knew what he had to do. The honorable thing—the thing he'd promised to do.

He had to set her up with another man.

Lucy woke up disorientated. The day before had been an emotional roller coaster, and she'd seriously looked forward to spending a lazy Sunday with Gideon, letting their time together ease her concerns over the whole thing.

Then she'd woken up alone.

She touched the side of the bed Gideon had slept on, but it was long since cold. Telling herself there was nothing to worry about, she went through her morning routine and then headed into the kitchen. A full pot of coffee sat waiting, along with a sticky note with a hastily written explanation. "Breakfast with Roman. Back soon." Lucy smiled a little and poured herself a cup of coffee. If he was occupied for a little bit, it wouldn't hurt to check her emails and make sure there was nothing requiring her immediate attention.

He still hadn't arrived by the time she was done with that, so she scrambled up a pair of eggs and went back to work on her files. Normally she had no problem losing herself in the facts she was compiling, but Lucy couldn't help keeping one eye on the clock as an hour stretched into two.

Did Gideon feel as strangely about what happened yesterday as she did?

Maybe he had regrets.

She wished he was there so his presence could keep her from second-guessing every single thing she'd said or done yesterday. Had she been too honest at dinner? He'd said he wanted honesty, but there was honesty and *honesty*. The sex had been even more outstanding than she'd come to expect, both the tender touches and murmured words and the rough and possessive…

"Stop it." She poured herself a third cup of coffee and headed for her living room. Obsessing over what Gideon did or did not regret would only drive her crazy. *Crazier.*

Work would steady her. Work *always* steadied her. It was her job that had gotten her through the worst times of her life, the ability to lose herself in the facts and how to use them to create the story she wanted the judge or jury to believe.

Except this time it didn't work.

Lucy kept glancing at her phone, waiting for a call or a text or, hell, a smoke signal. Something from Gideon. Something to prove that he didn't think this whole thing was a terrible mistake. Something to reassure *her* from deciding she needed to find a different way to accomplish her aims.

When her phone finally buzzed, she dropped the paper she'd been staring at for five minutes without reading and snatched it up. It was from Gideon, but only a few words.

The Blue Lagoon 7pm.

She hesitated, wondering if she'd missed something, and typed out a quick reply.

Dinner?

Yes. Wear something nice.

Lucy waited, but no information was forthcoming. She glanced at the clock. Two hours until he wanted her there. *Where has the day gone?* She could keep pretending to work, but the nerves bouncing in her stomach spoke of the futility of it. Something had changed with Gideon, and she wasn't sure it was a good sign.

Yesterday he'd been almost in her face with how much he wanted her—wanted *this*—and now he was playing least-in-sight. She'd thought Gideon was too direct a man to ever disappear on a woman, but she should have known better.

She'd watched him do it before, hadn't she?

She and Jeff even used to joke about the Gideon Special. He'd grow distant from whoever he was dating, showing up more and more at their place, and if the woman didn't allow him to fade gracefully away, he'd take her out for dinner and cut it off.

Kind of like the dinner he had planned with Lucy tonight.

She shot to her feet. "No. I'm being paranoid." Gideon wouldn't have said the things he'd said if he was planning on turning around and dumping her on her ass. He wouldn't have changed the perfectly good set of rules to push her to put her heart on the line.

Oh, my God. My heart is on the line.

She sat down heavily. She'd known she cared about him, of course—hard to be friends and not care about someone—but her heart being in danger had nothing to do with friendship and everything to do with deeper feelings.

Real feelings.

The same kinds of feelings that made a person blind to another's faults and left them emotionally bloodied and bruised. She didn't want that. She'd actively worked to *avoid* that.

And yet here she was.

She got ready, mostly to escape the doubt plaguing her. It was fear talking—it had to be. Having a meltdown about their first speed bump during this trial dating thing they had going was just going to prove how unready to date or marry Lucy really was.

Obviously something had come up with Gideon that required his attention and prevented him from coming back to spend the day with her. Just as obviously, if it was important enough to need his presence, then it would make his sending her a bunch of texts impossible. He'd arranged dinner tonight and paused in whatever he was doing long enough to let her know that they had plans, and *that* was a good sign.

She was overreacting.

Simple.

But she didn't feel any better two hours later when she stood in front of the Blue Lagoon, shivering in the cold beneath her thick coat. *This is fine. Everything is fine.* She walked inside and gave Gideon's name. The host smiled welcomingly and led her to a semi-private corner.

Lucy caught sight of a man sitting there already, but her steps stuttered when she realized he wasn't Gideon. *What the hell?* There was nothing to do but keep following the host. She started to reach for his arm to let him know that there had been some mistake, but as they came even with the table, she recognized the man. *Aaron Livingston.*

No. Oh, Gideon. Why?

She had to fight to keep her expression neutral as Aaron rose and smiled. "Lucy, it's been a while."

"I'm surprised you remember." She let him pull out her chair, her mind racing a million miles a minute. Gideon had set this up. It should have gone without saying, but she still couldn't wrap her mind around it. Twelve hours ago he'd told her that he wanted her to pick him—only him—and now he'd set her up with another man.

Aaron resumed his seat. "It's been a few years, but you're not a woman one forgets." He smiled charmingly, and though she could recognize why *BuzzFeed* had labeled him one of the hottest bachelors in NYC, his perfect features did nothing for her.

They also did nothing to explain why he was *here*.

You know why he's here, just like you know what it means.

If she was a better person, she'd sit and make small talk with Aaron and keep her eye on the prize—the whole reason she'd put this plan into motion in the first place. A husband.

But Lucy couldn't focus on anything beyond the fact that

Gideon had set her up. She lasted a full thirty seconds before she pushed back her chair and rose. "I am so sorry, Aaron, but I've got to go."

"Go...?" Those keen dark eyes took her in. "You didn't realize you were meeting me, did you?"

"I'm really very sorry." She headed for the exit as quickly as she could without actually running. Lucy made it onto the street before she found her phone at the bottom of her purse. She dialed Gideon's number and listened to it ring and ring and ring before clicking over to voice mail. She hung up without leaving a message.

That was the moment she should have stopped. It was clear Gideon didn't want her, that he'd misled her horribly. She didn't give a flying fuck. He didn't get to put her in this position and then avoid dealing with the fallout.

She scrolled through her contacts to find Roman's number. It wasn't one she'd used more than once, and that was years ago when she'd planned Jeff's surprise birthday party. *I was such an idiot. Apparently, I am* still *an idiot.* She dialed, holding her breath as it rang. He'd probably changed his number by now—most people did at one time or another.

But she recognized the cultured, masculine voice that answered. "Lucy?"

She lifted her arm to hail a cab. "You're going to tell me where he is, Roman, and you're going to tell me right this instant."

16

THE SECOND GIDEON HEARD THE BUZZER BEING pressed repeatedly, he knew it was Lucy. He hadn't even tried to hide. He'd known what he was doing today and, as sick to his stomach as it made him, Roman was right—it was the right thing to do. Hurt her a little now and set her back on the path she'd carved out for herself.

Knowing that did nothing to prepare him for the fury on her face when he opened the door. "Lucy."

"No, you do not get to *Lucy* me as if nothing's changed." She pushed into the apartment and spun to face him. "What the hell was that tonight, Gideon?"

He kept his expression stoic, knowing it would make everything worse. "I'm just doing what you contracted me for."

She actually took a step back. "You've got to be kidding me. You're going to take that stance now? What happened to you wanting me to pick *you*?"

"I was wrong." It actually hurt to say the words aloud, and it hurt more to see the naked pain on her face. He forced himself to keep talking. *A little hurt now, rather than a big hurt later.* "This was fun, but you were right when you pointed out that I'm not the keeping kind." She'd survived her breakup with Jeff. She'd bounce back even faster from this mistake with him.

Because that was how she'd see it in a few weeks—a mistake, a bullet dodged.

"You're serious." Lucy shook her head. "What happened between leaving my bed and writing me a note and..." She trailed off. "What did Roman say to you?"

She always had been smart. He let nothing show on his face. "He didn't have to say anything. A little distance was all I needed to realize that we aren't suited."

"Aren't suited." She pressed a hand to her chest as if he'd reached out and hit her there. Gideon felt like he had. She finally took a deep breath and lifted her chin. "You're a coward, Gideon Novak."

He flinched. "What the hell are you talking about?"

"You. Are. A. Coward." He could actually see her putting the pieces of herself back into place, though her bottom lip quivered, just a little. "Last night was too good and, I'll be honest—it scared me, too. But the difference between you and me is that *I* fought that fear and focused on how good it could be." She raked him with her gaze. "I'm not fighting for this. I spent too long fighting to be with someone who didn't even try. I won't do that again, Gideon. This was barely a bump in the road and you've already jumped ship. Fine. So be it." Her lower lip quivered again, but she made an obvious effort to still it. "I chose you, and you didn't choose me."

It felt like she'd stabbed him and twisted the blade. "Lucy—"

"No. Your actions speak just as clearly as your words and I'm not stupid. I understand." She drew herself up. "Consider our contract terminated. Keep the fee for all I care, as long as I never see you again."

Gideon watched her walk out of his apartment—and out of his life. He shut the door softly behind her and walked to his kitchen and stared blankly out the window. *It's done.* Something that took so much effort to coax into being, decimated in the course of a single day.

He braced his hands on the edge of the counter, an anchor to keep from chasing her down and trying to explain. There was no explaining this in a way that accomplished the severing of their relationship and left her pissed off enough to leave him behind for good. As much as he'd hated hearing it, Roman was right. Gideon hadn't been thinking straight from the second Lucy contacted him. If he had been, he would have set her up with someone else for her matchmaking needs. He wasn't qualified for either of the things she needed from him, and he sure as fuck wasn't an unbiased party.

Letting his own selfish needs overshadow hers, and then convincing her to see things his way...

Yeah, there was no explaining that away. Cutting Lucy loose was the best thing he could have done for her.

He let his head drop between his shoulders. The best thing for Lucy, but he'd be riding this wave of pain for the foreseeable future. Getting out of town might help, but the memories of what they'd done here and elsewhere would still be waiting to ambush him when he returned.

No, better to stay and push through the worst of it.

A band around his chest formed, blisteringly hot and so tight he exhaled in a rush. He'd just ended things with Lucy.

Ended for good.

Gideon slumped against the counter. He'd known that woman for six damn years. Had been respectful of her relationship with Jeff and never said so much as a word out of line. Had backed the fuck off and left her alone after things had imploded so she wouldn't have to look at his face and see a constant reminder of the lies she'd fielded.

Through it all, a small part of him had been sure that it would work out. One way or another, he'd find a path to Lucy. That he'd win her if he was just patient enough.

He huffed out a pained laugh. He should have known better. He'd been so busy putting her on a pedestal, he hadn't stopped to ask what *she* wanted. Worse. He'd ignored what she'd wanted in favor of his own desires being met.

She hadn't picked him.

If he hadn't forced the issue, if he'd just stayed in the place she'd designated for him, he could have maintained their friendship. Would it be painful watching her marry another man? Fuck yes. It would have ripped his still-beating heart out of his chest to smile and congratulate her on picking a man who'd do as a husband.

But less painful than standing there, realizing he was never going to see her again.

Lucy wandered the streets for hours. She'd intended to go home, but the thought of four walls closing her in was too much to bear. It wasn't any better on the street—the city itself boxed her into place, preventing her from running until she couldn't breathe, couldn't think, was too tired to process the level of Gideon's betrayal.

He blamed himself for not telling her about Jeff's cheating sooner. She knew that. She'd even used that to ensure he wouldn't say no to helping her.

She'd also foolishly assumed that, when push came to shove, he'd get over it.

Lucy looked up and breathed a sigh that wasn't quite relief. She dug out her phone and called. Her sister answered on the first ring. "What's up?"

"I don't suppose you're home?"

All joking disappeared from Becka's voice. "Yes. What's wrong? What happened?"

Burning started in her throat, making it hard to swallow. "Buzz me up?"

"Yeah, right away."

She hung up before her sister's concern had her breaking down in the street. The walk up the rickety stairs to the tiny apartment Becka insisted she loved was a lesson in torture. As if her body knew she was almost safe and had decided now was the perfect time to break down completely.

Becka opened the door as she lifted her hand to knock. Her sister wore a pair of brightly printed workout pants and a sports bra with more straps than was strictly necessary. Lucy stopped short. "You have class."

"I already got someone to cover for me, so don't even think of turning around." She stepped back. "Now, get in here and tell me everything while I make some tea I threw together this weekend."

That almost brought a smile to Lucy's face. "Is it better than the last batch?"

"The last batch was the exception to the rule, though thank you very much for reminding me of it." She made a face. "I couldn't get the taste of licorice out of my mouth for days, no matter how many times I brushed my teeth and drowned myself in mouthwash."

"Live and learn." Her voice caught, because living and learning was exactly what Lucy *hadn't* done. She'd been so sure she knew her path, and yet the first chance she had to take a detour that would ruin everything, she'd jumped in headfirst.

"Sit. Immediately." Becka took her coat and purse and tossed them onto the threadbare couch. Then she guided Lucy into a chair at the small dining room table and headed for the stove. The loft apartment meant Lucy only had to rotate a little to keep her sister in view.

Becka got hot water going in an ancient-looking kettle and doled out loose leaf tea into two wire tea steepers. The few minutes it took to get the water boiling was enough to calm Lucy's racing thoughts a little. "I'm sorry to drop in like this."

"What are sisters for if not to be there when you need them?" Becka poured the hot water into two mugs and brought them to the table. "This is about Gideon."

She started to deny it, but what was the point? She'd locked down everything after the Jeff fiasco, and all it had done was completely isolate her from the world. Maybe talking through it with her sister was the right choice.

"I… He changed the rules on me. I had a fully fleshed-out plan, and every intention of following through on it, but I didn't anticipate *him*. Our connection. He showed every evidence of wanting more with me—we even talked about it and he said so in as many words—and then I wake up this morning to find him gone." She had to stop and focus on breathing for several moments. Even with the break, when she spoke again, her voice was strained. "I thought we were meeting tonight, but when I showed up to dinner, he'd set me up with another man."

Becka's blue eyes, so like Lucy's, went wide. "I think you're going to have to rewind to the part when you woke up alone. You had *sex* with Gideon?"

She'd left out that part of the plan, hadn't she? Lucy cleared her throat and stared at the ever-darkening water of her tea. "We've been sleeping together since the initial agreement. It started out as a way to get my confidence back sexually, but things…changed."

"They'll do that when sex is involved." She shot her sister a look, and Becka gave her wide eyes. "Not that I would know, of course. Your dear little sister is most definitely one hundred percent a virgin."

She snorted. "I'd believe that if I hadn't caught you and… what was his name?"

"Johnny Cash." Becka laughed. "Don't look at me like that. I know it wasn't his real name, but I was eighteen and he was hot." Her smile fell away. "So Gideon pulled a bait and switch on you? That's seriously shitty, Lucy. I never pegged him for the type to play games like that, but I've been wrong before."

"We Baudin women don't have the best of tastes in men."

"You can say that again."

She was tempted to let them skirt into safer territory, but the raw feeling inside her only got worse with each minute that passed.

Lucy pulled her mug closer. "I promised myself that I wouldn't fall in love again—that I wouldn't even put myself in the position to do so. Feelings and caring on that depth only cause pain. I didn't expect him. I couldn't fight against the connection or the way he made me feel." The burning in her throat got worse. "I thought we had a chance, Becka. A real chance. That maybe I didn't miss my chance at a happily-ever-after, and maybe it could be with Gideon."

"Oh, Lucy."

She laughed, the sound vaguely liquid with unshed tears. "That's very foolish, isn't it?"

"It's hopeful. There's nothing wrong with hope."

Except it was hope that had gotten her into this situation. It was because of hope that every beat of her heart felt as if someone were stabbing her. Hope had driven her to lay her heart bare for Gideon, and it'd gotten crushed in the process.

She took a drink, ignoring the way the hot water scalded her mouth. A small pain compared to her emotional wounds. "Screw hope. I want nothing to do with it anymore."

17

GIDEON DIDN'T LOOK UP AS THE DOOR TO HIS
office slammed open. "Whatever it is, I don't want to hear about
it." Keeping the damn door shut in the first place should have
been enough to discourage anyone from coming in—anyone
except Roman, that was.

But when he finally looked up, it wasn't Roman kicking the
door shut behind him.

It was Becka Baudin.

He stared for a long moment and shook his head. "No. Whatever you have to say to me has already been said, so get out."

"It might have been said, but it wasn't said by me." She ignored his command and marched over to drop into the chair
across the desk. She wore tennis shoes and neon-green workout shorts tiny enough to have him concerned about frostbite.
When she shrugged out of her huge coat, she revealed a fitted
tank top in an equally eye-searing pink. How it managed not
to clash with her bright blue hair was beyond him.

"What the hell are you doing, walking around New York
in *January* wearing that? You're going to freeze your ass off."

She blinked and then shook her head. "You have a lot of
nerve. I could appreciate that if you weren't such an overbear-
ing, selfish asshole." Becka jumped back to her feet. Gideon

caught several of the men from the cubicles gravitating toward the windows of his office and stalked over to close the blinds.

"Put on some damn clothes."

She pointed at him. "Sit your ass down and listen to what I have to say, and then I'll leave and take my apparently in-adequately clothed body with me." Becka pulled her ponytail tighter. "What the hell are you doing with my sister?"

"Nothing."

"No, shit." She looked like she wanted to throw something at him. "You know, Lucy doesn't get why you pulled that sneaky little trick with the date."

"I—"

"But *I* do." Becka paced from one side of his office to the other. "I might not have been around her and Jeff as much as you were, but I was around enough. I know you've been holding a flame for my big sister for years, and I know *you* were the one who broke the news to her about Jeff being a cheating bastard."

He started to cut in, but she spoke over him. Again. "That must have been a head trip for you, huh? Hard to break up their relationship, even if it was the right thing to do, because you were in love with your cheating best friend's girl. That mud-dies the waters."

"Actually—"

"I am not through." She glared, her blue eyes practically lu-minescent. "When I'm done talking, then you get to talk. Until then, sit down and shut up."

He didn't sit, but he did give her a short nod. Obviously she wasn't going to be deterred from whatever she was trying to accomplish. After what he'd done to Lucy, the least he could do was stand here and take a verbal lashing from her sister. "Fine."

"Good." She took another lap from one side of his office to the other. "So, you're carrying around a boatload of guilt, and playing the martyr and letting her try to move on with her life." She shot him a look. "Martyrs aren't sexy, by the way."

She sure as hell wasn't holding back. "Noted."

"So, as my sister is telling me the insane deal she put together with you, I can't help wondering what your motivation was. For screwing her, I get that—it was fulfilling a lifelong dream."

He couldn't let that stand. "No."

She stopped. "No? Which part? Screwing my sister being a lifelong dream or—"

"Stop saying that. Fuck, Becka. I didn't manipulate your sister into bed with me. *She* came to *me*."

She propped her hands on her hips. "Aha. It wasn't the sex, then. It's the guilt." She pursed her lips. "Guilt isn't any sexier than martyrdom."

"Why are you here, Becka?" He needed her to get to the point of this verbal thrashing so she'd leave. She wasn't saying anything Gideon hadn't already gone over more times than he could count. He'd replayed every step and second-guessed every action. It all added up to a mistake he couldn't take back.

He still wasn't sure if the mistake was agreeing to help Lucy—or leaving her.

"My point is that you love the shit out of my sister and have for years, but you decided to be the guilty martyr and make an executive decision about what she *should* have." She stared him down. "Tell me I'm wrong."

"She should—"

"Sweet baby Jesus." Becka rolled her eyes. "Here's a tip— take 'should' out of your vocabulary when you talk about my sister and her future. You might care about her, but ultimately, you don't get a vote. She's an adult. She can make her own choices. And she chose *you*, you asshat." She shook her head. "The question is whether *you* are willing to choose her instead of your idealized version of her." She snatched up her coat. "If I had a mic, I'd drop it, but you get the picture. Woman up or don't, but unless you have a good grovel prepared, I don't want to ever hear about you contacting my sister again." She strode out the door, leaving a trail of startled and appreciative gazes behind her.

Gideon dropped into the chair behind his desk and stared at his dark monitor. Becka hadn't said anything he didn't already know. And yet…

And yet.

He drummed his fingers on the desk. The last twenty-four hours since the fallout with Lucy had been the worst of his life. He hadn't slept. Food wasn't of interest. He hadn't even been able to work up the resolve to get good and drunk. Every time he turned around, he caught a trail of her summery scent, and the few times he'd been on the street, he'd looked for her distinctive stride even though he knew better.

He'd had his dream in the flesh—Lucy in his bed and in his life—and it'd been better than he could have imagined. He already knew she was driven and kind and had a sense of humor. He knew she loved Chinese takeout and discovering little hole-in-the-wall restaurants no one had ever heard of. He knew her parents were MIA, but she had a wonderful relationship with her sister.

He couldn't have anticipated the passion that flared between them. Hoped, yes, but even that hadn't encompassed reality. Lucy met him every step of the way, *challenged* him every step of the way. She brought fun into the bedroom even as she made him crazy in the best way possible.

And now he'd never touch her again. He'd never be able to show her a new place that he discovered. Never call just to chat with her because he was thinking of her. Never spend those fantasy lazy Sundays they kept talking about.

He'd done that.

There's no one to blame here but me. I had it all and I shit it away.

Even if he tried to make things right, Lucy would likely tell him to get lost. She *should* tell him…

He went still. *Fuck me, Becka is right.* He and Lucy had been doing just fine before he'd started obsessing over what *should* happen rather than what *was* happening.

He'd done this. He'd ruined it.

Gideon had known that, but the truth drove home hard enough to have him rubbing the back of his hand across his mouth. He felt like the biggest piece of shit in existence to have been so close to everything he'd ever dreamed of romantically and for *him* to have been the one that made it combust.

He drummed his fingers faster.

Could he fix this?

Should—

No. There was no more room for *should*. He was head over heels in love with Lucy. If she'd have him—if she'd forgive him once again—he'd do everything in his power to ensure that he never hurt her again. Not like this. Never like this.

He straightened. He'd fix it. Tonight.

Right now.

18

LUCY CRASHED AND BURNED IN COURT. THERE was no other way to describe it. She'd bungled the opening statement and then made an ass of herself getting into it with the prosecuting attorney until the judge called a recess until the following day. She strode out of the courtroom, her throat tight with shame and her skin hot. *I screwed up.*

No matter how frustrating or crazy her personal life got, she had always—*always*—found refuge in work. With her clients, the world made sense. It didn't matter what case they had leveled against them, she had a knack for finding the right facts to turn things in their favor. That click was her favorite thing in the world.

She'd lost it.

Two days since Gideon had unceremoniously dumped her, and she'd spent the entire time going through too many boxes of Kleenex and watching movie after movie while clutching Garfunkel. She hadn't touched her files. She hadn't checked her email. She hadn't done anything other than sit there and feel sorry for herself.

It didn't make *sense*. Work was her everything. Work was the reason she had contacted Gideon to begin with. Dropping the ball there was inexcusable.

Why? Why can't I focus?

She knew the answer. She didn't want to face it.

But Lucy couldn't keep on like this indefinitely. If she didn't recover tonight and fix the mess she'd made today, she could kiss her promotion goodbye and it would all be for nothing. Facing down the ugly truth required more courage than she thought she had.

She hit the street and turned a direction at random, needing the movement to untangle her thoughts. Three blocks later and she was no closer to unveiling the truth.

Coward. Just like you called him.

Damn it. Lucy stopped short. "I love him." The comment earned her a few looks from people walking around her, but she started moving again before anyone could get pissed about her being a human roadblock. *I love him.*

She'd loved Jeff, but it was…different. Even if they'd been planning their wedding when she'd found out that he'd cheated on her, her connection with Jeff had never come close to what she felt for Gideon. Her heartbreak at the time hadn't made her miss a step at work. If anything, without the stress of trying to juggle her emotions over Jeff's nasty comments, she'd been free to focus solely on what was most important—her job.

The only problem? Her job didn't hold up against what she felt for Gideon. Every time she tried to work, she caught herself wondering where he was or what he was doing—or who he might be with.

The last was her own personal demon. Lucy didn't think for a minute that Gideon had dropped her on her ass and gone off to hook up with someone else. No matter what he'd said about not being the keeping kind, it was his fear talking—not reality.

He cared about her. He wouldn't have taken the noble route if he hadn't. It was a stupid choice, to be sure, but she understood that he was trying to protect her. He just wasn't giving her the benefit of making her own choices.

That was the problem.

That was the thing she didn't know if she could get over.

Liar.

Gideon might have pulled the trigger on ending things, but only because he'd beaten Lucy to it. She hadn't fought for him—for them. He'd tried to do the noble thing and, instead of telling him where to stick his high-handed attitude, she'd just walked away. So much easier to retreat than to put herself on the line and be rejected by him.

Lucy wove through the crowd of people on the corner and stopped next to the building, staring at the stream of yellow taxicabs. She'd projected herself. She couldn't even blame her history on her reaction. What she felt for Gideon scared the hell out of her. She *knew* he cared about her—loved her, even. They hadn't shared so much for it to be anything less than love. He wouldn't have told her to pick him unless he was one hundred percent serious. That wasn't how Gideon operated. He didn't play games.

Honesty. He demanded perfect honesty—and he'd given it, as well. She mentally played back everything he'd said to her. Nowhere in there was him telling her that all he'd wanted was sex. No, he didn't think he was good enough for her, so he'd cut her loose. *High-handed, but so very Gideon.* He'd chosen *her* happiness over *his*.

She needed to put herself out there. To tell him that *he* was her happiness. Lucy had lived a decent life the last couple of years. She'd been perfectly content, but she'd also cut herself off from anyone that would make her feel deeply enough to hurt her. She'd barely tried to date and hadn't attempted to reach out to friends she'd lost touch with.

She'd been the coward.

That stopped now. If Gideon didn't want her—didn't love her—he could damn well tell her to her face. That was the only acceptable reason for him dumping her. Anything else they could work past as long as they were together. Lucy would make him see that. The man might make her fumble her words a bit, but she'd power through it to get the truth out.

Her phone vibrated and she almost ignored it, but the only way to make her dumpster fire of a day in court worse was to ignore a call from her client or one of the partners. But when she dug it out of her purse, it was the last number she expected to see there. *Roman?*

Lucy frowned and answered. "Hello?"

"I owe you an apology."

She blinked. This situation kept getting weirder and weirder. Roman had never called her before, and she couldn't think of a single reason he'd have to call her now. Unless… Her heart lodged in her throat. "Is Gideon okay?"

"What?" His shock seemed genuine and then he laughed, breaking her tension. "Shit, I guess I owe you two apologies. Gideon is fine last I saw him, which was yesterday. I should have realized you'd think the worst."

Lucy let loose the breath she'd been holding. "Okay. Sorry. I just thought…"

"Logical. I should have considered it." He cleared his throat. "Look, I fucked up, Lucy. I never asked your forgiveness for not telling you about Jeff, and then I went and compounded the issue by letting my guilt prod me to give Gideon some truly shitty advice."

She'd known that something had happened while Gideon was with Roman to push him into action, but she didn't hold it against him. Any of it. "Gideon's strong-willed. He wouldn't have been pushed into doing something he wasn't already considering doing."

"Still."

She smiled at the stubbornness in that single word. It was no wonder the two men got along so well. They were cut from the same kind of cloth. "Consider yourself forgiven."

"I'd actually like to make it up to you. Before you tell me it's not necessary, know that I realize it's not necessary and that's how good apologies work."

Amusement curled through her, though she wished he'd get to the point so she could hang up and call Gideon. "What did you have in mind?"

"What are you doing right now? A friend is doing a soft opening of his restaurant and I have a table reserved so we can talk."

"Right now?" She looked around. "I guess that works." Damn it, she wanted Gideon, but if she was going to get him to come around, it wouldn't hurt to have Roman on her side. Maybe she could use the lunch to mine for information. The thought buoyed her disappointment a bit. "Text me the address, please."

"Will do. I'll meet you there." He hung up before she could ask him any further questions.

Lucy frowned. *Strange.* Her phone pinged almost immediately and she frowned harder because she recognized the address. It overlooked Central Park, though it used to be owned by someone else. It must have cost a small fortune—or large one—to purchase. She set the information aside and stepped to the curb to flag down a cab.

The ride was blessedly short, all things considered. Lucy kept looking at her phone, but now that she was going to meet Roman, she didn't want to call Gideon until afterward. Just in case he wanted to talk immediately. Her stomach did a slow flip-flop. *Please be willing to meet with me.*

To her surprise, the restaurant was actually the top floor of the building. After getting off the elevator, Lucy stood in the entranceway for a solid thirty seconds, just taking in the opulence of the place. It screamed wealth with its polished white-marble floors and subtle gold accents. Nothing déclassé, but there all the same.

A well-dressed man strode over, a practiced smile on his handsome face. "You must be Lucy. This way, please."

She followed, taking in empty table after empty table. "I thought this was a soft opening?" Surely there should be *some* people there. *Good Lord, did Roman invite me here to shove me out a window?* She pushed the thought away. Hysterical was what it was.

"It is." He chuckled. "Just a *very* soft opening."

That wasn't an answer at all, but she allowed him to lead her into what appeared to be a greenhouse. The air warmed enough that she unzipped her jacket. Flowers of every color and shape lined the walls. There were even trees in the corners, which made her smile despite everything.

She was so busy looking at the foliage that she didn't realize the man had left—or that she wasn't alone—until she turned around and found Gideon standing in the doorway. Lucy froze. "But—"

"I'm sorry for the cheap trick. I wasn't sure if you'd agree to see me if I called." His dark eyes drank her in and she actually felt his longing even across the space between them.

Lucy shook her head. "Gideon, you have to *stop*. If you want to see me, call me and say so yourself instead of trying to manipulate things into a perfect setup." Now that she had him here, though, she was just glad she didn't have to have this conversation over the phone. She lifted her chin. "And if you love me, you stay. You don't choose the self-sacrificing route because you think you know what's best for me. You sit down and have a damn conversation where we talk it out."

His smile wasn't all that happy. "I fucked up."

"Yes, you did." She wasn't about to let him off easily, no matter how much she wanted to cross the distance between them and feel his strong arms wrap around her.

"I'm sorry. There's no good reason to explain why I freaked out, but guilt makes people do crazy things—like walk away from the woman they love because they think it's what's best for her."

"*I* decide what's best for me."

His dark eyes took on a tinge of sorrow. "I know. And we both know that I don't deserve to kiss the ground you walk on. Not because I love some idealized version of you, but because you're *you*. You're a good person, Lucy. The best kind of person. You are funny and kind and sexy as fuck, and I might not deserve you..." He took a step forward and then another. "No, I *know* I don't deserve you."

"Stop saying that," she whispered.

"Maybe we both fucked up. Fear makes for all kinds of mistakes, and what we have between us is wildfire." Gideon stopped in front of her and went down on one knee. "But, Lucy, I'd gladly spend the rest of my life burning for you." He withdrew a ring box from the inner pocket of his suit jacket. "I love you. I've loved you for six goddamn years, and I convinced myself that the right thing to do was to stand back and let you be with someone you deserved. I fought every single damn day not to pull some underhanded shit and steal you from that douche."

She reached out with shaking hands and touched the ring box. "Gideon—"

"I know you wanted a safe and pat marriage to some guy you don't give two fucks about. I can't offer you that, Lucy. But I can offer you a husband who will love you beyond all reason, even if he occasionally screws up. I can offer you a safe harbor, a full life and more sex than you know what to do with. I *am* offering you that."

She couldn't catch her breath. In all the scenarios she'd played out over the last few days, she'd never once imagined Gideon, down on one knee, offering her everything she'd spent two years being too terrified to admit she wanted. "Gideon."

"Yes?" He didn't look scared while he waited for her answer. He looked totally and completely at peace for the first time in as long as she could remember. As if he was exactly where he wanted to be—where he was meant to be.

Lucy stepped forward and tangled her fingers in his hair. "Steal me."

His dark eyes went wide. "That's a yes."

It wasn't a question but she answered anyway. "That's a hell yes."

He gave a whoop and shot to his feet, sweeping her off hers in the process. "I love the shit out of you, Lucy. I'll spend the rest of our life making up for six years of missed opportunity."

She kissed him with everything she had. "Maybe it was good that it took us six years to get here and more than a few missteps along the way. There's a right time and place. This is *our* time and *our* place." Lucy kissed him again. "I love you, Gideon. So, so much."

He stepped back enough to slip the ring out of the box and onto her finger. It was…perfect. The simple silver band framed a princess-cut diamond that was big enough to have her shooting a look at him. "Wow."

"Funny, that's what I say every time I see you." He pulled her back into his arms. "Wow. This woman is mine. And I'm hers."

"Yes and yes and yes." She smiled up at him. "Always."

★ ★ ★ ★ ★

MAKE ME CRAVE

To Hunter McGrady.

You're an inspiration!

1

"I SHOULD CANCEL." ALLIE LANDERS THREW AN-other massive load of white towels into the washer and bumped the door closed with her hip. "Honestly, I shouldn't have let you talk me into this in the first place."

"It's cute that you think you let me do anything." Her best friend, Becka Baudin, laughed. She pulled another set of shoes out of the metal bin and paired them up with the appropriate-sized cubby. "And, besides, I already checked us in for our flight. It's too late to turn back now. Our classes are covered. Claudia is handling all the administrative work for the week—for both the gym *and* the shelter. If you stay, you'll just stand around and stress out because things are operating just fine without you." She slid another set of spin shoes back into their cubby. "When's the last time you took a day off, Allie?"

Allie sighed, because that was the one argument she couldn't win. She didn't take days off. Her gym, Transcend, and the women's shelter it helped support were her life. She even lived in the apartment above the building combining the two. When she wasn't filling in teaching a class for one of the girls she em-ployed, she was handling administrative work or doing what-ever was required for the shelter.

She preferred it that way. Being busy made her feel complete in a way that nothing else did. She was a vital cog in a perfectly operating machine.

Except little about it was perfect these days.

The few donors she'd had who helped keep the women's shelter afloat had dried up. The gym functioned just fine on its own, but she'd been using every bit of profit to keep the shelter going. Because of that, the gym was in jeopardy now, too. The result... She was in trouble. More trouble than she'd let on to anyone. Admitting it aloud was akin to making it real, and she couldn't do that. There was a way out. There had to be.

A way that didn't involve selling out to the vulture investors who'd been circling for months. Allie just needed *time* to figure it out.

The very last thing she needed was to jet off to the Caribbean to some private island for a week. But if she admitted as much to Becka, then she'd have to admit everything else.

She couldn't. Not yet.

Allie had just sunk what remained of her personal savings account into keeping the power bill paid at the shelter, which meant another month gone by without debt collectors calling. Or, worse in so many ways, without having to turn out any of the women currently living there.

"Hello? Earth to Allie." Becka waved a hand in front of her face, a frown marring her expression. "Where'd you go?"

"Nowhere important." She forced a smile and reached over to flick her friend's hair. "The blue suits you." It was just as bright as Becka's personality, several shades melded together to create something beautiful.

"Don't change the subject." Her friend frowned harder. "You aren't going to cancel, are you? If you try, I will hog-tie you to your suitcase and haul your ass to the airport myself. You're going to relax and enjoy yourself for a week even if it kills both of us."

Allie snorted. "If it kills both of us, that's hardly relaxing, is it?"

"Smart-ass." Becka's blue eyes were pleading. "I've already left our contact info with Claudia. I promise, if something happens and they need you, I'll pay for your flight back to New York without bitching about it once. And I'll never bully you into going on vacation again."

Allie raised her eyebrows. "How much did you have to pay Claudia to make sure she doesn't call me?" That was the only way Becka would make a promise like that. Her friend played to win, and she wasn't afraid to play dirty. Claudia was just as bad.

Becka all but confirmed it. "Claudia is on the same page as I am. We both agree that you need to get the hell away from this place for a little bit."

She sighed again, but a small part of her looked forward to seven days with no email, no phone calls, no weight of the world on her shoulders. The island had no internet access except in the main lodge, so she'd have no choice but to relax. "I guess I have to go, then."

"Yes, you do!" Becka gave a little wiggle. "Now help me get the rest of these shoes put away before your class. I'm going to pop in if it doesn't fill up. Seven days of drinking and sunning myself are going to add up quick."

Allie laughed and moved to help. She pushed away the worry and stress that had plagued her for months. It would still be here when she got back. What would it hurt to just cut loose for once in her adult life? "I'm looking forward to it." And for the first time since she'd bought the tickets, she actually meant it.

Roman Bassani glared at the pretty Chinese woman behind the counter. "You've been giving me the runaround for weeks. I know for a fact that Allie Landers is in here daily and she's actively dodging my calls. I just need to talk to her." He couldn't tender her an offer to invest in her business if he couldn't pin her down, and he'd been having a hell of a time managing that since his initial call to propose the idea. Coaxing reluctant business owners into seeing things his way was something that usually came easily for him. But Allie Landers was a slipperier quarry than he'd expected.

Apparently she'd successfully dodged him. Again.

"I'm sorry, sir." Claudia didn't look the least bit sorry. "She's out of town for the next seven days. Any business you have with her will have to wait until then."

"Out of town? Where the hell did she go? There's got to be some way to get ahold of her." He didn't actually expect Claudia to answer, but apparently needling him was too much of a temptation.

She leaned forward with a small smile. "She's on a private island with no cell service or internet. If you want to contact her before she gets back, I suggest smoke signals."

Cheeky.

He could use this. Roman plastered a disbelieving look on his face. "That's bullshit. There isn't a damn place in the Western Hemisphere without cell service or Wi-Fi, let alone without both."

"There is on West Island."

Aha. He didn't let his expression shift. "If you say so. You tell Allie to call me when she gets back."

"I'm sure she'll have you at the top of her list," Claudia said sweetly.

Roman turned without another word and stalked out of the gym. He breathed an audible sigh of relief once the door closed behind him. Everything about that place was so feminine, he couldn't walk inside without feeling like a bull in a china shop. It was more than the tiny instructors that he seemed to argue with the second he asked after the owner. There wasn't a single pink thing in sight, but the place was always packed with women.

None of that was a bad thing, but the looks they gave him—as if they expected him to go on a rampage at any moment—and the subtle flinches they made if he moved too fast… It grated. It wasn't their fault, and he applauded what Allie Landers was doing there, but their behavior left him painfully aware of how big his body was by comparison to theirs, and of the fact that no matter how carefully he spoke or how expensively he dressed, he was still a goddamn animal beneath the suit.

He didn't let anyone see it, but those women sensed it all the same.

A predator.

It didn't matter that he'd chop off his hand before he raised it to a woman or child. To them, he was a threat.

Roman cursed and started down the street. He should hail a cab, but he needed to work off his aggression more. The long strides helped clear his mind and ease his agitation, leaving nothing but cold purpose in its wake.

This Allie thought she could skip town for a week and ignore the fact that his deadline was bearing down on them. Two weeks until she had to make a decision, or other investors would make the decision for her. Normally, Roman wouldn't hesitate to play dirty, but his client wanted Allie to agree to the contract without him putting on undue pressure. *An impossible task.* He had a healthy bonus waiting for him if he could pull it off, but that was secondary. His client wanted full acquisition of the business with the shelter intact—the women in the shelter would scatter if they thought it was a hostile takeover. They trusted Allie, and they sure as fuck wouldn't trust *him*.

All of it boiled down to his needing the damn woman to go along with this buyout and he couldn't convince her to get on board if she wasn't here.

But he had a location.

Roman fished his phone out of his pocket and did some quick searching, his frustration growing when he realized that the resort was booked for the next year straight. The website promised a discreet paradise, which translated to the staff being unwilling to move things around to accommodate him. Since giving him guest names so he could offer his own incentive was against company policy, he'd hit a dead end.

Only one thing left to do. He called his best friend, Gideon Novak. "Hey, don't suppose you have any connections with West Island in the Caribbean?"

"Hello, Roman, so nice to hear from you. I'm doing well, thank you for asking."

Roman rolled his eyes. "Yes, yes, I'm being a prick. We both know that's not going to change. The island. It's important."

The slightest of pauses on the other end wouldn't have been there if he hadn't fucked things up royally six months ago. He and Gideon were mending that bridge, but rebuilding the trust was slow going. It didn't matter that Gideon understood where Roman was coming from—Roman had still almost cost his friend the love of his life, Lucy.

Finally, clicking sounded on the other end of the phone. "I haven't dealt with the owner specifically, but I've placed two separate clients with his company and they're both still working there."

It was better than he could have hoped. "I need one of the villas."

Another pause, longer this time. "Roman, if you need a vacation, book it yourself. I'm not a goddamn travel agent."

"No shit. This isn't pleasure—it's business. I need to find a guest arriving today. And offer the owner of the reservation a truly outstanding amount of money to reschedule. The resort won't give out that information to me, but if you have an in, they'll give it out to you."

"This better be *really* important."

It wasn't a question, but Roman had nothing to lose at this point. "Vitally. One of the businesses I've been trying to court for months is coming down to the deadline. If my client doesn't invest first, the other wolves circling will. They'll damage the integrity of this place and do irreparable harm to people's lives as a result."

"Sounds like you're playing the hero. A new look for you."

"Fuck no. I'm in it for the bottom line, and the bottom line is that with the right spin, this place could be making a significant amount of money, and the good press that comes from it being connected with a women's shelter would go a long way to opening doors to me that have previously been closed."

Gideon snorted. "Whatever you have to tell yourself. Give me thirty."

"Thanks."

His friend hung up without saying goodbye. Gideon would come through for him. The man was an unstoppable force, and Roman counted himself lucky to have him on his side.

Sure enough, thirty minutes later, a text came through with the reservation details—and the significant amount of money to be wired to the owner of the reservation he was co-opting. Roman wasted no time sending the money and booking the first flight out of New York.

He had seven days to track down Allie Landers and convince her to see things his way. How hard could it be on an island with only ten villas on it?

2

ROMAN TOOK FIVE MINUTES TO CHANGE AND
stalk through his villa, getting a feel for the place. It was all vacation luxury, heavy on the driftwood furniture and big open
spaces to maximize the view of his private beach and the foliage that surrounded three-quarters of the building.

And therein lay the problem.

He should have anticipated that an island with only ten villas would play heavily into privacy, but with the various activities open to all guests, he'd anticipated there would be plenty
of time to find Allie and make his argument.

He hadn't figured on not knowing which part of the island
she was on.

He strode onto the beach and looked around. The natural
curve of the island created a miniature bay that blocked out the
view of anyone else. There were bicycles and walking paths to
get to the main buildings, where there was a restaurant, a bar, a
yoga studio and a boutique gift shop. He could hang out there
and hope like hell that Allie would venture in for a meal, but
with the option to have dining brought to the villas, he didn't
like his odds.

No, better to get the lay of the land and plan accordingly.

A quick examination of the storage unit right off the sand—

designed to look like a weathered shack—gave him the answer. There was gear for a variety of water sports. He considered his options and went with the kayak. It was the fastest way to get where he needed to go and stay relatively dry in the process. He shucked his shoes off, paused and then dragged off his shirt, too. The summer sun should have made the heat unbearable, but as he pushed the kayak into the water, it was damn near pleasant.

Roman hadn't been on a kayak before, but it seemed easy enough. He experimented in paddling until he got a good rhythm, then set off, heading south around the island. He'd make a circuit and go from there.

The main problem lay in the fact that he didn't exactly know who he was looking for. He'd never managed to pin Allie Landers down into meeting him in person. The digging he'd done online had brought up precious little—both in details about her as an individual and pictures of her. Her social media accounts were both set to private, and the one photo he'd found of her was from ages ago. The Transcend website, which revealed more about the company's services and vision than its founder, didn't give more information than a contact email address. Considering it was linked with a women's shelter, *that* wasn't surprising, but it still irked him.

That said, Roman had secured deals in the past that began with even less information than he had now. He was confident he'd pull it off this time, too.

The first villa to the south had a family with two small-ish children making sandcastles, so Roman kept going, starting to enjoy himself despite the fact that he much preferred the city to anything resembling nature. This didn't feel like *nature*, though.

It felt a whole lot like paradise.

He made his way around the island, surveying beach by beach. There were two with families, two with groups that seemed to consist solely of men, three empty and one with a group of four women who catcalled him as he paddled past. He filed that information away to check on later. There was no telling how many friends Allie had come down here with, but he knew she wasn't married and had no children, so at least he'd narrowed down the search.

By the time he came around the north point of the island, he was fucking exhausted. Roman spent time in the gym regularly, but the heat and the constant paddling wore on him. He steered around the outcropping of rocks and let his paddle rest across the kayak in front of him, taking a moment to roll his shoulders.

Which was right around the time he saw the woman.

She lay on her back, her arms stretched over her head, her long blond hair stark against the vivid red of her beach towel. But that wasn't what made his breath dry up in his lungs.

It was the fact she was topless.

Her golden skin glinted in the sunlight as if she'd oiled herself before coming out to the beach, and the only thing resembling clothing she wore was a tiny triangle of indeterminable color. Her long legs bent as she shifted, her large breasts rising and falling with a slow breath.

He forgot what he was there for. Forgot that his muscles were damn near shaking with exhaustion. Forgot everything but his sudden need to see what color her nipples were.

What the fuck are you doing?

He shook his head. Going closer was inappropriate. Fuck, sitting there and staring like a goddamn creep was the height of inappropriate. It didn't matter how mouthwatering her curves were or the fact that she'd propped herself up on her elbows to watch him.

Roman took a deep breath, and then another. It did nothing to quell his raging cockstand, but he managed to pick up the paddle and keep rowing. Whoever that woman was, no matter that he wanted to spend a whole lot of time up close and personal with her...she wasn't Allie. The one picture he'd managed to source of the woman alone was several years old. Her goddamn senior yearbook photo. She'd been skinny to the point of being unhealthy with her hair chopped short and dyed pitch-black.

He highly doubted she looked anything like that currently.

The one defining characteristic of the women who staffed Transcend was that they were all tiny and chiseled and didn't have a soft spot on their bodies. Beautiful, yes. Roman could appreciate all body types, but none of them had made his hands shake the same way that woman on the beach did. Soft and curvy and with breasts he ached to get his mouth on.

Knock that shit off. You aren't here to fuck anyone, no matter how sexy she is. You're here for business.

He'd go to dinner tonight and see if he could sniff out which of the women on the island was Allie and make his plan from there.

And if he saw the mystery woman once he'd gotten the rest of it figured out?

Roman grinned. Maybe he'd make an exception to his rule and indulge in some pleasure along with business.

He was in paradise, after all.

"How are you doing, sweetie?" Allie pulled on a sundress and headed over to check on Becka. Her friend had indulged a little too heavily on the vodka on the flight down from the city, and the short plane ride from Miami to West Island had made her sick. She'd spent the afternoon sleeping it off, but she still looked a bit green around the gills.

Becka managed a shaky smile. "I think vodka and I broke up."

"It's temporary." She hesitated. "Do you want me to stay? Nurse you back to health?" She was pleasantly tired, but the draw of tonight's menu was enough to have her itching to ride to the lodge and get a better lay of the land. Becka had been so out of sorts when they arrived, it had been a rush to get checked in and settled in the villa so she could sleep off the worst of it.

"God, no. It's bad enough that I've brought shame on my family for ruining the first day of your desperately needed vacation. I'm not going to let you spend any time paying for my bad decisions. Go. Eat delicious food. Drink."

Allie still didn't move for the door. "Why don't I see if the chef can make up some broth or something easy on your stomach?"

"Go, go, go. You're on vacation. You're not required to mother me." She softened the words with a smile, still looking queasy.

Allie went. Becka wouldn't thank her for staying and would only feel guilty if she did, which would distract her from resting. Tomorrow would be soon enough for them to go exploring and try out the stand-up paddleboards Allie had eyed when she'd checked out the beach.

Her face heated at the fact she'd been caught sunbathing topless. Whoever that guy was, he'd been far off enough that she couldn't clearly see his face. Those shoulders, though… Allie shivered. Even at a distance, she'd seen the cut of his muscles and how purposefully he'd maneuvered the kayak through the turquoise waters. The island must have already gone to her head, because she'd spent a truly insane moment hoping he'd come to shore so she could get a better look at him.

Maybe more than a better look.

Allie laughed at her fanciful thoughts. Vacation hookups were all well and good, but if that was what she'd wanted, she'd chosen the wrong place to go. Isolation and relaxation were the name of the game on West Island, which was exactly what she'd craved when she let Becka talk her into booking the trip. It was the exact opposite of New York and her life there.

But now she found herself wondering if maybe something *slightly* more chaotic would have been a better choice. The sun and sea had soaked into her blood and the heady feeling had her convinced anything was possible. It was only a week. The perfect length of time for a fling...

If she wasn't on a private island in the middle of the ocean without a single man in sight.

She bypassed the little golf cart that was one of the main forms of transportation here. It felt good to walk after being cooped up on the plane and then lying prone while she sunned herself. She usually taught at least one class a day at Transcend— more if she needed to cover someone else's schedule—so being inactive wasn't natural for her. It was only a mile or two to the restaurant and the day had started to cool as the sun reached for the horizon. It'd be downright pleasant tonight.

She'd make sure to wake early and attend one of the yoga classes offered, and the rest of the day would be filled with activities that would keep restlessness from setting in. There was even scuba diving available, though Allie wasn't sure she was feeling *that* adventurous. Snorkeling? Sure. Going deeper with only a tank and a few tubes between her and drowning? That would take a whole lot more convincing.

The path was cleared and well maintained to allow the carts to drive without problems, so she let her mind wander as she fell into a natural stride that ate up the distance without tiring her out. Every once in a while, the path would branch off in different directions, some heading toward other villas, some heading deeper inland. There was a small selection of hiking trails that offered tours of the history of the island.

She made it to the restaurant easily and found it practically deserted. Allie paused in the doorway, wondering if she'd mis-understood the woman who'd checked them in. Maybe it was closed?

"Looks like it's just you and me."

She jumped and spun around. The man stood a respectable distance away, but his sheer size ate up the space and made her feel closed in. She froze. *I'd recognize those shoulders anywhere.* Confirming her suspicion, his gaze slid over her body as if he was reminding himself of what she looked like with nothing but what she'd worn on the beach. She tried to swallow past her suddenly dry throat. "You."

"Me." He finally looked her in the face, and she rocked back on her heels. The man was an Adonis. There was no other way to describe his blond perfection, from his hazel eyes to the square jaw to the cleft in his chin to the body that just wouldn't quit. He might be wearing a shirt now, but the button-down did nothing to hide his muscle definition.

He held out a wide hand with equally perfect square fingers. "Let me buy you a drink?"

"We're at an all-inclusive resort."

His lips twitched, eyes twinkling. "Have a drink with me."

Oh, he was good. Charm practically colored the air between them, and she had the inexplicable impulse to close the distance and stroke a finger along his jawline. To flick that cleft chin with her tongue.

Allie gave herself a shake. "Since we're the only ones here, it'd be silly to sit apart."

The look he gave her said he saw right through the excuse, and why not when it was pathetically flimsy? The truth was that this man was magnetic and she suspected she'd be drawn to him even in a room full of people. He waved a hand at the empty place. "Lady's choice."

"How magnanimous of you."

"I try."

She laughed and headed for the table in the middle of the small patio. There were half a dozen tables, and she picked a spot that put her back to the building and presented the best view of the ocean through a carefully curated gap in the foliage.

He eyed the view and then the chair on the other side of the table, and then he picked it up and set it adjacent to hers so they were sitting on a diagonal, rather than directly across from each other. "Nice view."

She turned to agree—and found him staring at *her*.

Allie wasn't falsely modest. Life was too short to play games with body shaming and pretending she didn't have access to a mirror. She was pretty—beautiful when she put some effort into it—but she'd given up being skinny or petite after the agony of high school, and she wasn't athletically built like some of the women at her gym. Sure, she had muscle beneath her soft- ness, and she could keep up with the best of them in her spin classes, but she loved food just as much as she loved to sweat, and her curves reflected that. Some guys had a problem with that, though she didn't keep them around as soon as comments like "Should you really be eating that?" started.

This guy looked at her like he wanted to put her on the table and feast on *her* for dinner.

The desire stoked the flame inside her that had kindled the second she saw him. She leaned forward, checking his left hand. No ring. No tan lines, either. "What brings you to West Is- land?"

"It's paradise, isn't it? Who wouldn't want to come here to get away from it all?"

That wasn't quite an answer, but she was distracted by the intoxicating way his mouth moved when he spoke. *Get ahold of yourself, Allie. You're in danger of panting for him.* She took a quick drink of water that did nothing to quell the heat rising with each minute she sat next to him.

Luckily, a waiter appeared to save her from saying some- thing truly embarrassing. He outlined the menu for the night and took their drink orders, then disappeared as quickly as he'd come.

They were in the middle of one of the most beautiful places Allie had ever seen, and she couldn't manage to tear her gaze away from this stranger. She licked her lips, every muscle in her body tensing when he followed the movement. She opened her mouth, but before she could speak, he took her hand, running his thumb over her knuckles.

The touch was innocent enough, but she felt that light movement in places that were most definitely *not* innocent. She didn't have to look down to know her nipples now pressed against the thin fabric of her sundress.

His smile was slow and sinful and promised things she never would have had the gall to ask for. "This is going to sound unforgivably forward, but what do you say we get out of here and go back to my villa?"

It was crazy. More than crazy. She didn't even know his name, and she sure as hell didn't know anything more pertinent about him.

But there on the softly lit patio with the tropical scent of some flower she didn't recognize and the soft shushing sound of the tide coming in, she didn't feel like Allie, gym owner and mother hen, the responsible one who could never afford to do anything out of line or make a misstep because too many lives depended on her.

Here, she was just Allie, a woman. A woman who desperately wanted the man staring at her mouth as if he was doing everything in his power to keep from kissing her right then and there. She licked her lips again, secretly delighting in the way a muscle in his jaw jumped. "Yes."

"Yes?"

"Yes, let's get out of here."

3

ROMAN TOOK THE WOMAN'S HAND AS THEY LEFT the candlelit restaurant and made their way to the golf cart he'd driven there. He'd considered walking, but he was so goddamn glad now that he hadn't.

She looked even better up close than she'd been on the beach. Her white floral dress displayed her large breasts to perfection, hugging her ribs and then flaring out to swish around her thighs as she walked next to him. Her long blond hair was a mass of waves tumbling just past her shoulders, and he could picture it all too easily tangling between his fingers as he thrust into her.

Slow down.

He took a careful breath, and then another, focusing on keeping his stride unhurried and his hand loose on hers. Roman was hardly a saint, but he'd never had a reaction to a woman on such an intrinsic level like he was having now. He wanted to kiss her pouty lips and run his hands over her body and…

Slow. Down.

Not happening.

Not when she looked at him from under thick lashes, her blue eyes devouring the sight of him. She wanted this.

But he had to be sure.

He pulled her into his arms when they stopped next to the

golf cart. She stepped against him easily—eagerly—and he let himself off the leash enough to run his hands down her back and to cup her ass, bringing her flush against him. Her breasts pressed against his chest, and he had to bite back a groan at how good she felt. "I'm going to kiss you now."

She didn't give him the chance to follow through. She tilted her face up and captured his mouth. It was chaste as such things went, her lips soft against his, but it didn't stay that way. Roman slid one hand up to cup the back of her head and deepened the kiss, tracing the seam of her lips with his tongue and delving inside when she opened for him. Her hands fisted the front of his shirt, pulling him closer even as her hips rolled against his.

Roman tore his mouth from hers. "Golf cart. Now." Or he was in danger of forgetting where they were and fucking her right here. Even ignoring the glaring lack of a condom, he wasn't a beast incapable of anything resembling control, and this beautiful wanting woman deserved better than to be bent over a goddamn golf cart.

At least for the first time.

First time? You're out of your damn mind.

He picked her up and set her on the golf cart, enjoying the way her lips parted in a surprised O. He was showing off and he didn't give two fucks about it, especially not when he slid behind the wheel, fired up the cart and started down the path leading toward his villa. He almost asked about hers, but just because she was alone didn't mean she was *alone*.

The thought brought him up short. He glanced at her. "Are you here with someone?"

"Just my friend." She correctly interpreted his expression. "I'm single. No boyfriend. No husband."

Thank fuck. "Same." He pressed the accelerator again. There were little eco-friendly lights scattered along the edge of the path to keep them from driving into a tree, and he made it back to his villa in record time.

Roman shut off the engine and turned to face her. "I—"

"Wait." She pressed a finger to his lips, and he instinctively nipped her lightly. Her eyes went wide. "Let's just...enjoy this. It's not like it's real life. It's the fantasy of this place." She motioned with her free hand.

He couldn't argue that, not with the low sound of some bird in the distance and the sky and sea fading from magnificent colors to true dark even as they sat there. He'd left on a scattering of lights in the villa, and he took her hand and led her inside. "Hot tub?"

"Maybe later."

There was no mistaking the intent in the way she watched him, so he didn't waste time. This was, after all, the fantasy. Roman embraced that and ignored the part of him that was curious about who this woman was and why she'd come to this place. About what her life was like wherever she spent her normal time. About a lot of things. He set it aside, because he craved another taste of her, and if he started talking about shit that didn't matter, he would ruin this perfect feeling of breathless need between them.

He led her into the main bedroom. It played up the island fantasy just as much as the rest of this place did: big windows overlooking the water, a massive mattress framed by a driftwood headboard. The white comforter was ridiculously fluffy, but he wanted to see her stretched out on top of it while he drove into her.

Slow, damn it.

Roman turned and framed her face with his hands. He kissed her, exploring her mouth as he took them deeper. She made a little helpless noise in the back of her throat that had his cock hardening even further. He licked along her neck and nudged off the strap of her dress before working his way across her upper chest to do the same to the other side.

As much as he wanted to rip the goddamn thing off her, he

dragged his mouth over the swell of one breast and then the other, shifting the fabric lower with each pass. Her fingers tangled in his hair, and she arched to meet his mouth, her breath coming as quickly as his.

He captured one nipple, sucking hard until her back bowed and she let loose a little cry. "I'm taking this off."

"Good." She shimmied out of the dress in a move that made his mouth water, her breasts bouncing a little.

And then she stood before him in only a pair of pink lace panties.

"Fucking perfection," he breathed.

It was hard to tell in the low light, but a flush might have appeared on her cheeks and chest. "Don't make a girl stand here while you stare."

He shook his head, trying to clear it. "Give a man a few seconds to enjoy the view. I didn't get a chance to on the beach earlier today." He knelt before her and ran his hands up her legs, enjoying the feel of her muscles flexing beneath his touch. He stopped at the generous curve of her hips and hooked his fingers into the edges of the panties. "It drove me fucking crazy that I didn't know the color of your nipples." The answer was a dusky rose, the contrast between her nipples and her tanned skin drawing him farther up onto his knees so he could see her better, could lick her there again.

She shook, just a little. "You could have come to find out."

"Mmm." He kissed her soft stomach as he drew her panties down her legs. "If I had, you would have run screaming up the beach and barricaded the door."

"Maybe." Her breath hitched as he ran his tongue around her belly button. "Or maybe I would have waded out into the water to meet you."

The image hit him with the force of a train. Of the waves cresting up to tease her breasts as she stood there waiting for him. Of him pulling her into his arms the same way he had here in the villa. Of her wrapping her legs around his waist and him tugging her bikini bottom to the side and— "Fuck, maybe I'll make another circuit around the island tomorrow and we can do it right."

She laughed softly. "Or maybe you can put that wicked mouth to good use and we can focus on the here and now."

That sounded even better. Roman moved, hitching one of her legs over his shoulder, and buried his face in her pussy.

Allie had half convinced herself that she was dreaming, but the feeling of his mouth latching on to the most secret part of her was all too real. She closed her eyes and gave herself over to his licks, long and slow as if relishing her taste and feel. It was the single hottest thing she'd ever experienced.

Right up until he turned them and toppled her onto the massive bed. She gasped, the sound morphing into a moan when he pushed a single finger into her, as slow and exploring as his mouth had been.

His eyes drank in the sight of her in a move she swore she could feel. He lingered on her thighs and pussy, hips and stomach, taking extra care over her breasts, before finally settling on her face. "Perfection," he said again.

"You're not too shabby yourself." She reached over her head to grip the comforter, knowing full well that it offered her breasts up for him.

He made a sound perilously close to a growl. "Thanks." A second finger joined the first, and he barely gave her time to adjust to that before he pushed a third into her. Stretching her. Readying her. "Fuck, woman, you feel good."

"You...too." She fought to keep her eyes open, to not miss a single second of the experience. This golden god looked at her as if he wanted to imprint himself over every inch of her, and she was more than happy to play sacrifice for the night. If he could bring such pleasure with his hands and mouth, there was no telling what he'd do with the rest of his body.

He twisted his wrist so that his thumb slid over her clit with each stroke of his fingers, the combined sensation leaving her feeling warm and melty. She let go of the comforter to reach up and cup his chiseled jaw. "I'm going to call you Adonis."

He barked out a laugh. "I'm hardly that pretty."

"You're even prettier." She never would have said it in real life, without the island and pleasure making her drunk on him. Allie traced her thumb over his bottom lip, slightly fuller than the top. "You call me perfect, but you're flawless."

Another laugh, this one strained. "Trust me, I have more than my fair share of flaws." He turned his head and kissed her palm. "But we'll pretend that's not the truth tonight."

"Works for me." She didn't ask about his flaws. That wasn't what this was. She didn't even know his name, which somehow made the whole situation hotter—because Allie never did this. Ever.

Tonight she was going to.

With that thought buoying her, she reached for his pants. "I need you."

"You have me." He pushed his fingers deeper as if to demonstrate.

"No, I *need* you." She managed to get his belt off and shoved his shorts down his narrow hips. His cock was just as perfect as the rest of him, long and thick, and she swallowed hard. "I'm tired of waiting."

"That's too damn bad, because I'm just getting started." He slid his fingers out of her and looped an arm beneath her waist, sliding her farther onto the bed until he could place her hands on the bottom of the headboard. "I'm not going to tie you down."

Her heart tried to beat itself out of her chest at the thought. "I don't know how I'd feel about that." *Liar.* She wanted it.

Allie didn't think she was particularly kinky before tonight, but the thought of being at the mercy of this man…

Slow your roll. He's a stranger. Getting tied up by a stranger is a bad idea, even in paradise.

He stopped, kneeling above her on all fours, his cock dipping down until it almost touched her stomach. Those hazel eyes were completely serious for the first time since she'd met him. *An hour ago. You met him an hour ago.*

He didn't touch her, though he was close enough that she could feel the warmth coming off his body. "If you've changed your mind, we can stop. I'll give you a ride back to your villa or, if you aren't comfortable with that, you can take the cart and the staff will return it to me tomorrow." No judgment in his tone. No trying to guilt her or pull some shady business. Just ensuring that this was exactly where she wanted to be.

She gripped the headboard. "I want to stay. I want you."

His grin had her breath fluttering in her chest like a trapped thing. "You won't regret it."

Before she could think too hard about what tomorrow would bring, he kissed her, long and slow. Reacquainting himself with her as if it had been days since they'd last touched instead of moments. Her Adonis worked his way down her body one torturous inch at a time, turning parts of her erogenous that she never would have considered before that night. The inside of her elbow. The bottom of her ribs. Her knees.

He stroked and kissed her body as if memorizing every inch, until she was a quivering mess. Her world narrowed down to where he would touch her next, to the only parts of her he *hadn't* touched—her breasts and the spot between her thighs where she ached for him. "Please. Adonis, please."

He chuckled against her inner thigh, and she felt it like a bolt to her pussy. "I like it when you call me that."

"I'll call you anything you want if you just *touch* me."

"I *have* been touching you." He shifted to lie next to her, his big palm coasting over her body, an inch off her skin. She shook with the need to arch up and feel him, but the slant of his brows told her that if she tried, he'd just move his hand farther from her. "Unless you mean something specific. Like here." His fingers drifted just above her nipples and then down until she could feel the air displacement above her clit. "Or here."

"Please."

The touch was so light, she thought she might have imagined it. But she didn't imagine the look in his hazel eyes. He leaned down until his lips brushed hers with each word. "I want to feel you coming on my cock."

4

ROMAN HAD LAUGHED WHEN HE'D FOUND THE stash of condoms on his initial exploration of the villa, but he'd never been so glad for them as he was in the moment when he ripped through a foil packet and rolled the condom over his cock.

He looked at her sprawled on his bed, her long limbs askew, her pussy so wet he could see it glistening from where he stood, her breasts reddened from his mouth, her hair a tangle over the white comforter... Passion personified. "Aphrodite."

She tore her gaze away from his cock. "What?"

"If I'm Adonis, then you're my Aphrodite." He wanted to know her real name, but Roman wasn't a fool—if he pressed her now about it, it would ruin the fantasy they played at. He ran his hands up her thighs as he climbed back onto the bed. "You look like her statue."

Her lips curved in a sinful smile. "You already have me in your bed. You don't have to go overboard with the compliments." She leaned up on her elbows and kissed his throat. "If you don't slide your cock into me right this second, I'm liable to expire on the spot."

Fuck, she kept surprising him. Roman laughed; the sound was harsh with need. "Can't have that."

"No, we can't." She nipped the spot where his neck met his shoulder and then her hand was around the base of him, guiding his cock inside her.

He fought to keep the stroke steady and not drive into her like a goddamn beast. She clenched around him, one leg looping around his waist to take him deeper yet. *Heaven*. There was no other word to describe her little whimpers and shakes that he could feel all the way to the base of his cock. Or for her hands sliding down his back to grab his ass and drive him the rest of the way into her. He tangled his fingers in her hair and kissed her hard. "You know what you want."

"I want you."

He pulled almost all the way out of her and she rose to meet his thrust, her body moving in perfect time with his. As if they'd done this a thousand times before.

It was good. Too damn good.

He pulled back enough to create a little distance between their bodies. "Touch yourself. I said I want to feel you come on my cock, and I meant it."

She didn't hesitate, one hand snaking between her thighs, her middle finger circling her clit. The sight of her seeking her own pleasure while they were still joined threatened to toss him headfirst over the edge. He thrust again, hard enough to make her breasts bounce with each stroke.

Once. Twice. A third time.

She came with a cry, her mouth opening in a perfect O and her pussy milking him. He had no choice but to follow her under. Roman grabbed her hips and fucked her, pursuing his own pleasure even as her orgasm went on and on. Pressure built in the small of his spine and his balls drew up as he came hard enough to see stars.

He managed to collapse next to her instead of on top of her, but only barely. They lay there several long minutes as their gasping breath settled into something resembling normal. Roman pulled her closer, driven by some desire he didn't have a name for, and kissed her again.

She shifted toward him and hooked her other leg around his waist. "God, I just came harder than I've come in living memory and I already want you again. Do you have some kind of aphrodisiac in your sweat?" She licked his throat. "I think you might."

He rolled onto his back, taking her with him so she sprawled on his chest. "If I do, then you do, too." Sure enough, his cock was already stirring.

She squirmed against him, her smile conveying that she knew exactly how hot the move was. "Is it still a one-night stand if we keep having sex until we're both walking funny tomorrow?"

He opened his mouth, reconsidered and shut it. Telling her to stay as long as they were both on the island was premature in the extreme—and would interfere with his business here. He couldn't forget his purpose, not even for this beautiful creature staring at his mouth as if she wanted it all over her body again.

Business would wait until tomorrow.

Roman coasted a hand down her spine, bringing her more firmly against him. "It's still night, so the possibilities are endless."

"I like the way you think."

"Trust me, I'll give you reason to like a whole lot more than that."

Allie woke up to his mouth on her pussy. Again. In the few hours since they'd passed out after having sex again, he'd woken her up three—*three*—times like that, and proceeded to ravish her until her promise that they'd both be walking funny today was definitely a reality rather than a possibility.

His big shoulders spread her legs wide and he fucked her with his tongue, his low growls just as hot as his actions. She slid her fingers through his hair without opening her eyes. "Yes. Right there. Keep doing that." He zeroed in on her clit, mimicking the movements she'd made when she touched herself and pushing her to the edge yet again.

She didn't stand a chance of holding out.

She came with a cry, back bowing and her hands clenching him to her to prolong the pleasure as if she was totally and completely wanton. Maybe she was. She certainly had played the part that night, with no thought to what he'd think of her words or actions because this was only temporary. They were strangers, which was freeing in a way she'd never anticipated. It didn't mean she'd ever do anything like this again, but she was going to enjoy every single second of her time with her Adonis before dawn came.

He left her for several precious moments, but then he was back on the bed, flipping her onto her stomach and drawing her hips up. The position left her exposed, but she loved every second of it, especially when he stroked her between her thighs and then his cock replaced his fingers.

He pushed into her with a smooth move, sheathing himself to the hilt. And then he began to move, thrusting roughly into her and then withdrawing, only to begin again. Allie gripped the comforter and shoved back to meet him, until the only sound in the villa was the smack of flesh against flesh and their ragged breathing. She tried to hold out, tried to keep from being overwhelmed with the pleasure, but he did something with his hips that hit a spot deep inside her, and her orgasm crested in a devastating wave. She cried out, distantly aware of him fucking her harder until he, too, came with a curse.

He dropped to the side and guided her down with him so that they lay spooning with him still inside her. He kissed the back of her neck and palmed her breasts. "Morning."

"Mmm. And a good one at that." She still hadn't opened her eyes, but as one of his hands trailed down to her clit, she laughed hoarsely. "You're insatiable."

"Only with you." He kept up those slow kisses to the nape of her neck. "You make me crazy. I just came and I want you again already." He cupped her pussy, the possessive move making her moan.

But then she opened her eyes and realized how light it was outside. Allie froze. "What time is it?" If Becka woke up and realized she'd never come back last night, she'd be worried. Allie was reliable and dependable, and she most certainly didn't stay out all night while having amazing sex with a stranger. As beyond amazing as it'd been, she hadn't stopped to consider that her friend might think she was hurt or that something bad had happened.

He picked up on her tension and removed his hand. "What's wrong?"

"I have to go." She rolled out of his arms, her body crying out at the loss of warmth, but if Becka wasn't already awake, Allie had to make sure she got back to the villa before that happened. If she *was*, then Allie had some explaining to do.

Either way, she couldn't stay there.

He sat up and watched her scramble for her dress, a frown marring his handsome face. "I know we joked about it being a one-night stand, but that doesn't mean you have to bolt the second the sun comes up. I thought we could have breakfast before you left."

It sounded just as wonderful and perfect as things had been since she'd taken his hand and embarked on this wild adventure.

Unfortunately, reality was calling—or as close to reality as a person got on West Island.

But she didn't like the look on his face—as if she'd somehow hurt him—so she paused. "I would love that, but my friend is back at our villa, and if she wakes up and finds me gone, she's going to think that I walked off the path and broke my leg or something and sound the alarm. I don't have an easy way to get ahold of her, so I have to go make sure she's not forming a search party."

His frown cleared. "I understand." He got out of bed and pulled on his shorts. "I'll give you a ride back."

She started to tell him she didn't need that, but the truth was she did. It was one thing to take his cart because she'd changed her mind about being with him and didn't want to walk the paths alone at night. It was another to want to skip a potentially awkward morning-after conversation. She was an adult. She could handle it.

She hoped. "Thanks. That would be helpful."

He threw on his shirt but didn't bother buttoning it. It gave him the look of a... She didn't even know, but she liked it. A lot. *Down, girl.* She found her shoes and followed him out to the golf cart.

Allie was so tense as she sat next to him, she was surprised she didn't jostle right out of the seat when he put the cart into gear, but he reached over and took her hand, interlacing their fingers as if they held hands all the time. She relaxed, muscle by muscle, but her nerves didn't calm. "I don't do that normally—any of it."

"You don't have to explain yourself to me." He squeezed her hand. "I had a good time last night."

"Me...too." She studied his profile. Adonis, indeed. "A really good time."

He shot her a look as he took a turn onto a path marked with her villa number. "I'm in danger of being pushy, but I'd like to have a repeat—or several. I'm here on business, but my nights are yours if you're interested."

Her breath caught in her throat, though she couldn't say why. To spend her days with Becka doing all the activities they had planned and her nights with her Adonis... That truly would be paradise. She licked her lips. "I... I'd like that."

He grinned and pulled to a stop where the cart path ended

and the walking path began. "In that case, would you gift a poor man with your name? You'll always be Aphrodite to me, but I'd like to know the true identity of the woman I plan to have coming countless times in the next few days."

She blushed and then called herself an idiot for blushing. "I'm Allie."

He went so still, he might as well have turned into a statue. Those hazel eyes focused on her with unsettling intensity. "Allie? Allie *Landers*?"

She jerked her hand back, her heart beating for a reason that had nothing to do with desire. "How do you know my last name?"

He laughed, but not like anything was funny. "This is so fucked."

"What are you talking about?"

Gone was the devilishly charming Adonis who'd seduced her with little effort last night, replaced by a cold man she didn't recognize. "Roman Bassani."

She knew that name. She *knew* that name. Allie scrambled out of the cart and took several steps back, though he made no move to touch her again. "The guy who keeps hounding me? What the hell are you doing *here*?"

His smile was as cold as any she'd seen. "I'm here to convince you to sell your business."

5

ROMAN WATCHED THE METAPHORICAL SHIT HIT the fan in slow motion. He looked at his Aphrodite—at *Allie Landers*—in disbelief. The horror in her expression, the way she took a step back and her body language closed down. Gone was the flirty siren he'd just had in his bed, replaced by a woman who didn't trust him as far as she could throw him.

Still, he tried to salvage it. "I can explain."

"Explain how you hunted me down to West Island and seduced me." She shook her head, blond hair flying. "Nope. Absolutely not. You pulled one over on me. Good job. Way to go. Points for being totally and completely unexpected. You don't get to stand there and tell me you can explain, because this is beyond explanation."

"I didn't know you were…you." He scrubbed his hands over his face. "I'm fucking this up."

"You think?" She took another step back. "Your reputation might be shady, but I never expected *this*."

He started to explain why he thought she couldn't possibly be Allie Landers, but cut the words off before they reached the air between them. Telling her that her glorious curves didn't fit in a specialized gym was both shitty and wrong, and he'd have realized that he shouldn't assume a single goddamn thing if he'd stopped thinking with his cock long enough to function. *There has to be a way to salvage this.* "I don't see why this has to change anything."

Her blue eyes went wide. "You don't think this needs to change anything." She drew herself up to her full height, somewhere close to six feet. "You're out of your goddamn mind. Get out of here. I never want to see you again."

"Like hell I will." He hadn't wanted to do it like this. In fact, he'd crafted several well-thought-out arguments about how she needed to listen to his investment proposal. All of that flew right out the window in the face of his frustration. "You're going to lose it all if you don't stop being so fucking stubborn and let my investor help you."

She looked at him like she'd never seen him before. "Wanting to preserve what I worked so hard to create isn't stubbornness—and not wanting to sell it out to someone like *you* doesn't make me an idiot." She motioned at him.

"Someone like me." She'd made it sound like an insult, and maybe it was. Roman played dirty. He'd never had any qualms about that truth. He still wouldn't have tried to seduce Allie into seeing things his way—but he would have done everything else under the sun. He still would.

But her obvious disdain stung. He laughed harshly. "Someone like me," he repeated. "Honey, look in the mirror. There's only one reason Transcend is going under, and it's not me. I'm just trying to save it."

Her lips twisted. "How noble of you. Well, you can take your apparent white-knight complex and shove it up your ass." She spun around and marched down the path toward her villa, her middle finger in the air.

Stubborn, frustrating woman.

Admittedly, he could have played that better. Roman pinched the bridge of his nose for a long moment and then turned the cart around and headed back for his place. If he could just tell her *who* his investor was…

Impossible. He'd signed a nondisclosure, which his investor had insisted on. Even if he wanted to tell Allie the details of what his client had planned for her gym and shelter, he couldn't. Judging by her reaction, it wouldn't have mattered anyway. She would have called him a liar and told him he was full of shit.

He'd miscalculated. It wouldn't have changed the reaction he'd had to seeing Allie in person—he didn't think anything could have altered that—but he'd have kept control enough not to try to seduce her.

Fool. He could almost hear his old man's voice as if the bastard sat next to him. *Took the easy way and look what happened— exactly what always happens. Failure.*

Roman shut that shit down. He didn't have time to wallow in shame for fucking up. He had to figure out a way around it. As tempting as it was to follow her back to her villa and continue the argument until she saw things his way, it wouldn't do anything but make her dig in her heels further. Allie had proved herself to be as stubborn as the day was long. For some reason, she was resistant to investors.

He needed to figure out why. It was the only way to get around her issues.

He took a shower and headed into the main lodge. It was the only place to get a call out on the island or to use anything resembling the internet. It took some convincing to get the woman on staff to give him access to the tiny business center, but he managed.

Roman sat down while the computer hissed and spit in the old-school dial-up sounds. He shook his head. Apparently paradise didn't like modern technology. Go figure. He considered his best options and dialed Aaron Livingston. It was late enough in the morning that the man should be at the office.

Sure enough, he answered on the fourth ring. "Aaron Livingston."

"Aaron, Roman here."

"Hey, Roman, it's been a while. What can I do for you?"

Roman hadn't spent much time out and about since the fiasco with Gideon and Lucy, and as a result, his social life had suffered a bit. He hadn't cared—it was a nice change of pace—but he hoped it wouldn't work against him now that he needed a favor. "I was hoping you could do a bit of a background check on a company I'm considering investing in. I've done the run-of-the-mill one, but the owner is being difficult and I need to know why."

"You mean they weren't down on their knees in awe at your greatness?" Aaron's amusement filtered through the line. "Color me shocked."

"You don't have to rub it in. I missed a step, and I need to figure out where."

Aaron laughed. "You'll have to give me a few minutes to get over my surprise that the vaunted Roman Bassani isn't perfect."

"Asshole."

"Without a doubt." Another laugh. "Give me the business name and I'll see what I can do. It might take me a few days, but I'll find the information you need."

"Thanks, man. I appreciate it."

"Yeah, well, I *am* charging you."

He grinned. "I wouldn't expect anything different." He hung up after Aaron told him to expect the information via email. It wasn't ideal, but he could wait through the long dial-up time to get it if that meant he had a leg to stand on with Allie.

Allie.

Roman sat back and scrubbed his hands over his face. It was time to deal with the fact that he'd fucked up. He might have fucked up badly enough that this account was lost...

No.

Damn it, *no.*

She was doing good work, but that good work could be increased exponentially if she allowed his client to invest and do the equivalent of franchising Transcend. It was a brilliant business model—or it would be if she moved a few things around.

Except she hadn't taken his meetings or returned his calls, and now she was doubly determined to stay the hell away from him. *Fuck me.* He had to fix this, to do something to get her to stop long enough to listen to what he had to say.

She was stubborn. She'd more than proved that. Well, it was too damn bad, because he could be a stubborn bastard, too.

Roman checked his email, verified that the sky wasn't falling back in New York and logged off. It was time to figure out a game plan to get moving again. They were trapped on this damn island together for the next six days, and he'd be damned before he let this opportunity pass because of one mistake.

Though he'd be lying if he considered last night a mistake. He should have gotten her name immediately, but if he had, the night wouldn't have happened. Having Allie in his bed... He stomped down on his body's reaction to the memories that rolled through him, one after another. Her taste on his tongue. The feel of her generous hips in his hands. Her pussy clenching around his cock. The little smirk she gave him when she knew her saucy attitude was flat-out doing it for Roman.

He'd give his left hand for a repeat. *Get your priorities in order, asshole. She might be hotter than sin and amazing in bed and funny as fuck, but she's still business.*

Roman couldn't afford to forget that—or let the lines blur.

"Roman Bassani followed you *here*?"

Allie adjusted her balance on the paddleboard and dipped her paddle into the water. "I already said that." She glared at the gorgeous water. Stupid paradise, making *her* stupid. She knew better than to go home with a man whose name she didn't even know. *You didn't go home with him, because neither of you are home right now.*

Not helping.

"I just… That's ballsy. Even for Roman."

She twisted so fast, she almost fell off the damn board. "You say his name like you know him." Something resembling jealousy curled thorny vines through her stomach. She had no right to the feeling, and it made no rational sense, so she ignored it.

"Well… I kind of do." Becka shrugged. She wore a bikini so tiny, it must have taken an act of God to keep it in place. It was a bright neon green that managed to complement her equally bright blue hair. "Or we have one degree of separation, but I've met him once, I think. He was a friend of my sister—*is* a friend of my sister." She shook her head. "You know the story, but yeah, he's really good friends with her boyfriend and so they all hang out sometimes now. But I know him by reputation, at least, and he's the best at what he does."

That was part of the problem—Allie wasn't one hundred percent sure what he *did* do. He'd contacted her about investing in Transcend, but it quickly became clear he was a middleman for someone else and… She didn't know. Trusting an investor was difficult enough without them hiding behind a third party. That extra distance didn't bode well for her being able to maintain control of the gym and shelter if she signed on the dotted line. She'd come to West Island to escape real life for a little bit, and it'd followed her here despite her best efforts.

And then she'd slept with it.

She frowned. *Way to make the metaphor weird, Allie.* "It doesn't matter. It was a mistake and I'm going to enjoy the rest of my damn vacation without worrying about him." She was lying through her teeth, but she sent a look at her best friend, daring Becka to call her on it.

Becka dipped her paddle into the water, moving farther away from the beach. "I don't know, Allie. He's one sexy golden god of a man. What would it hurt to bang him like a conga drum while you're down here and go back to hating him when you get home?"

"He's *Roman Bassani*. He's the enemy. I can't just separate things like he apparently can." Though he'd been just as shocked at her identity as she was at his. Allie knew that for a fact. The man might be a good actor, but no one was *that* good. She didn't believe for a second that he'd tried to manipulate her through sex, but that didn't mean she was about to roll over and offer herself and everything she'd worked so hard for to him just because he was beautiful and had an amazing cock and—

Not helping.

"What would a little hot and smoking sex hurt?"

She splashed water at Becka. "It wouldn't *hurt*, but the man already doesn't take me seriously. If he thinks he can seduce me into seeing things his way, who's to say he won't do exactly that?"

Becka sighed. "You're right. I know you're right. It's just so… This place. It makes everything sexier and less complicated, and even though vodka and I broke up, vodka would most definitely agree that it's a good idea."

"Then it's a good thing you and vodka broke up." They reached the mouth of their little bay and paused, letting the paddleboards shift with the water. She lay back on the board and closed her eyes, willing the sun to soak in and chase away her tension. "It's not fair. I am so damn furious that he pulled this shit, but my body hasn't got the memo. He's just so hot. It makes me crazy." She was pretty sure she had the self-control to keep her hands off him going forward, but Allie wasn't all that eager to put it to the test.

"Yes…yes, he is."

There was something in her friend's tone that made her open her eyes. Allie shot up to a sitting position. "Tell me that the sun has gone to my head and I'm hallucinating."

"If you are, we're sharing the view." Becka adjusted her kneeling position like she was going to war. "I can distract him if you want to make a break for it."

That ugly jealousy rose again, even though there'd been nothing resembling insinuation in her friend's tone. Anyway, Allie had *just* said that she wanted nothing to do with him. She couldn't have it both ways. And Becka was... Becka was a force of nature. *Stop that right this second. She's your friend, and he's not anything to you.*

The "he" in question rowed his kayak toward them in smooth movements that made the muscles in his shoulders and chest flex—kind of like they had when he was hovering over her and thrusting...

Her face flamed, and she shook out her hair, doing her best to pretend it was just the external heat and not his effect on her. When Roman got close enough for her to see his face clearly, she went still. He wasn't looking at Becka at all. His attention had focused on Allie like a laser beam, and he cut through the water, effortlessly back paddling to coast to a stop next to her paddleboard. "Allie."

"I'm not sure of the exact laws in this place, but I'm pretty sure they frown on stalking."

His lips quirked. "It's a small island. We're bound to run into each other."

How could he sit there so calm and collected while she fought between the desire to tip his damn kayak and to jump him where he sat? She steadied her grip on her paddle and fought for control. It was easier—so much easier—to be angry than it was to deal with the conflicting emotions inside her. "Is that what you call your kayaking past our villa—again?"

His grin was quick and unrepentant. "The view isn't as good this time." She sputtered, but he didn't give her a chance to reply, turning instead to look at Becka. "I know you."

"Not really. But you know my sister—Lucy Baudin."

He flinched—actually *flinched*—though he covered it up quickly enough that Allie wouldn't have noticed it if she wasn't watching him so closely. Becka had said her sister and Roman were friends, but it appeared to be more complicated than that. Allie filed that away, and irritation rose all over again. "We're trying to have a relaxing time, and you're ruining it."

Roman turned the force of his attention onto her again. His wearing sunglasses should have diluted the effect, but she swore she could feel his gaze dragging over her, taking in her high-waisted vintage swimsuit. It was a flirty black with pink polka dots, and she knew she looked damn good in it. From the way his grip tightened on his paddle, he agreed.

A strange sense of power rolled through her. He wanted her just as much as she wanted him. She'd known that, of course, but the shock of his true identity had twisted everything up in her head. Roman might be considering trying to seduce her into submission, but… What if she turned the tables on him?

Or maybe you want any excuse to get into bed with him again.

She ignored the internal voice and leaned forward, giving him a good view of the excellent cleavage the underwire top created. A muscle ticked in his jaw, and she reveled in the power for a breath before reason kicked back in. "Get lost, Roman. You don't have anything to say to me that I want to hear."

"We both know that's not true." His wicked grin widened, leaving no illusions to what he meant.

Her irritation flickered hotter. He was sitting there, the smug bastard, and thinking he had her number just because he'd made her come more times last night than she'd thought physically possible. Thinking he could railroad her into doing what he wanted.

Well, fuck that.

Allie lifted her chin. "I don't know anything of the sort. It was a forgettable experience across the board." She jerked her chin at Becka, who watched them with jaw dropped. "Let's go. Something stinks out here."

6

ROMAN SPENT THE REST OF THE DAY CONSIDER-
ing his game plan. Cornering Allie was all well and good, but
from the look she'd given him before she paddled away earlier,
if she thought he was trying to talk business, she'd cut him off
at the knees. *Misplayed the hell out of this.*

There was no use bitching about it. The ideal situation was
long gone, so he had to work with what he had.

What he had was smoking-hot chemistry with Allie Landers. Seeing her in that cocktease of a swimsuit with her hair in
beach waves around her shoulders hadn't done a damn thing
to help remind him why he couldn't have her.

He decided to give her until tomorrow—or, rather, to give
himself until tomorrow—to figure it out. Rushing this wasn't
going to accomplish the end he wanted.

He checked his email, more to distract himself than because
he thought there'd be any information yet. There wasn't even
a single fire for him to put out. Roman ran his hand through
his hair. Paradise was all well and good in theory, but it was
fucking boring here by himself.

On a whim, he made his way to the patio where sunset yoga
would be held—and stopped short at the sight of Allie in a pair
of yoga pants and a tank top that seemed to have too many

straps but showed off her body to perfection. As he watched, she pulled her hair back into a ponytail and unrolled a mat.

The instructor—a tiny woman with dark eyes, curly hair and a wide smile—caught sight of him. "The mats are against the wall. Pick a place that feels best for you, but we do prefer to have classes in a single line when there's a small number of people."

Allie turned and her eyebrows shot up, then lowered just as fast. "What are you doing here?"

"Yoga." There was no backing out now, even if he wasn't going to get the relaxation he'd craved. He'd wanted to get time with Allie to talk, but this wasn't what Roman had in mind. He grabbed one of the mats and flung it out with a snap a decent distance from hers. On her other side, Becka looked between them as if she wasn't sure how she was supposed to react.

The instructor was all smiles and gentle hands as she picked up his mat and scooted it until it was only a few inches from Allie's. "Yoga is meant to be experienced as a group. We like to keep it intimate here—which we can't do if someone is creating distance." Once she was satisfied he'd obey, she moved to the front of their line and started her intro.

Roman tried to do yoga a few times a week. He spent too much time sitting behind a desk, and he preferred boxing as his outlet—both activities wreaked havoc on his joints. Yoga helped, and it settled his racing mind like little else, he found.

Today, there was no settling to be had.

He had too much awareness of Allie next to him, her body flowing through the positions effortlessly, her breathing deep and even. *She* didn't seem the least bit bothered to have him so close. It aggravated him in a way it shouldn't have, but he wanted to force her to acknowledge that he was *right there*.

"Roman, you seem distracted." The instructor—he couldn't remember her name, but it was something like Tiffany or Tracy—stopped next to him, using a light touch to adjust his Warrior I stance. "Focus on your breathing. Inhale deeply."

She demonstrated, exhaling slowly through her nose in an audible sound. He followed suit, and she nodded. "Exhale your thoughts. Let your breath center you. You gave yourself this time today. Don't waste it."

He tried. Fuck, he tried. But each inhale brought a faint strain of Allie's lavender scent, and when she turned to face the side of the patio, he found himself captivated by the faint sheen of sweat on her golden skin.

It was too much.

With his being so goddamn in tune with his body, there was no fighting the threatening cockstand. Roman turned on his heel and stalked away, into the main building. He needed distance from that woman, but fuck if it helped. Her scent was in his system, her body a siren call he had no business hearing. She didn't want him—not now that she knew who he was.

He shouldn't want her, either.

But he did.

Roman considered heading straight back to his villa, but the thought of being alone right now only increased his agitation. *This was a mistake.* Which part was the biggest mistake was up for grabs, but he was considering chalking the entire situation up as a loss.

With nothing left to do, he walked into the bar. It was a small space—no more than a serving counter with a handful of lounge chairs facing the ocean—as everything on the island was. He motioned to the bartender. "I need two shots of whiskey, and a double seven and seven."

The man's eyebrows rose. "Sure thing. You've got the run of the place, so post up wherever you like." He turned back to select two bottles from the wall behind him.

Roman didn't want to sit, but standing there and hovering while the guy made his drinks wasn't going to win him any goodwill. He had enough people pissed at him currently, so he strode to the middle lounger and dropped into it.

Lazy streaks of color teased the darkening blue of the sky, the first sign of day giving way to night. Roman welcomed the change even as he dreaded what it meant. Another day down. Another night closer to failure.

It might not be the end of the world if he didn't secure Allie's cooperation in franchising her gym model, but her gym *would* go under. He'd seen the financials. She couldn't keep it afloat much longer, and it'd be a goddamn tragedy to see it fail. He knew she didn't look at it that way, but if she'd stop fucking *reacting* and listen to what he had to say, she might see things differently.

Right. Because I've been the very essence of calm and collected.

Her rejection stung. He wasn't about to lie and say it didn't. It sure as hell did. She hadn't just rejected the professional persona he displayed for work—she'd rejected *him*. The sex changed things, for better or worse. *Looking like for the worst at the moment.*

The bartender brought his shots over and lined them up, quickly followed by his drink. Alcohol wasn't the best choice— not when he needed to be sharp and fully present—but he wasn't going to be around Allie tonight, and the rest of the island could sink into the sea for all he cared. Roman downed one shot and then the second. The fiery burn of whiskey did nothing to chase away his... He didn't even know what the fuck to call what he was feeling. It wasn't pleasant—that was all that mattered.

Women's voices carried over the beach, and he tensed. Before she walked around the corner, Roman already recognized Allie's voice. She stopped short when she saw him, but Becka rolled her eyes and gave her friend a small shove. "Enough, already. I get it—he's a jerk. I won't even argue with you." She winked at Roman, not looking the least bit repentant. "But I want a drink, and this is the quickest way to get what I want." She gave a brilliant smile to someone behind Roman. "Hey, gorgeous. Can we get something fruity and alcoholic?"

"Sure thing, ma'am."

Becka launched into how horrified she was to be called "ma'am" while she walked to the bar, but Allie stopped at the foot of Roman's lounger. "You ran off pretty unexpectedly."

He gave her body a slow caress with his gaze, from her bright pink painted toes to her yoga pants to the tank top that offered her breasts up to perfection. "I was preoccupied."

She inhaled sharply, and he didn't miss the way her nipples pebbled against the fabric of her shirt. "Don't play games with me. It happened. We're done. End of story. Stop bringing it up."

"I didn't bring it up." He climbed to his feet slowly and then closed the distance between them. "A word."

"Excuse me?"

"We need to have a goddamn conversation, so get your panties out of a twist long enough to unstopper your ears and hear what I have to say." He grabbed her hand and towed her into the growing shadows beneath the palm trees framing the walkway to the beach. Roman didn't stop until they were out of sight of the bar and far enough away that Becka's flirting with the bartender was barely audible. Only then did he release Allie and turn to face her. "Now, where were we?"

Allie was so furious, she could barely put two words together. "You don't get to just decide that we're having a conversation and haul me out here to do it."

"If I was going to *haul* you anywhere, it'd be over my shoulder."

Her body clenched at the thought of him doing exactly that, but she fought her reaction back. "You are insufferable. Do you know when the last time I had a vacation was? Ten goddamn years ago when I was still in freaking high school and on spring break. Ten. *Years*. Becka had to twist my arm to get me here, but I was enjoying myself—"

"I know *exactly* how thoroughly you were enjoying yourself."

She ignored that because if she tried to deny it, she'd be a red-faced liar. "That changes nothing. The point is that I'm *not* enjoying myself now, and the only one to blame for that is *you*." She went to push him back a step, but her hands had a will of their own. They stayed on his chest, and she sucked in a breath at how warm his skin was. The man might be a corporate suit, but he looked perfectly at home in his shorts without a shirt on here in the growing darkness near the beach. It was almost enough to forget all the reasons she never wanted to see him again.

Allie stepped closer and lowered her voice. "Nothing you say can make me believe you're anything but a goddamn shark."

"Who said I'm trying to convince you of anything?" The words brushed her mouth as he leaned down, just a little. "I *am* a shark, Allie. I've never pretended to be anything else."

She started to call him a liar, but he was telling the truth. He hadn't tried to seduce her with sweet words to get her into his bed—he'd offered her exactly what she wanted in as many words. Black-and-white. Simple.

It wasn't simple at all.

"I despise you."

"You want me." His hands rested lightly on her hips. "It tears you up inside that you crave my cock, but you can't fight it no matter how hard you try." He backed her up, step by slow step, until she bumped a tree. Roman kept coming, the side of his face brushing hers. "Did you think about how good it'd feel to have my fingers sliding into these yoga pants?"

"No."

"Who's the liar now, Allie?" His lips caressed her earlobe. "I'd love a private yoga session. Just us. No friends, no instructors, no clothes. How long do you think we'd last before I was on my back and you were riding my cock?"

She couldn't breathe. Her skin felt too tight, as if it were several sizes too small, and her core pulsed in time with her racing heart. "I would never—"

"No, Allie. No more lies between us. You're pissed that I'm here—I get that—and you're even more pissed that you want me. Trust me, I know the feeling. I was never supposed to fuck you, and if I'd known who you were…"

She leaned back enough to look at his face—or what she could see of it in the darkness. "If you'd known who I was, you wouldn't have gone there with me."

Roman cursed. "Even if I'd known your name, that wouldn't have stopped me from wanting you. Needing you."

She stroked her hands down his chest to the waistband of his shorts. "Do you need me now?"

"I never stopped."

This was the worst idea. She needed her head clear, and it was nothing but muddled around Roman. He was too big, too beautiful, too overpowering. Even now, she leaned forward, the few inches between them too much distance. He let her, his hands on her hips branding her—but not trying to guide her. Allie inhaled deeply. "Do you drug your cologne? Because, seriously, how am I supposed to think straight when you smell so good?"

He chuckled. "I'm not wearing any."

He was gorgeous and a god in the bedroom, and he had to smell good naturally. Because of course. "I don't like you."

"You don't know me."

She could argue that, but it didn't feel completely accurate. Allie traced the waistband of his shorts with her fingers. She shouldn't…but she was going to. She unbuttoned his shorts and slipped her hand in to grip his cock. "I don't have to know you—I know this."

"You're playing with fire."

"Maybe." Definitely. If she was smart, she'd release him, walk away and spend the rest of her vacation in as close to bliss as she could get, throwing herself into relaxation before she had to go back to reality. She stroked him again, liking the way his body went tense but his hands stayed still on her hips.

As if he was waiting for permission.

The realization sent a thrill through her. She kept stroking his cock, teasing him. "Did you really think it would be that easy?"

"What would?" He spoke through gritted teeth, and her body gave another thrill of pleasure.

"Getting your way." She squeezed him around the base and nudged his pants down a little farther so she could cup his balls with her free hand. "You thought you'd show up here, interrupt my vacation and what? I'd fall all over myself to give you exactly what you wanted?"

Roman released one of her hips and braced his hand on the tree behind her. The move brought him closer to her, but not so close that he impeded her movements. She stroked him harder as he slid his cheek against hers, his breathing hitching with every downstroke. He nipped her earlobe. "Isn't that exactly what happened last night?"

She glared and gave his balls a squeeze that was just shy of vicious. "You're awfully cocky for someone who's got their nether bits in my hands."

"They're very capable hands." He shifted to press butterfly kisses along her jaw and down her neck even as his hand on her hip squeezed her. "Don't stop."

"I should." She didn't. "I should stop right now and leave you with a wicked case of blue balls." Why was her breath coming as harshly as his? He'd barely touched her, but having his cock in her hands and him so close… Intoxicating. There was no other word for it.

Roman gave her collarbone an openmouthed kiss and dragged his hand up her side to palm her breast. "I'll just go back to my villa and jack myself off thinking of your sweet pussy. Not as good as the real thing—nothing is—but you gave me more than enough inspiration to get the job done." He tugged the strap of her tank top off her shoulder. It was one of those things with a built-in bra, so the motion freed her breast. He repeated the move with the other side, and she shivered as the breeze coming in off the water teased her nipples. "Beautiful," Roman murmured.

"You go overboard with the compliments." She kept up her leisurely stroking. It was like the rest of the world ceased to exist outside their little sphere. It was just her and Roman, driving each other crazy.

"I give credit where credit is due." He bent and sucked one nipple into his mouth. The position meant she had to let go of his cock, which she did with reluctance. He cupped her through her yoga pants, the coolness of the tree against her back only highlighting how warm his body was. "If I slipped my hand in here, would I find you wet and wanting? I think so." He traced a single finger up the seam of the pants—right over her clit. "I think having my cock in your hands turned you on as much as the fact that we're ten yards away from the bar and anyone coming up from the beach will get the show of their life."

She pushed back against him even as her hips rolled into his touch. "That's not true."

"Liar." She felt more than heard the word as his breath caressed her neck. "You get off on this as much as I do." Another stroke through the fabric. "Would you take my cock right here, right now?"

She started to say yes, but common sense reared its ugly head. "I'm not fucking you without a condom."

"Mmm." He kissed her neck. "I know." Roman pulled her pants down in a swift movement. She started to protest, but he went to his knees in front of her and yanked her foot free. *Oh.* He looped one leg over his shoulder and she caught the glimpse of white teeth when he grinned. "Have a little faith, Allie. I'm not a complete monster." And then his mouth was on her pussy and she didn't have the breath to argue.

7

ALLIE FORGOT ALL THE REASONS SHE WANTED nothing to do with Roman under the slow slide of his tongue. He tasted her pussy as if he'd been years without it and wanted to imprint every last detail on his memory. She bit back a cry and covered her mouth with one hand even as her other laced through his hair and pressed his face closer to her.

His dark chuckle vibrated over her clit, nearly sending her to outer space. What was he *doing* to her? She didn't act like this. She didn't screw strangers, and she definitely didn't let a man she was pretty sure she didn't like give her oral while in clear view of anyone who happened by.

He pushed two fingers into her and zeroed in on her clit, sucking and then flicking it with his tongue in a rhythm she couldn't have fought even if she wanted to. His fingers deep inside her circled that sensitive spot and he mirrored the movement with his tongue, driving her ruthlessly over the edge. Her hand muffled her cry, but only barely. Allie slumped against the tree and watched him press his forehead to her stomach as if trying to get control of himself.

As if fighting not to rise and drive that glorious cock into her right then.

Finally, he helped her get her foot back into her yoga pants and stepped back while she righted her clothing. Roman didn't speak, didn't look at her, and she couldn't help the dip of disappointment deep in her stomach.

Allie took a fortifying breath and turned for the bar. She needed a drink and to get the hell out of there. She could smell him on her skin, and between that and the orgasm, she was having a hard time remembering why Roman was off-limits.

So off-limits that I just had his mouth all over me.

She managed one step before a hand closed around her arm. Allie looked back, waiting to see what he'd do. Roman finally cursed and released her. "We need to talk, Allie. Actually talk."

Disappointment warred with righteous anger. "Wrong. As I've said half a dozen times already—I am on vacation." Her orgasm-induced high brought more words. "On the other hand, if you want this." She motioned to herself. "Then that's something we can negotiate." At the look on Roman's face, Allie almost took the offer back.

He stepped closer. "You want to separate business and pleasure."

"Business and pleasure should always be separate." She lifted her chin, half-amazed at how brazen she was being, but it wasn't as if she had anything to lose. Roman wasn't going to give up—the limited interactions she'd had with him up to this point reinforced that belief—and she also wasn't going to back down. They could either blow off some steam here on the island before they got back to her dodging his calls and his trying to buy her business out from under her, or they could go their separate ways now.

There was no happy medium. Not for them.

His gaze dropped to her mouth. "I can't promise that. The timeline is too tight and—"

"I don't want to hear it," she cut in. "If you can't promise you won't talk about business, then don't talk at all."

That delicious muscle in his jaw ticked. "You make it sound so simple."

"It is. It's exactly that simple."

Roman stared at her long enough that she had to fight not to squirm. He smiled, the expression doing nothing to quell the urge. She crossed her arms over her chest. "What?"

"I don't have to make any deals with you, Allie."

Again, disappointment tried to take over. She fought it back down, but she was less successful this time. She had to make a conscious effort not to let her shoulders dip or her spine bend. "And why's that?"

"Because you want me as much as I want you." He traced a single finger down her throat and over her sternum. "You want me so badly, if I crooked my finger, you'd be back at my villa, naked and coming on my cock. You say you'll draw the line in the sand, and that's fine, but you'll be fighting yourself more than you'll be fighting me to keep from crossing it."

Her growing anger was almost a welcome relief. Allie knew how to be angry. She didn't let it control her, but most of her successes in life could be chalked up to doing things out of spite. A trailer trash girl from upstate New York couldn't go to college? Like hell she couldn't—and she'd get the majority of it paid for while she was in the process with volleyball scholarships. Having a forward-thinking women's-only gym that paired with a women's shelter was unconventional? Sure, it was. But that wasn't going to stop her from going for it full throttle.

Roman thought he could sit back, kick up his heels and let the lure of his cock draw her in after she'd laid out her terms?

Not fucking likely.

She pushed his hand away from her. "You're wrong."

"Am I?"

She wanted to smack that smug look off his face, but that wasn't how she operated. She stepped back and then stepped back again. "The terms are what they are. If you can't respect that, stay the hell away from me."

He blinked, as if he hadn't expected her response. "Allie—"

"No, you will not 'Allie' me as if I'm being irrational. I want you. We both know it. What *you* don't seem to be able to wrap your brain around is that while you might be ruled by your cock, *I* am more than capable of making decisions that aren't based in sex." She forced herself to turn around and walk away from him. "If you change your mind, you know where to find me."

She didn't give him a chance to respond before she picked up her pace and made her way back into the lantern light now illuminating the bar area. Becka turned away from the handsome bartender and raised her eyebrows. "You look like you've been up to no good."

"I have no idea what you're talking about." She took the bar stool next to her friend and downed the tequila shot waiting for her without hesitation.

"That was mine," Becka said mildly.

"I'll get you the next one." She shook her head. "What am I saying? They're included." She'd lost her damn mind. There was no other explanation for how she was acting—like a horny teenager who didn't care what was at stake as long as she got hers. Allie was better than that. She had to be.

The bartender poured them each another shot and set a fresh margarita in front of Allie. "Ring the bell if you need me."

"Sure thing, sweetie." Becka barely waited for him to walk out of eyesight before she swung around to face Allie. "Explain yourself. I didn't think you needed assistance, but I can't tell if you've been in a fistfight or fucking against a tree."

Allie's face flamed. "We didn't have sex."

"But you did *something* against a tree." She shook her head. "For a woman who says you despise that man, you are having a hell of a time keeping your hands off him."

She started to protest, but what was the point? Allie could chalk up the night before to her not knowing who he was, but she didn't have that excuse this time. She knew who Roman was and why he was here, and she'd still stuck her hand down his pants. "I get around him and my rational brain shuts off. It's like I have a lady Neanderthal in there, and she's decided she really likes the look of Roman and wants to bang his brains out and to hell with the consequences."

"This is a new thing for you." Becka downed her shot and set the glass on the bar with a faint clink. "It's disconcerting, huh? To have rational Allie who follows all the rules overrun by the hindbrain."

That was exactly it. She kept saying she didn't do things like this, but only because it was the truth. Back in New York, Allie never would have laid down the offer she'd just given Roman. She wouldn't have gone home with him in the first place. She glared at her tequila shot. "I think they pump something into the air on this island to make people act irrational."

"Or maybe…just maybe—" Becka nudged the shot into her hand "—it might *possibly* be that you've been wound so tightly for a seriously long time that the first situation that arose where no one was depending on you, you let yourself live a little. You don't have to play whipping girl about this, Allie. It's okay to want him."

But it *wasn't* okay.

She didn't know how to reconcile the person she was back home and the woman she was acting like here. "I'm not supposed to want him. Anyone but him."

"Ah." Becka nodded and took a long drink of the pink thing in front of her. "I don't have an easy answer for that. You going to his place tonight?"

"No." She might want him more than she had a right to, but that didn't change the fact that she *didn't* want to talk business with him—or, rather, fight about business. If he couldn't agree to that bare minimum, then the pleasure wasn't worth the pain.

She just had to keep reminding herself of that.

Roman didn't sleep well. Every noise brought him fully awake, sure that Allie had changed her mind. He knew she wouldn't. She had drawn that line in the sand and she was stubborn enough not to cross it. He might have bullshit her yesterday, but he knew the truth.

The ball was in his court.

He woke early and attended the sunrise yoga class. There were a few people there he didn't recognize, but neither Allie nor Becka showed up. It was a relief to turn off his mind for a bit, but the feeling lasted until he walked into the tiny business center and went through the irritating process of checking his email.

Aaron had come through for him.

Roman stared at the document for a long time before he printed it. Even if he decided to take Allie up on her offer, he still had his eye on the prize for when they got back to New York. That meant he needed the deeper research so he could figure out how to play this. They were down to the wire.

It wasn't completely his fault, but that didn't change the bottom line.

He gathered the papers, double-checked to make sure the document hadn't downloaded on the computer and logged off. There was plenty of time to get his reading done and then figure out how he'd plan the rest of the day. Accidentally running into Allie might be entertaining as fuck, but it wasn't accomplishing anything. He had to figure out a better way to go about this.

I could take her up on the offer.

Roman hesitated in front of his cart. It seemed simple enough—leave business out of things. It meant passing up valuable opportunities to talk to her, but...it wasn't like Allie was talking to him at this point. She wasn't going to, either. She'd made that more than clear.

There was no goddamn reason not to say yes.

He turned around and headed back into the main building. The hostess smiled when she saw him coming. "Mr. Bassani, are you enjoying your stay?"

"Very much so." He was about to enjoy it a whole hell of a lot more. He stopped next to the desk she stood behind. "I was hoping you could help me with something."

"Of course." She smiled brightly, her brown eyes lighting up with the rest of her face. "Let me know what you need and I'll take care of it."

"I'd like to send a message to one of the other villas—villa six."

Her face fell. "Oh, I'm sorry. We do our best to create an iso-lated and relaxing atmosphere here. If guests choose to come into the lodge, that's one thing, but we don't seek them out unless they need something." And she clearly thought that whatever he wanted to send wouldn't be relaxing.

Roman put on his most charming smile. "It's just a little note. If they order dinner tonight, there would already be someone going out there. You can just include the message with the food."

Still she hesitated. "I'm not sure."

"If it makes you feel better, you can read the note. Just to ensure it's all on the up-and-up."

Another hesitation, shorter this time. "I suppose…" She passed over a thick piece of island stationery. Roman accepted the pen and scrawled a quick note. The hostess frowned. "That's it?"

"She'll know what I mean."

She smiled, obviously put at ease by the fact he hadn't writ-ten anything inappropriate. Roman could have corrected her assumption, but he needed Allie to get that note. *Passing notes. That's what I've been reduced to.*

It would be hours yet before he knew what *her* answer was—possibly longer if she decided to make him wait. The entire thing was beyond his control, and it irritated the fuck out of him. What was he supposed to do with this? Roman was used to seeing what he wanted and going for it—and heaven help anyone who thought they could stand in the way.

He wanted his client happy, and the only way that would happen was acquiring the gym.

He wanted Allie, too.

Therein lay the issue—he couldn't have both. There might not be any sort of future with Allie, but there sure as fuck wasn't one if he kept pushing her. She'd made that more than clear.

If he stopped pushing her, they could relax into the insanely hot sex, but he'd have to let his plan for Transcend go. It might not be the end of the world, but Roman's career was built on the faith that he could provide exactly what he promised. He'd never met an obstacle he couldn't account for and overcome.

Until now.

He turned and strode out of the main building and to his cart, gripping the stack of papers. All the information he could come up with for Allie and her gym—something Roman should have done a long time ago. Oh, he'd done the basic background check and pulled the available financial statements he could get ahold of, but he hadn't dug deeper than that, even when she'd refused to meet him.

Stupid of him.

He didn't need to navel gaze for the rest of his goddamn life to know why he hadn't pushed as hard as he normally did. *The shelter.* He admired the hell out of what she was doing there, and he knew it was pretty damn likely that she had some kind of history that drove her to create a safe space like she had. Having a man try to bulldoze her might trigger shit that he'd have to be a monster to pull up.

He'd played softball with her.

Now that he'd met Allie, he was forced to reevaluate. She wasn't anything like he'd expected. She wasn't a wilting flower that would crumble at a sharp word. The woman had thorns, and she had no problem using them. Roman gripped the papers. The gloves were coming off. Now.

8

ALLIE BARELY WAITED FOR THE MAN TO LEAVE their covered food before she yanked the lids off. "I'm starving." If she'd spent any time wondering if she'd be active enough while on vacation, she needn't have worried. Swimming and paddleboarding had left a pleasant soreness in her muscles and an equally pleasant tiredness.

Also, she'd been ready to wade into the ocean and try to catch her own fish if dinner hadn't shown up when it did.

Becka laughed and bumped Allie with her hip. "They also brought vodka. Your priorities are suspect."

"Food always trumps vodka." She speared a glazed shrimp with her fork and then grabbed a chair. "I'm glad to see that you and vodka are back on speaking terms."

"We're taking it slow." Becka pulled up a second chair and sank into it. "My shoulders are killing me. I obviously need to add more push-ups to my routine."

Allie laughed. "The girls will love that." Her friend had a reputation for being a brutal fitness instructor—a reputation she'd more than earned—and this would only cement it. One of the biggest draws Transcend offered was high-energy spin classes with combined exercises that worked the entire body.

She reached for the pitcher of cucumber water in the middle of the table and froze. "What is that?"

Becka reacted first and snatched up the little folded note. She read it and frowned. "What the hell *is* it?" She turned it around, and Allie's heart skipped a beat.

Yes.

The word had been scrawled with a careless masculine hand, and even though it wasn't signed, she had no doubt who had written it. *He accepted my terms.* A flush spread over her skin, and even though she tried to fight it, Becka saw.

Because of course she did. She dropped the note and pointed a finger at Allie. "It's from Roman. You sly fox, I thought you were calling the whole thing off."

Allie pushed her food around the plate with her fork. "I told him if he could keep from badgering me about business—or even talking about it—then we could spend more time together."

"That was the tamest euphemism for banging your brains out that I've ever heard." Her friend slouched back into her chair and laughed. "Vacation has done wonders for your stress level. I told you so."

"The guy trying to convince me to sell the gym that I worked my entire adult life to get started and keep running followed me to another country to pitch his sale, and you call this trip a success."

Becka shrugged, completely unrepentant. "You took care of that by removing business from the equation. Now there's only the hot monkey sex to worry about, and I think you two have proved that you're more than capable of keeping your eye on the prize." She made an obscene gesture.

Allie spit out the sip of water she'd just taken. "Oh. My. God."

"Just calling it like I see it." Becka winked. "But seriously—

if he's willing to shelve that big black mark against him, are you going for it?"

There was no reason to think he was telling the truth. He could be trying to pull a bait and switch to get her alone. But that didn't make sense. He could have found a different way. Roman had more than proved how capable he was in tracking her down. He had no reason to agree if he wasn't interested in exactly the same thing she was—sex.

Her body clenched at the thought. Allie set her fork down. "I think so."

"Woot!" Becka gave a little wiggle. "That's my girl. In that case, I'm bringing that delightful bartender, Luke, back here for some of said hot monkey sex."

She shot her friend a look. "You wouldn't, by chance, be throwing me at Roman so you can hook up with Luke?"

"Oh, please. We both know that I'm more than capable of finding a suitable place to get under that uniform if I have to." Becka sobered. "But I don't want to get him into trouble, so the villa is a better option." She held her straight face for all of two seconds. "What are you waiting for? Go! Get your..." Becka stopped short, her expression turning wicked. "He's stacked, isn't he? You can just tell by how he carries himself that the man is packing serious heat."

"*Becka.*" Allie laughed, which broke the tension that had been building from the moment she realized Roman had changed his mind. She sat back in her chair. "You did that on purpose."

"You're stressing, which is the opposite of what you're supposed to do here." Becka popped a strawberry into her mouth. "I helped."

"Yes, you did." She looked at the food, but her stomach was tied in too many knots to think about eating right now. Allie pushed back her chair and stood. "I guess I should...change?"

Becka picked through the food and added more to her plate. "You want my advice?"

"As if saying no would stop you from giving it to me." She snagged one of the bright red strawberries and took a bite.

"Wear that." Becka waved a fork at her.

Allie looked down at her muscle tank top and sleep shorts. "This is not sexy."

"Lose the bra and whatever you're wearing under the shorts." She grinned. "If he doesn't take you right there on the floor, I'll give you twenty bucks."

Allie walked across the warm sand to Roman's brightly lit villa. Soft music emerged, and though she couldn't quite place the lyrics, the lilting melody drew her in. She made her way up the porch stairs and stopped just outside the ring of light from the foremost lamp.

"You're teasing me."

She jumped and then silently cursed herself for jumping. Allie searched the spot where his voice had come from, only making him out of the shadows when he moved closer. "How long were you lurking there, waiting to make your grand entrance?"

"Would you believe me if I said I went for a swim to burn off some energy and just got back?"

She started to call his bluff, but he walked into the light and, sure enough, he wore wet swim trunks and his hair dripped tiny rivers down his shoulders and chest. It took more effort than it should have to drag her gaze to his face. "Swimming in the ocean at night is stupid."

"I survived." He held out his hand, as imperious as a king. "Come here."

Allie had never been one to make an entrance, but she found herself wanting to prove Becka right. She threw her shoulders back and put a little extra hip into her walk, knowing it would make her breasts sway more than normal.

Sure enough, as soon as she breached the circle of light, her chest was exactly what held Roman's attention. His hazel eyes went wide and then hooded. "AC/DC."

"I'm a fan." She looked down and pulled at the hem of her shirt, which drew the fabric forward and revealed a bit more side cleavage. "They're classic."

"How attached are you to that shirt?"

The question brought her head up. She found him closer than before and stopped. "I've had this shirt since I was thirteen."

"Mmm." He circled her, and she didn't bother to try to keep him in sight. Allie already knew what he'd see. The tiny sleep shorts that her ass filled out, the slits in the sides teasing even more skin. The carefully ripped sides of the shirt that showed her breasts and part of her side. She normally wore the shirt for sleeping or working out—*with* a bra. It was practically indecent without one.

Which was the point.

Roman stopped in front of her, closer than before. He reached out and ran his hands slowly down her arms, his thumbs caressing the sides of her breasts. "I'll show the required restraint not to rip it off you right this fucking second."

Allie shivered. "If you did, we'd have a problem."

"Noted." His hands moved back up her arms, thumbs again making the movement a tease. "Were you wearing this when you got the note?"

"I might have made a few alterations." *Thanks for the tip, Becka.*

"Mmm." The sound was somewhere between a purr and a growl. Roman released her arms and hooked his fingers into her shorts. A swift yank and they hit the deck. "No panties. Allie, I think you're going to fucking kill me."

She started to pull her shirt off, but he stopped her. "Keep it on. It's just as much a tease as you are."

"If anyone is a tease, it's you."

"Is that so?" Roman undid the ties at the front of his suit and slid it off without taking his eyes from her. "You came earlier, Allie. I suffered."

She smacked his hands away when he reached for her again. "Don't pull that shit with me. You said you'd jerk yourself. If you didn't, that's your problem, not mine." She tried to make herself believe the words. She wasn't some idiot teenager who thought blue balls meant she owed a guy something, but the thought of Roman suffering didn't sit well with her, even if he was the enemy outside of this island.

"If you think my hand can compare to your pussy, you're sadly mistaken." He went to his knees right there in front of her and lifted her skirt to bare her completely from the waist down. "It's been hours, Allie. Fucking *hours* that I've wanted you and haven't been able to do a goddamn thing about it." Roman dragged his mouth from one hip to the other, just below her belly button. He inhaled deeply. "I crave you. What are you doing to me?"

"Me?" She didn't get more than that out before he nudged her legs wider and gave her pussy a long lick. The position didn't leave her open nearly enough, and she tried to spread her legs farther without toppling over.

Roman hooked the backs of her thighs and lifted her to straddle his face. She blinked down at him, but he was too busy taking advantage of the access. He delved his tongue into her, and pleasure made her stop worrying about if he was going to drop her. She clung to his head and gave herself over to what he did to her, trusting him.

He fucked her with his tongue the same way he fucked her with his fingers and cock. Thoroughly. She could barely shift against him in her current position, though, and frustration warred with desire. "Not enough. I need more."

His growl vibrated through her and seemed to center on her clit. He shifted and she let loose a cry as he stood and walked them to one of the lounge chairs arranged to look out over the beach. With the light of the villa, the contrasting darkness felt absolute, but Allie didn't have a chance to think too hard on that before he laid her on the lounge chair and lifted his head. "Not enough."

"That's what I said."

He pushed two fingers into her. One stroke. A second. A third finger joined them. Roman used his other hand to tug her shirt to reveal one breast. He flicked her nipple with his tongue as he plunged his fingers into her again and again. "Is this enough, Allie?"

Yes. No.

She thrashed, shaking her head. "I need *you*."

He nipped the underside of her breast. "You missed my cock. You've been empty and aching for me since you left. That orgasm earlier only made it worse, didn't it?"

"Yes," she sobbed out. It was the truth. Instead of taking the edge off, she'd been acutely aware of what she was missing, rather than what she'd gotten.

"You need me, Allie." He kept up the punishing rhythm with his fingers. "You need what I can give you."

"Yes! I need you." She grabbed his shoulders. "Tell me you have a condom nearby."

She felt his grin against her skin. "I stashed some earlier." He reached under the lounge chair and she heard the familiar crinkle of foil. Roman ripped it open and stopped touching her long enough to roll it on. "Up."

Allie scrambled to obey, already anticipating what came next. He took her place on the lounge chair and guided her to straddle him. "That shirt won't last much longer." He cupped her exposed breast and went still as she positioned his cock at her entrance. "That's it, Allie. Take what you need."

I need you.

She didn't say it again. It felt too big, too vulnerable, to give voice to, when she was going out of her mind with what he was doing to her. She sank onto his length, enjoying teasing them both by taking it slow. Only when he was sheathed completely inside her did she breathe out. "Yes. This."

He pulled her shirt up. "I want to see all of you while you ride me."

There were no shadows to hide in out here on the patio. Anyone who walked up could see them, but that was the point of paradise—there was no one but them. She liked the thought of being interrupted, though—more than she wanted to admit.

Allie took her shirt off, braced her hands on his chest and began to move. A long slide up, and another down while she rolled her hips. It felt so fucking good, she had a hard time keeping up the rhythm. Roman's grip on her hips urged her on, her pleasure cresting all too soon. She dug her nails into his perfect chest. "I'm close."

"I know."

So damn cocky. It would have been unbearable if not for the way he watched her, as if she was something he wanted. Needed. Allie couldn't close her eyes, couldn't look away, couldn't do anything but ride him with one slow stroke after another, pushing them both toward oblivion.

"I love your body." He skimmed his hands over her stomach and up to her breasts. A few breathtaking seconds spent plucking her nipples and then he coasted his hands back down to her ass. "Fucking phenomenal."

"Stop talking." She had decent self-confidence, but that didn't mean his showering her with compliments made her comfortable. Allie knew Roman wanted her—he wouldn't have acted the way he had since meeting her if he didn't. He sure as hell wouldn't have compromised his business plans to give them a reprieve. She might not know him well, but she knew that much. But the way he spoke to her—about her—was as worshipful as if he really thought she was Aphrodite.

But she was only a woman, and not one that he'd like all that much outside of paradise.

Allie might not be sure of a lot of things, but she was sure of *that*.

9

ROMAN HELD ALLIE'S BODY, BUT HER MIND WAS a million miles away—just like it'd been since they'd finished having sex. He had no right to push her. He knew that. The agreement that had brought her here in the first place was the same one that kept him from asking anything that might link back to New York.

Except...

"What are you thinking about?"

"Hmm?" She blinked those impossibly blue eyes at him and gave herself a shake. "Sorry. I was mentally wandering."

It was tempting to let it go. Hell, it was the right move to make. But when Roman opened his mouth, that wasn't what came out. "Tell me."

"It's just boring stuff." She shifted off him and climbed to her feet. A small petty part of him was pleased to see her legs shake a little. The sex had been...beyond words. Desperation—that was what he felt for her. He'd hoped she'd respond favorably to the note, but Roman hadn't been sure she'd actually come to him.

He wasn't sure of a lot of things when it came to Allie.

She scooped up her clothes but made no move to pull them on. He liked that. She was so comfortable in her body, and that confidence was just as attractive as her looks were. But all that was surface-level shit. He wanted to know *her*.

Roman stopped short. Knowing her wasn't part of the bargain. It was supposed to be just sex—strictly physical with nothing else involved.

She didn't say no emotion. She said no business. Apples and oranges.

He steadied himself and followed her into the villa. She meandered to the kitchen and pulled a bottled water from the little fridge. Allie watched him as she took a long drink. "What?"

"What?"

She frowned. "Now you're the one mentally wandering. What's going on in that devious brain of yours?"

He grabbed his own water and contemplated it. "I was thinking about the terms of our agreement."

She went still. "And?"

This was the moment he could back off, change course and keep them in a safe spot. But Roman had never met a woman that both turned him on and called him on his shit the same way Allie did. He might never again. Letting her slip through his fingers without at least poking at the potential for more was a stupid move.

Roman didn't make a habit of making stupid moves.

"And I want to know more about you." He watched her closely, noting the tension that crept into her shoulders.

Allie set her water bottle down on the counter. "Why?"

"I haven't connected with a woman the way I've connected with you. Ever. I want to know if it's just lust that will run itself out or if it has the potential to be more."

"Normally..." She shook her head. "There is no normal in this situation. In another world, I'd think that sounded downright nice. But this isn't another world, this is ours—and no matter how great the sex is or how compelling the connection, there remains the fact that you want to buy my business out from underneath me."

"Ah-ah." Roman held up a finger. "No business talk. That was part of the agreement."

She glared. "That was before——" Allie cut herself off and looked at the ceiling. "Damn it, you're right."

"Taking business out of it——"

"Roman, that's crazy."

"You keep throwing around that word. Maybe you're even right." He set his water bottle next to hers and placed his hands on either side of her hips on the counter. "But what if you're not, Allie? Do you run into this kind of thing so often that you're willing to pass it up?"

She frowned harder. "Your argument is compelling. Irritating, but compelling."

He'd given her a lot to think about, but he wasn't planning on giving her recovery time to think *too* much. Roman traced her collarbone. "Any siblings?"

"Only child." Her expression closed off, as clear as if she'd lit a neon sign warning him away.

Family is off-limits. Got it. It was almost enough to confirm that Allie's pushing so hard for the women's shelter had something to do with her past. He set the thought aside—for now. He wanted her to tell him when she was ready. He might have the file on her history, but he decided right then that he wouldn't read it. Better to hear from Allie whatever she wanted to share with him.

What happens when we get back to the mainland?

We'll figure it out.

She pulled her hair off her shoulder to give him a clear path to stroke to her arm and back again. "You have siblings?"

"No. I always wanted one or two, but my parents had other priorities."

"Like what?"

He glanced at her face, but there was only curiosity there. Roman stroked her knuckles. "They're both from old money, and while I was growing up, their only priority was making the family even richer. My old man was a stockbroker, and my mother was a consultant like I am."

"Was?"

He shrugged. "They retired a couple years back. I haven't seen them since, but they bought a boat and have been traveling the world. It's large enough to house a small army, because my parents never do anything halfway. They'll come around again when they get tired of the travel, but I don't expect them to stay. They're nothing if not restless. Always have been." He loved his parents, in a way, but it was a distant sort of feeling that meant talking to them once every few months and the occasional Christmas card if they stayed in one place long enough to receive it. He had friends who'd grown up with loud families filled to the brim with messy love that manifested in jokes and hugs and the occasional heated fight. There was no room for that in the deep stillness of the Bassani household. "Even when I was little, they traveled regularly. They'd be gone for weeks at a time."

"That must have been hard to deal with as a kid." She looped her arms around his neck, bringing them chest to chest. "I don't know anyone with perfect parents—mine included—but at least most of them were *there*. The absent figures must have sucked."

"I thought it was a grand old time when I was in high school. Parties every weekend and girls staying over most days of the week." He tried to give the comment lightly, but it came out bittersweet.

Allie saw it. She smiled and ran her finger along the shell of his ear. "You turned out all right—except for the whole business thing that we aren't talking about."

He laughed. "Except for that—which is my life."

"Seriously? You don't have anything else going on but work?"

He squeezed her hips. "Do you?"

She opened her mouth but seemed to reconsider. "That's a

fair point. I could argue that my business is more honorable, but… I'm not in the mood to argue."

Roman liked this side of her, playful and almost coy. He turned them so he could lean against the counter with her in his arms. "What, pray tell, are you in the mood for?"

"I'm so very glad you asked." She kissed his throat, his shoulder, his pectoral muscle, sliding to her knees in front of him.

The wood floor would be hell on her knees, but she gave him a look from beneath her lashes that stilled the words in his chest. Allie knew exactly what she was doing, and she wasn't about to let him drive the show this time. The sight of her stroking his cock with an exploratory hand had him in danger of swaying. It was only the promise of her wetting her lips that kept him pinned in place.

"Your cock is ridiculous." She gave him another stroke. "There isn't another word. Just *ridiculous*."

He tried to laugh, but the sound came out strangled. "Thanks?"

"You're welcome, but seriously, with you packing this around, it's no wonder you're an arrogant ass." She flicked her tongue along the underside. "You've gone down on me like a dozen times in the last few days and I haven't had you in my mouth even *once*."

"Show me."

She gave him a saucy smile and then his cock was between her lips. Allie sucked him down, down, down, until he bumped the back of her throat. Roman gripped the counter, using every ounce of self-control he had to keep from moving other than to brace his legs a little wider.

She took the move as an invitation and cradled his balls with one hand while she kept sucking him. Just when he thought he couldn't take another second of it, she released him. But Allie wasn't done. She gripped him around the base of his cock with her free hand and licked him like he was her favorite flavor of lollipop. That evil, wonderful tongue of hers damn near made his eyes roll back in his head. "Fuck, Allie."

"We're about to."

Allie barely got the words out before Roman was on her. He paused long enough to pull a condom out of a candy bowl she hadn't noticed before and then he was between her thighs, his cock sliding home. He cradled her head with one of his big hands, saving her from knocking herself silly against the hard-wood floor with the strength of his thrusts.

It was…brutal. There was no other word to describe the way he moved over her—in her.

She loved every single second of it.

She was the reason he'd lost control.

Allie clung to him, rising in time with his strokes. "I should give you head more often."

"Every single goddamn day." He kissed her, which was just as well because she didn't have a response to that. *Every day* sounded a whole lot like time after they left West Island. Allie couldn't promise him that. He *knew* she couldn't promise him that.

She kissed him back with everything she had. Their limited time only made the whole thing hotter—or that was what Allie told herself as Roman rolled them. She slammed down onto him without missing a beat, leaning back to brace herself on his big thighs. The man was a monster in the best way possible. The wood floor bit into her knees, but the faint pain only spiked her pleasure higher. She bent down and kissed him without throwing off their rhythm. *Yesyesyesyesyes.*

"After this. Bed."

"Yes."

Roman palmed the back of her head and pressed a hand to the small of her back, effectively caging her. He thrust up, fucking her from below while she was helpless to do anything but take it. Allie took his mouth even as he took her pussy, the pleasure so intense there was no holding out. She came with a cry that he ate down, her legs shaking from the strength of her orgasm. He followed her over the edge with a curse, his rough grip at odds with the sheer pleasure written across his face.

They lay there for several long moments before he shifted her to the side. She gave a small cry of surprise as he climbed to his feet, lifting her into his arms in the process. "What are you doing?"

"We might not be too old to fuck on wood floors, but it's hell on the back." He shifted her and pressed a soft kiss to each of her knees. "And on you."

"Totally worth it."

"Without a doubt." He chuckled. "We'll call the bed a nice change of pace."

But he wasn't going to the bed. He turned left inside the bedroom and walked through the doorway leading into the bathroom. It was similar to the two in her villa, but the coloring was all soft grays and a bright blue that reminded her of the ocean surrounding the island. The tiled walk-in shower was large enough to fit ten people, with two sunflower shower-heads and a bench that made her think filthy thoughts despite the exhaustion that broke over her in a wave.

Allie lay her head against his shoulder. "I should get back."

"I don't think so." He set her on the bench. "It's late, and it's dark, and I promise to let you get some sleep tonight if you stay."

She raised her eyebrows. "*Some* sleep?"

Roman turned on the water and shot her a look. "You can't honestly expect me to have you in my bed and keep my hands to myself."

"God forbid." She stood and ducked under the closest shower-head. The water was the perfect temperature, and Allie let herself just *be* for a few seconds. She could hear Roman washing himself, and as tempting as it was to watch, her thoughts kept her feet rooted in place. *He wants to know me.*

The thought shouldn't scare the shit out of her. Roman was gorgeous and successful and… It would never work. Irreconcilable differences about summed them up. Those differences might not matter while they were on West Island, but they would be glaringly obvious when they got back to New York. He was a rich…whatever the hell he was…and she was having to rob Peter to pay Paul and make ends meet. They lived in two different worlds.

They always had.

He'd grown up rich with distant parents. Her heart ached a little for the boy he must have been. So alone. In that, at least, there was a thread of similar experiences. The main difference was that Allie would have given anything for her parents to be gone and leave her alone. Well, her father at least. She shuddered.

"It's okay." His arms slid around her from behind. She tensed, waiting for him to ask what was wrong, but Roman just turned her to face him and held her closer. Comforting her without prying.

Even though she knew better, Allie clung to him. She wasn't weak for wanting to lean on someone for just a few seconds. *It's so hard being strong all the time. I don't know if I can take it. I'm about to fail, and when I do, I'm going to take so many women down with me.* Words pressed against the inside of her lips, all her worries and fears that she never gave voice to bubbling up inside her. She clamped her mouth shut and buried her face against his shoulder.

No matter how good the sex, or how wonderful he seemed to be, she couldn't afford to forget what Roman's ultimate goal was—the gym and shelter. He might have shelved his ambition temporarily, but that was all it was. Temporary. Spilling her fears would just give him ammunition later.

What if he could actually help?

He can't. No one can.

Worse, his version of help might be to sell the damn thing out from underneath her. It wasn't as easy as that, but once she started missing bills, it opened a door she couldn't close. If she didn't figure something out, and fast, she wouldn't have any choice at all in the matter. *I need a plan…a better plan than just pushing forward and hoping for the best.*

"It will be okay," he murmured and stroked a hand down her back. "Whatever it is, it'll be okay, Allie."

She wished she could believe him.

Allie took a breath, and then another. Self-pity wasn't her MO. She was the fighter, the one who took people under her wing. She stepped back, and Roman let her go. To hide her embarrassment, she ducked under the spray again. By the time she cleared the water from her eyes, Roman had turned off his showerhead and was drying himself off with an oversize fluffy white towel. He returned with a second one, and she stepped into it after turning off the water.

Roman kissed her forehead. "Come to bed with me, Allie."

Despite the turmoil in her head, there was only one answer. "Yes."

10

ROMAN WOKE TO FIND ALLIE GONE. HE SIGHED
and rolled onto his back. It shouldn't have surprised him that
she'd bolted, but disappointment was sour on his tongue. He
stared at the vaulted ceiling for a few long moments before he
forced himself out of bed. Lying around all morning wasn't
going to do anything but give him more time to debate what
the fuck he was going to do.

Accepting her terms was probably a mistake. But the thought held
no strength against the memories from last night. He wouldn't
take that choice back, no matter how thoroughly it might bite
him in the ass later.

He pulled on a pair of shorts and headed out into the main
living space of the villa. It was a sprawling room contain-
ing a kitchen and furniture artfully arranged around the wall
that opened to the beach. Roman stopped short at the sight of
Allie walking up the steps, sand on her feet and her blond hair
windblown.

She grinned. "The sunrise is seriously beautiful today."

She didn't leave. He tried to get his reaction under control
and to smile in return. "It *is* paradise."

"That's true." Allie dropped a kiss on his lips as she walked
past. "I got coffee started. How do you take yours?"

Roman had never lived with a woman before. Even when he'd dated—occasionally seriously—his schedule prevented this kind of casual morning interaction. It had never felt like a loss until that moment. He followed Allie into the kitchen. "Black."

"I should have known." She'd reclaimed her shirt and shorts, and they looked even better in the daylight than they had the night before. She brought two mugs from the open-faced cupboards and poured coffee into them. After setting his in front of him, she doused hers with enough cream and sugar to make his teeth hurt. She shot him a look from beneath her lashes. "What can I say? I like sweet."

"I see that." Even this early in the morning, he was smart enough not to comment on it. He took a cautious sip. "You stayed."

She stirred her coffee. "I almost left, but it didn't seem right to sneak out like a thief." Allie made a face. "Plus, Becka was otherwise occupied last night, so I don't expect her up and around until a little later. I do *not* need to walk in on some kind of morning-after shenanigans."

He almost asked, but Roman was… He didn't know how to term his relationship with Becka's sister anymore. They were friends once, albeit not close ones. They might be friends again if Gideon ever forgave him for meddling in their relationship. At this point, he'd be lucky if he was invited to the wedding.

Either way, it was none of his damn business who Becka Baudin went to bed with. He wasn't her brother, and he wasn't her friend. Her sister might have an opinion on that, but Lucy wasn't here and Roman wouldn't win any points by running back to her and telling tales. No, Becka was a grown-ass woman and he was going to stay the hell out of it.

Roman leaned against the counter. "Big plans today?"

"We were going to go snorkeling off the reef on the other side of the island. They have a boat that takes you out and they provide lunch, too." She hesitated. "Do you want to come?"

Yes.

He tempered his reaction almost as fast as it arose. Jumping at her and yanking her into his arms was only going to spook her and make him look like a fool in the process. Instead, he saluted her with his mug. "Only if I'm not intruding."

Allie raised her eyebrows. "As if you'd let that stop you."

He laughed. "Fair point. Yes, I'd like to come snorkeling with you." Saying it felt like he was agreeing to something more serious than a daytime outing, but Roman didn't let himself think about that too hard. He liked Allie. He liked spending time with her. She wasn't going to let him get any ground on talking business while they were down there, and even if he went back to New York, he couldn't make any forward progress without her. All that aside, he *wanted* to be on West Island. With her.

"When's the last time you had a vacation?"

He shrugged. "I visited my parents in Morocco a couple years ago."

Those blue eyes saw too much. She gave a soft smile. "When's the last time you had a real—*relaxing*—vacation?"

"Ah, that's something else altogether." He thought hard and came up blank. "I don't know. Maybe spring break in college, but that's hardly the idea of relaxing you're talking about." He'd had his eye on the prize even back then, so Roman had used the time to network. Nothing brought people together as much as getting drunk and doing stupid shit, and those relationships had panned out nicely in the years since.

But an actual vacation? Just to relax?

He cleared his throat, not quite able to meet her gaze. "Never."

"That's what I thought." Allie set down her mug and slid into his arms as if she'd made the move a thousand times before. "We have four days left on West Island. Why don't we treat it like a real vacation and just enjoy ourselves?"

It sounded a whole hell of a lot like she'd just smacked an expiration date on them. Roman wasn't surprised at that. What *did* surprise him was how her words made him feel—like he wanted to bend her over the counter and fuck her until she admitted that there might actually be something *there*.

Instead, he palmed her ass and gave her a light squeeze. "You'll stay here at night."

"Yes." No argument for once. Her gaze dropped to his lips. "I have to talk to Becka, but judging by how excited she was by my leaving last night, I don't think she'll have a problem with the change of plans. Especially if it leaves the villa open for her to have her own vacation fling."

I'm not a fucking fling.

Once again, he smothered the response. Roman didn't know what he wanted from this yet, other than more time with Allie, but he'd be damned before he did or said something to spook her. There would be plenty of time to hash it out later. Right now, they were just talking about the next four days.

He smoothed her hair back. "Why don't you bring your things here for the duration—it'd save you the multiple trips."

"Trips I'll still have to make to arrange things with Becka for our daily plans." Allie shook her head. "No, this is better with clear boundaries. I'll bring enough stuff for overnight—toothbrush and that kind of thing—but the rest stays."

Stubborn woman.

"You're being difficult."

She grinned. "What I'm being, Roman, is noncompliant. I get the feeling that you don't get told no a lot, but you should get used to it. You might have a magical cock, but that doesn't mean you get a permanent free pass to run my life."

"You think I have a magical cock?" He pulled her closer, lining up their hips so she could feel exactly what she'd just described.

Allie's eyes went wide. "I might have said that." She palmed him through his shorts. "Then again, my memory is a bit faulty. It's been ages since I've had you inside me."

"Woman, it's been a few hours at most." He laughed and scooped her into his arms, liking the little yip sound she made. "But never let it be said that I don't take care of your needs."

"Heaven forbid." She arched up to murmur in his ear. "I'm desperate for you, Roman."

His cock went rock solid and he tightened his hold on her. "In that case, I think your friend can wait another hour or two." He strode for the bedroom.

Allie sat as rigid as she was able to while the boat wobbled its way through the waves away from the island. When she'd invited Roman along to go snorkeling, she hadn't really thought it through. Becka hadn't seemed to mind, so it didn't really sink in until they'd left the island that this was…a date.

No, not a *real* date.

But it was as close as she'd come to a date in *years*.

Not loving what that says about my social life.

What social life?

It was different when it was just her and Roman in his villa. She didn't have to think too hard about the implications, because it was clearly just sex. Or maybe the sex just fuzzed her mind and *that* was why spending all that time with him didn't bother her.

Either way, it was different now.

They were out in what passed for public on the island. The little boat was maxed out with her, Roman, Becka and a trio of giggling women who kept shooting Roman significant looks. All three had wedding rings, but that didn't look like it'd stop them from taking him somewhere to be alone if he so much as crooked a finger.

Allie clenched her fists and stared pointedly at the ocean. Roman wasn't hers. If he wanted to run off with someone else, she didn't have a right to be pissed. She certainly didn't have the right to punch him over it. *Get it together.*

"You look like you're about to shove someone into the ocean." Roman's murmur was barely loud enough to be heard over the waves they cut through. "What's wrong?"

"Nothing's wrong." She'd answered too quickly. *Might as well have put a sign over my head claiming the opposite.*

"Allie."

She glared at the horizon. If she was smart, she'd fake a smile and play this off. Admitting to feeling something as damning as jealousy would give Roman even more ammunition than he already had. Then again, if she'd wanted to prevent him from having ammunition, she shouldn't have slept with him a second and third time…and she shouldn't be planning on doing it again at the earliest available opportunity. There was no taking back those actions, and she had no intention of stopping until she really had to.

"Allie." He pressed his hand to the small of her back. "You've been checking out on me ever since last night."

"Maybe it's just what I do. You don't actually know me, so you don't know that it's not something I don't do." It sounded just as jumbled as her head felt. She battled the truly ridiculous urge to cry. Allie shook her head. "I'm sorry. I think it all just became real to me and I'm trying to come to terms with the fact that I'm not really protected against you and it's my own damn fault."

Roman moved closer, his body blocking her from the rest of the people on the boat. "You think you need protection from me?"

She couldn't read his tone, but the words didn't sound any happier than she felt. "Not like *that*. I know you'd never hurt me, but…" But once they left West Island, all bets were off. She also knew that. She'd known that going into this thing with him.

So why did it bother her so much now?

I like him.

It was as simple as that. It might have started with just sex, but it wasn't *just* sex. She'd never been all that good at compartmentalizing, and even if she had been, Roman's sheer presence would overwhelm whatever barriers she put up between them. It was easier when she could pretend she loathed everything about him except for his body.

That fallacy hadn't held up against their interaction that morning. He wasn't just an unfeeling suit. He was a man, with a past and a present and a future, and they had at least a few superficial things in common. She understood his loneliness, because she held the twin feeling inside her. He spoke to her as if he cared what she thought, even if most of the time they'd been too busy to talk about much of anything. It didn't matter. That focus was *there* and he'd have her confessing her deepest desires if given half a chance.

She turned to face him, putting her back against the boat railing. His expression wasn't a happy one. He hadn't had a vacation, and she'd invited him out here to continue their feel-good time together...and now she was ruining it. She hated that, hated that she'd been the one to damper his enjoyment of the boat ride. *Of the sight of those women.*

Stop it.

She bit her lip, but there was no holding back the torrent of words. "I hate the way they look at you."

He blinked and then blinked again as comprehension dawned. "You're jealous."

"I wouldn't say *that*." That was exactly what she'd say.

Roman moved closer and skated his hand up her side until his thumb brushed the side of her breast through her swimsuit top. "Do you honestly think I have the slightest interest in anyone else?"

She didn't really know. That was the problem. It was entirely possible that the only reason he'd come on to her the first night was because they were literally the only two people in the restaurant. *Oh, for God's sake,* stop. Allie gave herself a shake. She didn't do this. Crippling self-doubt was exactly that—crippling. She hadn't had time for that nonsense up until this point, and she'd be damned if she would let it prevent her from enjoying her remaining time with Roman.

She took a long, slow breath, and then another. "Okay, yes, I'm jealous. You might not be mine, but you're mine right now, and I don't like them looking at you like you're a piece of meat they'd like to share over dinner."

Roman burst out laughing, the sound taking up residence in her chest...and lower. His thumb dipped beneath her swimsuit, wandering dangerously close to her nipple. "You know damn well that you're the only one who gets to have me for dinner."

She couldn't find the air to laugh. Not when he pressed his hips into her, letting her know *exactly* how much he wanted her to have him for dinner. Allie ran her hands up his chest. "There isn't anywhere private on this boat."

"If there was, we'd already be there, and I'd be inside you." Roman's thumb found her nipple. "I wouldn't even tell you to be quiet, Allie. I'd fuck you hard enough to make you scream as you came around my cock, so everyone within hearing range would know exactly who it belongs to."

Belongs to.

She didn't know what to say to that, so she went onto her tiptoes and kissed him. Allie looped her arms around his neck and pressed her body against his and tried to tell him without words how hot he made her—how much she appreciated the distraction.

Distantly, she was aware of the boat turning and stopping. The guy driving it cleared his throat. "We'll gear up here and you can explore the reef." He went on, but she was too focused on the heat rising to her cheeks to pay attention.

Roman backed off just enough to fix her top and then slid behind her and wrapped his arms around her waist. His cock pressed against her backside, the hard length preventing her from focusing fully on the instructions. He knew it, damn him. His lips brushed her ear. "Pay attention."

"Stop distracting me." She rolled her hips a little, rubbing her ass against him.

The instructor finally finished up and started handing out snorkels and life vests. Allie slipped out of Roman's grasp and headed for Becka. Her friend gave her a significant look. "I thought you two were going to go at it right there."

Her face flamed, but she tried to laugh it off. "Don't be ridiculous."

"It's not ridiculous if it's true." Becka grinned. "Get it, girl." Her gaze went over Allie's shoulder and her eyebrows inched up. "Would you look at that?"

She turned around in time to see one of the other women saunter up to Roman. Her bikini was tiny enough to border on indecent, and she wore it with utter confidence. Normally, that would have been enough for Allie to want to give her a high five, but with the way the brunette was eye-fucking Roman, the only thing Allie wanted to high-five was her face—with a chair. She sidled up to him, all flirtatious moves and sweet smiles, and placed her hand on his arm, leaning in so her barely covered breasts pressed against his biceps.

He took off his sunglasses and looked down at the spots where she touched him with such coldness that she actually jumped back a step. Roman gave her one last long look that wasn't in the least bit friendly and then turned to take his snorkel gear from their guide. He donned it quickly, dropped his sunglasses on top of his towel and slipped into the water.

All without saying a word.

Becka whistled under her breath. "He gets a nine for takedown, with a plus-two bonus for dramatic exit."

Allie snorted and then tried to cover the sound with a cough. "You're horrible."

"No, what's horrible was that attempt to poach your man." She spoke just loud enough that there was no way the other woman didn't hear her. "Who the hell does that? He was two seconds from dragging you into the ocean to bang you against the side of the boat and *she* thinks she has a chance?" Becka tsked. "Girl's got issues."

Allie smacked her friend lightly even though she agreed with everything Becka had said. All her worries seemed silly in the face of what had just happened. Hell, they were silly even before Roman rebuffed the woman. *A fling in paradise. Don't complicate things for no damn reason.*

Easier said than done.

11

ROMAN ENJOYED THE HELL OUT OF THE DAY. THE weird tension riding Allie disappeared once they got into the water, and they spent several hours exploring the reef and then floating in the waves. By the time the boat dropped them back to the island, she was tucked comfortably under his arm and chatting animatedly with Becka. Roman kept expecting her friend to say...something...about their arrangement, but Becka seemed content to hang out as if this was the most normal thing in the world.

He drove them both back to their villa and left the women there. Though he wanted to take Allie back to his place, he recognized that she needed a little space.

Frankly, he could use a little space himself.

Roman had never been more conflicted in his life. He liked Allie. He wanted to see her succeed. Fuck, he just flat-out wanted her. But she was right this morning. There was a lot more to take into account than what they'd experienced together on West Island.

With that in mind, he strode into his villa and sat down with the papers he'd stashed there the day before. As much as Roman wanted Allie to give him the information voluntarily, the truth of the matter was that she was blocking him. She had her reasons for not wanting to open up, and he respected that, but this wasn't about his growing feelings for her—it was business.

He had to separate the two.

He couldn't afford not to.

She needed his help. She just didn't know it yet. If he let her wait until she was comfortable talking about this stuff with him—*if* that ever happened—the opportunity would pass and she could lose everything.

He needed to know what he'd missed about that damn gym, and he needed to know now. Stomping down on the guilt that tried to dissuade him, Roman sat down and fanned out the papers. He started at the beginning—with Allie and her family.

A story that he'd seen played out before. Alcoholic father. A mother who fled with her child when the abuse transferred to her daughter. A hard life lived, but which didn't stop Allie from graduating from college with honors and very little student debt. She'd worked her ass off to get Transcend up and running with money her mother had left her when the woman passed away three years ago. The shelter was set up under a nonprofit bearing Allie's mother's name.

But a successful nonprofit took a lot of work and shmoozing, and Allie obviously didn't have a taste for it. It didn't bring in enough to cover the costs, so she'd been draining the income generated by the gym—and her own personal savings.

Roman shook his head. It was an easy fix. Pass off the nonprofit to someone else, franchise Transcend and things would even out—and transfer from red back into the black.

So why was she so resistant to the idea?

Once he knew the answer to that, he'd know how to play things. He sighed. *Except it isn't that simple.* This wasn't a prospective client he could manipulate into doing what he wanted without remorse. This was Allie. He didn't want to hurt her, even if it was ultimately for her own good. He wanted her to trust him—to let him help her.

He kept reading. Her abusive father was horrible, but it didn't explain why she was so determined to do this alone. The woman Roman had started to get to know over the last couple days was strong and smart, but not a control freak like he'd expected. That was the only thing that would explain her insistence on not allowing the investor he represented to buy into the company.

Frustrated, Roman flipped through the papers again. Nothing, and he'd essentially breached her trust by doing this search to begin with. *Fuck*. He'd done the basic background on her when he first found the business, but Allie Landers kept her nose clean and, aside from the business's financial records and her school history, he hadn't dug deeper before.

He wished he hadn't now, either.

Roman threw the papers back into the folder and tucked it into a drawer under the kitchen counter. There was no easy answer here. He'd promised that they would leave business in New York, but the only way he could figure out what was stopping her was to *talk* to her... Some fucking businessman he was. He'd painted himself into one hell of a corner with this.

Enjoying their time together was the only option. If he tried to push her, she'd call an end to the whole thing. Allie didn't care about the pending deadline, since she had no interest in selling her business.

Which was a problem, because the whole damn ship was sinking. She'd be underwater inside of six months and then she'd lose everything. If she would just trust him, he could take care of everything. That was the problem, though. Roman knew he wanted what was best for the gym and Allie, but *Allie* didn't know that. It didn't matter how many different ways he tried to tell her, the truth was that he hadn't done anything to earn her trust, and it was doubtful he'd manage that feat sometime in the next four days.

Roman sat there and contemplated it for nearly an hour,

no closer to finding a solution by that point than he had been when he'd first started thinking about it.

What the fuck am I going to do?

Come to dinner with me. Dress to the nines.

Allie looked at the masculine scrawl on the note that had been delivered to their villa with the snack Becka had ordered. She felt a stupid grin pulling at the edges of her lips and tried to fight it. A single note from Roman shouldn't be a highlight of her day—especially after the glory that was snorkeling off the coast of the island—but her heartbeat kicked up a notch knowing that he was thinking about her…and planning something for tonight.

"He sent you another note, didn't he?" Becka stepped out of her room, wearing a wrap dress that showed off her legs and lean frame. She'd pinned her blue hair up into a style that could only be described as shabby chic. And she was grinning like the cat who'd eaten the canary. "I don't know if that's adorable beyond measure or cheesy as hell."

"Both." She tried to sound unimpressed, but the stupid smile wouldn't go away. "It's lame."

"It is not lame. He's smitten." Becka eyed her. "You're both smitten."

"I can't be smitten with Roman Bassani. We only have a few days left and then it's back to being enemies again." The thought dimmed her smile like nothing else had been able to. It was strange to think a time would come when she and Roman would be adversaries, but there was no real alternative. He wanted her gym. She would never give it up. End of story—end of them. Nothing that happened while they were on the island would change that.

Becka poked at the snacks that had been delivered and chose a selection of fruit. "You know he has a client who wants to invest in Transcend. Do you know why?"

"For the same reason all the other investors came around when they realized I wasn't making ends meet as well as I would have liked. They think they can jump on the trendy fitness-nutrition combo and franchise it. They don't care about the shelter—and they'd probably cut it out completely if they had control. It's a money pit, after all, and it's not like they're invested in any of those women's futures." Allie shook her head sharply. "No. I can't risk it. Business isn't so bad that we have to give in to the kind of offer Roman and people like him are bringing us. We're doing just fine." *Not really fine at all.* She should have organized a fund-raiser or something for the shelter, but she was so busy running the gym that the thought of adding anything else to her plate was too much to deal with. So she'd put it off.

She was regretting it now.

Too little, too late.

"How do you know?"

She pulled herself back into the present. "What?"

"How do you know what Roman has planned for Transcend?" Becka popped a piece of pineapple into her mouth. "Have you talked about it?"

"No. And we're not going to." At her friend's incredulous look, she glared. "You wanted me to have hot vacation sex, and hot vacation sex includes not talking about work. That's the only condition Roman and I put on this thing, so hell if I'm going to break the rules. It's just going to end in another fight, and this one we might not be able to screw our way out of." She ran her hand over her face. "What am I doing? This whole thing was a mistake."

Becka jumped to her feet. "Oh, no, you don't! I'm sorry I pushed buttons. I thought I was just asking a question." She hurried to Allie and guided her toward her own room. "Go get ready. Then get your ass back in here and have a shot with me for sure mutual courage. Then we'll never speak of this again—at least for the next few days."

"You don't have to be sorry. I'm the one acting batty." She paused just inside her doorway. "I like him."

"I know you do, honey."

She didn't know if that was comforting or worrisome, so she didn't comment on it. She just gently shut the door between them and dug through her suitcase for something that would be qualified as dressing to the nines. She'd packed a couple nice dresses, just in case, and she laid them both out on her mostly unused bed. One was a simple little black dress that was flowy and showed her cleavage to perfection. The other was a two-piece with a stretchy nude pencil skirt and a cropped bustier top that showed a sliver of skin between them. Normally for something resembling a first date, she'd play it safe with the LBD and leave the trendier choice for once she'd figured out if the guy was a douche or not.

But she already knew what Roman was—and what he thought of her.

Allie's grin reappeared. The cropped top and skirt it was.

She took extra time getting ready, styling her hair in perfect beach waves and keeping her makeup light enough that it wouldn't melt off her face the second she left the villa—or once she and Roman got to whatever he had planned for dessert. She finished off the look with her strappy wedge sandals. With their three-inch heel, she'd be almost as tall as him, and the idea pleased her more than it probably should have. Roman's masculinity wasn't so fragile that he needed her to cut herself down to make him feel better. It was one of the things she liked about him.

I like a lot of things about him.

Stop it.

Becka grinned when Allie walked back into the main area

of the villa. "Ooooh, someone has their seductive panties on tonight."

"I'm not wearing any."

Her friend laughed. "Which just serves to support my point. After that little show on the boat earlier, if he doesn't fall on you like a starving man the second he sees you, I'll eat my shoe."

Allie wasn't prepared to take Roman's response to seeing her—whatever it would be—for granted, so she just shook her head and started for the exit. "See you in the morning?"

"As long as by morning you mean after eleven." Becka set her fork and plate in the sink. "Luke is meeting me here after his shift, and I plan to rock him all night long."

"You like this guy?"

Becka shrugged. "I like parts of him. He doesn't have the most stimulating of personalities, but he's got a monster cock and magic hands, so he's perfect for the time and place." Her smile was sunny but didn't quite reach her eyes. "You know me—I don't do that messy emotional bullshit. I like my life how it is. I don't have time for some needy dude expecting me to bend over backward to rearrange it for him."

There was a story there, but in all the years Allie had known Becka, she'd never got to the heart of it. Despite her friend's carefree spirit, Becka had a hard line when it came to anything resembling a relationship. She liked to laugh away the serious stuff whenever they got close to talking about it, and Allie respected the unspoken request to not bring it up.

Then again, Allie hadn't done more than casually date in that time, either, so she wasn't one to talk.

"Shots!" Becka poured vodka into two glasses and passed one over. "To a night of wall-banging sex and living our vacation to the fullest."

They clinked glasses. "Tomorrow, why don't we do something with just us?" Allie suggested.

"Sure…as long as you aren't using me as a shield against

Roman." Becka downed her shot without a grimace. "If you want to spend the rest of this trip with him, then you should. I'm more than capable of keeping myself occupied, and it's not like we don't spend more time with each other in New York than we do with anyone else in our lives."

There was no arguing that, but... She took her shot, closing her eyes as the alcohol burned its way down her throat and created a comforting warmth in her stomach. "I don't want to abandon you." She wasn't sure she wanted to be that close with Roman, either. It was already hard to keep the boundaries in her head between them—between the island and New York, between the present and the inevitable future. Getting to know him better would make it worse.

Except...

"I'll think about it."

"Do that." Becka plucked the shot glass from her hand. "Now get out of here. Five bucks says he bangs you right there on the patio."

"You really need to stop making bets about how quickly Roman and I get to banging." But she laughed all the same. She could shelve all her worries about what the future held—at least for a few more days.

Allie would figure out the rest when she got back to New York.

12

ROMAN HAD EVERYTHING PREPARED FOR ALLIE.
A table set up on the patio overlooking the sunset. The food
prepped and ready in its various warming plates. Candlelight.
The best of intentions.

And then she walked out of the jungle and the blood rushed
out of his head and took up residence in his cock. She wore a
skintight beige skirt that his hands were itching to slide over,
and her little crop top bustier thing offered her breasts up as if
begging for his mouth. The sandals had a little heel on them,
which only served to highlight the muscles in her legs and…

He rubbed the back of his hand over his mouth. "Fuck,
Aphrodite."

Her sweet smile was reward enough, but he wasn't going to
be the gentleman he'd planned to be originally. Not with her
looking at him with those come-fuck-me eyes and strolling
right up to slide her arms around his neck. Her smile widened
as she pressed her hips against his. "Hey."

"Hey." He cupped her ass with one hand and her hip with the
other, dragging his thumb along the exposed few inches of her
upper stomach between the skirt and top. "You look amazing."

"Thanks." She looked him over. "You, too."

It was too hot for pants, but he'd chosen a pair of khaki shorts and a linen button-down that passed as dressed to the nines for island fashion. "Are you hungry?"

"Starving." She hooked her fingers into his belt loops. "But not for food. I've been thinking about you since we were on the boat." She gave a delicate little shiver that had his cock hardening further. "Dinner will hold. I need you now." Allie had his belt undone in the space of a heartbeat and shoved his pants down his legs.

Shock stole his reasoning when he recognized the look on her face. "You're still jealous."

"No, I'm not." She knelt in front of him and wrapped her fingers around his cock. "I was. It wasn't anything you did, and it wasn't anything I have a right to feel, but it was there all the same."

He laced his fingers through her hair. "You're entitled to feeling anything you damn well please."

"Yes, I'm aware."

He watched her lick her lips, his heartbeat kicking up a notch. She was jealous of the woman on the boat. Roman hadn't bothered to remember her name, but she had been beautiful and confident and someone he might have looked at twice if he wasn't totally and completely wrapped up in Allie. "Do you really think another woman can compare when you're in the room?"

"We were on a boat." She gave him another stroke but seemed content to talk for the time being.

"The point stands."

Allie pinned him with a look. "I'm not interested in competing with another woman for a single damn thing. Life isn't a zero-sum game, and too often we're pitted against each other when it's not beneficial for anyone but the men around us." When he just looked at her, she relented. "*Fine*. I hated seeing her touch you. I wanted to march up and toss her over the railing. I'm not proud of that."

He wished he'd seen the obvious fury in her gaze when it all went down, though it was probably for the best that he hadn't. Roman had no business being pleased with the fact she was jealous, but he was all the same. He slid his fingers deeper into her hair and lightly massaged her scalp. "I'm not interested in anyone but you."

"For the next few days."

For always. He couldn't say it. Even with all the extenuating circumstances, it was too soon. Roman had never shied away from what he wanted, though—and what he wanted was Allie Landers.

He just had to give her a reason to give him a shot.

Focus.

"Suck me, Aphrodite. Show me how disinclined you are to share."

She arched a perfectly shaped eyebrow. "I find myself very disinclined to share." Allie licked the underside of his cock like a lollipop and then sucked him down.

Roman had to fight to keep his eyes open, to watch her pretty pink lips move over him. She licked and sucked, her gaze never leaving his face. She worked him like she was laying claim to his cock in a way that had lightning sparking at the small of his back and pressure building in his balls. He wasn't going out like that, though. Not without touching her. "Come here." He guided her off him and lifted her onto a chair.

Roman hit his knees and slid his hands beneath her skirt, pushing the soft fabric up. She wore nothing beneath it, and his breath caught in his throat when he found her wet and ready for him. *Not yet.* But a taste couldn't hurt. He hooked her legs on the outside of her chair arms and dipped his head to drag his tongue over her. As long as he lived, he'd never get enough of the taste of Allie on his tongue.

She moaned and arched her back, offering herself further. "Stroke your cock, Roman. For me."

He froze, nearly coming on the spot at her words. *Fuck, woman, I'm keeping you.*

Keeping one hand bracketing her thigh, he made a fist around his cock and stroked hard. He was already close from her sucking him off, but he wasn't about to let himself come before she did. He flicked her clit with his tongue, alternating between circles and those vertical motions that he knew she liked. A frenzy took hold and he devoured her, driven on by her moans and writhing. She was close. So fucking close. His balls drew up, and he fucked her with his tongue, growling against her pussy. Needing more.

Needing *her.*

Allie laced her fingers through his hair, riding his mouth and crying his name as she orgasmed. He gripped his cock harder, roughening his strokes as he followed her over the edge, coming hard enough that he saw stars. He drew back enough to kiss first one of her thighs and then the other, then he pulled her skirt back down over her hips. "Now it's time for dinner."

Allie slouched in her chair, feeling completely boneless. "That's one way to start a meal."

"Mmm. Yes." Roman kissed her stomach and then adjusted her clothing to its correct place. He did up his pants just as efficiently, and she mourned the loss of the sight of him. The man was built magnificently and as good as he looked in clothes, he looked even better out of them.

He set about doling out food onto two plates with an easy, almost professional quickness. When he nudged a crooked fork back into place, she knew it had to be true. "How long were you a waiter?"

"Six years. My parents paid for my college, but they are big believers in working for anything worth having, so the rest was up to me. I handled room and board and books and all the other bullshit expenses that show up when you're in college by working at a local restaurant." He shook his head. "I will never do it again. Lifetime food service workers are either saints or insane, because nothing brings out the asshole in people as much as the little power they think they have when they're out to dinner."

From the comments he'd made, she'd assumed he'd grown up with money, but knowing he'd had to work for at least part of it made her like him better. "Bet you tip really well."

"I can afford to." He shrugged as if that made a damn bit of difference.

Allie examined her food, giving him a brief break from a subject that obviously made him uncomfortable. *Interesting.* He hadn't minded talking about working the job, but anything resembling evidence that he might be a good guy and he was suddenly closemouthed. She took a sip of wine. "I was a bartender my college years. O'Leary's." She saw from his look that he knew it. "Rich guys are the worst tippers out there—unless they think they have a shot at getting into your pants. Trust me, it's not something that your waitstaff take for granted."

"You don't have to do that."

"Do what?" She set her glass down and gave him her full attention.

Roman studied her. "Convince me that I'm not a total piece of shit. I already know I'm not. I might not be the best guy out there, but I'm a far cry from the worst. I'm solidly average."

Allie snorted before she could stop herself. "Roman, you are many things, but average is not one of them." And she wasn't just talking about the size of his cock. He was obviously driven and smart and clever, and he'd done well for himself.

Even though she knew better, she still asked, "Why are you in this brand of investments? Why not stockbroking or something that—" Allie cut herself off before she could finish that thought aloud. *Why not something that doesn't involve taking from other people?*

From the look he gave her, he knew exactly where her mind had gone. "I know it doesn't seem like it, but I'm not the enemy—not yours and not any of the others whose businesses I help pair up with investors. Most of them thank me in the end."

She had no doubt about that. Roman was hardly a snake oil salesman, but the force of his personality was often in danger of eclipsing all else—like common sense and reason. If he focused the entirety of it on a person, eventually he'd have them convinced that the sky was green and up was down. Even now, *she* was trying to find a way for it to make sense that he was the good guy and not the boogeyman under the bed that she'd assumed for months.

In truth, he was neither the bad guy nor the dream vacation fling—at least not in full. Reality was a lot more complicated.

Allie took a long drink of her wine and poked at the food on her plate. "You understand where I'm coming from with this."

He didn't answer for several beats. "You want to talk about business?"

Did she? The longer they were together, the clearer it became that they'd have to talk eventually—probably before they actually left the island…but she didn't want it to be tonight. She shook her head. "No. I'm sorry I brought it up."

Another of those searching looks. "We can talk, Allie. We're both adults, and as much as I enjoy the hell out of fucking you, I want to get to know you better."

That sounded like… She didn't know what that sounded like. It didn't fit in with her preconceptions of their boundaries. It didn't fit with *anything*. Allie swallowed against the panic welling inside her. It was just a conversation. She wasn't agreeing to anything just because she was talking with him. She'd *been* talking with him this entire trip. It just felt different this time.

Meaningful.

She took a breath, and then another. "Do you have…hobbies?"

Roman smiled gently, as if he knew what the question had cost her. "I work a shit ton, so I don't have much in the way of time. But I box a couple times a week at my gym—nothing crazy or competitive. Just sparring."

She could see it. He certainly had the upper body of a boxer, though his legs were just as solid as the rest of him. "Boxing and yoga. That's quite the combination." He was experienced with yoga. She'd been doing it for years, and she still had trouble with some of the poses he'd pulled off the other morning.

"They both help with my stress level, albeit in different ways."

"I bet they do." She cocked her head to the side. "Doesn't leave much time for social stuff." Like recognized like—between running the gym and teaching classes, she had nothing in the way of free time.

"How did you get into the gym business?" He held up his hand before she could speak. "I'm not talking about your business right now—I want to know why you chose that route."

She started to consider how she wanted to answer that, but exhaustion rolled over her. Allie was so damn tired of having to watch what she said around him. If she trusted Roman enough to give him full control of her body, she should trust him enough to have a conversation without worrying that he'd twist it around to use it against her.

Maybe it was time for a tiny leap of faith.

Allie took a bite and chewed slowly, finally swallowing the food, though she couldn't have begun to guess what it was she'd eaten. Her entire focus was on Roman and their conversation. He had no way of knowing that the seemingly innocent question would open a whole Pandora's box of history for her. She finally set her fork aside. "When I was growing up, I didn't have the healthiest of childhoods. It could have been a lot worse than it was, but the only high points during those years were when my mom would let me tag along to the gym. When she was there, she was…" She had to search for the word. "Free. In control in a way that she never was while married to my dad. When that relationship ended for good, it was a new city, a new gym, a new sense of purpose. It was in that place that I saw her find herself again, make friends, start the long road to what healthy looked like."

She tried a nonchalant shrug, but every muscle in her body was tense. "I initially started going so we would have something in common, but I really liked it. I never got super into the nutrition aspect of it, but I eat healthy enough." She motioned at her body. "I like food. I like working out. I like giving women like my mom a safe place. It all came together in Transcend."

Roman was so still, he might not have breathed the entire time she spoke. "I'm sorry your father was such a piece of shit."

"Me, too." Once upon a time, she'd wondered if her being born was the thing that ruined her parents' relationship, but Allie had seen too much—heard too many stories out of the same playbook—for that guilt to hold any water. Her father would have been the same if it was a different woman, whether there was a child or not, regardless of the external stressors he liked to blame for his flying off the handle.

She looked at Roman and tried to picture him drinking so much he actually hurt a woman—anyone, really—and couldn't wrap her mind around it. Maybe she was being naive, because he had a ruthless streak a mile wide, but nothing about him rang that warning bell. *Why am I even thinking about this?*

Because you can't afford not to.

Except this ends when we go back to New York, so it won't matter what he's like when he's not on vacation because you won't be around to see it.

The thought had her sagging in her seat. She poked at her food again. Wanting more with Roman was out of the question. The whole condition of their being together was *not* to

talk about the most important thing in their respective lives—
her gym and his work. It wasn't sustainable.

But part of her wanted it to be.

13

ROMAN SAW THE EXACT MOMENT ALLIE STARTED to shut him out. He'd been pushing it with that question and he'd known it, but there was too much he didn't know about her. He *should* be prodding her with questions to help spin things to his advantage, but the only reason Roman had asked was because he genuinely wanted to know.

He cleared his throat. "I envy you, in a way."

"Why's that?" The distance in her blue eyes retreated, leaving her present and accounted for.

In for a penny, in for a pound. She'd bared part of herself with that little window into her past—he couldn't do anything less than the same. "I mentioned before that my parents weren't around much when I was a kid." He snorted. "I might have understated it. They were gone more often than they were there. There was nothing traumatic about my upbringing, other than a bit of benign neglect, but when I was younger, I would have given my left arm to have designated time with either of them like you had with your mom."

Allie leaned forward, now fully engaged. "Why didn't they have more kids, if only to give you someone who wouldn't leave?"

"My mother didn't like being pregnant all that much, and

she wasn't a fan of what came after, either." He made a face. "Hearing that at the tender age of five was eye-opening, to say the least."

"Oh, Roman."

"No, none of that." He casually slashed his hand through the air. "I don't need pity any more than you do. All my needs were met and my parents loved me in their own way. They just loved each other and travel a bit more. I had a whole staff of people who ensured I didn't turn out a monster, though I wager my nanny, Elaine, would feel differently if she'd lived to see me as a business acquisitions consultant." At her raised eyebrows, he continued, "She found money to be a necessary evil but always told me that she hoped I'd pick a good honest job that didn't revolve around it."

He hadn't thought about that conversation in over a decade. Elaine had passed when he was in his first year of college, and by that time he was firmly in his rebellious stage. Too much drinking, too many girls, too many attempts to do something crazy enough to force his parents to acknowledge him. Elaine's death had snapped him out of it like being thrown into a freezing ocean. He'd taken a good hard look at his life and realized that the only person he was hurting was himself. His parents would never change who they were, and trying to push them to be different was a lesson in futility.

Roman shook his head. "This got heavy. Sorry."

She tucked a lock of hair behind her ear. "I appreciate your sharing. It's kind of strange that we don't know much about each other, but..." Allie motioned between them.

"We fuck like we were made for each other." He wished he could recall the coarse words the second they were out of his mouth. He and Allie had bypassed mere fucking days ago. This was something on another level and cheapening it was a shitty thing to do.

She smiled. "Exactly that."

It stung that she agreed with him so quickly, but had he really expected anything else? In an effort to distract them both, he said, "So how did you meet Becka?"

As she launched into a tale of two broke college students desperate enough to take second jobs at the scary campus gym, he sat back and indulged in watching the animated way she spoke. Allie really was beautiful. He'd known that, of course—he had two eyes in his head, after all—but she was beautiful right down to the core. A genuinely good person.

Let me help you.

He couldn't say it. Even talking about the gym in more abstract forms had caused her to shut him out. Trying to talk more explicitly was a recipe for disaster. He had to play the game within the terms they'd set out. It was the only way.

"You're not even listening." She didn't say it like she was mad—just stating a fact.

"I am." Roman managed a smile. "That boss you had at the campus gym sounds like a real piece of work—though he should have been reported for forcing you to be in those conditions."

She raised her eyebrows. "Okay, that's a neat trick. You were a million miles away, but you still retained everything I said. That's nuts."

"Necessary evil." Though he'd never once been called on it before now. "I learned early in my career that it's best to have several options for plans by the end of a meeting with a new client—that means listening to what they're saying while still thinking strategically to create a game plan. They fill out preliminary information, of course, but until I meet them face-to-face, I rarely know exactly what they're looking for." He shrugged. "Some things sound better on paper than they are in reality."

Allie bit her bottom lip, and he could see the conflict clear on her face. "Okay, I'll bite—tell me about your job. Broad strokes, please."

Easy enough, though he couldn't help feeling it was a test. "I am a glorified numbers monkey. I research various businesses that look like good investments and then line up investors that will fit well with them. The ultimate outcome varies. Sometimes they take it to the ground level and build it up again. Sometimes they expand. Sometimes they franchise. Usually it's successful for both business and investor and I get a nice fat bonus."

"Depends on your definition of *successful*, doesn't it?"

He knew where she was going with this, and as much as he didn't want to fight, maybe it was better to get it out there now and expose the elephant in the room. "I won't pretend that every business owner is thrilled with the process, but most of the time the alternative is rock bottom and losing everything they worked their ass off to accomplish. Sometimes compromise is necessary."

She looked directly at him with those big blue eyes. "And do you ever compromise, Roman?"

Allie should have…well, she should have done a lot of things. She regretted the question as soon as she put it to voice—like she regretted much of what she'd said around Roman since they'd met. She pushed to her feet. "Never mind. We just got through saying we shouldn't talk about this—should keep it light—and we keep doing the exact opposite of that."

There was one thing they were good at—better than good at.

She slid her thumbs into the band of her skirt and pushed it down in a smooth move. The top took a little more effort, but she managed to unhook it and drop it without looking like a total fool. Roman hadn't moved once, but his knuckles were white where he held on to the table. He managed to tear his gaze from her breasts to her face. "What are you doing?"

"We're going to ruin this by talking too much. I don't want to ruin it."

Still, he didn't move. "It's okay for us to disagree on things. It's unrealistic to think that we'd match up on every subject the way we match up physically."

She knew that. Of course she knew that. Only a child or an idiot thought there was such a thing as a perfect relationship. Everyone had problems, though most of the time they weren't as catastrophic as her parents' had been.

But this wasn't a relationship. She had to keep reminding herself of that, and *that* was as much a problem as anything.

She shook her head. "That's the thing—this is fantasy. There is no room for disagreements in fantasy. I want you. You want me. Let's just leave it at that."

"Allie—"

She turned and strode into the darkness. He'd follow. He'd be unable to help himself. And then they'd get their hands on each other and all her conflicting feelings would disappear for a while. *That* was what she wanted. She already had a complicated life. She didn't have room for *more* complications—even if they arrived in a package that made her body ache and her heart beat too hard.

Sex was easier. Sex was safe.

Even if it didn't feel particularly safe as she hit the sand and kept going. The wildness of the island was closer to the surface here, with the villa lights seeming at a distance and the stars a blanket overhead. The soft shushing sound of the water sliding over the sand let her draw her first full breath since she and Roman had started talking about things better left unsaid.

She tilted her head back and inhaled deeply, taking the salty air into her lungs and letting it chase away her worries. She was still on vacation, no matter how stubbornly real life kept trying to intrude. Relaxation was the name of the game and Allie would be damned if she was drawn back into all the crap before she was good and ready.

Footsteps padded behind her, and she didn't turn to watch

Roman approach. She wouldn't be able to see more than the outline of him, and it was better to soak up what little peace she could as she waited to see if he'd let the conversation go.

He stopped next to her, close enough that his shoulder brushed against hers. "You can't run from this forever."

"I'm not running from anything." *Liar.* "I'm holding to the arrangement we made. Everything can wait until we leave West Island." What happened then… No, she wasn't going to talk about it. She wasn't even going to *think* about it.

"Allie…" His exhale was lost in the sound of the small waves hitting their feet. "This is what you really want? For me to fuck you until neither of us is capable of words and we just ignore everything unspoken between us?"

This was the moment of truth. If she said she'd changed her mind about their bargain, she had a feeling Roman wouldn't judge her for it. He seemed to want to talk—actually talk. Maybe he was starting to feel the same thing she was—that this thing between them wasn't just about mutual orgasms.

That maybe it could be more.

All she had to do was tell him that she was willing to talk.

But when she opened her mouth, it was cowardice that won. "We can talk when we're in New York."

He turned to face her, his expression lost in the darkness. "Promise me that we will."

"What?"

"Promise me that you won't run when we get back. You'll have dinner with me and we'll talk."

It'll never happen. It sounded good in theory right now, beneath the stars and with their bodies gravitating toward one another, but once they got back to the city and were grounded in their real lives, it wouldn't hold up. He'd get busy. She'd have to cancel a few times. They'd both lose interest and move on with their lives.

The thought made her chest ache, but she set it aside just like everything else she'd set aside since she came here. "I promise."

Roman shifted closer, sliding his hands over her hips and up her back, fitting her body against his. He'd stripped before following her out here, and all his skin against all of hers sent a delicious thrill through her. He kept calling her beautiful, but he was a work of art. "Adonis."

"Aphrodite." He lifted her easily so she could wrap her legs around his waist. "Let's go swimming."

She didn't protest as he walked them into the ocean. Roman didn't go far, stopping as the water lapped the bottom of her breasts. It felt absolutely wicked to be out here in the dark with him. Even if it'd been broad daylight, no one would have seen them, but the thrill of the risk still heightened every sensation.

The water teasing her breasts. The slick slide of his skin against hers. The feel of his breath ghosting across her lips.

She arched against him, trying to take his mouth, but Roman dodged her kiss. "Do you know the legend of Aphrodite?"

She blinked. "Yes, of course. She came from the sea." The words were barely past her lips when Roman launched her away from him. She was airborne for a single breathless second and then she hit the water and went under.

Allie surfaced with a curse that turned into a laugh. "You're crazy."

"Come on. You can't skinny-dip in the Caribbean without horsing around a bit." He splashed her and then disappeared beneath the surface.

Allie skittered back, searching the inky water for a sign of him, but the only warning she got was a hand around her ankle and then he pulled her under. They twisted beneath the surface and tangled together. She used his shoulders to shove him farther down and push herself up for a breath.

And then his arms were around her waist and he was hauling them closer to shore. His cock pressed against the small of her back and her breath hitched in her throat. "Playtime's over."

She laughed at the cheesy line, but the sound came out strained. "You just wanted to get me all wet."

"Mmm." He cupped her breasts and rolled her nipples between his thumbs and forefingers. "Come on. As much as I need you right here, right now, the condoms are back in the villa."

She almost threw caution to the wind and said it didn't matter. Allie clamped her mouth shut to keep the words inside and nodded sharply. Unprotected sex with Roman, no matter how much she wanted him in that moment, was the worst possible idea. "Yes. Villa. Now."

Before she did something they'd both regret.

14

ROMAN CARRIED ALLIE ACROSS THE SAND. HE ignored the tension bleeding into her body the farther they got from the waves. *Too much time to think.* They were being so damn careful not to edge too close to subjects that would put them at odds with each other, but he craved that part of her as much as he wanted the rest. Allie wasn't just the beautiful siren who looked so at home in the sun and sand, with the turquoise water creating the perfect backdrop.

She was a strong woman who hadn't let circumstances beyond her control beat her. She'd fought tooth and nail to accomplish so much in such a short time, and it was a fucking tragedy that it hadn't gone according to plan. He didn't want her to lose Transcend any more than she wanted to lose it, if only because he now recognized the pain it would cause.

Roman would go to extraordinary lengths to save Allie from whatever pain he could.

He padded up the porch steps and headed straight for the bedroom. She wouldn't thank him for ruining their good mood with serious talking, and she might go so far as to leave if he tried to broach the forbidden topic. There wasn't a damn thing Roman could do to change that, and he wasn't used to being so effectively painted into a corner.

He couldn't use words to reassure Allie.

But he could use his body.

"Roman?" The hesitance in her tone killed him.

He set her on her feet but didn't release her. Naked and wet from the ocean, she really did look like a siren who'd been sent to tempt him. Allie blinked those big blue eyes. "Are we okay?"

"Yeah." *Not as okay as I want us to be.* He *liked* Allie. He admired her strength. He wanted to bolster it, to be the immovable object she could lean on when she needed it. If there was one thing he was sure about when it came to the woman in his arms, it was that she didn't allow herself to rest, to pass the burden on to another.

He wanted to bear all her burdens, at least for a little while.

Roman framed her face with his hands and stroked his thumbs over her cheekbones. "I want it to be just us while we're here. No past, no worrying about the future. Just you, Allie, and me, Roman. Two people enjoying their time together."

"That sounds good." She bit her bottom lip. "But I don't know if it's possible to just put all that aside and pretend it's not there."

"Aphrodite." He kissed the spot on her lip where there was still an indent from her teeth. "Nothing exists but us. The goddess of love and her Adonis."

She laughed a little. "You know that myth didn't end happily, right?"

"It's Greek mythology. There are no happy endings." He shifted to kiss her stubborn chin. "Fuck them. This is our story."

Her hesitation was so brief, it might not have existed. "Yes. Tonight. The next three days. You and me. I'm in."

As much as Roman didn't want any kind of limit, he knew when not to push his luck. Allie had given him more than he'd hoped, and he'd have to be happy with it. "I'm taking you to bed now."

"Finally." She gave a dramatic sigh. "I thought we'd never get to the good part."

"All of it is the good part." He walked her back to the bed and laid her down, leaning over her. "Tell me what you want. Your wish is my command tonight."

"Just tonight?" There it was again, the slightest hint of vulnerability.

Not just tonight. Always. Promises he had no business making rose, pressing against the inside of his lips like live things. He'd known he wanted Allie, but the realization that he had only three days left with her pulsed up inside him, desperation building with each heartbeat. He looked down at her, her open expression of need cleaving into his chest as if she'd actually struck him. *I don't want to lose you.* He swallowed hard. "We'll start with tonight and see how it goes."

Her grin brought out an answering one from him. "Kiss me, Adonis." She arched up, pressing all of her body against all of his. "Touch me. Hold me. Fuck me."

There was no room in this night for fucking. They'd passed that point days ago, though he couldn't pinpoint the exact moment when Allie went from a gorgeous woman who drove him out of his mind to a woman whose inside was just as compelling as how she felt when she rode his cock. It wasn't just sex between them, no matter what lies she told herself.

Maybe it never had been that uncomplicated.

Roman joined her on the bed and kissed the long line of her neck. "Here." He shifted to the side so he had full access to her body, and moved to the curve of her shoulder. "Perhaps here."

She shivered. "I could think of a few places I'd like."

"I bet you could." He urged her onto her side so he could fit himself against her back. The position gave him free reign, and he wasted no time cupping her full breasts, weighing them in his hands. "Open your eyes."

She obeyed and froze when she met his gaze in the reflection of the windows across from the bed. The deep darkness outside and the single lamp he'd left on inside created a mirror of the glass.

Roman pressed an openmouthed kiss to the back of her neck and retreated just enough for his breath to ghost over the damp skin. She shivered and arched her back against him, pressing her breasts more firmly into his hands. "That feels good."

"I'm just getting started." He lightly pinched her nipples, rolling the tight buds between his fingers. "I love how rosy your skin gets when you like what I'm doing to you."

She lifted her head and frowned. "The reflection isn't that damn good."

"No. It's not." He skated a hand down her stomach and hooked her thigh, lifting her leg up and setting her foot behind his legs. It left her open for him and he delighted in her shiver. "Cold?"

Allie reached back to run her fingers through his hair. "I'm burning up. Touch me, Adonis."

He loved it when she called him that. It was something they alone shared. Something special and meaningful. Roman dragged a single fingertip over the inside of her thigh, teasing her. "Where do you want me to touch you?"

"You know where."

"Mmm. I might." He palmed her pussy, and cursed when he found her warm and wet and wanting. "This is where you want me." He traced her opening. "Where you're aching with need."

"Yes." She shifted her hips to guide him, but he nipped her shoulder. Allie hissed out a breath. "Bossy."

"Always." He spread her wetness up and over her clit and circled the little bud of nerves with the pad of his finger. "You love it."

"Maybe."

"Definitely." Roman pushed two fingers into her, stroking her leisurely while he watched her face. Her sinful lips parted and her blue eyes went hazy. "My Aphrodite." He released her long enough to reach over and snag a condom.

"Let me." Allie turned in his arms and plucked it out of his hand. She ripped it open and then gripped his cock. A stroke. Two. The desire in her eyes a match to the furnace inside him. "You shouldn't be this perfect, you know? It's got to be a mathematical improbability."

He barked out a laugh. "Not perfect. Never that." He had more than his share of faults. He always had. Too selfish. Too driven, often at the expense of his relationships. Too stubborn by half.

"Well, obviously." She rolled the condom over him, taking her time. "I was talking about your cock, Adonis."

That surprised another laugh out of him despite the fact she started stroking him again. "Quite the backhanded compliment."

"Only if you want to look at it that way." She nudged his shoulder, pushing him onto his back. Allie climbed on top of him and ran her hands up his chest. "Seriously, though. You don't have a single physical imperfection. I've never had a man take my breath away just by looking at him, and you do."

He looked at her, this woman that he'd never planned on. She was trying so fucking hard to keep as many barriers up between them as she could. Easier to focus on the physical than to admit that he might not be as evil as she'd assumed. To admit that she liked him for more than his ability to make her come hard enough to see stars.

Allie positioned his cock at her entrance and sank onto him in a slow movement. Her eyes fluttered closed and her pink lips parted. "Oh, God." She rolled her hips a little, adjusting. "I always think I can anticipate how good it will feel, and I'm always wrong."

"Because it's me."

Her eyes flew open and she frowned down at him. "What?"

"You lose your fucking mind every time I touch you because it's me. Just like I can't keep my goddamn hands to myself when I'm in the same room as you. We make each other crazy, and yeah, some of that has to do with how smoking hot you are. But it's more and you know it." He reached between them to circle her clit with his thumb. "I'm not a glorified dildo or a blow-up doll. I'm *me*."

Allie stared down at Roman. All she wanted was to lose herself in the perfection of the moment, of how good it felt to have him inside her, his big body between her thighs. She didn't want to turn this into something it wasn't supposed to be. *Too little, too late.*

"I know it's you." As if she could detach the man from his body. She couldn't. She'd tried. Roman's personality was just as overwhelming as his good looks. "Damn it, I see you."

Driven by the pounding pleasure in her blood, she shifted, swirling her hips a little in a move that made them both gasp. "I see you," Allie repeated. "You're not a bad man, no matter how much you pretend to be." He might not be a *good* man, but that wasn't something she could determine inside of a week.

Liar.

She leaned down to kiss him, answering the temptation of his mouth as much as she wanted to silence the little voice inside her. *You won't be able to take this back. It's already complicated and it's only going to get more so.* She didn't care. She'd worry about complications when she came to them. All that mattered in that moment was removing the flicker of hurt she'd seen in Roman's hazel eyes.

She tasted the ocean on his lips, felt the warmth of the sun in his skin. Roman was like this island personified, beautiful and more than a little bit wild beneath the carefully cultured exterior.

"It stopped being just sex with you. You know it. I know it. We're still not talking about it."

He hesitated but finally nodded. "I can play the patient hunter, Aphrodite. We won't talk about it tonight. Maybe not for the next three days. But we *will* talk about it."

That was what she was afraid of. "Guess you really *are* Adonis," she murmured against his lips.

"Only when it comes to my Aphrodite."

She didn't want to talk anymore. Every time he'd spoken tonight, he'd chipped away at the fragile balance she'd worked to keep in place. Boundaries were there for a reason and, damn it, Roman seemed determined to trample all over them. He'd stopped playing by the rules, but he hadn't pushed so hard that she could call him on it.

Do I even want to call him on it? What's the harm in enjoying this? It won't last.

What if it does?

She kissed Roman again, pressing her body into his. She rode him slowly, not worried about the destination. They'd get there eventually. They did every time. No, right now what Allie wanted was to be fully present in the moment. Right there. With him. The rest of the world could wait.

He dug a hand into her hair and grabbed her ass with the other, guiding the long slide of her strokes. Sweat slicked their skin, and the drag of her nipples across his chest made her moan. *So good. Everything* about them was *so good.* Nothing else mattered but how his tongue moved expertly against hers, the feeling of him inside her, big and full and almost too much, and where he would touch her next. "I need more."

He rolled them, and the second her back hit the soft mattress, Roman began to move. He rolled his body like the waves they'd just been playing in. Smooth and steady and hitting all the right places. He ground his pelvic bone against her clit, the friction drawing a moan from her lips. His big body kept her pinned even as he wrapped himself around her. All she could feel was Roman. All she knew was Roman. The feel of his strong hands gripping her hips, the pounding of his cock between her thighs, the little curses he uttered with each exhale.

Glorious. So incredibly glorious.

"Yes. *There.* Don't stop."

"Come for me, Aphrodite," he growled against her neck. "Come for your man."

She was too lost to the pleasure of what he was doing to her to think too hard on his words. Or that was what she told herself as she buried her face in the curve of his neck and orgasmed hard enough to shake the earth on its axis. Roman pounded into her, wild with a need she felt to her very soul.

This isn't going away. I don't know if it's real or not...but I want it to be.

Roman tucked her against him and held her tightly, as if he expected her to leap out of bed and flee into the night. Considering how hard her heart pounded in a way that had nothing to do with the outstanding sex, she wasn't sure his fears were unfounded. "I don't know how to do this."

"Do what?"

She kept her face pressed against his chest. It was easier to be honest when she wasn't looking directly into those hazel eyes. "This. You. Us." *Us.* One little word, but it somehow changed everything. The realization that this wasn't simple vacation sex had been growing inside her every time Roman touched her. Every time she came with his name on her lips.

He smoothed a strand of her hair back from her face, tilting her head up so she could see him. "Why do you have to do anything at all?" There was something in his expression, something tight and guarded despite his warm smile.

"What's wrong?"

He hesitated and sighed. "Look, Allie, I like you. A lot. But I can tell that this whole thing freaks you out, so I'm trying to not put any pressure on you while we're here."

While we're here.

They wouldn't be on West Island forever. Hell, they wouldn't be here this time next week. This thing they had was temporary. She knew it and he knew it. Allie took a careful breath as the knowledge settled in her chest like a stone. They had an expiration date. There would be a time in the very near future when she'd no longer have the right to spend her nights tangled up with Roman.

I have to shore up enough memories during these last few days to last me a lifetime.

The thought made her want to cry, but she shoved the feeling down deep. There would be plenty of time for tears later. Right now, the only thing that mattered was gorging herself on everything Roman. On the little touches. On his kisses. On the feeling that rose inside her as she came apart around him.

"Aphrodite?"

She tangled her fingers in his hair and pulled him close for a desperate kiss. She put all her frustration and fear into the slide of her tongue against his. Three days. She had so much living to pack into three tiny twenty-four-hour periods.

Roman pulled her closer yet, his big hands cupping her ass and grinding her against him. He broke the kiss to nip at her jaw. "This is what you need, isn't it? Not to think anymore."

"Yes." He always seemed to know what she needed, even when she couldn't put it into words. "I just want to feel you. To be here and present and not worried about what happens when we get back to New York."

"Consider it done." He captured one of her nipples in his mouth, sucking hard. "Trust me, Aphrodite. I'll take care of you."

For the next three days, she finished silently, even as he rolled her onto her back and began kissing his way down her body. She couldn't bear to think about what happened after.

So she didn't.

15

ROMAN SMOOTHED ALLIE'S HAIR BACK FROM HER face. "You'll have to get moving if you're going to make your flight."

She swatted at his hand without opening her eyes. "Screw it. I'm not going back to New York. I'll just stay here until they kick me out."

He felt the same way, though it wasn't the island that had Roman wishing he could make this moment last forever. He wasn't ready to let this thing with her go. It was a truth he'd been working toward for some time, but this morning, knowing that they were going to board their respective flights back to New York and go back to their normal lives... The stakes were suddenly sky-high. "Come out with me tonight."

"What?" She finally opened a single eye. "What are you talking about?"

"Tonight. After we're both settled. I want to take you on a date." He didn't exactly form it as a question, but Roman knew all too well how fragile the limb he stood on was. They'd spoken about changing the rules, but he'd just thrown every single one of them out. Roman stroked his hand down her arm and laced his fingers with hers. "I'm not ready for this to be over."

"Roman, we talked about this. Our lives don't match up

outside of this island. Our worlds are too different—our world-*views* are too different. We wouldn't last the week before something happened that ruined us for good." She shifted to look down at their joined hands. "And that's not even getting into the whole 'your investor's trying to buy my gym out from underneath me' thing."

She was determined to see the worst in that situation, and he hadn't had the chance to convince her otherwise because every time it came up, suddenly they were having sex. Roman knew damn well that Allie was trying to keep them both distracted, and he couldn't exactly be pissed at the side effect, but he wanted to *talk* to the infuriating woman. "Have dinner with me. We'll talk about all the shit we've been avoiding up until now. If at that point you're sure you don't want me to facilitate someone investing in the gym, then I won't."

"Just like that?"

"Just like that." It wouldn't be just like anything. His client was interested in the gym and she had a clear vision over what she wanted for its future—a vision Roman shared. It wouldn't be easy to find a replacement, but he'd make it work. *If* Allie actually talked to him. "What do you say?"

Still, she hesitated. He could practically see her weighing her desire not to go to that dinner against the chance to get him to back off once and for all. Finally, Allie nodded. "I can't do tonight, but tomorrow I'm free."

"Tomorrow it is." He pressed his lips to her forehead. "As much as I want to seal this with a kiss, if I start kissing you, we won't stop until lunch and you have a plane to catch." He bit back the impulse to tell her to stay—that they really could just live on the island indefinitely and leave their lives behind. That peace wouldn't last. No matter how effectively they'd checked out of reality for the week, given enough time, real life would come creeping into their time here. Hell, it already had. Allie had done her best to avoid it, but Roman was a realist—they needed to get their shit out in the open so they could deal with it.

They had no chance of a future without that.

Before he could reconsider kissing Allie, she was out of the bed and pulling her clothes on. "I'd better go. If left to her own devices, Becka will pack my stuff and her version of packing is to shove everything in and wrestle with the bags until the zipper is in danger of breaking. Better for both me and my luggage if I do it myself."

"Give me your number."

Again, the slightest of hesitations. She grabbed a piece of stationery from the nightstand and scrawled her number on it. "See you tomorrow."

Tomorrow. In New York.

No matter how much he wanted to pretend otherwise, it was a big fucking deal to bring their budding relationship home. Roman managed a smile. "Have a safe flight."

"You, too." And then she was gone.

He listened to her footsteps leading out of the villa, and only after they'd faded did he climb out of bed and throw on a pair of shorts. His flight was in a couple hours—the early one off the island—so he wouldn't have a chance to see Allie again beforehand.

It took fifteen minutes to pack everything he'd brought and comb every room twice to ensure he didn't miss anything. He took extra time to shred up the information he'd gotten about Allie. He didn't need it. She'd given him everything when she spoke about why she'd started the gym. He knew what pressure points to push to incite the reaction he wanted…but he couldn't do it.

She wasn't just a stubborn business owner who needed a little pressure to do things his way. This was *Allie*. For her, he'd bypass the manipulations and shady dealings for plain old honesty.

Roman grabbed his bags and made his way to the lodge. It

was time to get this show on the road, and he had a shit ton of work to do on the trip. All the pieces had to be in place before he saw Allie again.

The stakes were too high for it to be any other way.

Allie couldn't wrap her mind around being back in New York. It was more than the weather, more than the sheer amount of people. It was almost like her life didn't quite fit the same way it used to, as if it was a sweater with a tag she'd never noticed before but that itched every time she moved. To distract herself, she taught an early-morning spin class and spent the rest of the day holed up in her office going over bills and the budget for next month.

It was a shitty distraction. Nothing lined up. They'd taken their usual summer months hit in attendance to the classes, which meant less income. She was already in the red, but both the gym and the shelter were rapidly reaching the point of no return. Allie would have to start laying off her girls soon—like next week—and the thought made her sick to her stomach. The only other option was to turn away some of the women in the shelter, which wasn't an option at all. It was like having to choose between two of her children and she didn't even know where to begin.

She set it aside to work on later. She couldn't call Becka, because Becka would quit on the spot. She wouldn't worry too much about finding another job—Becka was the type of woman to jump out of a plane and figure out how a parachute worked on the way down. It was part of her charm, but Allie couldn't ask her to make that decision.

No, who she really wanted to call was Roman. They'd spoken briefly last night—mostly to arrange a time and place for their date today—but it was nowhere near enough after having him within arm's reach for a full week. She wanted to be wrapped up in him and have him tell her that it'd all be okay and that they'd figure it out together.

Weak. I shouldn't have to lean on a man for strength. I should be strong enough to stand on my own.

Especially since Roman's solution would undoubtedly be to try to convince her to sell the business and let it become someone else's problem.

For the first time, she was actually tempted. She'd been shouldering the burden alone for so long. It was no one's fault but her own that both the shelter and gym were in danger of going under. Running either of them was a full-time job and Allie was trying to do both by herself. If she'd just been willing to find a business partner she could trust…

At twenty-two, she'd been sure that the only person she could trust was herself. She'd needed some way to work through her grief over her mother passing, and this seemed like the best option. She *was* doing good; it just wasn't working like the well-oiled machine she'd anticipated. *There has to be a better way.* She just didn't know what it was.

Frustrated, she headed out. The evening classes were already covered, so there was nothing holding her there except a strange sort of guilt. There had to be something *more* she could be doing, but hell if she knew what it was. Maybe if she scrambled, she could throw together a fund-raiser or two this month, before it was too late. It would mean relying on her girls to run the gym while she devoted herself to event planning, which had never been her strong suit. Making cold calls to the few donors who'd helped her get the shelter off the ground was the next step, but it had always made her feel awkward and shameful—like she was begging for charity. As it was, her presence at the gym was totally and completely unnecessary at that moment, and all she'd accomplish by staying was working herself further into a spiral of worry.

Allie went upstairs to her apartment. She took her time showering and getting ready, battling nerves that told her this date was a giant waste of time and would only end in heartbreak for her. Roman had his eye on the prize—and the prize wasn't her. It was her gym and the investor interested in it.

Knowing that didn't douse the slow excitement building in her stomach at the thought of seeing him again. It hadn't even been forty-eight hours and she already longed for his touch. *Dangerous.*

She checked the time and decided that being a little early wasn't a bad thing. Nerves were in danger of getting the best of her as she made her way to the restaurant, but she knew Roman well enough at this point to know that he'd find a way to get ahold of her if she no-showed him. What was more, he wouldn't make the same offer twice. This was her chance to get what she wanted—freedom.

Too bad the thought of that didn't fill her with the expected relief. Free meant she wouldn't be seeing Roman again. How could she when he represented such a different set of priorities than she had? Even if she was willing to give it a shot, their respective schedules would mean dates were few and far in between. If things didn't fall apart because of their differences, they'd fall apart because neither one of them could come up with the time to make it work.

Wow. Talk about being fatalistic.

No, I'm being realistic.

She walked into the restaurant Roman had chosen. It wasn't one she was familiar with, and she stopped just inside the door to take it all in. Everything was very modern and minimalist, which was a far cry from the shabby beach chic clutter of West Island. Nothing about the choice screamed Roman to her, but that could very well be because she didn't know him nearly as well as she would have liked to pretend. *You're seesawing all over the place. Get ahold of yourself.*

She told the waitress she was meeting Roman Bassani and

was led back to a little booth tucked into the side wall facing the street. The windows weren't big, but they offered plenty of fodder for people watching. Or they would if she could look anywhere but at Roman's perfect face. He rose to meet her, and she couldn't help comparing this man with the one she'd felt so connected to on the island. *Her* Roman was there, beneath the expensive suit and the perfectly styled hair. She could see a hint of him in those hazel eyes, but even the way he held his shoulders was different here. Harsher.

"Hey." She wrapped her arms around herself, wishing she'd worn something fancier. But that wasn't Allie any more than the relaxed guy in the cargo shorts was Roman. Her wrap dress was nice, but if she didn't miss her guess, he could pay her rent for several months with that suit.

"Hey." He took her hand and pulled her gently closer. The quick kiss he dropped on her lips made her heart ache because it was different, too. Cursory. Distracted. Lacking the heat she'd grown used to that was present in even the smallest of touches between them before.

She disengaged her hand, forced a smile and slid into her seat. "You look nice."

"You're stealing my line." His lips quirked up as he sat across from her. "How was your day?"

Horrible. I can't pay my bills. I'm realizing I care about you a whole lot more than I expected, and the writing is on the wall that both this budding relationship and my ownership of my gym will end awfully. I'm in a funk I don't know that I'll ever get out of. She tried to smile. "It was okay."

Roman's brows slanted down. "What's the truth, Aphrodite? Because that's not it."

She tensed. "Let it go. Please." The last thing Allie wanted to do was rip herself open for him. She didn't do that for *any-one*. She was the strong one. The one who got through things that would break other people and came out the other side swinging with everything she had. It couldn't be clearer that this dinner was the end. Roman wanted things she couldn't give him—and she wasn't talking about her gym and the shelter. He wanted parts of *her*.

No way.

She gritted her teeth and resolved to get to the end of this date so she could secure Roman's promise to leave her business the hell alone. Then she'd walk. Better to end things here and now instead of letting them drag on and enact any one of the horrible scenarios she'd tortured herself with earlier.

The waitress appeared to take their drink order, and Allie was pathetically grateful for the distraction. She ordered a white wine and Roman had whiskey. Then the woman was gone and there was nothing to stand between them. She took a steadying breath. "I'm ready for your pitch."

16

_____

ROMAN STARED AT ALLIE ACROSS THE TABLE from him, feeling like he was on a boat headed for a storm, watching the receding shore of paradise and knowing he'd never see it again. Regardless of what she'd told him when she'd agreed to this date, it was clear she'd already made up her mind about both his proposal and him. It made him want to shake her, to force her to see that good things were within reach if she'd just lower the barriers the slightest bit.

If she'd let him in.

He sat back. Might as well get this over with, because he could already see that she wouldn't let him get anywhere near anything personal until they'd both fulfilled their part of the bargain connected to her beloved gym. "I don't have to tell you about the stats of women who feel harassed in their gyms, let alone their daily lives. With Transcend you've created a unique hook that my investor thinks will go over well as a small franchise. Something exclusive to a handful of big cities at first—LA, San Antonio, Seattle, Atlanta, Chicago. Boutique gyms are in right now, but this has the potential to last longer than the fad does, especially if there's some kind of health plan and smoothie bar that goes hand in hand with it."

"That's not what Transcend is about."

"That's exactly what Transcend is about. You are a bastion of safety for women. They flock to that gym because it's one of the few places they can let their guard down a little. *You* are the reason they feel safe, and the little community you've created." He leaned forward and braced his forearms on the table. "Don't women outside this city deserve that feeling, too?"

She met his gaze directly. "There are other women-only gyms out there. Mine is far from unique."

"But yours is the only one connected with a shelter for battered women." This was it. He'd lose her or have her based on this last part. "My investor is interested in continuing and expanding the work you do with the shelter." The hope in her eyes killed him, so he spoke quickly. "With the caveat that you sign over the nonprofit entirely."

"What?"

No use pussyfooting around it. "It's not your passion. The brainchild was all yours, but the delivery has been lackluster at best. You help those women, and *that* is your passion, combined with the gym. But a successful nonprofit requires shmoozing and networking, and that's a full-time job—a job it couldn't be clearer you are not interested in. You haven't done much with it up to this point."

"That's not fair. I—"

He held up a hand. "That wasn't a criticism. You're running two full-time businesses by yourself. It's natural that things have fallen through the cracks as a result. My point—my investor's point—is that if you delegate and hand off a few things, the whole operation could expand and run smoother as a result."

Allie sat back, the golden tone of her skin going pale with worry. "Even if I was interested in signing away everything I've worked for, what guarantee would I have that this investor of yours wouldn't turn around and do exactly the opposite of what they're proposing now?"

"It's something that could be stipulated in the contract." He found himself holding his breath while she seemed to think it over.

But she shook her head. "No. I can't risk it. Those women depend on me to keep them safe, and I don't know a single damn thing about this investor of yours. I've seen how flimsy paperwork can be when it comes to protection—might often makes right, and your investor has all of it."

She was technically right—even with the protections written into the contract, there were limits to what Allie could demand—but Roman knew this investor and he knew that the offer was legit. He wouldn't have fielded it otherwise. "Trust me. I wouldn't have brought this to you, especially after the last week, if I didn't think it would honor what's important to you."

"You keep saying that—to trust you. You haven't done a single thing to earn this level of trust."

And fuck, that stung. He'd shared things with her last week that he didn't talk about with anyone. Even though Allie was still guarded, he'd thought she'd shared shit with him, too. He wasn't a sappy romantic, but that *meant* something.

Or at least, he'd thought it had.

Roman forced the tension from his shoulders. "I have only your best—"

"No."

He waited for some kind of explanation, something he could work with, some sign that she wasn't just shutting him out without explanation. None came. With a slow sinking in his stomach, he sat back. "And if I ask you on another date—if I want this to go somewhere—am I going to get the same answer?"

Allie fiddled with her fork and then set it aside. "I'm sorry, Roman, but I just don't see how this could possibly work out. We're too different."

A nice pat explanation—and it was bullshit. "How are we supposed to give this a shot if you won't talk to me? If you *never* talk to me. You came to dinner tonight with your responses already planned out. It didn't matter what I said, because you were always going to tell me no to investing in the gym, and no to us dating."

She flinched. "I'm saying no to your investor because I don't trust their intentions. And there is no *us*. I had a wonderful time with you on West Island, but that wasn't reality. This?" She motioned between them. "This is reality. You in your expensive suit and me in my secondhand dress. I do whatever I can to help people, and you hurt them *for your job*. We're just too different."

"That's bullshit and you know it." Frustration grabbed him by the throat. She was determined to see the worst in his choice of career, no matter what evidence he provided to the contrary. It didn't matter if he laid out a list of all the happy business owners who had benefited from him doing his job—Allie would pick out the one from the bunch who was pissed and then use it as proof that he was a monster. "You're being a chickenshit. News flash, Allie—I'm not your father. I'm as far from that bastard as a man can get, but if you can't see that, then maybe you're right—we don't stand a chance."

Roman wasn't saying anything Allie hadn't said to herself, but somehow hearing those words—that condemnation—come out of his mouth sucked all the air out of the room. "That's not fair."

"Neither is sacrificing a potential future with me because you're scared." He spoke low and fiercely, and part of her wanted to give in and just let him take the wheel. Roman was more than capable of taking care of both of them and guiding the relationship toward…

What am I thinking?

She knew what came from having to depend on a man. Even if Roman would never hurt her—and he wouldn't—he was too overpowering and overwhelming. He would swallow her whole and all that would be left of her identity would be connected to him. Roman's woman.

Not Allie, strong and mostly confident business owner who didn't need to lean on anyone. That person would be gone, and she'd never be able to get her back.

If Allie didn't have her gym, she didn't have anything. She'd be starting over from scratch, selling her soul in the process. It was easy for Roman to tell her to trust him, to talk to him, when *she* was the one making all the sacrifices and he was making none.

"Is that what you really think?"

She hadn't realized she'd spoken all those thoughts aloud, but she'd put it out there and she wasn't about to take it back now. "Isn't that the truth?" Roman had all the chips in this scenario—he had since they'd met. *No, not since we met. That first night, we were on equal footing.* There was no going back now, though. They were who they were, and neither of them could really change that.

He clenched his jaw hard enough that she feared for his teeth. "Talk. To. Me."

"That's exactly what I've been doing this whole time. Just because I'm not saying what you like doesn't mean I'm wrong." She slid out of the booth and stood. "This was a mistake."

"Allie, if you walk out that door, that's it. I'm not going to chase your ass down just so I can keep bashing my head against the same damn wall." He said it with such finality, her throat burned and her eyes prickled.

Because this was it. They'd been hurtling toward this moment since the first time they'd realized each other's identities. Part of her had thought they'd find a way around, but he was too uncompromising, too sure that he knew what was best for her.

And he was right—he was nothing like her father or the abusive men who drove the women to her shelter in flocks.

Roman would never hurt someone like that, no matter how angry. She'd stake her life on it.

No, the damage he dealt wasn't physical. It wasn't even intentional. That didn't stop her from feeling like he'd reached into her chest and ripped out her heart. "Goodbye, Roman."

"Allie, wait."

Her feet stopped, even as her brain demanded she keep moving. Almost against her will, she turned and looked at him.

Roman stood and glanced around them. She'd been vaguely aware that they had an audience before then, but the reality of the situation came crashing down on her. She was having a very public breakup with a man who wasn't even her boyfriend. *This is what my life has come to.* "If you have anything left to say, now's the time." She waited, holding her breath, wondering if maybe he'd say something that would override her fears and put them back on something resembling solid ground.

He stepped closer and lowered his voice. The warmth was gone from his eyes, leaving the cold businessman in his place. "If you don't take this investor's offer, you'll be sentencing both your gym and the shelter to death."

Allie flinched. She knew that she was in trouble better than anyone, but that didn't mean she'd put the women who depended on her at risk. Not until she'd exhausted all other options. "I'll find another way."

"Good fucking luck." He shook his head and walked around her. "I do mean that, Allie. It'll take a goddamn miracle to save you at this point, and you just turned down the helping hand I offered. That's on you—not me."

She watched him walk away, a pit opening up inside her with no end. Allie had hit so many snags since she'd set herself on the goal of opening her own business and nonprofit, and every single one of them she'd fought her way through. By all rights she should be furious at Roman, and that should drive her to figure out a solution to this problem.

But all she wanted to do was go home and cry herself to sleep.

She turned to pay for their drinks but caught sight of a fifty that Roman had left on the table. Even pissed as hell, he had ensured that he held up his end of the bargain, at least when it came to this. *Stop thinking about that.* She'd given him the only answer she could. Ultimately, his investor could paint whatever pretty picture they wanted, because when push came to shove, money talked. Once the papers were signed and Allie was no longer in control, the investor could do as they pleased and she'd have no power to stop them.

She'd made the right call. She was sure of it.

She just didn't know why it felt so freaking awful to have pulled the proverbial trigger and put an end to both the investor talk and her time with Roman. She should be relieved. It was over. She'd held up her end of the bargain, and she was free. Not to mention a vacation for the record books, the kind she'd remember fondly for as long as she lived...

Even if all she felt right at that moment was overwhelming sadness.

Allie left the restaurant, thought about grabbing a cab and ultimately decided to walk. She needed to expend some energy, to work her way through the crap circling in her head. Roman's words kept ringing through her mind, telling her that she'd never figure out how to save her gym and the shelter on her own. That she was destined for failure.

Fuck that.

It was easier to focus on business than to deal with the yawning chasm of loss taking up residence in her chest. It didn't matter how much she told herself that she and Roman would never work—she'd secretly hoped that he'd have a solution that would take care of her fears. *Depending on Roman to shoulder all of that was totally fair.* It wasn't that... Allie shook her head and picked up her pace. Maybe it was partly that. She didn't want to depend on him for everything—for anything—but she had still kind of been on the verge of doing exactly that. *Weak.*

She couldn't afford to be weak. Not in business, and not in her yearning for Roman.

Allie still had to fight not to call him as she strode down the block toward her apartment. She wanted to talk to him, to yell, or cry, or...something. Connect. She'd been adrift for so long, and she hadn't realized it until his grounding presence had slammed into her life. The fact they'd spent only a week together should have been a bucket of cold water on her, but it didn't seem to make any difference. They had a connection, and it scared her. It didn't seem to scare him as much, but what did he have to lose? The scales of their risk were not equal.

Roman would move on with his life after this. She had no illusions that he'd be happy to leave her behind, but he was a driven individual who wouldn't let a little heartache stop him from reaching his goals. He'd find a better-fitting investment for this client. And the next, and the next.

Eventually he'd start dating. Even as chaotic as his schedule had to be, he was too much of the full package *not* to find a woman willing to put up with it. They'd date the appropriate amount of time and then he'd propose on an island a whole lot like West Island. Hell, maybe he'd actually propose *there.*

The thought made her sick to her stomach.

Just get home. You can break down when you get home.

She flagged down a cab and rattled off her address. Through the entire drive, Allie focused on breathing, putting every bit of concentration she had on that single task. It got her as far as her front door and then she slumped to the floor. "Oh, God, what am I going to do?"

17

"YOU'RE IN A PISSY-ASS MOOD."

Roman stared at his drink. It was his second, and he forced himself to sip it instead of shooting it like he wanted to. No matter how good of a friend the man next to him was, he still couldn't afford to lose control. *Mostly because I'll end up drunk texting Allie and making a damn fool of myself.* "I'm fine."

Aaron Livingston snorted. "You're about as far from fine as a man gets. I've never seen you this out of sorts about a deal falling through."

The deal and Allie were all twisted up in his head, and he couldn't untangle them. That investor would have *helped* her. He couldn't divulge details until the contracts were set, but his client, Clare Belford, was the perfect fit for that company. She had one of the biggest nonprofits for abused women in the country, and she'd loved the idea of Allie's gym being linked up with several of them.

Because of a nondisclosure agreement he had with Clare, he hadn't been able to tell Allie that, but if she'd just trusted him, she would have found out shortly.

Except she hadn't trusted him.

He was good enough to fuck, but anything beyond that was strictly off-limits. The thought had him downing the rest of his drink despite his best intentions. He motioned to the bartender to refill the glass, doing his best to ignore the curious look he could feel Aaron giving him. "I don't want to talk about it."

"Holy fuck." Aaron leaned against the bar, blue eyes narrowed. "It's not business at all—it's woman trouble."

"What part of 'I don't want to talk about it' don't you get?"

"You do want to talk about it. You wouldn't be here otherwise." Aaron waited for the bartender to slide the newly filled glass over before continuing. "You weren't seeing anyone before you left for the island, and that place has a limited population of guests, so there was only one woman there who'd be twisting you up like this." He whistled softly. "You and Allie Landers? I thought you didn't mix business with pleasure."

"I don't—didn't." He eyed his glass but didn't pick it up.

"You might as well get it off your chest. I can't say I've ever had that look on my face, but I have three sisters, so I know a thing or two about women."

Roman almost commented on the fact that if he had to recall his sisters for advice instead of his own dating history, he wasn't much help. But the truth was that Roman had a varied dating history and he'd never been this fucked up over a woman. Even his worst breakups and the respective aftermaths had been filled with a sense of peace because it was the right call.

There was no peace in this.

He nudged his glass farther away. "I had all the answers. The solution to everything she needed. All I got for my trouble was a kick in the ass as she showed me the door." When Aaron made a noncommittal noise, he kept going. "I never planned on her. Fuck, man, she's strong and gorgeous and smart as hell. I'm talking full package. I thought we were on the same wavelength, but she didn't even try to see that I might actually be right. She's so determined to do things her way, she won't even give us a shot."

"You want the bro-supportive view or real talk?"

He finally looked at Aaron. Roman could have called Gideon to come drink with him, but his other friend was so deep in his romantic bliss with Lucy Baudin that he wouldn't be able to commiserate. Aaron, at least, was single. All Roman really wanted was someone to drink with who wouldn't press too hard, but he'd underestimated Aaron. It was tempting to say he wanted the supportive viewpoint, but Roman had never shied away from the shitty side of things, so he went with the hard truth option. "The latter."

"You fucked up."

He blinked. "How do you figure?"

"Look at this from her perspective—you crashed her vacation and, yeah, maybe your intense chemistry made everything else take a back seat for the week, but nothing really changed. You were still the conquering enemy force once you two got back to New York. You have the standard contract with the prospective investor?"

"Yeah. Always."

Aaron nodded. "So even if it's the best fit, you aren't telling her shit about this person and you're expecting her to just take your word for it. From all accounts, Allie Landers is a woman who's been holding the world on her shoulders and dealing with every issue that's arisen on her own. You can't seriously have expected her to just flip on a dime and put everything she's worked years for on the line on your word alone."

"I expected her to trust me," Roman snapped. The fact she hadn't still stung like a bitch.

"Why?"

He growled. "Because I would never hurt her or what she cares about."

"Maybe you know that. Maybe she even knows that on some level." Aaron shrugged. "If your delivery was anything similar to the one you've given tonight, you can't blame her for telling you to fuck off. Maybe the sex changed things for you both, but if you didn't tell her that, how's she supposed to know? She's not a damn mind reader."

He wanted to rail at his friend—at Allie—that she should have trusted him anyway, but... What had he really done to earn that trust? A multitude of orgasms was great, but it didn't translate—a fact he damn well knew. He'd opened up about his past a bit, but he hadn't exactly made himself overly vulnerable to her. He'd held back. They might have established a connection, but it certainly didn't earn him the amount of trust he could expect her to stake her business on. He drank some of his whiskey, forcing himself to go slow. "I care about her."

"And it's making you stupid. Don't worry—you're not the only one who's done it. She made mistakes in this, too, but we're not talking about her. We're talking about you." Aaron took a pull of his beer. "The question remains—what the hell are you going to do about it?"

Allie cared about him. Roman would bet everything he owned on that fact. His pride might be demanding he let the whole thing go and move on with his life...but he couldn't wrap his mind around moving on from this. Allie was special. More than what he felt for her, he wanted her to succeed in the vision she'd put into play. He wanted to be by her side when she saw it realized. If he walked now, he wouldn't do any of that.

What was his pride when compared with his happiness—and hers?

He checked his watch and stood. "I'm going to go get my girl."

"There you go." Aaron toasted him with his beer. "Though I'd recommend waiting for morning, since it's after ten."

Roman was already turning for the door. "I have a few calls to make. I'll catch up with you later." He had several things to line up before he could talk to Allie. If he wanted a chance to succeed in winning her back, he had to be able to present new information—to change the narrative.

A pounding on the door brought Allie out of her light doze. She shot to her feet before she realized that she wasn't in her bed, and nearly tripped over the coffee table. She scrubbed a hand over her face and headed for the door as whoever was on the other side kept knocking. For one crazy moment she was sure it was Roman, coming to find her after last night to say... She didn't know what. Something.

But when she opened the door, it was Becka on the other side. Her friend took one look at her and shook her head. "Oh, God. It's worse than I thought."

"What?"

Becka nudged her back into the apartment and shut the door. "You. You are worse than I thought. Look at you—you're wearing holey sweats, you have powdered sugar on your shirt and there are ink stains all over your hands. Something is going on with you, and I want to know what it is. Did Roman do something? Do I need to kick his ass to Brooklyn and back?"

"What? No." *Yes. Sort of.* She smoothed her hair back, belatedly realizing that she hadn't showered today and her messy bun was more mess than bun. "Roman and I had a vacation fling and it's over now."

Becka narrowed her eyes. "Bullshit."

"Excuse me?"

"You heard me. You were well on your way to head over heels for that guy, and from the way he looked at you, he was right there with you. So what gives? Because you were fine when we flew back to the city, and now you're on the verge of a breakdown."

She opened her mouth to make some excuse and change the subject just like she always did when Becka put her on the spot, but despair got the better of her. "I'm in trouble, Becka. Big trouble."

Instantly, her friend's half-joking demeanor disappeared. "Tell me so we can fix it."

"I don't know if there's any fixing this." She walked back to the couch and sat down, waiting for Becka to join her before she started in. Allie detailed how far behind they were on bills, how she'd been borrowing from her own income to supplement both the gym and the shelter, how she was almost drained dry.

How she'd told Roman no even though he'd offered her a potential way out.

"Well, yeah." Becka nodded. "He didn't give you much in the way of assurances, and I get why you said no." Before Allie could relax, she continued. "What I don't get is why this is the first time I'm hearing about all this."

"I thought I could handle it." Even when she'd realized she couldn't, putting that burden on someone else went against everything Allie was. She was the problem solver, and she knew she could depend on herself. *Other people* depended on her—she didn't depend on other people. She didn't know how to reach out when she was in trouble.

Becka gave her a look. "You know, it's not the worst thing in the world to ask for help. You're allowed to not be perfect."

"I know I'm not perfect."

She snorted. "But you don't know how to lean on other people. As your best friend, I'm all about blindly hating anyone you hate, but I have a question and I want you to answer it honestly."

Even knowing where this was going, she couldn't help nodding. "Okay."

"Did you even stop to consider for a second that maybe Roman was on the up-and-up? That maybe he cared about you and was telling the truth about his investor and he only wanted to help?" She held up a hand. "I mean, the man is not a saint. He went after this account because he knew it would make his investor happy, and he didn't really care about what you wanted before he met you—but that doesn't mean that the investor is an evil mastermind who wants to destroy everything you've worked toward. Did you ask Roman if you were going to be able to stay on in any capacity?"

"No." Heat climbed her chest and throat to settle in her face. Embarrassment. "He wanted me to compromise on everything and just have faith that he wasn't screwing me. I just…reacted."

Becka nodded. "I mean, I'm not saying you were one hundred percent in the wrong. He played that poorly from beginning to end. But I also think that maybe, just maybe, you reacted instead of thinking it through. I know you want to be able to do this all yourself, but there's no shame in letting someone else share your vision—and help you realize it."

She took a slow breath. "All those women are depending on me to help them."

"Whoa. Slow down there, Wonder Woman. Those women are grateful for a safe space, yes, but they're not helpless. They're not children who need you to see to their every need. You can't put all that on your shoulders." She leaned forward. "Let's be honest here for a second, okay?"

Allie managed a half smile. "We weren't being honest before now?"

"You know what I mean. I love the shit out of you, but you can be bullheaded to a clinical degree. Roman scared you. He made you feel things and he offered you something you want desperately but are afraid to take because it might blow up in your face. I get that. I do. But I also think you latched on to any reason why it wouldn't work and just ran with it, ignoring any indication that you might be—just maybe—dead wrong."

She didn't want to admit that. Roman was as bullheaded as

she was—if not more so. She couldn't afford to show weakness because he'd steamroll her.

Except by not showing weakness, she'd put them in a position where it was all or nothing. There was no compromise because *she* hadn't tried to compromise. She'd just turned him down and cut things off because it was easier than putting herself out there and trying. Becka's words wouldn't smart so much if they didn't have more than a grain of truth in them. "Damn it, you're right."

"I often am." Becka slouched back onto the couch and pulled her legs up to her chest. "So, to simplify—you like Roman a whole hell of a lot, and you're in trouble with the gym—the kind of trouble an investor would solve, but only the right investor."

"That about sums it up." She twisted a lock of hair around her finger. "I guess if I had the right investor, it wouldn't be hard to sign over control—at least partial control. Someone who has the same vision I do, and who wants the same things."

"That makes sense." Becka grinned. "Good thing we know someone with a whole list of people wanting to invest in start-up companies that have promise. I imagine if you went to Roman with a counteroffer, he'd fall all over himself to give you whatever you want."

Since Allie couldn't imagine a scenario where Roman fell all over himself, she just nodded. She could go to a different person to make this connection, but that seemed the height of stupidity—and cowardice. Facing Roman and admitting that she was wrong shouldn't be the end of the world. It wouldn't be comfortable, but what if he really had been serious about giving them a real shot? She'd spend the rest of her life wondering if she'd missed the love of her life because she was too stubborn to ask for help. "I should call him, huh?"

"If you think so."

She considered it for a full thirty seconds. "I'm going to shower and *then* I'm going to go find him."

"That's my girl!"

18

ALLIE'S INTENTIONS WERE ALL WELL AND GOOD, but she couldn't find Roman. He wasn't in his office, and no one seemed to know what his schedule was—and he hadn't answered any of her calls. By the time the afternoon rolled around, she was on the verge of despair. *Maybe I misread the entire situation and he really wasn't interested beyond the gym and now he wants nothing to do with me.*

Not sure what else to do, she sent him a quick text. I'm sorry. I'd like to talk. Can we meet somewhere?

Her phone buzzed before she had a chance to set it down. Where are you?

He wouldn't respond to any of her calls, but he responded to a text—because of course. Down was up and up was down, just like it had been since she'd met Roman. The gym.

Stay there. On my way.

Her heart leaped into her throat and she had to swallow several times before she was able to force her thumbs to type out a reply. Okay.

She tried to busy herself with paperwork, but she kept watching the clock and wondering what was going on. Allie wanted to talk, for sure, but Roman's abrupt texts made her wonder all over again if this was a mistake.

No. Stop it. You care about him, and you're going to fight for him, damn it.

She clung to that thought for the next twenty-five minutes. When someone knocked on her office door, she nearly bolted out of her chair. "Come in!"

Roman walked through, and the sight of him was like coming home. He wore a pair of dark slacks and a button-down shirt that did wonders for his shoulders, and the look he gave her when he breached the door was one of a returning hero. As if he had craved the sight of her as much as she'd wanted him.

She opened her mouth to say all the things she'd had running through her head for the last day, but stopped when she registered that he wasn't alone. A petite silver-haired woman stepped into the room. Her face was ageless enough that Allie couldn't tell if her silver hair was trendy or all natural, but she could only be termed a handsome woman. Her bone structure was a little too strong to be merely pretty, and she carried herself with a confidence that filled the room.

Roman shut the door and turned to Allie. "I'd like to introduce you to Clare Belford—the investor who hired me."

She froze. "I know that name... You're the woman who runs Safe Places."

"I am." Clare's voice was low and melodious. "I'm really impressed with the operation you're running."

"I— Thank you. I love your work. You make such a difference in so many women's lives."

Clare moved closer to her desk. "Roman here told me about your concerns—which are perfectly valid—and I wanted to meet you to reassure you that I have every intention of staying true to your vision. I would like to incorporate your shelter into Safe Places and expand Transcend to pair new gyms with the current shelters in the cities Roman suggested. And I would also like to hire you to stay on as general manager of both the local shelter and the original gym. I know it's not the same thing as owner, but I'm prepared to allow you full autonomy provided you operate within the parameters you've already established."

Allie couldn't breathe. She couldn't think. It was everything she could do not to cry. In all her imaginings of how things would go down with her shelter and gym, *this* wasn't even on the list of possibilities. She cleared her throat. "That sounds wonderful."

"Don't give me an answer now. Think it over and let me know by the end of the week." Clare reached out and shook Allie's hand. Her grip was just as confident as her personality. "I'm glad we were able to meet."

"Me, too."

Roman waited for the door to close behind Clare to speak. "I'm sorry."

She still couldn't quite process the turn of events. "I thought you couldn't talk about who your investor was."

"I signed a nondisclosure agreement. It's standard because the job can get a little sticky when it comes to negotiations and some investors would rather not be identified beforehand for their own reasons."

The dots connected with a snap she could almost hear. "You asked her to talk to me."

He hesitated. "While it would have been great if you'd trusted me on this, I understand why you didn't now. You have more than just your life at stake, and going into the situation with only my word isn't sufficient. I knew if you met with Clare, you would understand that this will only mean good things for both the shelter and the gym—and more women than you can reach on your own."

Allie took a breath, and then another. "Roman, I don't know what to say."

"Then just... I have to apologize—actually apologize. I was pissed that you wouldn't trust me, but I was asking you to do all the bending and I wasn't putting anything on the line to keep us on equal footing. So here it is—I love you, Aphrodite. I know it's too soon and you have reservations, but I'm willing to do whatever it takes to be with you. If that means you need time, then I'll give you as much time as you need." The tense look on his face conveyed how much he liked that idea, but he charged on. "We can go as fast or as slow as you want, but *I* want *you*. So unless you don't want me back, this is happening."

God, she was more than a little in love with him, too.

Allie stood and rounded the desk to stand in front of him. "If we're going to restart this on the right foot, I have to apologize, too. I went with my knee-jerk reaction to take care of things myself and didn't stop to think that maybe it's okay to lean on someone or to ask for help." She shifted closer to him, not quite willing to touch him yet, but wanting to. "I was actually calling you today to ask if you'd help set me up with an investor." She smiled. "I guess we were on the same page, after all."

Roman took her hands, his expression serious. "If you aren't comfortable with what Clare is offering, we can find someone else. I'm not going to push you on this. I promise."

"I'm going to take her offer." She'd known it the second Clare had made it. As much as it had initially been her dream to own her own business, being the GM wasn't much of a step down. If she was able to keep control and be assured that all the women who came through her shelter were cared for... It was worth it. It was more than worth it. "Thank you. I'm sorry I didn't trust you."

"You have nothing to apologize for."

She slipped into his arms. "I do have one other thing to say."

"Just one?" A smile flirted with the edges of his lips.

"I love you, too." She kissed him, showing him she meant the words, putting everything she felt into the contact. "This might be too soon, and it might be a little crazy, but I wouldn't have it any other way."

★ ★ ★ ★ ★

OUT NOW

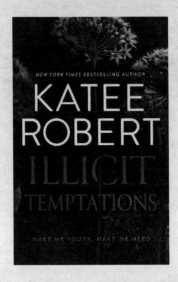

Don't miss another 2-in-1 book from Katee Robert...

Make Me Yours

Three months ago, fitness instructor Becka Baudin gave Aaron Livingstone the most satisfying night of his life...and then walked away. But now, she's pregnant with his child. Although he manages to persuade her to move into his Manhattan penthouse, Becka want nothing to do with Aaron and his flashy CEO lifestyle. They are total opposites – with different jobs, interests, lives. But their chemistry keeps pushing them together...

Make Me Need

Trish Livingston desperately needs her new job. Which means putting up with the world's grumpiest boss, Cameron O'Clery – who is also her brother's best friend and business partner. The way he looks at her is pure disdain...but when he touches her, it's pure fire. With family and business ties at stake, they are not supposed to be together. There's a fine line between hate and lust, and they are going to cross it...but at what cost?

LET'S TALK
Romance

Follow us:

- Millsandboon
- @MillsandBoon
- @MillsandBoonUK
- @MillsandBoonUK

For all the latest titles and special offers, sign up to our newsletter:

Millsandboon.co.uk